MENGELE'S APPRENTICE

ROBERTA KAGAN

PROLOGUE

A quiet suburb on the outskirts of Paris, 1943

A SINGLE LIGHT BULB HUNG IN THE CENTER OF THE ROOM. IT hummed and flickered threatening to extinguish itself and leave the area in total darkness.

Five people were gathered in the living room of that small, sparsely furnished apartment. In the corner stood a sofa, its edges worn, and beside it a coffee table made of dark wood, scratched from years of wear. A young, pretty mother with thick black hair, and blue eyes the color of the ocean, stood trembling beside an old woman. She anxiously stared at her husband, a distinguished older man. Around her neck hung a delicate chain with a golden Star of David that sparkled in the dim light. Her husband gently gripped her arm in an attempt to keep her calm. He wore a dark, tailor-made, wool suit and carried his expensive hat in his hand. A magnificent maple-colored fur coat hung open to reveal a modest dress on the small, slender body of the old woman. She held the hand of one of the young boys, and he held the hand of his brother. Except for the husband, they each carried a small suitcase. The husband had a

1

larger suitcase and a corrugated valise, which he'd set down on the floor in front of him.

A beautiful blonde woman stood across from the family. "It's good to see you again. In case you forgot my name, I am Gisele." She smiled at the two little boys. "Don't be afraid." Then she turned to the adults and said, "Dr. Eugene is going to help you. He is a good person. You'll see. You will like him."

"Have you been working for him for a long time?" the husband asked.

"No, not too long. You are the second family I assisted Dr. Eugene with to help escape from France. But Dr. Eugene has been doing this for much longer. He has helped many, many people. Both he and I are very invested in helping Jews to get away from the Nazis."

Just then a man walked into the room. He took off his coat and smiled at the family reassuringly.

"Good evening. I'm Dr. Eugene. You must be the Rosenblatts." Dr. Eugene stretched out his hand to shake Mr. Rosenblatt's hand.

"It's a pleasure to meet you," Mr. Rosenblatt said.

"I hate to seem petty, but I must know. Do you have the cash? I only ask because we need the money to keep our mission going."

"Yes, Dr. Eugene," the husband replied. "I have all of it. Twenty-five thousand francs apiece. Payment in full, for each of us."

"Good. Like I said, it's not that the money is so important to us, it's just that we need it to fund our next family. I am sure you understand."

"Of course." Mr. Rosenblatt handed the corrugated valise to the doctor. "It's all in here."

"Good. Just give me a few minutes to count it." The doctor sat down on the sofa. He pulled the coffee table over so that it was in front of him. The screeching of the legs of the coffee table, as it was pulled across the floor, broke through the quiet in the room. Then he opened the valise. His wild, dark hair wrapped around his head like the tentacles of an octopus. He stared at the money with dark, intense eyes. Then he began to count. No one made a sound. The room was silent except for the buzzing and flickering of the light bulb. The doctor's face was serious. Mrs. Rosenblatt took her husband's hand and squeezed it. She looked into his eyes. "This is our only chance to escape from the Nazis," she whispered.

"Don't worry. Every penny is there. I counted it carefully this morning," Mr. Rosenblatt whispered to his wife.

"Perfect. It's all here," Dr. Eugene finally said, looking up at them and smiling.

"Thank you for this. We are so grateful to you, for your help. We know what a risk you are taking with what you are doing for us," the pretty, young Mrs. Rosenblatt said. "Not many people will help Jews these days."

The doctor closed the valise. Then he said, "I think it's a dirty shame how the Jewish people are being treated by the Germans. You are not only Jewish, but you are French, like me. Being a good Frenchman, I feel it is my duty to do what I can to help you. I hate the Nazis as much as you do. So, I do my part by helping oppressed people to escape out of France and to get to safety, far away from the Nazis." Dr. Eugene smiled at her. Then he cleared his throat and continued. "Now that we have all of the finances in order, I will tell you the plan. I have set up an escape route out of France, headed to South America, where you will be going to live in Argentina. When you arrive in Argentina, you will be greeted by members of my staff who will help you to get settled in your new home."

"Is this a dangerous trip?" the old woman asked.

"Well . . ." The doctor sighed. "Of course, there is always some degree of danger when the Gestapo are involved. However, don't be afraid. I've helped other Jewish families escape, and so far, we have not had any problems. I don't expect any with your family."

The old woman smiled. "Good. I mean, we have the children with us, as you can see."

"Yes, I do see. And they are handsome young boys. Are they your grandchildren?" the doctor asked.

"Yes, and this is my son and his wife." The old woman indicated the couple. "They are the children's parents."

"I assumed as much," Dr. Eugene said. "What a beautiful family you are."

"Thank you."

"Shall we get started?" the doctor asked.

"Yes. The sooner the better," the man said.

"I agree. The sooner we can get you out of France, the better," the doctor said, then he added, "You are going to need to be vaccinated."

"Vaccinated?" the husband asked. "What kind of vaccines?"

"Yes, you will need to be vaccinated. You won't be able to get into Argentina without tropical vaccines. The government won't allow it. Besides, you would want to be protected from any disease."

The husband nodded. "Very well. You're the doctor. You know best."

"Gisele," Dr. Eugene said. "I've found that the vaccines make the patients tired. Why don't we give them the shots as we are all getting into the car? That way, they will be able to take a long nap while we drive to our first safe-house destination."

"Yes Doctor," Gisele said.

Dr. Eugene smiled as he held the door for everyone. "Follow me to my automobile." He said "It's quite comfortable. You'll have no trouble getting some rest on our way to the safe house."

Everyone followed Dr. Eugene to a black car that was parked a few feet from the door of the building.

"Why don't you give them the injections," Dr. Eugene said to Gisele.

"I'm not sure how to do it," she said.

"Ahhh, all right. There is really nothing to it." Dr. Eugene smiled. "I'll give the man his shot first. Then you can give the injections to the rest of the family. Watch me now, all right?"

"Yes, Doctor," Gisele said.

Dr. Eugene administered the first shot. Gisele administered the rest. It really was as easy as Dr. Eugene said it would be.

Then the entire family climbed into the back seat. Gisele got in beside Dr. Eugene, who started the engine.

"You were right when you said that the vaccine would make me tired. I am very sleepy" the wife said, her voice barely a whisper.

They drove slowly, and by the time they arrived at their destination, the entire Jewish family was dead.

To the poor Jewish families who looked to him with hope in their eyes as their only chance for survival, his code name was Dr. Eugene. To his wife, Georgette Lablais, and their son, Gerhard, and to his colleagues at the mental hospitals where he worked, he was called by his given name: Dr. Marcel Petoit. And although his cruelty could not compare to the brutal and savage Dr. Josef Mengele, to those who truly knew him and knew him well, he could be known as no other than Dr. Satan.

BOOK ONE

CHAPTER ONE

The outskirts of Berlin, Germany

ERNST WAS THE NEIDERS' ONLY SON, THEIR ONLY CHILD, AND THEY wanted the best for him. His parents were not wealthy, but they took great pains to make sure that Ernst never felt their financial struggle. They adored him and doted on him as he grew up. Ernst was spoiled, but he did not behave like a spoiled child. He was kind and loving to his parents, but he was shy and unpopular with the other children. His parents found ways to give him things that most other boys in his working-class neighborhood only dreamed of, like his own bicycle, which they gave him as a gift for his tenth birthday.

And even though both of his parents worked long, hard hours at the bakery his family owned, he never lacked for attention. On Sundays after the family attended church, his father took him to the park to play fußball. Ernst was not very athletic, but his father never made him feel incapable. He encouraged his son in every way. And then, each month, his mother took an afternoon off from the bakery. It was a special day for Ernst because she took him into town to the cinema. Afterward, they ate ice cream cones and walked home together.

There was never a doubt in Ernst's mind that he was the light of their life. It was because they explained to him how he came to them like a miracle. After years of trying to have a child, they had finally accepted that they were to be a childless couple. And then a miracle happened: when Adele was almost forty and Franz forty-five, Adele became pregnant. At first she hadn't thought she was with child; she just assumed that she was losing her period early. Never in her wildest imagination had she considered that she might be pregnant. But by the third month, when she saw her belly begin to extend, she went to visit the midwife. And to her surprise and delight, she returned home with good news. She and Franz were going to have a baby. For the next six months, Franz would not allow his wife to lift anything heavy. He pampered her as much as a poor man can pamper his wife. And even though they could hardly afford it, they hired one of the local girls to help them in the bakery when Adele was too tired to work and needed to stay at home and rest.

Once Ernst was born, they put their own needs aside and did without in order to make sure that he was well cared for and had everything he needed. Ernst was a chubby child, pink cheeked, and rarely cried. He was healthy, a good eater, and slept through the night almost immediately. It was a good thing, because the Neiders didn't have money to spare for doctors. But if Ernst had needed anything, they would have found a way to get it. No one would have called little Ernst a pretty baby, but he was robust and always smiling. And his parents thought he was the most beautiful child in the entire world.

The Neiders weren't educated people, but they wanted better for their son. Before they were married, they both had to leave school and go to work to help their families. Then after they were married, they worked long hours at the bakery just to make ends meet. But both of his parents were in agreement; they wanted Ernst to have the education they'd both been denied. So they decided that when he was old enough, he would not come to work with them. Instead, they would insist that he continue in school even if they needed his help at the bakery.

His mother was able to read but at a very basic level. She'd had a few years of school, just enough to learn to read a little. So, although she could read to him when he was young, she was unable to teach him. He enjoyed being read to. He would lay his head in his mother's lap and listen intently to the stories that she read. And so, because he wasn't very popular with the other children his age, he found books made good friends.

When he was old enough and he started school, both of his parents stressed the importance of education. Ernst was a good student, because he wanted so much to please them. He had grown up adored, and in turn he loved his parents who were older than any of his classmates' parents. Instead of going out to play, he always made sure to finish his homework. He loved the smiles his parents gave him when he brought home a good mark on one of his papers.

But then Ernst became a teenager. And those were difficult years for him. He was still very shy and had grown even plumper, eating pastries his mother brought home from the bakery each evening. And to make matters worse, when he got nervous, he stuttered. When he had to speak out loud at school, he would stutter so badly that the other students would laugh until he sat down red faced and embarrassed. The teachers liked him because he was a good student. They knew he had a speaking problem that caused him to stutter, so they stopped calling on him to answer in class. He was relieved. But he was the prime target for the class bully, Otto Schatz, who loved to single him out. He'd nicknamed Ernst Arschgeige, or ass violin. The name had stuck, and soon everyone was calling Ernst by it. Ernst did what he could to avoid Otto, but Otto always found ways to imitate his stuttering until the other students were laughing so hard that Ernst wished he could crawl under the floor and die.

Many nights, Ernst would lie awake in his bed and dream of going to one of the school dances with Ilse, who was considered the prettiest girl in school. But he knew it was little more than a fantasy. He would never have the nerve to attempt to speak to her. Ernst was certain that if he even tried to speak to Ilse, he would be unable to control his terrible stutter. So he watched and admired her from a distance. One afternoon during lunch break, Gerta, one of the less-attractive girls, walked over to Ernst and tried to speak to him. She asked if she could sit with him. He felt his face turn hot. He couldn't answer her. "May I sit here?" she asked again.

He wanted to say, "Sure," but he couldn't speak. He found himself so tongue tied that he got up, took his books, and then ran away.

In the autumn before the snow of winter fell upon Germany, the other boys his age played fußball in the park after school. Most of the girls, including Ilse, stood around watching. When Ernst passed two of the boys in the hallway, he heard them talking about a fußball they were planning to play after school that day. One of the boys mentioned that Ilse would be there watching. When Ernst heard that, he yearned to be a good athlete. He imagined himself scoring a goal, and it made his heart ache to think of her pretty face looking at him with admiration. But he knew that he did not have the skills. In fact, no one would want him on their team. And to make matters even more painful, everyone knew that Otto was a great athlete. There was no doubt in Ernst's mind, that Otto would score many goals. In his mind's eye, Ernst could see Ilse looking at Otto and cheering him on. It made Ernst feel terrible. So he made a great effort to avoid walking by the park on his way home from school. He took a roundabout way even though it took him ten minutes longer to reach his destination.

Then when his church began to host parties for the young people his age, Ernst found excuses not to attend. Deep in his heart he wished he could go because Ilse would be there. But so would Otto. And Otto knew just what to do and say to make Ernst's life miserable. So rather than go to parties like the other young people in his town, Ernst devoted his time to studying. It was important to him to keep his grades up because he would have hated to disappoint his parents.

No one would ever know that deep in his heart he secretly yearned for a girlfriend. No one ever knew that he secretly dreamed of Ilse. He hid it from everyone by pretending not to care about girls. He did this because he felt that no girl, and especially not one as pretty as Ilse, would ever be interested in him. But when he was alone in his room at night, he ached with yearning. He couldn't help but wonder what it would feel like to kiss Ilse, or to touch the soft pillows of her breasts. His heart skipped a beat when he thought about looking deep into her soft blue eyes. But the idea of being rejected terrified him. And he was not a courageous or outgoing sort of person, so he knew that he would never speak to her. Instead, he began to concentrate on building a different dream. Ernst had always loved science. And he'd always dreamed of doing something wonderful with his life. He longed to be someone who was respected, needed, and loved even if he wasn't the most attractive boy in his class. This thing that would gain him respect and admiration, he decided, was the pursuit of a career in medicine. Everyone in town respected the local doctor. And eventually, everyone, rich or poor, would find they needed the doctor.

There would always be disease, and therefore, Ernst was certain that a good doctor would earn a good living. A man who was loved and needed could be bold and outspoken even if he was not attractive. A man like this would have a lovely wife and a good family. All of this was very attractive to Ernst. And as he grew older, he came to realize that he did not come from money. His parents provided everything they could, but he was seeing reality now, and he knew how poor his family was. He looked at his home and compared it to the others he'd seen, and he began to realize all of the sacrifices his parents had made for him.

He loved them—he loved them for so many reasons—but he was awestruck at how they had worked so hard, so he would grow up never wanting for anything. And because he wanted to find a way to pay them back, to make them proud, to let them know that their always believing in him had not been in vain. He knew that he must become a great doctor. *Someday I will give them all of the wonderful things they gave me when I was a child*, he promised himself as he watched them growing older. In spite of their age, they were forced to continue working at the bakery, and carrying heavy sacks of flour was getting to be too much for his father. *I will someday earn enough money to buy them a home of their own somewhere quiet where they can forget about working and just enjoy the outdoors.*

To become a doctor, he knew he must attend the university. But the university was expensive, and he didn't have the money. However, because his grades were good, and he worked very hard to please his teachers, they were eager to help him. They made every effort to ensure that he was awarded scholarships which would enable him to attend the university in Berlin. When the time came for him to leave home and go away to school, he could see in his parents' eyes that they would miss him. He knew that he was their entire world. However, he also knew they loved him so much that they would never stand in his way. They encouraged him to go.

When the day came to leave, both his father and his mother stood beside him on the train platform. He'd never noticed how poorly dressed they were before that day. But now as they stood on the platform with the other travelers, he could see how worn their clothing was. Then his mother, her eyes glassy with unshed tears, turned to him and gave him her biggest smile. "Ernst, you have grown into a man so quickly. Your father and I are so proud of you. Our son, going off to university. It's like a dream come true."

"I know, Mutti. I am glad to be going. But I am sorry as well because I have to leave home and leave both you and Vater. I will miss you both," he said. He was trembling with nervousness, but he didn't want them to know how afraid he was.

"I know that you will miss us, Ernst. Your father and I will miss you too. But, we don't want you to live your life the way we lived ours, getting up in the morning before dawn to stand in front of a hot oven. We want better for you. We don't want you to break your back in the bakery. You've seen how hard it has been for us over the years. Whether we were sick or well, rain or shine, it made no difference. Either way, we had to open the store and serve our customers. Your father and I want better for you," his mother said, then she put her arms around him and held him tightly.

His father tried to smile as he swallowed hard, holding back the tears. "This is your chance to have a better life than we could give you. Now, I know you're smart. But sometimes when a young man is away on his own for the first time he can be tempted to get into trouble. Make sure you stay on a straight path; don't get involved in any kind of nonsense while you're at the university. Remember that if you get into trouble, you can get thrown out of school. And we wouldn't want that to happen. So, in case you are tempted to do things that you know are wrong, just remember that you must make sure you never lose sight of your goals and your dreams. Work hard, and keep up your marks," his father said. "You'll graduate with honors in no time. Your mother and I are quite sure of it."

Ernst nodded and shook his father's hand. "I will work very hard. I will not lose sight of what is important. I promise you," Ernst said. He wiped his eyes with the back of his hand before the tears slid down his chubby cheeks. "You'll see, Vater, I won't disappoint you and Mutti," Ernst said, then he picked up his suitcase and boarded the train to Berlin.

CHAPTER TWO

1935

THE TRAIN RIDE TO BERLIN WAS NERVE WRACKING. AS HE STARED
out the window listening to a baby crying a few seats in front of
him, he wondered if he had made a mistake. He was all alone now,
embarking on a new career, a new life. It would have been easier to
go to work for his parents at the bakery. He knew what to expect.
But now everything in his world was about to change. His stomach
felt queasy from nerves. *I've been working for this my entire life thus far.
And now that the time has come to fulfill my dreams, I am terrified*, he
thought.

Being away from his parents and living in a small dorm room
was strange and difficult for Ernst. Not only was he lonely, but he
had never taken care of himself before. And now he was washing
his own clothes and making sure to keep his class schedule straight.
He had never had any real friends. So he didn't miss them. But at
least when he was at home, he had his family. Now he spent all of
his time studying.

His roommate, Walter, came in from Frankfurt a few days after
Ernst. Walter was a handsome, wealthy boy, from a good German

family, who was more interested in getting into a fraternity than he was in studying. He had an easy laugh, and when he talked about the girls on campus, he talked as if he planned to sleep with all of them. Ernst listened quietly, but he found that Walter made him uncomfortable. Walter was always dressed impeccably, and he had a devil-may-care attitude that Ernst found repulsive. Unlike Ernst, who needed to graduate to further his dreams, Walter was only interested in momentary pleasures. "If you can find a way to get yourself accepted into a good fraternity, the girls will fall at your feet. Or, shall we say, fall into your bed." Then he looked at Ernst, and said, frowning, "However, with your background and, well, the way you look, this just might not be possible for you. I don't mean to insult you, but you will find that I am always honest."

Ernst resented Walter. He resented everything about him. But he didn't say anything. Instead, he just nodded. He had no plans of rushing a fraternity. Ernst knew he would not be chosen, and he was afraid he might even be laughed at. So he kept to himself. Late one night during rush week, Walter returned drunk to the room he shared with Ernst. He'd been beaten up; his eye was bloodshot, and his lip was split.

"What happened to you?" Ernst asked, appalled at being awakened by such a sight.

"I got the shit kicked out of me by a bunch of no-good Hitler thugs. I told them exactly what I think of their leader and how he is not qualified to be a chancellor. I told them that he is nothing but a thug like them, and that he was in prison. And this is what they did to me. Cowards. It took four of them to take me. But I wasn't afraid. I stood up to them. I told them I would fight any one of them individually, but they laughed. Then three of them held me down and the other one punched and kicked me. Men like that have no character; they are only brave when they are in groups."

Ernst didn't want to get into any trouble with any of the political groups at the university. He wasn't political at all. However, he had read the papers and found that he liked the things he'd read about the new chancellor of Germany, this man called Adolf Hitler. He had read a great deal about him. How he excited the crowds with the very idea of restoring Germany to a world power. Hitler promised that the German people who were poor, like Ernst's parents, would have a share in the wealth. Although he didn't necessarily share the hatred that Hitler was directing at the Jews, he didn't allow it to change his mind about the chancellor either. He'd known a few Jews in his lifetime, not many, and he hadn't cared for them one way or the other.

A few weeks later, Walter was happy to announce that he was accepted into a fraternity. He smiled as he packed his things. Then he left with a cheery goodbye and moved into one of the frat houses on campus.

It was two days later when Ernst was studying that there came a knock on the door.

"Yes, come in," Ernst said, annoyed at being interrupted.

The door opened. "Hello, it's nice to meet you. I've just been assigned to this room. I'm your new roommate," a tall, dark-haired young man, with a winning smile, said. Then he extended his hand. "Ancel Ahronson," he said.

"Er-rnst Neider," Ernst stuttered.

"Nice to meet you," Ancel said. He didn't seem to notice Ernst's stuttering. He just tossed his corrugated valise on the bed, which had been Walter's.

Ernst smiled at Ancel, but then he noticed that Ancel wore a Star of David around his neck. *I should have known by his name that Ancel is a Jew. I hope that having a Jewish roommate isn't going to turn the other students against me.* The poison of Hitler's speeches had already found its way onto the campus. Jews were not popular at the University of Charité in Berlin, even though several of the professors were Jewish. And that's why Ernst was surprised when Charité had allowed Albert Einstein, who was a professor at Humboldt, a neighboring university, to come and speak. Ernst and Ancel attended the speech, and Ernst had to admit that he was impressed. Einstein, he decided, was quite possibly the most brilliant man he'd ever heard.

A few days passed, and Ernst found that his new roommate was considerate, friendly, smart, and quick witted. He, too, was a medical student, and Ernst enjoyed studying with him. By the second week of school, Ancel had introduced Ernst to a group of Jewish medical students who accepted him without question. And since Ernst did not make friends easily on his own, he was grateful for his roommate and this newly found group of friends. Ernst shared classes with some of these boys. And now for the first time in his life, he always had a table of friends to sit with at lunchtime. When he was with these boys, he felt comfortable, so he almost never stuttered. But they were a small group, and one afternoon when they were having lunch, Ancel explained why. "Neider, you know why there are so few Jews here?"

Ernst shook his head.

"It's because they only accept a small quota—five percent, to be exact. You know what that means? It means we're the cream of the crop. We had to get the highest marks, or we wouldn't be permitted to be here," Ancel said.

About a month later, on a Friday night, Ancel invited Ernst to have a Sabbath dinner with him and the rest of the Jewish medical students. "I spoke with the other fellows, and we decided it would be nice for us to have a Shabbos dinner together. We're going to a little restaurant in town. They don't announce it, but they have some kosher entrées. So, we go there sometimes. Would you like to join us? I think you would enjoy it," Ancel said.

"No, thank you. I don't have money to go out and eat."

"It's all right. We can each put up a little to pay for you. The fellows all like you, and we'd love for you to come. Come, join us; it will be nice," Ancel said. "It's a kosher restaurant, and as you know, I don't keep kosher. But I love the taste of traditional Jewish food. And from what I hear, this place has the real thing, just like my bubbie used to make: potato latkes, brisket, stuffed cabbage." He smacked his lips. "I really think you'll enjoy it."

But Ernst refused. Not because he didn't want to go—in fact, he did. He thought it would be nice to get out with a group of like-minded friends. But he was afraid of what the other non-Jewish students might say if he was seen in town eating with a group of Jewish students at a Jewish kosher restaurant. Ernst didn't care that they were Jews. It made little difference to him. But he knew that if he was seen with them, a stigma would follow him, and he was afraid it might hurt his chances of finding a good job after he finished school. *I have been courting danger eating at the same lunch table with them,* he thought. *The Jews are ostracized by everyone. I have been telling myself that I should break off this friendship I have with them because I don't want to be ostracized too. If only I had the courage to make friends with the non-Jewish medical students, I know it would be better for me in the long run. And it's a shame that I have to break away from these boys, because I really like them. They're kind to me, and I feel comfortable with them. But the truth is, I am glad that I am not one of them. And I know that my parents would say that I should be friends with people who are my own kind. Pure German, Aryans as we are called now. But, I feel so inferior to the other pure Germans. I am not athletic or handsome. And then to make matters even worse, that damn stutter starts. I just don't know how to talk to the Aryan students, but I know I should find a way.*

When he went into town to buy food that weekend, he saw a group of Aryan students from his pre-med classes sitting at an outdoor biergarten. They were talking, laughing, and drinking dark German beer. *This is my opportunity to make friends,* he thought. *I wish I had the courage to walk over to them, introduce myself, and start talking.* But he couldn't bring himself to do it; he felt so awkward. So out of place. And he was sure that if he tried to talk to them, he would stutter, and he was afraid they would laugh. *Then who knows, my stutter could be discovered by another boy like Otto, who would torture me for the rest of my time here at school. Better to keep to myself. And I should make an effort to stay away from the Jews.*

Before he had left for school, Ernst's parents gave him all the money they could spare. However, he knew the small sum of reichsmarks that he had would not last forever. He was grateful to have scholarships to pay his tuition, but he needed spending money, and that meant he needed to find work. The only work he'd ever done in his life was to help out at his parents' bakery. So one morning before his first class, he went into town to one of the bakeries to ask for a job.

"I have plenty of experience. My parents own a bakery," Ernst said, trying to sound confident. "I will work for a lower wage than anyone else you could hire. You see, I am a student, and I really need the money. I can come in before dawn in the morning and start the baking. But I do have to be back at school for my first class by ten."

The baker scratched his bald head. "Yes, there's no doubt that I could use the extra help. My health has not been good lately. I'm getting older," he said, sighing, then added, "and mornings before the shop opens is my most hectic time." The baker studied Ernst, then he said, "All right, I'll give you a job, but I can't pay you much."

"Pay me what you can. It's more than I have now."

"Good, so we are in agreement. You can start work tomorrow morning. Is that all right with you?"

"Yes, of course. I'll be here," Ernst said. He was happy to have any income at all.

CHAPTER THREE

1938

ERNST GOT INTO A ROUTINE. HE WOKE UP EARLY TO GO TO WORK AT the bakery, then ran all the way back to school to make it to his 10:00 a.m. class. After that, he ate a quick lunch before attending his afternoon classes. After class, he took a nap before eating his evening meal. And while the other boys were out drinking or meeting girls, he studied until he fell asleep with his nose in his book. Sometimes he would wake in the middle of the night still sitting at his desk, and climb into bed. But before long, it was time to awaken and start the whole process over again.

Getting up early to go to work at the bakery left Ernst exhausted. But as the years passed, he earned the trust of the baker, who now allowed Ernst to open without him in the morning. Ernst needed the money, but he needed his medical degree even more, so no matter what he had to do, he didn't allow his grades to suffer. He found that he had less time to spend with his Jewish friends. His lunch was a quick sandwich, which he ate on the way to his next class; there was no time to sit at a table with a group of fellows to discuss what they'd learned. And his dinners were in the school cafeteria, but he ate them alone, quickly, so he could return to his room to get in as much study time as possible.

At first, he missed the camaraderie he'd shared with the Jewish medical students. He missed it terribly. He'd never had friends before, and it had been a very enjoyable part of his life. But he reminded himself that it was probably for the best; they were Jewish, and it was a good thing that he had been forced to distance himself from them. They still invited him to dinners and to study groups, but he was just too busy; he couldn't attend even if he wanted to. The loneliness he'd felt his entire life had been gone for a short time, but now it had returned, and he wished things were different. However, he forced himself to remember that he had a goal, a dream, and he wasn't going to allow anything to get in the way.

That summer he had saved enough money to surprise his parents and return home for a week during his birthday. He was excited to see them. When he walked into the bakery, where they were both busy at work, his mother ran out from behind the counter and excitedly threw her arms around his neck. He felt sick when he looked at her. He couldn't help but notice how pale and thin she had gotten. Her face was lined with wrinkles, and gray hair had started to come in at her temples.

His father, whose clothes were wet with sweat and his brow deeply lined from years of hard work, saw his son, and his face lit up. The old man shook Ernst's hand and then drew him into a bear hug. Ernst wished he could stay home and help them in the bakery. They needed him, but he knew he couldn't. His dream of becoming a doctor was right on the horizon, and he couldn't give up now.

As he walked through the small town where he had grown up, he noticed that anti-Jewish sentiment was everywhere. There was a poster of a man with curly black hair and a big nose trying to lure blond-haired, blue-eyed children into a dark room where a cauldron stood burning. There were other posters, too, that said things like, "Never trust the Jew." Nazi flags hung from the buildings. When he went to a bier hall to have beer with his father one afternoon, he found that people spoke openly and often about their hatred of the Jews. They spewed lies as if they were the truth, lies that the Jews were responsible for Germany losing the Great War. Lies about how the Jews were enemies of the German people. Ernst knew that all of this wasn't true and wished he had the courage to tell them about his Jewish friends, but he didn't. He just sat there silently sipping his drink.

There was no doubt that Ernst felt guilty at betraying his friends. But even so, he remained silent. The week with his parents was delightful. His mother prepared all of his favorite dishes, kartoffelpuffer, a potato pancake that she fried until it was crispy on the outside and fluffy within, and homemade bratwurst, a slightly spicy sausage which she stuffed into the casing until it was near bursting and, of course, his most beloved spaetzle, a dumpling she prepared with just the right amount of cheese. The time sped by so quickly that his heart ached with each passing day. And then it was over, and once again, he stood on the train platform and waited for the train to come, with his parents beside him.

WHEN ERNST RETURNED TO SCHOOL, his Jewish friends had a birthday cake for him to celebrate his birthday. He really liked them; he enjoyed their company so much. And he wished that things were different for them. Having friends had been one of the most enjoyable parts of his life on campus. But he knew he must continue to distance himself from these boys. It was dangerous to allow these friendships to grow; they were not good for his reputation. *It's nice to have friends here on campus, a group of fellows who I can talk to, even depend on in an emergency. But unfortunately, I must keep my distance. If only these boys weren't Jewish.*

CHAPTER FOUR

September 1938

ERNST NEVER RECEIVED TELEPHONE CALLS AT WORK. SO WHEN HIS boss told him that he had a call, Ernst looked at him puzzled. A sting of alarm shot through him. His hands trembled as he picked up the phone.

"Allo," Ernst said.

"Ernst, it's your vater. Mutti is very sick. She is not doing well at all. Can you come home?"

How can I get home? I have no money. I have no way to get back. I spent every penny I saved to make that trip home on my birthday. And, even if I had the money, what about my classes; how can I leave my classes? But my mother needs me. I must find a way. What am I to do?

"Ernst."

"Yes, Vater."

"There isn't much time. You must get here as quickly as you can."

"I'll find a way," Ernst said. He felt sick to his stomach.

When he hung up the phone, he turned to the owner of the bakery who had been listening. "I must go home. I must get there as quickly as I can. My mother is very sick. I know that this is a lot to ask of you, but can you loan me some money? I have none left. I spent everything I had saved to go home a few months ago."

The old baker drummed his fingers on the wooden table. "I don't have much money to give you. Business has been slow, and we had a roof leak last month, if you recall. It set me back."

"Yes, I know. But anything you can do to help would be greatly appreciated."

"How long do you think you will be gone?"

"I don't know. I wish I did."

"Yes, I understand. And don't worry, your job will be here waiting for you when you return."

The baker walked over to the safe he kept in the back of the bakery and opened it. He handed Ernst a few reichsmarks. "I'm sorry that this is all I can spare. I wish it could be more."

Ernst nodded. "Thank you." *It's hardly enough. It won't even get me a one-way train ticket.*

It was a hectic day. But Ernst finished his shift and returned to his dorm room, weary, frightened of what would become of his mother, and worried that she might pass away before he could find a way to get home to see her.

"You look terrible," Ancel said when Ernst walked in. Ancel was getting ready to leave for class, but when he saw Ernst, he stopped and put his books down on the desk. Then he turned to look at Ernst. "What's the matter with you?"

Ernst told Ancel everything. Ancel listened; he did not interrupt. Ernst knew Ancel was going to be late for class. "You'd better go. Classes are starting."

"Yes, I know. Are you coming?"

"I can't. I wouldn't be able to concentrate anyway," Ernst said.

"I completely understand. And I sympathize with you. But don't worry, Ernst. I'm going to see what I can do to help you." Ancel patted Ernst's shoulder.

Ernst spent the entire morning and afternoon staring out the window of his dorm room. He held his head and thought about his mother, remembering the fairy tales she told him and the songs she sang to him when he was small. He remembered the strudels she'd baked for Christmas, and her laughter that filled the house with joy. Tears fell down his cheeks. *I wasted time being here at school, time I could have spent with her if I had known what was in store* , he thought.

At four thirty that afternoon, Ancel returned with the other Jewish students who were their friends. He walked into the apartment and handed Ernst an envelope. "All of us fellas wanted to help you, so we got together and, well . . . here's some money. It should be enough to pay for train fare for you to get home and back," Ancel said. Then he patted Ernst's shoulder.

Ernst took the envelope. He felt tears welling in his eyes. "I don't know how to thank you."

"It's all right. No need for thanks. We know you appreciate it. We all have family, and we understand how hard all of this must be for you. Take the money and go home tonight. Take the next train, and get home to your mother."

Ernst nodded. Then he thanked them again. Throwing some clothes in his suitcase quickly, he put on his coat and left. Then he ran all the way to the station where he boarded the next train, which arrived an hour later.

CHAPTER FIVE

ADELE NEIDER WAS LAID TO HER FINAL REST UNDER AN ELM TREE IN the backyard of her home. Her son, Ernst, and his father stood beside the preacher. It was a rainy autumn day, cold and gray. But the ground was covered with a blanket of color from the autumn leaves. This was the most difficult day of Ernst's life. He didn't know how he was going to go on without his mother. She'd always been there beside him. Even when he was away at school, he knew she was at home supporting him. Now, she would be gone. His vater would have to go on alone and knowing that weighed heavily on Ernst's mind. He considered not returning to school. But he couldn't do that because the last thing his mother said to him before she closed her eyes forever was, "I am so proud of you. Who would have ever thought my son, my little Ernst, would be a doctor? When you finish school, you go out into the world, and make a name for yourself, Ernst. You will be the first person in either your father's family or mine to graduate from the university. What an accomplishment."

Ernst stayed with his father for a week following the funeral, helping him in the house and in the bakery. He knew his father could use his help, but he had to get back to finish his classes. Every day that went by, he was getting further and further behind. So this time, it was just his father who stood beside him on the platform at the train station. Both of them were feeling the loss of his mother deeply, but neither of them mentioned it.

The whistle blew as the train pulled into the station. "I guess it's time for you to go," his father said as he reached out and shook Ernst's hand. But then his father pulled him into a bear hug. "I'll see you again soon," he said.

Ernst nodded. He didn't want to look at his father's face because he knew that he was crying.

CHAPTER SIX

IT TOOK A GREAT DEAL OF EFFORT TO CATCH UP ON HIS WORK. HE'D been gone from school for a little over a week, but the workload was tremendous. His boss at the bakery understood that Ernst needed a few extra days off to get himself situated with his classes. Because he liked Ernst, he allowed him to take the extra time. And so Ernst caught up on his schoolwork and, even though Ernst's heart was heavy at the loss of his mother, his life went back to the way it was before. Busy.

On a chilly November morning, Ernst returned to his room at the dormitory from working at the bakery. He would have liked to lie down for a half hour before his next class, but he really didn't have time. He hardly had time to change his clothes and make it to his first class. When he entered the apartment, all his Jewish friends were gathered there. Ancel stood in the corner; his face was ghost white.

"What's wrong? What's going on here?" Ernst asked, looking around the room at the unusual situation.

"Something happened last night. In the mitte, where my family lives," Ancel said.

"And mine too," one of the other boys added.

"What happened? Was it a fire?" Ernst asked.

"More than one. There were many fires. From what we have heard, there was an attack on the Jewish community. We are hearing there have been attacks on Jews all over Germany."

"What? Attacks?" Ernst asked, sitting down on his bed.

"We don't know what happened exactly. Of course, we do realize that the hatred for our people has been growing. Anyone can see that. But an attack like this is so barbaric. It reminds me of the pogroms we hear about that happen in Russia. I would never expect it in Berlin," Ancel said.

"Who did it?"

"We don't know that for sure either," Ancel said. "But we do know that the Jewish community was targeted."

Ernst stared at him and his mouth fell open. There were so many things going through his mind. But he said nothing.

CHAPTER SEVEN

One afternoon, without much warning, when classes were in session, all of the Jewish students and professors were expelled from the university. And from that day on, no Jews, professors, or students were permitted on campus. Ernst was unaware of what happened. He was so busy with his hectic life that he didn't realize what was happening. That morning at work, his boss, the baker, had not been feeling well. "I'm having a lot of pain in my chest and legs," he told Ernst. "I need to lie down."

"I understand. I'll stay here through my ten o'clock class. But I have to get to school by one. I have a test this afternoon," Ernst said. He hated to miss his morning class, but he couldn't leave his boss in this condition.

"That would be very helpful," the baker said. "I need to lie down. Can you handle the customers, alone, when they come in?"

"Of course. Don't you worry about anything. I'll take care of everything."

Ernst kneaded dough and stood in front of the counter all afternoon. The baker was not able to return to work, and he could not leave the bakery. So in order to help his boss, who had become a friend, he missed his test. *I'll speak to my professor tomorrow and explain.*

Hopefully he will allow me to make up the test, Ernst thought. Meanwhile, he had no idea that his Jewish friends had received notices that Jews would no longer be allowed to attend school. When he returned to his room late that afternoon, he found Ancel's bed made and all of his things gone. On the small desk that stood in the corner, Ernst saw a note. The envelope was addressed to him, and it was sealed shut. He opened it and read:

My good friend,

When you return to our room from work today, you will find that my things are no longer here. You may have heard that myself, along with several of our dear friends, have been expelled from school. This is because it has become law that Jews are no longer permitted to attend. It's hard to believe that something so preposterous is happening here, in Germany. All of the Jewish professors have all been discharged from their positions. And you know as well as I do, that some of them are wonderful, brilliant men, with so much knowledge to share. I can't imagine how this is good for the country. I believe that the repercussions of this action will be devastating to Germany's advancement as a country. But there is nothing I can say or do. I must leave here and return home. So it is with a heavy heart that I leave you. I enjoyed the time we shared learning together. We had such thought-provoking discussions. You have a bright mind, Ernst, and I will always remember you. I hope you will remember me too. I have no doubt that someday you will be a wonderful doctor. I wish I could say the same for myself. I don't know if I will be denied this opportunity, but I will try to attend a Jewish university and continue my educational pursuits. Perhaps we will meet again; who knows what this life has in store. But for now, I must bid you goodbye and I wish you well.

Ancel

. . .

ERNST PUT the paper back down on the desk. His fingers tingled; his hands trembled. *Ancel is a good person. I like him. He has been a friend to me, a true friend, when no one else would be. I know he would make an outstanding doctor. This is insanity. I can't understand what the German government is thinking. And I don't know what will become of my friends. It's hard to believe that all of their talent is lost because they are Jews. It doesn't seem logical. Still, I don't dare say a word to anyone about my feelings. If I do, everyone will turn against me.*

His boss recovered. He was weaker than before, but he managed to take care of the business, allowing Ernst to return to his regular schedule.

Three days later, a young man was assigned to Ernst's room. He was to be Ernst's new roommate, a student of literature and poetry. The two of them had little in common. They were civil, even friendly, but never friends. And, Ernst found that as the days went by, he was lonely. He missed Ancel and the rest of the fellows. But there was nothing he could do.

Each week he composed a letter to his father, and many times as he wrote those letters, he wished he could just go home. In one such letter, Ernst confessed that he wanted to return home and work with his father at the bakery. He explained that he knew how difficult things had become for his father now that he was working alone without his mother's help. His father wrote back promising he would hire someone to help him and insisting that Ernst finish school: ***You have come so far, you must do this, you must become a doctor, not only for yourself but to honor our family name.*** But, unbeknownst to Ernst, he never hired anyone.

CHAPTER EIGHT

A MONTH AFTER ANCEL HAD BEEN SENT HOME, ERNST WAS IN CLASS when a young man entered the classroom. He was tall and thin and very confident. "I'd like to speak with Ernst Neider," he said.

"Herr Neider," the professor called his name. "This gentleman would like to speak with you."

Ernst stood up and walked to the front of the room. He was concerned that he might be in trouble for having befriended the Jewish students who were now gone. "Y-yes. I-I'm Ernst Neider."

"Nice to meet you. I'm Hans Bruder. I'm with an organization called the Carl Schurz Society. Would you like to have a beer with me after class?"

Ernst would have liked to decline. But he was afraid it would draw attention to him so he said, "S-s-sure, but w-w-what is the Carl Schurz Society, may I ask?"

"I'll tell you all about it when we go for a beer," Hans said.

After class ended, Ernst and Hans walked to a local biergarten. They sat down and Hans ordered for them both. Then he smiled and said, "You have a good reputation. Your professors like you; they tell me that you are very smart."

Ernst blushed. "I t-t-try."

"Well, you are well respected among your peers and your teachers. I think you have a lot of potential."

"Me?" Ernst asked, surprised.

"Absolutely! You are the kind of man we are looking for," Hans said. Hans was so friendly and warm that Ernst felt comfortable around him. No one had ever complimented Ernst so openly, then Hans added, "So, how would you like to help the fatherland?"

"You mean Germany, of course," Ernst said. He didn't notice that he wasn't stuttering.

"Precisely. You are a German, an Aryan, and Germany is proud to have you as one of us."

Ernst beamed. His entire life, he'd felt like an outsider. But now Hans was making him feel like he was a part of something. He felt accepted. And he liked it. He wanted more of it.

"Anyway, let me explain," Hans said. "We have a group of about seventy-five American students scheduled to come and visit our beautiful country. This is not the first time we've done this sort of thing. The Carl Schurz Society had arranged tours like this before. But this time the students will be coming here to the Charité University to see how we educate our doctors in Germany. And since you are so intelligent, I've been sent here to ask you if you would like you to speak to them. Our main goal is to let them see how wonderful it is to live here in the new Germany, under the Third Reich. It's important that the world can see the progress Germany is making in the process of an economic and cultural renewal. Once they see it, they will return home to America and tell their families, their friends, and their fellow students just how much we are growing here in the fatherland."

"I-I-I see," Ernst said. He was stuttering again because he was thinking about speaking to a large group of people, "A-a-and I w-w-would love to help y-y-you. But, as y-y-you can see, I h-h-have this terrible stutter, and b-b-because of it, I d-d-don't feel comfortable speaking in front of an audience."

"I completely understand. So, how about this. What if I can get you a speech teacher? Someone who can help you to get rid of that stutter once and for all? Would you do it then?"

Ernst thought about it. He had longed to be rid of his stutter for a very long time. "I'd be willing to try."

"Good. Then I'll arrange it. The Americans won't be here until the end of next month so that should give you plenty of time to correct this problem," Hans said, then he added, "Don't you worry about a thing. I promise you will be just fine."

CHAPTER NINE

HANS RETURNED TO HIS HOTEL ROOM AND PICKED UP THE PHONE.

"Allo." It was a female voice.

"Greta. It's Hans. I need your help with something."

"What is it?"

"I am at Charité University in Berlin. The students are coming here next month, with the Carl Schurz program. I just met with a brilliant medical student, who happens to be just a little odd and awkward. He has a terrible stutter. But, I truly believe it can be easily cured by the attention of a beautiful woman."

She laughed. "Why do men think everything can be cured by a woman's attention?"

"Because it's true. Now, listen to me. I want you to come here and work with him. He thinks you are a speech teacher. You won't need much to fix him. All you have to do is flirt with him, compliment him, and give him the confidence he lacks. He'll be fine once you do that."

"And what do I say when he wants to continue things with him and I? I mean, if I have been flirting with him, he is going to think I want more."

"You tell him that you find him attractive, but you are his

teacher, and that sort of thing is unethical. This man is the type to understand and accept that as an excuse. He is the type of person who is trying very hard to do the right things."

"I'll be there in two days. What's his name, and where do I find him?"

CHAPTER TEN

It worked. Greta's compliments and kind words gave Ernst the confidence he required to speak to the American students. He found he enjoyed their questions. Their interest in his career made him feel important. They wanted to know all about Germany and what the führer was doing to bring about economic recovery. Although it haunted him, Ernst was careful not to mention the attack on the Jews in November or the fact that they had been expelled from all public schools including the university. Instead, he told them how two years ago, Hitler had begun a program whereby every German citizen would have an automobile. They seemed impressed. And when Ernst finished speaking, Hans and Greta took him out for dinner. They told him that he had served his country well. And he liked the way it felt to finally be a part of something.

CHAPTER ELEVEN

Spring 1939

Finally, Ernst was ready to graduate. He'd done well in school and had achieved honors. It had been a long, arduous road for him. It was difficult to work at a job and study at the same time, but he'd done it, and he was also proud to say that he had saved enough money for his father to come to Berlin for his graduation. Ernst sent his father the money. They were both excited about seeing each other because they hadn't been together since his mother's passing. But two weeks prior to Ernst's graduation, he received a phone call at the dormitory from a woman who had been a friend of his mother's.

"Ernst? This is Marta, your mother's friend. I live a few houses down from your parents. Do you remember me?"

"Yes, of course," he said.

"I'm sorry that I have to be the one to call you and tell you this. But there was no one else. I am afraid I have bad news." She sucked in a deep breath, then in her strongest voice, she told him, "You see, I went to go to your father's bakery. I went for several days, but each day I went, it was closed. So, I went by your house, and I found something terrible. I am sorry, Ernst, but your father passed away. There was an envelope with money and a letter from you on his table. Should I send you the money, or will you be coming here to the funeral?"

It was as if a dark cloud just fell like a bomb upon him. *I am alone in the world now.* He didn't want to return just to see his father's body laid in the ground. *There is nothing for me there anymore.* "Just send me the money, please," he said. Then he managed to say, "Thank you."

"Of course," she replied. And the phone line went dead.

CHAPTER TWELVE

1939

By August, Ernst had gotten a job at a local hospital. He had rented a room above a store in town and was still working at the bakery part time, when he received a call from Hans. "It just so happens Greta and I are right here in town. We'd love to see you," he said.

"Yes, I'd love to see you both," Ernst said. Ernst was happy to hear from Hans and even happier to hear that Greta was with him.

"What time do you get off work tomorrow?" Hans asked.

"Seven o'clock. Is that too late?"

"Not at all. Where are you working?"

"A hospital in town. I can meet you at the biergarten right around the corner from the University. You know the one?" Ernst said.

"Of course. And, it sounds perfect. Eight o'clock."

Hans and Greta were waiting when Ernst arrived. They'd brought a young, handsome soldier with them, who introduced himself as Werner. The three visitors bought Ernst several beers to celebrate his graduation. Greta had positioned herself in the seat beside Ernst, and every so often she rubbed his forearm. He was enjoying his new friends: the laughing, the joking and the feeling of belonging, when Werner said, "You know, it would be a good idea for you to join the army."

"The army, why?"

"Well, the fatherland has been expanding. As you know, we are short on land. We've taken Austria, and now we are moving our troops into Czechoslovakia."

"Oh, but I am not a soldier. I have never been very athletic," Ernst admitted.

"No, of course not," Hans said. "But you are a brilliant doctor. And whether or not you agree with Hitler's choice to invade Czechoslovakia, you must admit it was a very good idea to rid ourselves of the threat of their large, imposing army."

"I am not a very political man," Ernst said.

"But you must know how pleased Austria is that we have annexed them into Germany. I know Czechoslovakia will feel the same in time."

Ernst was squirming a little in his chair. Greta reached over and rubbed his forearm. Then in her throaty, sultry voice, she said, "It's not about the war, Ernst. You are a doctor. Our German soldiers need you. If they are injured, you have the power and the knowledge to save their lives. You must help them. We—all of us—me included, of course, are depending upon you."

She had a way of making Ernst sit up straighter. When they had worked together to rid him of his stutter, she'd made him feel like he could do anything. How he'd wished that she would be his girl. But he hadn't had the nerve to ask her. And she never mentioned any sort of future with him. But even now when he knew that she was going to leave and go home to Munich, he still wanted to please her. "So, I would be a medic? I wouldn't have to fight?"

"Of course not. You are a doctor; you would be there to help the wounded," Hans said.

Ernst considered this. He sipped his beer.

"You would make me so proud," Greta said, smiling at him. "And we could write letters to each other, you and I."

This was the first time Greta had ever given Ernst hope that she might consider a relationship with him. "You would be proud of me?" he repeated as he looked into her eyes. "Would I be in danger?"

"Never. Germany is so powerful that there is no actual fighting. The countries we occupy surrender to our power quickly, without a fight. The truth is, I think they want us to take them over," Hans said. "We offer them stability."

Greta took Ernst's hand and raised it to her lips. She planted a warm kiss on his palm. He felt a bolt of sexual energy surge through him. "If you don't join, you'll be conscripted, drafted, anyway. Wouldn't you rather show how loyal you are to the party by joining?"

"As always, Greta, you're right. I'll join," he said.

Greta leaned over and kissed him. He felt his entire body trembling.

CHAPTER THIRTEEN

Autumn 1939

ERNST JOINED THE ARMY. HE WAS SENT FOR MILITARY TRAINING. Although he was not an athletic man, his trainers overlooked a lot of his shortcomings because they needed trained doctors, and he was a brilliant one. Once he completed his training, Ernst received a brown leather bag to carry his medical supplies, and then he was fitted for a uniform that he thought made him look almost handsome.

Idealistic, and hopeful that he was going to make a positive difference, Ernst marched east with his troop. At first he could feel that he had a purpose for being in the military. Even though the long walks were strenuous for him, he felt useful. There were soldiers who fainted due to the long marches, and he was happy to be able to help. But then, unexpectedly, Hitler broke the promise he made to Poland. He'd promised he would never invade them. But now, Germany was bombing her Polish neighbor, and the troops were on their way to march into Warsaw.

Ernst wrote to Greta as often as he could. But as of yet, he had not received a return letter from her. He told himself that this was because he was constantly moving around, and soon her letters would find him. They didn't. There were no letters. Ernst was alone facing a frigid, miserable winter as his troop headed east.

CHAPTER FOURTEEN

Russia 1940

BY THE END OF 1940, ERNST WAS BATTLE WEARY. HE'D SEEN enough blood and suffering to make him consider returning home and going back to working at a bakery rather than using his medical degree. He had held young men as the life left their bodies. He'd watched them cry in the arms of their troop leaders. And as he did, all of his secret dreams and ambitions of being a godlike healer evaporated. War had humbled him. He knew now that he was limited, very limited in just how much he could do to help another human being. And he'd also come to realize just how vulnerable he was when he'd faced death more than once during the battles. He knew the lasting effect it could have on a man to witness someone blown to bits who stood right beside him. And all the while, as he looked at the mass of blood and bone, he was thinking, *That could just as easily have been me.*

Then in the fall of 1941, Ernst and his troop found themselves in a city called Rzhev just about 140 miles outside of Moscow. The Germans had a plan—they named it Operation Typhoon. A terrible, bloody, battle between Russia and Germany ensued. Germany was victorious.

It was still only autumn, and the brutal Russian winter had not yet overtaken the under-equipped German Army.

Russia named this battle the Rzhev Meat Grinder.

By early January 1942, Ernst and his troop, along with many other German battalions, had arrived at the gates of Moscow.

The Russians fought hard, and now the bitter cold of the Russian winter was upon them. This was a chill that was deeper and more penetrating than anything Ernst had ever experienced. Hitler had not equipped his troops sufficiently to endure this weather. He had thought that Germany would have taken Russia by now. And so, the tides began to turn. Germany was in trouble; they were losing the war.

The gunshots, the blood, and the dead bodies continued to accumulate as the Germans shivered in their too-thin winter coats.

Then one afternoon, Ernst saw another man who wore a doctor's uniform get shot down. Ernst knelt down on the ground. Bullets flew above his head and all around him. But he had to see if the man was alive. He placed his fingers on the man's neck. There was a pulse; the man was wounded but not dead.

"Help me." The man opened his eyes. "I'm a doctor."

"I am too," Ernst said. "Don't worry. I will help you."

Ernst carried the man's wounded body away from the front lines and back to the makeshift hospital. He removed the bullet that had entered the man's body, and stitched him up. Then he stayed with the man until the man was fully awake.

"Thank you," the man said. "I'm Josef Mengele. Who are you?"

"Ernst Neider."

"You saved my life, Neider. I am going to have you promoted to the Waffen SS."

And so it was that Ernst became a member of the SS. Then only a month later, Ernst was kneeling beside a boy who had been fatally shot, when a bullet fired by the enemy found its way into Ernst's leg. He crawled all the way to the makeshift hospital, where he was immediately taken to have the bullet removed. But when he recovered, his leg was permanently damaged. He walked slowly and with a severe limp. However, he wasn't disappointed at losing his mobility. He was relieved because his platoon leader suggested that he put in for a transfer. "You are surely eligible to get out of this mess. With your leg being the way it is, you shouldn't go back into battle," he said.

Ernst was placed at a desk job in Berlin. He moved back, but before he started work, he received a telegram:

Neider, this is Mengele, the man whose life you saved. I'd like to speak to you about you coming to work with me. I am on my way to Berlin for a conference. I was hoping we could meet. I'll be there next week.

Ernst replied immediately. He said he would be happy to meet with the doctor. Then he told his superiors that he was considering a job with Dr. Josef Mengele, so he wasn't going to take the desk job.

CHAPTER FIFTEEN

Mengele telephoned Ernst the following Monday to say he was in town. They met at a small, intimate restaurant for dinner that evening.

"Neider," Mengele said, smiling, when Ernst walked in. "It's good to see you."

Ernst sat down. They ordered sauerbraten, potato salad, and large mugs of dark beer.

"I was looking through the transfer requests for an assistant, when I came across your name," Mengele said. "I have a good job offer for you."

"In a hospital?" Ernst asked.

"You could say that. You will be working in the hospital there," Mengele said. "Are you willing to move to Poland? The money is excellent as are the benefits."

"I would be willing to move."

"You will be given a place to live that you will not be required to pay anything for. Uniforms are provided. You will find that this is a very coveted position that I am offering you. Are you interested?"

"I am," Ernst said.

"Good. Then it's settled. You're my new assistant."

"What's the name of the place?" Ernst asked.

"It's called Auschwitz-Birkenau." Mengele smiled.

CHAPTER SIXTEEN

MENGELE TOOK A FOUNTAIN PEN OUT OF HIS JACKET POCKET, AND A small notebook. He tore out a piece of paper and wrote down an address. I expect you to arrive at Auschwitz on Monday, two weeks from today. I think two weeks is long enough for you to finish any business you have here in Berlin."

"Yes, two weeks is plenty of time. Thank you, Doctor. Thank you. You won't be sorry you chose me. I promise you that." He looked down at the address Mengele had given him and then tucked the paper into his jacket pocket. But when he went to ask Mengele for a little more information about the job and what would be expected of him, Mengele had already laid several reichsmarks on the table to pay the bill and was on his way out of the restaurant. Ernst watched him walk across the street. Then Ernst looked down at the paper he held in his hands. *My future lies right here*, he thought. *I am going to be someone important.* Mengele didn't give him any additional information, so he had no idea what to expect. All he knew was that he had been chosen for an important and coveted job.

When Ernst arrived at Auschwitz early on a Monday morning, he was shocked to see a facility that was surrounded by an iron gate with a sign: Arbeit Macht Frei, Work Sets You Free. *What a strange place*, he thought. *I was expecting a hospital. But this is not a hospital, nor is it a research facility. It appears to be a prison of some kind.*

He felt a little strange as he approached the guard at the gate. "I am Dr. Ernst Neider." Ernst loved the sound of that. He loved to hear the word "doctor" before his name. It represented all of his hard work, and for a moment he forgot the strangeness of the facility, and his chest swelled with pride. "I am here to see Dr. Mengele. He is expecting me."

The guard looked Ernst over, up and down, slowly. Then he picked up a pad of paper and silently read through a list. "Yes, I see your name right here. Dr. Mengele is expecting you. Excuse me for a moment," the guard said to Ernst, then turning to his coworker, he added, "I am going to escort Dr. Neider to the hospital. He's here to see Dr. Mengele. I'll be right back."

The other guard nodded.

"All right, follow me, please," the guard told Ernst.

Ernst entered the grounds and looked around him. It was not at all what he had expected. He'd thought he was going to a hospital where everything would be clean and sterile. Instead, this place was filthy. There was strong, unpleasant stench, which made him gag; it was something he'd never smelled before, and he could not identify what it was. Sickly, emaciated-looking people walked around in striped uniforms surrounded by armed guards, who were everywhere.

"Welcome to Auschwitz," the guard said to him. "Hell on earth." Then he laughed and waved to another guard who was sitting in an overhead tower. Ernst saw the guard above was armed. *This has to be a prison. Or it could be a hospital for the criminally insane?* He would have asked the guard, but before he had a chance to say another word, they had arrived at a building. "This is it. This is the hospital. You'll find Dr. Mengele in here," the guard said, smiling, as he held the door for Ernst, who walked inside.

This is the hospital where Dr. Mengele works? I would never have thought that he would work in a place like this. This place is filthy too, Ernst thought, disgusted by his surroundings, as he followed the guard to the front desk where a young blonde nurse was sitting. She looked up from the papers in front of her as they approached.

"This is Ernst Neider. Dr. Mengele is expecting him," the guard said. Then he turned to Ernst. "She'll help you from here."

"Thank you," Ernst said. But the guard was already gone; he was outside the door.

"Wait here, Dr. Neider. I'll let Dr. Mengele know you have arrived," the young nurse instructed.

Ernst nodded. He looked around the room as he waited. *Dr. Mengele is a well-respected physician. Why would he ever choose to work here when he could work anywhere he wanted? This is all very strange.*

"Heil Hitler," Dr. Mengele said as he saluted when he walked into the room.

"Heil Hitler," Ernst responded with a salute.

"Welcome, Ernst," Dr. Mengele said in a friendly tone. He was smiling brightly. "I'm glad to see you." Once again, Ernst was struck by Dr. Mengele's good looks and confidence. "We just opened this place this past spring, so we're still getting organized. There's a lot more that needs to be done. It takes time. But we are working on it. Come, let me show you around," Mengele said graciously.

"Is this a prison?" Ernst asked as he walked beside Dr. Mengele.

"Yes, in a way, it is. These people who you see here are enemies of the Reich. We can't allow them to wander the streets; they would poison the entire population. So, we keep them here."

"These are the barracks where the prisoners are housed." Dr. Mengele pointed to several buildings. Then he showed Ernst the Gypsy camp. "A Gypsy camp? Why a Gypsy camp?" Ernst asked.

"That's easy. The Gypsies are lazy and filthy. They bring disease and drain the government of money. They pose a huge problem to the Reich. Besides that, their morals are questionable, so we need to be sure they don't go around seducing young Aryan women. Their blood is tainted."

"But there are women there as well as men. Old women too. They could hardly seduce anyone."

Mengele turned to Ernst and gave him a look that let Ernst know that he had gone too far. And if he wanted to stay on Mengele's good side, it was best that he not ask any more questions. "They are enemies of the Reich. That's all you need to know. That's all that needs to be said," Mengele said curtly.

Next, Dr. Mengele led Ernst to a room filled with little people. They were small in stature, and from the back, they could have been children. But from the front, they were of varying ages. "Dwarfs?" Ernst asked.

"Yes, dwarfs. They are deformed. And, once again, we can't have them out in the world polluting our new Aryan nation, now, can we?"

Ernst looked at Mengele, puzzled. He had heard all of this propaganda about inferior races, on the radio, and read about it in the papers when he had time to read the papers. But he'd ignored it for the most part. He was too busy with school and then the war to take any of it too seriously. However, now that he was seeing evidence of it, he was finding it disturbing. He said nothing.

"We are trying to prove to the world that we are the master race. We can't have this sort of thing infiltrating our pure Aryan blood, now, can we?"

"So, you mean to tell me that these people live here, in a prison, because they are dwarfs?"

"There is so much you have to learn," Mengele scoffed. He avoided directly answering Ernst's question. Then he said, "Just be glad you are a pure Aryan man with a good head on your shoulders. If you don't ask too many questions and you don't delve too deep into things that don't concern you, you will go far. Heed my warning," Mengele said. He was staring intently into Ernst's eyes. There was something about Mengele that made Ernst shiver. But then Dr. Mengele broke his gaze and smiled. He patted Ernst on the shoulder and said, "Now, come, follow me. I have something very special to show you."

Ernst followed Mengele into a large room filled with children. But not just any children; these little ones were all twins. *It's like seeing double*, Ernst thought. Every child had an exact look-alike.

"I love twins," Mengele said, ruffling the hair of a little boy who sat beside his brother, "because they are exactly alike. They are perfect for our experiments."

"Experiments?"

"Yes. As I said, you have much to learn. But that's enough for one day. Don't you agree?" Mengele asked. Then without waiting for Ernst to answer, he added, "Let's go and have a cup of coffee."

They walked back to Dr. Mengele's office where he told his pretty young secretary to bring them refreshments.

"Yes, Doctor," she said. "I'll get it right away." Ten minutes later, she returned with a tray.

It was real coffee, with real cream and sugar. *I can't remember the last time I had real coffee,* Ernst thought.

"Would you care for a pastry?" Dr. Mengele asked.

Sweet rolls. Ernst's mouth watered. Sugar was so expensive, and even though he worked at the bakery, he wasn't permitted to eat the sweets. They only baked a few pastries each day due to how difficult it was to get the ingredients, and these were saved for paying customers. So he hadn't had a sweet roll in years. "Yes, thank you," Ernst said, taking one of the rolls from a plate Dr. Mengele held in front of him.

"Good?"

"Very."

"We get them from the local bakery. They are only for the doctors."

"Not the nurses?"

"Sometimes, you can give a nurse one, if you find a girl who you like. If you know what I mean," Mengele said, winking.

"And the prisoners?"

"Never for the prisoners."

"Not even the little children, the twins?"

"No, never. Although sometimes I give them candy. They love it." He laughed. "Would you believe that they call me uncle? I give the candy to the children, the twins, the Gypsy children too. They are all very sweet. Especially the Gypsy children. You haven't seen them yet. Although I must advise you not to become attached to

57

them. You must remember that although they look human, they are not. It's just an illusion. They are all untermenschen, subhumans: Jews and Gypsies."

Even though Ernst had been locked away at school, engrossed in his studies and then in the army, he'd heard the term untermenschen before, and he knew what it meant. He didn't agree with it. Still, he knew better than to voice his opinions if he wanted this job. And he did want this job. Even if he only worked with Mengele at this terrible place for a year or two, it would be like a star on his résumé.

Once they finished eating the coffee and sweets, Dr. Mengele began to explain Auschwitz. "All right, let me make some things clear to you. This is a sort of prison, as I said before. Most of the inmates are Jews and Gypsies."

"So, it's a prison for Jews and Gypsies?" Ernst repeated what Mengele said. He was trying to act as if he were in agreement with all of this. But for a moment his thoughts traveled back to his Jewish friends at the university.

"Yes, Jews and Gypsies. But not only Jews and Gypsies. Also, any other unsavory elements that Germany must be cleansed of. Political prisoners, criminals of all kinds, prostitutes, homosexuals, thieves, you understand. And Jehovah's Witnesses. Let me tell you about them. They are a stubborn bunch for certain. Have you ever met a Jehovah's Witness?" Mengele asked.

"No, I'm afraid I haven't."

"They would rather die than renounce their god. Fools, I say. Do you believe in God?"

"Yes," Ernst said. "I have seen too many miracles not to believe."

"I don't. The only god I believe in is myself," Mengele said.

Ernst swallowed hard. *This is a difficult man*, he thought.

"So, you have a hospital here in case they get sick?" Ernst asked.

"Yes, and also, well, as I said before, we can use them to learn."

"To learn?"

"Yes, it is our right to use them to further our scientific knowledge. We experiment on them in ways we would never be allowed to on actual humans. And because they react like humans, we can learn things we need to know from experimenting on them."

"I don't really understand."

"All right, let me make this clear. Now, being that you are a doctor, you are also a scientist. Is that not true?"

"I suppose it is."

"Well, how would you like to have the opportunity to test any medications or theory on living, breathing human beings rather than animals? I mean they are not actually human, in the way we are, of course. They are inferiors. However, their bodies respond the same way ours do, and that gives us plenty of opportunity to test our theories. And if you have made an error in your theory, and the subhumans die, you don't have to be concerned. No one will question you. There will be no repercussions. Don't you see the benefit? Can't you see how having this ability is tremendous for us? There are no limits to what we can learn, what we can achieve without having to answer to anyone."

"It seems morally wrong," Ernst said.

"Perhaps. But you must not forget that they are untermenschen after all. And besides that, the end justifies the means, as they say. What if the work we do here saves good German lives? What if we are able to find cures for diseases that have plagued mankind? I know the idea of experimentation is ugly because these subjects look and act human. But believe me they are not, and the results could have a marked effect on the future of the world. Our world. A world where our führer rules, and the fatherland is the greatest power on earth. In this new world, the Aryan man's well-being will be the highest priority. And it is only right."

"Yes, I have to admit. I can see the value," Ernst said. And he did see it. Yet the very idea of experimentation on humans still bothered him. He couldn't see these victims as untermenschen. He'd had Jewish friends; he knew they were as human as he was.

"Well then, now that you can see the importance of our work, I know you'll do just fine here."

Early one afternoon, a few days after Ernst started working at Auschwitz, Dr. Mengele came into the room where Ernst was finishing his morning rounds.

"You're just the man I was looking for," Mengele said. Then he took Ernst to the side of the room where the two young twins he'd been examining could not hear him and said, "A transport is scheduled to come in later today. I'd like you to accompany me while I do the selection."

"I am not sure I understand what you mean 'the selection.'"

"You will understand," Dr. Mengele said curtly. "You do ask a lot of questions, don't you, Neider? You really should try to curtail that. It's rather annoying. Anyway, I am busy, and I don't have time to explain it to you right now. But you'll understand once you attend a transfer. I promise you." He managed a strained smile as he walked away.

An hour later, Dr. Mengele found Ernst sitting at his desk documenting everything he'd done when he had completed his rounds.

"Allo, Ernst," Mengele said cheerfully. There was no trace of his earlier disdain toward Ernst. In his hand, Mengele carried a horseback-riding crop which he gently rapped against his thigh. "The train has just arrived. It's time for you to witness your first transport. Follow me."

Ernst put his clipboard down on the desk where the nurses sat, then he and Mengele were on their way out of the building. Once outside, he followed Dr. Mengele. They walked for a while until they came to the train tracks where a boxcar awaited their arrival.

"This is the ramp where we greet our new inmates." Mengele winked at Ernst as he climbed up the ramp. Ernst followed silently. Then one of the guards, who stood at the front of the first boxcar in the row, nodded to Dr. Mengele. The doctor tapped his thigh with the riding crop. Then he nodded back to the guard.

Ernst heard the metal doors of the train cars being pushed open.

Crowds of people were forced from the train by armed guards who were accompanied by large dogs. Dead bodies fell out of the train cars as the people rushed out. Some were standing paralyzed by fear. The guards nudged them forward with their guns. Others were crying. But most of them were running. Women held tight to their children's hands. One woman fell to her knees clutching what Ernst thought for sure was a dead infant. A guard stood over her and demanded her to leave the child's body and get into the line. But she ignored him and began to wail like a wounded animal. He took his gun and shot her. Ernst gasped at the sight. Mengele turned to look at him for a moment. Then Mengele let out a laugh. "It's quite a spectacle the first time you see it," he said. Ernst didn't answer because he couldn't speak.

The guards were pushing the people into a line. At the front of that line stood Dr. Mengele with Ernst at his side. Mengele turned to Ernst and smiled, then he said, "Shall we begin?"

Ernst stared at Mengele.

"Don't look so frightened. You'll get used to this. Besides, we don't have to do it all the time. Sometimes one of the others handles the selections. I don't mind doing it myself. In fact, I prefer it. However, even when someone else is in charge of making the selections, I make sure to be here. Just in case there are twins. We never want to miss a set of twins. Or some interesting deformity," Dr. Mengele said.

Ernst watched as the terrified people were lined up. The guards were yelling, "Mach schnell, hurry," and "Zwillinge, twins. All zwillinge come to the front."

"Look at this." A young guard walked up to Dr. Mengele. He was holding the arm of a slender teenage girl as if he had found a rare gem. "Look at her eyes, Doctor. One of her eyes is blue; the other is brown."

"Good work in finding that one," Mengele said, patting the guard on the shoulder. "Good work indeed." Then he looked at the girl, who was shaking. "This is your lucky day. Don't be so frightened. I am sending you to my special misfit room." Then he turned to the guard and told him, "See to it she is sent to my misfit room."

"Did you see that heterochromia? I love those. As soon as I saw her I knew that I would use her to turn that brown eye to blue. I've been working on something that can turn brown eyes to blue. Can you imagine? If I succeed, we would have a completely blue-eyed world. No good German would have to endure brown eyes ever again."

"Can that really be done?"

"I believe it can," Mengele said. "Unfortunately I haven't had many heterochromias come into this camp. The last one I had died from an infection from the chemicals I injected into her brown eye, trying to change the color. I will try something different with this one. I have been working on this for a while, but for the most part, I have been using brown-eyed children. So far, I haven't found the right chemical combination. I did have some success at one point; the eyes turned blue, but then the subject went blind. I had to euthanize it." He shook his head. "It was a bit of a failure, I am afraid. But, all it means is that I must try another method. Isn't that right, Neider?"

Ernst didn't answer; he was mesmerized by a young woman holding a small child in her arms. She was looking right into Ernst's eyes. For a moment, a single second, she caught his gaze. In her eyes, he saw pleading. He felt sick to his stomach. *I should do something*, he thought, but couldn't. He felt weak and powerless. So he looked away from her. Dr. Mengele smiled warmly at the frightened prisoners. Then Mengele glanced at Ernst. "So, now we begin," he said. Then without waiting for any reaction from Ernst, he began to quickly glance over each person as the line moved in front of him. "Left," he said to one. "Right," he said to another. And the prisoners were forced into two lines, one to the left and one to the right.

It wasn't until later that day that Dr. Mengele took Ernst into his office to have lunch to explain. While they were eating their afternoon meal, Mengele explained that anyone who had been sent to the left was on their way to a gas chamber, where they would be euthanized, and then their bodies would be burned in the crematorium. "Those are the weak and sick ones. The ones who are too young to work. Basically, useless eaters," Mengele said. "Now those who are sent to the right are those who are capable of work." He took a bite of his roast beef and cheese sandwich, then went on to say, "In the end they will all die."

Ernst shivered. "I was sorry to see that we didn't receive any twins other than that one with the bicolored eyes—no oddities today. Nothing else of great interest." Mengele sighed as he sipped his beer. "Would you like more cheese?" he asked Ernst.

Ernst shook his head. "No, thank you." He had lost his appetite. *This is not a hospital. This man is not a doctor. I don't know what this is, or who Dr. Mengele is. But he is a monster. That much I know for sure.*

Mengele eyed Ernst. Then he said, "You must realize that I have given you a hell of a good opportunity. I did this because you saved my life. However, don't make me regret my decision. The look on your face tells me that you don't appreciate what I have done for you. But I am warning you, Neider, don't be an ingrate."

"I'm sorry," Ernst managed to say. "It's just a lot to take in. I don't mean to be ungrateful."

All afternoon, gray ashes fell over the compound covering everything: the ground, the tops of the buildings, Ernst's clothes.

"I'm afraid we have to endure all of this filthy ash from the crematorium," Mengele said. "It's rather unappealing, I know; however, you'll get used to it."

Ernst felt his skin crawl as the ashes fell upon his hair and shoulders. He thought of the young mother whose eyes had met his and of her child who had been torn from her arms. Her child had been sent to the left. *Perhaps this bit of ash is the little boy that was in her arms,* he thought and felt his stomach turn.

"Now, let's go and explore the specimens in my special rooms, the ones I showed you briefly this morning," Dr. Mengele interrupted Ernst's thoughts. "First, we can look in on my misfits of all sorts, you know, the dwarfs, and that sort of thing. And then we'll go and see my twins. If you remember, most of them are children. They are of the utmost interest to me." Mengele smiled. "As a young doctor, I know you will find them fascinating. You see, Ernst, we are so fortunate to be able to work here. Why, this place is a doctor's dream. We can do any medical experiments that we like, and there are no restrictions. We have an opportunity to make medical advancements that have never been made in medicine before. We can make history. The world will thank us for years to come for all the wonderful discoveries we make here."

CHAPTER SEVENTEEN

ERNST FOLLOWED DR. MENGELE INTO THE ROOM WHERE THE dwarfs sat in a corner together. The young girl with the two different-colored eyes was there too. Her face was red from crying. There was a very tall young man, perhaps seven feet in height. "Good afternoon, you misfits," Mengele said. Then he let out a laugh as he glanced at Ernst, who managed to smile back at him.

"Look at these deformed bodies, will you? Do you ever wonder what causes this? I mean, what causes things to go wrong in the womb to create such monsters?"

Ernst didn't answer. But he managed to nod. He had often wondered why some people were born deformed, but unlike Mengele, he felt sorry for the man who was far too tall to be considered normal, and for the family of dwarfs, and the poor girl with the mismatched eyes.

"I once got my hands on a child who was born without limbs, would you believe? It was born here. What a treasure that was, but it died. I was sorry to lose it."

Ernst said nothing. In his mind's eye, he saw the infant born without limbs, and he felt such pity for it. He wondered how it was that Mengele, who had been trained as a doctor, could have no sympathy for the suffering.

Mengele didn't notice the way Ernst was looking at him. He seemed entranced by his room filled with unfortunates. Then Mengele pulled a young boy out of his bed and pointed to his foot. Look at how deformed it is. It was twisted in the womb, but why? And how?"

Ernst had read somewhere that Dr. Goebbels, Hitler's Reich minister of propaganda, had been born with a clubfoot. He wondered why Goebbels was in a position of power while this child was imprisoned. The only reason he could come up with was that the child was a Jew.

It was as if Mengele read his mind. "We can't tolerate deformities. And this one is not only a monster, but he's a Jew too. Not only can we not tolerate Jews, but we must eliminate anyone who is imperfect, especially Aryans. That is why it is so important to find out what causes these mishaps so we can avoid them. We want to breed the strongest and healthiest Aryans. Do you understand?"

Ernst nodded. He longed to ask about Dr. Goebbels, but he knew that it was best that he didn't. *Perhaps when I get to know Dr. Mengele better, I will ask him. But for now, I'll keep my mouth shut and agree with whatever he says. This job pays very well, better than any other job I would have found as a new doctor right out of medical school. And, of course, working with Dr. Mengele will improve my chances for better opportunities later, when I am ready to look for something else.*

Mengele greeted his "little monsters" as he called them, treating them like children even though they were adults. He ruffled the hair of one of the dwarfs who was short in stature but was a full-grown man. Mengele smiled warmly at each of them. But Ernst could see their lips quiver when they tried to return his smile, and he knew they were afraid of Mengele.

"This is my new assistant, Dr. Neider." Mengele indicated Ernst. "I know you met him already when he came in to examine you this morning, but I thought perhaps a formal introduction was in order. You will be seeing a lot more of him." As he patted Ernst's shoulder, he said, "All right, we're done in here for now. On to the next room."

The room filled with the young twins was next. *These children don't act like children. They are too quiet and well behaved. I have a feeling it's because they are terrified of Mengele..* The twins were not emaciated like the other inmates Ernst had seen walking around the grounds. They appeared to be well fed. Their hair had not been shaved, and they were cleaner than the others as well.

"I love my twins the most of all," Dr. Mengele said, smiling like a benevolent father. "Won't you just look at how amazing they are? Each pair is unique, yet there are two of them who are exactly alike. Do you realize how perfect a situation that is for testing? It's like having a ready-made test group. And besides that, what if we could find out what causes twins to be created. Then we would have the power to create double the number of Aryan children. We could impregnant Aryan women and assure they would give us two rather than one offspring for the Reich. As you know, we just can't produce pure Aryan children fast enough. Why, we could create an entire world filled with blond-haired, blue-eyed children in no time if we could produce twins. We would be able to double our output, so to speak." Mengele's eyes lit up.

Ernst nodded, not knowing what else to say or do. He'd heard about the government's desire to produce a perfect race. But he had been so busy at school, that he hadn't had time to think much about it. But now that this project of creating children was staring him in the face, he was having questions as to the ethics of it.

"This is Dr. Neider. He will be visiting with you each morning and taking your blood. I think you have probably met him already." Mengele smiled. Then he said, "What have we here?" as he pulled a handful of candy out of the pocket of his coat. "Candy! Who wants candy?"

The children didn't move. But Mengele began handing out pieces of candy. They took it and thanked him almost robotically. He noticed that the twins sat very close to their counterparts. Some of them held hands; others had their arms around each other.

"We're done here. Let's go," Mengele said.

They left the twins and took a short walk to the Gypsy camp. When they arrived, Ernst followed Mengele into a room where they kept the Gypsy children imprisoned.

"Uncle," the very young ones screamed when they saw Mengele.

Dr. Mengele let out a laugh as he picked a small boy up and held him high in the air. The child let out a giggle. He was too young to be afraid. Most of them were. Then the rest of the children gathered around Dr. Mengele. "Who wants candy?" Mengele asked.

"Me."

"Me."

"Me."

The children were all screaming at once. Mengele turned to Ernst and smiled. Ernst returned the smile nervously. "Aren't they sweet?" Mengele said. "Won't you just look at how they love me?"

Ernst said nothing. But Mengele didn't notice. His eyes were bright with joy. However, behind the joy, Ernst was sure he saw true madness.

These Gypsy children were dirty and hungry, but they were loud and boisterous. Ernst thought that they behaved more normally than the children he had seen in the two other rooms.

"All right, I can see how excited you are." Mengele laughed a little. "Come closer, here is candy for all of you." Dr. Mengele emptied his pockets of the candy he'd brought. The children eagerly grabbed for it.

"Now we must make sure that everyone gets a piece," Dr. Mengele said to the children. "Who didn't get one?"

He's not so bad, Ernst thought. *He loves these children, and they love him.*

"Do you want to hear the new song I learned?" a pretty little girl with black curly hair asked Mengele.

"Of course. I would love to hear your new song," Mengele said, taking the little girl onto his lap as he sat down in a chair.

The child began to sing.

After the child finished, a little boy said, "I'm learning to play the violin."

"Would you like to play for us," Mengele said.

The child nodded and grabbed one of the violins that belonged to one of the men who was a musician in the Gypsy camp orchestra. The man had allowed him to use it to practice during the afternoons when he didn't need it.

The child played a simple Gypsy tune.

Mengele smiled and clapped his hands. "That was very good. Soon you'll be playing Wagner." Then he turned to the group of children who looked up at him with open and innocent faces and said, "Have you met my new assistant?" Mengele put his arm around Ernst's shoulder.

"Yes. We met him," they all screamed.

"I just wanted to come and make sure he was treating you well."

"He is very nice," one of the children said.

"I am glad to hear it. I am glad you like him. Well, as much as I would like to stay with you, I am a busy man, so, I must go now."

"Goodbye, Uncle. Will we see you tomorrow?" the children yelled.

"Perhaps," Dr. Mengele said. Then Ernst followed him. But before they left the Gypsy children's room, Dr. Mengele said to the guard who was standing at the door, "Gas them all today. A new group will be arriving tomorrow morning, and we will need the space."

Ernst couldn't believe what he'd just heard. *Gas them? Kill them? I couldn't have heard him right. He was so affectionate with these little ones. They love him. How could he do that? Should I ask him? What should I say?* Ernst had no idea what to say or do. He was struck silent by what he'd just witnessed.

They walked side by side without speaking, all the way back to Dr. Mengele's office. It was a bright, sunny day. The brightness of the day contrasted against the gray darkness of the camp. "I don't know how to ask you this," Ernst said. He had to ask. He couldn't bear it anymore.

"Go on. Ask," Mengele said openly.

"Did I hear you tell that guard to gas those children? Do you mean send them to the gas chamber? Kill them?"

Mengele nodded. "We only have so much space. That particular group of children is not involved in any of my experiments. So, I don't need them." He glanced at Ernst. "You'll get used to it. You'll see. Don't look so shocked. The poor little things won't know what hit them. Right now, they are so excited about the candy that they won't even realize." Mengele smiled warmly at Ernst.

Ernst couldn't look at Mengele's face. He stared at the ground and just nodded.

CHAPTER EIGHTEEN

OVER THE NEXT FEW WEEKS, ERNST CAME TO REALIZE THAT Auschwitz was even worse than he'd originally thought. If he tried very hard, he could justify some of Mengele's experiments. For instance, he told himself that when Mengele injected diseases like tuberculous and typhus into one of a set of twins, and he examined the effects, he was only doing this for the sake of science. But as the days passed, he witnessed unnecessary amputations, castrations, and organ removal, without anesthesia, and he began to realize that although the Nazi Party thought of Mengele as a brilliant doctor, he was little more than a sadist. This realization bothered him and sometimes he wondered if things would have been better in the world if he hadn't been there to save Mengele's life during the war.

Ernst had to constantly remind himself why he was there. The pay was good as were the accommodations. He couldn't have found a better-paying position. Ernst was treated with respect by the guards and his peers. And the prisoners did whatever he asked. *I know they are terrified of me. They think I am just like Mengele. I am not. Or am I? If I don't say or do anything to stop his monstrous behavior, doesn't that make me as bad as he is? Damn, but this certainly wasn't what I had in mind when I was in medical school. It's true that I wanted to earn a lot of money, but*

I wanted to do some good with my life as well. I wanted to be a healer. And, instead, I am a part of a team led by a sadist who does little more than inflict pain and suffering. And I am ashamed to admit it, but I am too afraid of Mengele to discuss my feelings with him. I feel trapped.

He sat staring out the window at the people returning home from work. It was after hours, and he'd gone back to his room to have his evening meal. Tonight he ate a sausage sandwich that he'd brought home from one of the local restaurants. But after a few bites, he found his appetite was gone. And he had always had a good appetite. But now the greasy meat was turning his stomach. He wrapped the sandwich and put it away, thinking he might be hungry later.

Sometimes he would wake up in the middle of the night starving and eat whatever he could find. This was happening more and more. In fact, Ernst could not remember the last time he'd slept all the way through the night. *It's obvious to me that I am feeling guilty about my work. I took the Hippocratic Oath, and what I am doing certainly goes against it. Still, I must not quit. If I do, it could ruin my career. I should try to stay at least for a year or two so I can put this job on my résumé. Any hospital would be happy to have me, knowing I'd been Mengele's apprentice.* He shuddered at the very thought of it. *Mengele's apprentice.*

During the next several months, Ernst felt himself becoming more and more unraveled. The things he was seeing take place under Mengele's direction, left him feeling frightened and ill. Besides that, he was lonely. He had no one. Not even a friend he could talk to. There was no one in his life who he communicated with except Dr. Mengele. And Ernst was terrified of him. If anyone knew how mentally deranged the man was, it was Ernst. So he was always guarded around the doctor. Always careful of every word he said. And although he could see the humanity in his patients, he dared not befriend any of them. He thought about his Jewish friends when he was in medical school, and he found he was suddenly longing for the camaraderie they'd shared.

When Ernst first arrived at Auschwitz, he had found himself befriending one of the dwarfs, as Mengele referred to them: Kurt, a man close to his own age. For about two weeks, Ernst enjoyed conversations with the young man. And he found that Kurt had shared many of the same feelings and experiences that he did.

"I fell in love once," Kurt told Ernst in confidence. "But she never knew it. She was not one of us dwarfs; she was a woman of normal height. And she was kind. She spoke to me like I was a man instead of an overgrown child. I was so in love with her that I couldn't see straight."

"So, you never told her?" Ernst asked.

"No, are you kidding? She was so beautiful that I knew she would never be interested in me that way. Deep down, I knew her kindness came from the fact that she pitied me. But I didn't want to hear her say it. So, I never told her how I felt. Instead, I pretended in my mind that she was my girlfriend. Of course, that was until I met her fiancé. What a blow that was. I thought my heart had burst; I was in such emotional pain."

"I understand." Ernst patted Kurt's shoulder. "When I was young, I used to look at the girls I went to school with and wish I was handsome. I longed to be loved. But I wasn't handsome, and no one wanted me. I was chubby, and, well, I had these thick glasses. Still do." Ernst reached up and touched his glasses. "I felt the same way you did. I didn't think any of them would want any part of me, and I certainly didn't want their pity. So, I kept to myself and studied a lot."

"Do you like working here?" Kurt asked.

Ernst looked at the floor. "It's a good job. I have a good position."

"But do you like it?"

"No," Ernst admitted. "I don't. I hate it."

"Then you should probably look for another job. You're not like the others. You're a human being. I sometimes wonder what that Dr. Mengele is made of. I would have to say it's not flesh and blood. I think he's made of poison."

Ernst nodded in agreement, but he didn't say a word.

Then Kurt went on, "I have to admit, I am glad you're here. And I sure would hate to lose you if you left and got another job. You are the only one of those Nazis who has a heart."

Ernst shrugged. "I'd like to leave. But I can't for many reasons. And I find that change is difficult for me. I get settled into a situation and I can't move. If my parents were still alive, I would return home. I miss them so much. But even if I returned to my old neighborhood, I know that there is nothing there for me anymore."

"I understand. And I am glad to have your friendship. I treasure it," Kurt said.

The next day when Ernst finished his rounds, he went to see Kurt. But when he entered the room where Mengele kept the dwarfs, he found Kurt's bed empty. "Where is he?" he asked one of the nurses, indicating Kurt's bed.

"He has been taken care of. He was of no more use to us. So, he won't be returning."

"Taken care of? What do you mean?"

"Dr. Mengele gave the order. He said if you had any questions that you should speak to him."

"Order for what?" Ernst said. His face was red. His fists were clenched, and he was angry. He didn't want to believe that his only friend was dead.

"I'm sorry," the nurse said as she hurried out of the room.

Ernst walked out of the room, too, and followed her to the nurses' desk where he left his clipboard. Then he headed straight for Dr. Mengele's office.

"Come in," Mengele said when he saw Ernst at the door.

"What happened to Kurt, the dwarf?"

"I noticed that you were quite taken with him. And I could see he was manipulating you. Yesterday, I overheard the two of you talking, and I realized that he was becoming a problem. So, I eliminated him."

"What exactly do you mean, 'eliminated him'?" Ernst was so angry that he forgot to be afraid of Mengele.

"What do you think I mean?"

"I think you mean he's dead? I think you killed him."

"Yes. I'm sorry, but it was for the best."

Ernst couldn't look at Mengele. If he did, he was afraid he might punch him. And Mengele was bigger and stronger than himself. Ernst walked out of the office and ran to the bathroom where he lay his head against the wall and wept. He blamed himself for what had happened to Kurt, and at that moment he vowed never to make friends with any of the prisoners again. *My friendship cost Kurt his life.*

CHAPTER NINETEEN

EACH MORNING AFTER HE FINISHED HIS ROUNDS, ERNST WAS expected to go into the room where Mengele kept the twins and draw blood from each of them. Then in the afternoon, for no apparent reason, Dr. Mengele performed blood transfusions, taking the blood from one twin and transfusing it into the other. One morning as Ernst was drawing blood from a small girl, her twin sister asked, "When will you doctors stop hurting us?"

Ernst turned to look at the child's face. She was so small that she couldn't have been more than five. Her eyes were wide, and she was so innocent.

"How old are you?" he asked.

"Eight," the child said boldly.

Poor thing, Ernst thought. *She is so small that she looks five.* Then he asked, "What's your name?"

"Sarah, and my sister's name is Devorah," the little girl answered. "And I don't think you're as bad as the other doctor, the one who makes us call him uncle. I can tell he likes to hurt us. But you don't."

"No, I don't," Ernst said, surprised at his candid response.

"So, why do you do it?" Sarah asked.

Ernst didn't hear Dr. Mengele come in. He was just about to speak when Dr. Mengele came up behind him.

"Good morning, Sarah," Dr. Mengele said. Then he turned to her sister who had just finished having her blood drawn. "And good morning to you, too, Devorah. Today I have a special surprise for the two of you," Mengele said.

Sarah and Devorah looked at Ernst. He turned away, ashamed of his own weakness. He had no idea what Mengele had in store, but he knew that when Dr. Mengele said he had something special for a patient, it was never a good thing.

"Well, Ernst"—Mengele slapped Ernst on the shoulder—"have you finished your morning blood draws?"

"Yes, this is my final blood draw for the morning," Ernst said.

"Good, then let's go and have some coffee and a pastry."

Ernst saw the child's eyes light up at the mention of a pastry. But he looked away because he dared not give the little girl anything. If Mengele thought he liked the child, it could be dangerous for little Sarah. Then Mengele smiled at the twins and pulled two pieces of candy out of his pocket. "Here's one for each of you." His eyes twinkled.

Ernst felt a cold chill run up his spine. When Mengele gave the children candy, it was never really a gesture of kindness. He'd learned that.

"Let's go. We're done here for now. I could use that coffee," Mengele said. Then he smiled at Ernst. "I'm starving." Ernst followed him out of the room without looking back at the girls.

That afternoon, Mengele demanded that Ernst join him in his operating theater.

"Make sure you are present in my operating room at one this afternoon," Mengele said.

"Yes, Doctor," Ernst managed.

When Ernst arrived, each of the twin girls was naked, and they were strapped to separate cots. They stared at Ernst with pleading eyes. He had to look away.

Sarah began to cry. Ernst felt his heart race. He couldn't help the child, yet he knew she was hoping he would do something. He hated himself for being so weak. Yet he could not speak up.

"This won't hurt at all," Mengele said to Sarah's sister, Devorah. Then he injected a long needle into the child's chest. Devorah let out a scream. Within seconds, the little girl lay motionless. Sarah began to scream loudly. She struggled against the leather strap that held her to the table, but she was too small and weak to break free. "Now it's your turn," Mengele said, smiling at the screaming child. Ernst was leaning against the wall, trying to hold himself up. He was dizzy and afraid he might faint.

Mengele inserted the needle into Sarah's small white chest. Within seconds, she was quiet.

"That was phenol. They didn't suffer. Both of them died immediately. I want you to send their bodies to that Jew doctor, Maximillian Samuel, and tell him I said to do an autopsy. Have him remove the eyes and some tissue samples. I am planning to send these things to my professor."

Ernst couldn't look at the two small dead bodies. He was trembling so badly that his teeth were chattering.

Mengele tapped the cot where Sarah lay. Then he turned and walked out of the room. Ernst felt himself cracking. He was alone in the room with the dead bodies of two children who had been healthy and alive only minutes before. Inside he was screaming. A tortured sound only he could hear. *I am going mad*, he thought. *I am losing my mind here in this horrible place. I can't take much more. I have to get away from here. I must or I'll go crazy. I am going to have to ask Mengele for some time off. I need to be far away from this hell, so I can decide what to do with my future. I can't go on like this.* Then he remembered that Mengele had told him to have Maximilian Samuel, a Jewish prisoner, dissect the two bodies. Trying to compose himself, Ernst left the bodies and went to give Samuel Mengele's orders.

Samuel was sitting on a stool in the back of the lab. He was a stern-looking man who spoke very little. But his eyes were always alert, and he was observant. Ernst had watched him over the last several months, and in doing so he had discovered that Samuel was secretly trying to help Dr. Mengele's patients. Ernst knew this because he would sometimes notice that supplies would go missing. And once he'd seen Samuel sneaking some painkillers into the pocket of his uniform. Ernst purposely looked the other way. He was glad that Samuel had more courage than he did. He was glad someone was willing to risk their own life trying to help.

When Mengele had first introduced Samuel to Ernst, he told Ernst that he didn't really care for Samuel, but he found him useful. Then he added, "Samuel was an obstetrician and gynecologist in his former life. Before the war, I mean," Mengele said. "When he first arrived here on his transport, he volunteered to help me in the hospital. Didn't you?" Mengele said to Samuel.

Samuel nodded. "Yes, I did."

Mengele smiled at Samuel, then turned to Ernst. "I would have sent him to the gas, but I thought, well, why not. He could be of use, you know? I can always dispose of him later. Right?"

Samuel looked away.

Ernst had just nodded, not knowing what else to say.

But when Mengele turned around, Ernst studied Samuel and wondered what this young Jewish doctor was like before he came to Auschwitz. Max Samuel brought back memories of the Jewish medical students who had been Ernst's friends, the young potential doctors who had been so kind to him when he was in medical school. It made Ernst's heart ache to think that those bright young medical students might be suffering at a facility somewhere like this one. That they might be treated the same way poor Samuel was being treated.

"Nice to meet you," Ernst managed to say to Samuel.

"Yes," Samuel answered. That was all he said.

"How nice. Just like a real doctors' meeting." Mengele laughed a short laugh. "I love to play pretend with the inmates. It amuses me greatly."

Neither Ernst nor Samuel said another word.

That was months ago. Since then, Ernst had only seen Samuel a handful of times. Samuel had always been respectful, and he carried out any orders that Ernst passed on to him from Dr. Mengele. But he wasn't ever friendly.

Ernst cleared his throat, then he said to Samuel, "There are two female twin children in the operating theater. They are deceased. Dr. Mengele wants you to perform autopsies and dissections on both of them. He wants you to remove their eyes and to get him tissue samples."

Samuel looked into Ernst's eyes for a second, and Ernst felt his blood run cold. It felt like the Jewish doctor thought he was as much to blame as Mengele.

"Children, huh?" Samuel said. "Little girls. Just innocent little girls."

Ernst nodded, feeling ill.

"Nebuch, such a pity, the poor little things must have been very sick to die so young," Samuel said with a hint of sarcasm in his voice. And Ernst knew that Samuel knew Mengele had murdered the children.

He knows they weren't sick. He knows Mengele is a sadist. And he probably thinks I am too, Ernst thought as he left the barracks.

On Ernst's way back to the hospital, he passed Mengele who was sitting in his office. "Neider, come in here for a minute. I want to talk to you," Mengele called out.

Ernst shivered. *What does he want now? I can't stand to look at him. He just killed two little girls for no reason, and he is sitting behind his desk acting as if he has done nothing wrong. Does he really believe in his heart that what he did was all right? Could he possibly believe that those two children were really not human beings?* Ernst thought as he glanced at Mengele, who was sitting behind his desk running his fingers over the ashtray. Ernst looked at the ashtray. Only the top officials in the Nazi Party had one. Not that he would have wanted one. The idea made him sick. It was a special conversation piece because it had been made from the pelvis of a woman. Ernst made a special effort to divert his gaze from the monstrosity Mengele's eyes glittered as he looked up at Ernst who walked into the office, feeling a sense of dread come over him. "Yes, Doctor." Ernst choked on his words, as he approached him.

"Heil Hitler." Mengele stood up and saluted.

"Heil Hitler," Ernst replied and saluted.

"Sit down," Mengele instructed.

Ernst took the chair across from Mengele's desk.

For a moment Mengele did not speak. He watched Ernst carefully. Then he sighed and said, "I have been thinking. Perhaps it would be best if you take a week or two off from work. I'm expecting a visit from a few friends, high-up officials in the party. And, let's face it, you're very overweight, and that just won't make a good impression. I'll admit that you're a good doctor, even brilliant at times, but highly unstable and very awkward. To be quite honest, I have been thinking about letting you go. Now, that would be a shame, wouldn't it? After all, this is an excellent job. I mean, the benefits are outstanding."

He wants to see me squirm, Ernst thought as he tried to compose himself. But he felt the sweat beading on his brow and in his armpits. The last thing he wanted to do was stutter, yet he couldn't control it. And that was exactly what he did. "I-I don't w-want to lose the job," he said, although he wasn't sure it was the truth. *I would love to get out of here. But being fired by Mengele would certainly hurt my chances of finding a good position anywhere in the future. I am trapped by him, and he knows it, and he loves to trap people. It's part of his sadistic nature.*

"There you go again with that stuttering. Yes, I think it's best that you take a week or even two off. I need some time away from you. You're beginning to get on my nerves," Mengele said.

Ernst nodded. *What can I say to him? He hates me. He instinctively knows, like a predator, that I am weak, and I can't stand the things I see here. He sees my weakness, and it makes him want to go for my jugular.* "Y-yes, Dr. Mengele. I-I'm sorry."

"Go on, get out of here. Get out of my office. I can't bear to hear that irritating stutter again. It grates on my nerves."

Ernst stood up; he was trembling. He dared not speak again for fear he would stutter. He just nodded his head and began walking toward the door, tripping on the handmade rug and almost falling down as he stumbled out of the office.

That night, Ernst lay in bed awake and thought about the two little girls who Mengele murdered that day. He thought about the pelvis ashtray, and the selections when the trains arrived. He thought of Kurt who had died needlessly, and of the people with dwarfism. He remembered the murders of the little Gypsy children who had run to Mengele and called him uncle. Everything that he had witnessed since he'd begun his work under Mengele raced through his mind like a film reel.

He had never been a drinker, yet over these last several months, he'd begun to need a glass or two of schnapps to help him sleep. Getting out of bed, he went into the drawer of his nightstand to look for his bottle. Then he remembered that he'd finished it the previous night. *I need a drink*, he thought. *Maybe it would do me some good to get out of here. Maybe I should go somewhere where I can sit in a tavern, have a beer or two, and listen to some music. I'll buy a bottle of schnapps on my way home. If I still can't sleep, I'll have some more.*

He got dressed and walked to a local biergarten. It was busy, filled with people drinking and laughing. *I need this to forget*, he thought as he sat down. It was a cool autumn night, and although it was a little chilly to sit outside, he liked the freshness of the air. It was so much cleaner than the air inside the compound at Auschwitz.

Ernst had heard about this place from his fellow coworkers. It was an establishment that was often frequented by the German guards who worked at Auschwitz, so the beer was German. And the food was too. Even the entertainment was geared toward their enjoyment. It was like being in Germany. There was no evidence at all that he was in Poland.

Ernst sat at a table in the back sipping his dark beer while a group of four musicians played German folk songs. The lively music made him think of home. He began to tap his foot to the music and sang along softly to himself. He remembered how much he'd loved living with his parents, and he wished he could go back to those days. But it was impossible; they were gone now. There was no point in returning to his hometown. There was no one there who he missed. However, he would have liked to go back to Berlin. When he thought of his days at the university, he had fond memories of the city. *I'll bet I could find a job there. After all, it's a big metropolis. The job probably won't pay as well as the position I have now, but I might find a job that makes me happy, as a doctor, a real doctor. A job where I could be helping people rather than torturing them. Work that would let me sleep at night and would not drive me insane. Mengele's given me some time off, and I have plenty of money. I think I'll make a trip back to Berlin and see what I can find. In fact, I'll leave tomorrow morning.*

CHAPTER TWENTY

1943

As Ernst rode the train into Germany, he thought about Auschwitz. It was not what he had anticipated when he'd agreed to take the job. It was a horrific nightmare of a prison where the inmates had no say in anything. They could be used and murdered without any thought at all. And from what he'd seen, except for Dr. Mengele's collection of twins and other oddities, the rest of the prisoners were severely underfed. In fact, they were starving. They walked the grounds looking like half-dead skeletons. Their hollow, dark eyes had begun to haunt Ernst when he left the facility at night. That was how he had started drinking. And he could find no justification for the experiments. As far as he could tell, the experimentation had nothing to do with science and everything to do with power and control. *Mengele thinks of himself as a god. He thinks it is his right to decide who lives and who dies. Not only that, but he gets a sick pleasure from torturing these poor souls, even the children. The doctor may be well respected by the Nazi Party and the government, but I can see that he is nothing but a sadist. And the more I work with him, the less I like him. However, I know he is power hungry, and it's important that he never finds out how I feel about him. Because I have no doubt that he wouldn't think twice about murdering me too. And knowing him, I have no doubt he would get away with it.*

The train rattled along the tracks as it entered the city of Berlin.

BOOK TWO

CHAPTER TWENTY-ONE

1938

A LARGE SHTETL BUSTLING WITH EXCITEMENT AS THE HASIDIC Jewish residents finish their kosher food shopping before sundown on Friday, the day of the Sabbath.

Shoshana Aizenberg giggled as she and Neta Fiszbaum, her oldest and dearest friend, waited for Samuel Kleinstein, the vegetable vendor, to finish his weekly transaction with their neighbor, Mrs. Klausky. Shoshana hated it when she was in line to see one of the vendors and behind Mrs. Klausky. Everyone in the village knew the woman was a talker. When she went shopping for her weekly food supplies, she arrived at the market early. As she visited each of the vendors, she argued prices all the while spreading vicious rumors about everyone in town. Sam rolled his eyes at the young girls and made a funny face. They both tried to suppress their giggles. They knew Sam's look of annoyance was due to Mrs. Klausky's long-winded story about the betrothal of a young couple that had been called off because the girl wore clothing that was immodest. It was not a new story. Everyone in the shtetl had heard it before. But Mrs. Klausky loved to gossip. And the obvious annoyance that Samuel felt toward this gossiping woman made Shoshana smile because she felt the same way about her.

"Here is your purchase," Samuel said to Mrs. Klausky.

"I tell you, Sam, what kind of a girl shows her elbows so freely? Of course, Hermy's parents were going to be forced to break the engagement. What did the girl's parents think would happen with a daughter like that. Nu? Who would want such a girl in their family? What kind of a mother would she make?"

"All right, Mrs. Klausky, that's enough. I don't want to hear all of this gossip. Aren't you a frum and pious woman? You are always judging everyone else's piety. So, you of all people should know that it's a sin to gossip. Now, go and have a good Sabbath," Sam said, then he turned away from the old woman. Mrs. Klausky, was embarrassed at having been reprimanded. But she knew Samuel was right. Gossip was the greatest sin. But everyone did it—at least almost everyone. The old woman frowned at Sam. She looked as if she'd been struck across the face. But she did not move. She stood staring at Shoshana as Sam reached over, and careful not to touch Shoshana's hands, he took the vegetables from her. Humming to himself, Sam began to weigh Shoshana's purchases of carrots, sweet potatoes, raisins, and dried prunes.

"I see from what you're buying that your mother must be planning to make tzimmes for Shabbos dinner tonight?" Sam said.

"Yes," Shoshana answered.

"Mmmm, how I love a good tzimmes," Sam replied to Shoshana, smiling. He knew that Mrs. Klausky's feelings were hurt, and he should probably apologize if he wanted her business next week. But he found her repulsive, and instead of trying to say something to ease the tension to make her feel better, he ignored her.

Finally, Mrs. Klausky shook her head in disgust. "All right. I've made up my mind. You obviously don't need my business, Sam Kleinstein. So, I'll buy my fruit and vegetables from Yakov Goldstone next week. You think you're important, but you're not. I don't need you, Samuel Kleinstein. And neither do my friends. I'll tell them how rude you were to me. They won't want to buy by you either. No one will buy by you. You just wait and see how your business suffers," she said, but when he didn't answer, she clicked her tongue, picked up her purchases, and left. Shoshana watched her walk a few feet over to the shop of the fishmonger. *She is a terrible gossip. And Sam was right to refuse to listen to her story. I am sure she'll try to tell the fishmonger that same story about that poor girl,* Shoshana thought.

Sam shook his head as he added up the purchases and then carefully put them into the cloth bag Shoshana had brought with her. He had been selling his wares in that same location for as long as she could remember. As a child, she and her mother had visited his vegetable stand. He was a younger man then, and he always had a big smile ready for Shoshana's mother. But she never returned it. She portrayed herself to the world as a modest woman, who spoke to men outside of her home as little as possible. Even so, Sam was always very kind to them. And Shoshana assumed that he knew all the town gossip because everyone bought their vegetables from him. So, when he smiled at Shoshana because he knew that she and her friend were watching Albert Hendler, who worked in his father's butcher shop across the street, Shoshana knew why. *Sam knows that Albert and I are betrothed,* she thought.

Albert looked up from his work and waved when he saw the girls eyeing him. Shoshana felt her face grow hot and red. But Sam just let out a short laugh.

"I'll bet someone is going to have a chicken for their seder tonight?" Sam said. "All you have to do is go and ask your betrothed. I'm sure he'd be happy to give you one for your family."

"Ouch!" Shoshana let out a soft cry when Neta pinched her. She was so embarrassed by all of this that she couldn't speak.

"He waved to you," Neta said. "Wave back."

"I can't," Shoshana whispered, elbowing her friend.

Sam shook his head. "Nu? Today, she's shy?" He was speaking to Neta, but he was talking about Shoshana, and her face grew even redder.

I wish the earth would open up and swallow me, so I don't have to stand here feeling so uncomfortable, Shoshana thought.

Shoshana didn't answer Sam. She just paid him the money she

owed him and took the small bag. He laughed a little, but she didn't look him in the eye.

Then, with her purchases in hand, Shoshana and Neta began walking toward home.

"You know, Albert really is handsome," Neta said. "You are lucky. So lucky. I mean, your father really made a good match for you."

"Yes, he is. And you're right, I am fortunate."

"My father is looking for a match for me. I can only hope mine will be as handsome as yours," Neta said nervously. "But who knows what my father will come up with; you know how much he drinks. I can't trust his judgment."

"He will do a good job. You'll see," Shoshana said, trying to comfort her friend.

"Alevei, from your mouth to God's ears," Neta said.

They walked silently. Each girl lost in her own thoughts for a few moments.

I remember how awkward and afraid I felt that first night my father brought Albert home. I was so afraid he would be old, or ugly. And even though Jewish law says that I have the final say as to whether I will marry him or not, I could never stand up to my papa. He's not the kind of man to say no to, Shoshana thought. *I remember when Papa introduced me to Albert that first time. Papa had that look on his face that told me that I would marry Albert, like it or not. And it just so happened I was lucky. Albert was young and handsome, but he easily could have been otherwise, and I would have had to marry him anyway.*

To introduce Albert to Shoshana, her father had made arrangements with Albert's father for Albert and his parents to come to a Shabbos dinner one Friday night in early June. Once the plans were in place, her father demanded that Shoshana and her mother make the finest Shabbos table they had ever prepared. The entire day, they'd slaved over the meal and the table. They'd cleaned the house so thoroughly that there wasn't a speck of dust to be found. Shoshana looked around at the fuss her mother was making, and she grew more and more nervous. She wished she had more time. But she was already fourteen, and if she was to be married next year, her parents said it was a wise decision to choose the young man as soon as possible.

When the Hendlers arrived, Shoshana had been in the kitchen checking on her challah to make sure it didn't burn. She heard Mrs. Hendler and her mother talking.

"You have a lovely home, Mrs. Aizenberg," Mrs. Hendler said.

"Oh, it's just a humble little house," Mrs. Aizenberg answered. But Shoshana knew from the sound of her mother's voice that she was feeling proud of her home.

"Shoshana," her father called. His voice was firm.

"Yes, Papa," Shoshana said. She was trembling as she wiped her hands on a kitchen towel. "I'll be there in a second."

She walked into the room with her eyes cast down at her shoes.

"This is Mr. and Mrs. Hendler. And this is their son, Albert."

For a split second, she glanced up at him. He looked at her admiringly. A slight smile came over her face. He was truly handsome. And although she would have liked to have more time, more years as a single girl, marriage no longer seemed as terrifying a prospect.

Her seven-year-old twin sisters, Bluma and Perle, sat quietly on the sofa, holding hands. They wore their best dresses. Shoshana smiled at how adorable they were. She knew that the twins had been instructed by their father that they were not to make a sound throughout the entire dinner. Bluma looked at Shoshana questioningly. Shoshana smiled at her sister to reassure her that she was all right.

Everyone gathered around the table as Naomi, Shoshana's mother, lit the Shabbos candles and covered her eyes as the prayers were being said. Shoshana stole a glance at Albert. He was watching her and smiling. She felt the heat rise in her cheeks and looked away. But she couldn't help but smile.

And that was how it began. She and Albert were betrothed.

They hadn't had any time to talk alone yet, but the families had dined together several times, and during these dinners, she and Albert had exchanged glances. Shoshana knew Sam, the vegetable vendor, was right; if she had gone into the butcher shop to say good

Sabbath to Mr. Hendler, he would have probably offered to give her a chicken for her family's dinner. But she couldn't do it. And once again, Sam was right; she was shy.

Shoshana and Neta hadn't spoken at all; they'd walked side by side in silence. When they arrived in front of Shoshana's small wooden house, which looked just like all of the other small wooden houses in the shtetl, Shoshana turned to Neta and asked, "Do you want to come in for a cup of tea?"

"I can't. I wish I could, but I have been out too long already. I must hurry and get home to help my mother cook. It's almost sundown."

"So tomorrow you'll come and eat by us for lunch? I would love it if you could."

"I will," Neta said.

"Good, I'll see you then," Shoshana said, then she turned and walked into the house.

The twins stood side by side; they were kneading dough for challah. *My sisters are such beautiful girls.* They would be considered identical to anyone who didn't know them well. But to Shoshana, they were as different as the colors blue and green. She adored them, and she knew they were her parents' pride. Although her father would have loved to have had a son, the twins came to the Aizenbergs after seven years of trying unsuccessfully to have another child. During those seven hard years, Naomi Aizenberg had suffered from two miscarriages and a stillbirth. When Naomi and her husband, Herschel, had finally resigned themselves to having just one child, Shoshana, a miracle had happened. Naomi got pregnant, and nine months later, delivered two healthy twin girls. Papa rejoiced. He made a nice donation at the shul, and from that day forward, he always referred to them as his miracle babies. The twins were overly protected. They were not permitted to ever leave the house without a red ribbon tied to their undershirts. It was due to an old superstition. It was believed that if they wore a red ribbon, then no jealous person could give them a kinehora, which was another word for the "evil eye."

CHAPTER TWENTY-TWO

August 1939

ORIGINALLY, BOTH FAMILIES HAD AGREED THAT THE COUPLE SHOULD be married in a year. But as the wedding grew closer, Shoshana convinced her mother to ask her father for more time to arrange things. She was scared of marriage and in no hurry. Her mother agreed to speak with her father, and to Shoshana's surprise and delight, Herschel agreed. But he hadn't agreed because Shoshana wasn't ready for marriage. He agreed because he liked to show off his success. He wanted everyone to know that he earned a lot of money. So when Naomi told him that she wanted the best of everything at Shoshana's wedding, and that took time, he agreed.

Now the wedding was scheduled to take place in the summer of 1940, the following year. But once the marriage had been agreed upon, both families of the young couple made plans to spend the upcoming high holidays together. They made plans to have dinner together on Rosh Hashanah, the Jewish New Year, at Shoshana's home, and then the following week they would break the fast on the highest of holidays, Yom Kippur, at Albert's home. It was a joyous time for Shoshana's parents. And although Shoshana did not feel that she could tell them, she still felt uncertain about the marriage. It wasn't Albert she was not sure of. It was just the idea of getting married. She didn't feel ready, yet she knew if she said something to either of her parents, they would laugh and tell her that she would never be ready until she was married. They would say that once she said "I do" she would find that this was what she'd been born for. Yet the idea of it, and all of the changes that would take place once she became a wife and mother, terrified her.

But then at the beginning of September, a day shy of two weeks before Rosh Hashanah began, something even more terrifying than marriage happened in Shoshana's life. Nazi Germany broke the promise they made not to attack Poland, and suddenly Poland was under attack. Bombs rained upon the land like giant earthquakes. There was gossip in the streets about the cruelty of the German Army. And in the tiny shtetl where Shoshana grew up, the very fabric of the life the Jews who lived there had known was threatened, and the people were terrified. When Shoshana went to the market early one morning, she saw her father talking to several men whom she knew he attended the shul with. She stood close so that she could hear what they were saying.

"They are persecuting Jews in Germany. They had a terrible pogrom last year. And since then, the Jews have been forced to register and give up their personal possessions," one of the men said.

"How do you know this?" another man asked him.

"Because my brother-in-law and sister live there. They fear for their lives. And now, the Germans are coming here."

"A pogrom in a country as civilized as Germany?" one young Torah scholar asked.

"Yes," the man said, "a pogrom. It was last fall, in thirty-eight. Thugs ran through the streets of Berlin and broke all the windows from the stores. Then they attacked and killed any people they could find. It was a terrible thing."

"Our lives in this small village have gone on for centuries in the same way. I don't believe the Nazis would want to be bothered with us. We are too small for them to even notice," Shoshana's father said, "and that's why we keep to ourselves, and we follow the old ways."

"Eh, who can be sure? The goyim get such pleasure from torturing us," Mr. Fishman, one of her father's closest friends said.

"Nu, so, if there should be a pogrom, God forbid, we'll survive it. We'll find a way. We always do. Pogroms are not new to our people," Herschel Aizenberg said to his friend Mr. Fishman as he patted him on the shoulder.

As Shoshana walked home, she thought about the future of her family and herself. Until Poland was bombed, Shoshana hadn't given much thought to anything but her upcoming wedding. She'd been focused on all of the things that would be expected of her, like the cleansing she would have to endure at the mikveh the day of the wedding, followed by her mother shaving her head the day after the wedding. She'd been worried about how ashamed she would feel standing naked in front of the old ladies at the mikveh, and she prayed that she would not feel so reluctant about giving up her long, black hair. The thought of how she would look with a bald head concealed by a scarf, made her sick to her stomach.

Then it happened. The first time a bomb exploded near the small village where Shoshana lived, she had been in the kitchen cutting potatoes. She'd been looking out the window and wondering what it was like to live a different life. She knew it was a sin, but she wondered how it would feel to be a secular Jewish woman, to go to school, and to make her own choice of when and whom she would marry.

Without warning, there was a deafening sound, and then earth shuddered. At first Shoshana felt that it was Hashem, God, and he was angry with her for her thoughts. She was so stunned that she didn't even realize that she'd cut her hand. Her heart had never beat so hard in her chest. When the twins came running into the kitchen, it woke Shoshana out of her self-absorbed thoughts. They ran to her, and Perle yelled, "Mama? Where's Mama?"

The twins were sniffling. Bluma grabbed onto Shoshana's skirt. "I'm scared. What's happening, Shoshana?"

"I don't know," Shoshana said honestly.

Their mother had gone to the market a half hour earlier. Shoshana thought of her mother and trembled. *Dear God, is Mama all right? What about Papa, he is at the shul.* She knelt down to be at the same height as the twins. Then chilled by her fear, Shoshana clutched her sisters to her breast as the children wept. Another bomb fell. Perle screamed. "Shhh, it's all right," Shoshana said, but she didn't believe it. Something was terribly wrong. Outside, people had gathered in the streets. They were running around confused, and Shoshana could see no reason to go out there and talk to them. Her sisters needed her here. The girls sat huddled together on the kitchen floor, frightened and anxious, hoping that their parents would come home soon.

An hour later, their mother came into the house; she was clearly shaken. The children ran to their mama and clutched at her dress. But Naomi did not reach down and embrace the children the way she normally would have. Instead, she stared at Shoshana with terror in her eyes. Neither of them said anything for several seconds. Then her mother turned to the twins and said, "Go on, get cleaned up. Papa will be home soon."

"But Mama, what is happening? Why is the earth shaking? What were those sounds? Is Hashem angry with us? Did we do something bad? Are we being punished?"

"I don't know. I don't know anything, except that you should go and get cleaned up for dinner. Go, now."

Reluctantly, but always obediently, the twins took each other's hands and went to get ready for dinner.

It was only a short while later that the girls' father walked into the small house. He didn't say a word. He didn't look at Shoshana or her mother. He just walked into his bedroom and shut the door. More bombs followed that night. There were screams coming from the streets, and Shoshana knew that the entire town was terrified.

In the weeks that followed, the bombings escalated. But no one got used to them. Instead, the fear only increased. And the plans for Shoshana's wedding seemed trivial now. For a month, Germany terrorized Poland, her neighbor, until finally two weeks later in the autumn, as the trees turned brilliant colors, the Polish surrendered.

And although Shoshana didn't know it at the time, on that day, her life would change forever.

Poland was divided into two sections, one owned by the Soviet Union, the other owned by Germany. Shoshana and her family fell under German rule.

Life in the small shtetl was changing rapidly. By November, all Jewish-owned businesses were required to display a Star of David on their doors and windows. When Shoshana went to the market, she saw several of the store owners whom she'd known all of her life painting Stars of David on their windows. They didn't seem concerned, but then things escalated and, only a month later in December, all Jews over ten years of age were required to wear an armband.

People no longer stood out on the streets gossiping, kibitzing, and planning shitachs—arranged marriages. The people in the village had grown quiet. Even when they went to market, they said very little, and most of them rushed to return home as soon as they made their purchases. It was easy to see the fear in their eyes.

Herschel had stopped going to work. He was afraid to leave his family alone, so he stayed at home with them, but he had heard that in Warsaw the Jews were now forbidden to use public transportation. And he began to see the writing on the wall; the hatred for the Jewish people was growing. He just couldn't be sure how bad things would get. It was hard for him to believe that a country as advanced as Germany would take things much further. But although he didn't admit this to anyone, he just wasn't sure.

Once in a while, Shoshana would see a cluster of old men gathered on the street in front of the shul after services, their faces lined with worry. She assumed they'd gathered to discuss their fears of an upcoming pogrom. But then in January, a law was passed, and it was now illegal to hold services. There were no more communal prayers. The Germans said that they implemented this law in order to prevent the spread of disease, but the Jews knew better. They knew it was because they were Jewish, and the Nazis hated them.

The younger men talked quietly among themselves as they walked home from their classes at the yeshiva. They were careful to whisper so that the women did not hear them. They didn't want to alarm the women any more than they were already alarmed. The women didn't speak openly about this with each other. But when Shoshana saw them in the market clutching their babies, or holding the hands of their children, they looked worried all the time. Even Shoshana's mother was quiet, and Shoshana knew it was best not to ask her any questions.

Then one afternoon, Shoshana's father came home from speaking with Albert's father. He explained that since they were both concerned about all of the frightening new demands that the Germans were putting on the Jews, the wedding was to be postponed. Shoshana was not happy about what was happening with Germany, but she was relieved not to be getting married.

The persecution of Jews didn't begin in the small villages. It began in the cities, but the news of how the Jews were being treated, filtered quickly to the shtetl. And everyone wondered if or when the Germans would come to their little village. And, more importantly, what would happen when they did.

It was over a year later in December of 1940, that a troop of German soldiers wearing heavy wool coats, shiny black boots, and carrying guns, marched into the streets of the shtetl. The woman who lived next door came over to tell Shoshana's mother that she had been in town at the market, and she saw that the Germans had arrived. It was less than a half hour later that the troops marched by the front of the Aizenbergs' house. Shoshana held on to her sisters' hands as they watched the troops from the window.

Shoshana looked at her mother, terrified.

The Germans were strong and overpowering. They forced the Jewish people, who feared for their families and their lives, to surrender anything they had that was of value. Shoshana's mother who had been trained as a seamstress wished she had more time so she could sew her silver candleholders into her coat. But there was no time. The Germans took everything.

A week later, just as everyone had begun to settle back into some form of normalcy, the Germans returned. This time, it was worse. They'd taken everything of value from the people in the shtetl. So no one expected them to return. However, on this snow-covered winter afternoon, a troop of uniformed Nazis strutted through, up and down the streets, crying out in their harsh, guttural German, "Jewish swine. Miserable, filthy Jewish swine. Come out of your houses, or we will drag you out."

Then a man who seemed to be the leader said that everyone living in the shtetl had just five minutes to pack a suitcase and gather their families together. "You must come out and line up in the street. Anyone who attempts to escape will be dealt with harshly," the Nazi said. "If you are wise, and you want to keep yourselves and your families safe, you will do as you're told."

Naomi, Shoshana's mother, quickly packed warm clothes for the entire family, into suitcases. She and Shoshana had helped the children to dress warmly by layering their sweaters.

Herschel stared at them for a moment. Then he said, "I must go outside, so I can see exactly what is going on."

"Be careful, Herschel," Naomi said.

"I will," he answered and then walked out the door.

Naomi watched through the window as Herschel spoke with a young man for a few minutes. But then a soldier came and forced both Herschel and the young man into the back of the truck. She turned to look at Shoshana, who was as pale as a ghost. They stared at each other for several moments. Shoshana felt her heart beating so hard in her chest that she was light-headed and nauseated. Her sisters ran to her and took her hands. She held on to them tightly. "What's happening?" Perle asked. "Where are they taking Papa?"

"I don't know," Shoshana admitted.

Neither of the twins said another word; they just moaned like two tiny, terrified kittens.

Then there was a loud crash as a Nazi soldier kicked in the door of the house. He entered and pulled Naomi out by her shoulder. She let out a scream as he tossed her onto an open-air truck. Another soldier grabbed Bluma who tried to resist. He hit her in the face with the butt of his rifle. Her lip poured blood. Then the Nazi turned the gun on Shoshana and her sisters. "Get in the truck," he said.

They did as they were told. When Naomi saw Bluma bleeding, she ran to her. The Nazi hit Naomi in the hip with the butt of his gun. She fell facedown onto the ground. And as she did, she remembered that this was the same hip where the Nazi had hit her in her dream. She shivered, but she forced herself to get up and gather her children to her. Naomi used the hem of her skirt to wipe the blood from Bluma's face.

It was still snowing. Shoshana couldn't help but see the beauty in the dusting of the white, lacy flakes that fell on her sister's hair and then melted. It made such a lovely contrast to their shiny, raven-black locks. *How could such horror be happening even when there is such beauty in the world?* Shoshana thought as tears fell down her cheeks. *Which is real? The horror, or the beauty? How can they exist side by side?*

"They are taking us away. Where are we going?" one of the neighbors said to no one in particular.

Naomi looked at Herschel, who was in the back of the truck in front of them. His eyes met hers. He tried to look reassuring. But she was not reassured. She could see that he was frightened too. And she wondered if they were all going to the same place or were they being separated, and if they were, would she and her children ever see Herschel again.

The trucks formed a line. As they were about to drive away, Naomi saw Frieda, Herschel's secretary, lying dead, facedown in the dirt. She glanced over at Shoshana, who saw it too. But neither of them mentioned what they had just seen.

"Where are we going? Please, tell us. Where are we going?" an old woman said to the soldier, who was holding the entire truckload of people at gunpoint. He didn't answer.

"What will become of us?" she said to the others.

"Hashem will watch over us," a young yeshiva student said.

"But how can you be so sure?" the old woman asked.

Then the Nazi hit her in the stomach with the gun and she was silent.

Shoshana saw Neta riding in the truck behind her with her parents, and Albert with his family. Albert sat defiantly with his arms crossed over his chest. His feet were apart, and he was staring at the German guard angrily. Albert was looking around, watching the Nazis, when his eyes caught Shoshana's. She looked down immediately. But when she glanced back up, she found he was still staring at her. His eyes were wide. She could see that he, too, was afraid. But he was hiding his fear with a strong façade of impertinence.

As the truck pulled away from the village that the Aizenbergs called home, Perle tugged at Naomi's sleeve, and in a whisper, she said, "Look over there, Mama. Look at that flag that soldiers left behind. Do you see it?"

Naomi nodded.

"It's the same flag that I saw in my dream. Do you remember?"

"Yes, Perle. I remember," Naomi said. But that was all she could manage to say, because she already knew that flag. She had seen it in her own frightening nightmare, and she had never been able to forget it.

CHAPTER TWENTY-THREE

Warsaw Ghetto, February 1941

WHEN THEY ARRIVED AT A SECTION OF WARSAW THAT WAS A PRISON built to house Jews, they were forced to get down from the truck bed quickly. Once on the ground, Shoshana looked around her. She saw Neta a few feet away, standing beside her parents, looking frightened.

Perle and Bluma clung to Shoshana's skirt and to each other. They begged to go home. But all she could do was comfort them with hugs. Then Herschel found them. Although he didn't admit it, because Herschel never admitted to weaknesses of any kind, he was relieved. Shoshana could see it in his face. "Nu, so at least we are together again. We'll face whatever we must as a family," Herschel said.

Albert and his family had just arrived. They were only a few feet away from the Aizenbergs. She could see the defiance growing in his gaze again, and she was afraid for him. But she was also very shy, so she looked down at the ground immediately. But when she glanced back up, she found Albert was still staring at her. Then to her surprise, he walked over to where she and her family waited their turn to see the Judenrat, the Jewish council: these were Jews who worked with the Germans.

"Mr. Aizenberg," Albert said to her father. "I am here to help you with anything you might need. After all, I am almost your son-in-law."

Herschel Aizenberg nodded. "Thank you," he replied.

"And I will protect Shoshana with my life." Albert stood up straight and tall. "We shouldn't have to put up with this treatment from these Germans."

"I agree with you, Albert. But don't be reckless. You could lose your life in an instant. The Germans have conquered Poland. And . . . we are Jews. You know what that means."

"I don't know what it means. I know that we have been persecuted since the beginning of time. But I also know that it's wrong."

Shoshana's father didn't answer. He just patted Albert on the shoulder.

Neta walked over to Shoshana. She had overheard Albert. She whispered in Shoshana's ear, "You are so lucky that Albert is your betrothed. He is fearless. He's just like Daniel when Daniel entered the lion's den."

Shoshana gave Neta a trembling smile. But she didn't say anything. She was listening as Albert was arguing with a Nazi. *Sometimes Neta is so childish. How is it possible that she doesn't realize that Albert's pride is putting us all in danger?*

"What are you planning to do with us?" Albert boldly asked one of the guards.

The guard was a young man, not much older than a boy. He was trying to sound strong and intimidating, but Shoshana could see he, too, was frightened. "Get back into the line," the guard commanded.

"I want to know where we are and what you plan to do with us," Albert said fearlessly.

"Get back into the line," the soldier repeated. "The Judenrat will tell you where you are to go from here."

"I will not get in line unless I know what you are planning for us."

"*You* will do as I say," the young soldier said. His authority was being threatened, and he was shaking.

"I don't take orders from you. I only take orders from Hashem," Albert said. "Now, tell me what is going on here."

"I don't know about any Hashem. I only know what Hitler says, and he has commanded that you get in line. Now, do as you're told."

Just then an older, more seasoned soldier walked over. He shook his head. "What is going on here?" he asked the younger man.

"This Jew refuses to do as I say."

"Ahhh, and you stand here like a pansy and allow this?" the older soldier asked in a mocking voice. "Who is in charge here? You or a Jew? Kill him. Make him an example for the others. Let them know you won't tolerate their insolence."

"No. please. I beg you. Let him be." Shoshana found her voice. She began to walk forward toward the soldiers and Albert. But her father grabbed her arm and pulled her back.

"Quiet," her father said. He held on tightly to her arm.

The soldiers ignored her. "Come on, are you a man, or are you a coward?" the more seasoned guard asked the younger one.

The young guard's hand was shaking as he lifted his gun and pointed it at Albert. Albert did not back down. He looked the young guard straight in the eyes. Shoshana couldn't believe that Albert was still unafraid. He was still staring directly at the guard. His eyes were dark and insolent. And he did not drop his gaze. Then the soldier cocked his gun. Shoshana gasped. Naomi let out a short cry. And then, Albert covered his eyes with his right hand and began to pray softly in Hebrew. He was reciting the Shema, the prayer for the dead. Shoshana gasped again. *He has accepted that he is about to die*, she thought. But she didn't speak.

"What is he doing?" the young soldier asked the older guard. He was clearly shaken by this young, courageous Jew. "It seems to me that he is casting some kind of a Jew spell on me."

The seasoned soldier let out a gruff laugh, then he said, "Do you actually believe that he can put a curse on you? Do you think he is that powerful? You are a strong Aryan man. You are in power here. Kill him."

"I don't know if I should. What if he is that powerful? I am sure you've heard what Dr. Goebbels says about these Jew people. They consort with the devil," the young guard said. He swallowed hard, and his Adam's apple bobbed up and down. "You do know that they drink the blood of Christian babies; it makes them more powerful."

"Nonsense! Now, I've had enough of your behaving like a child. You are a pure Aryan man. Live up to your birthright. Either you kill him, or I'll see to it that you lose your position. If you are nothing but a weak coward, you don't belong with the rest of us."

The young guard continued to point the gun at Albert. His hands were shaking. Shoshana's father was holding tightly to her shoulders to keep her from running toward Albert. Then the roar of a gunshot shattered the air. Everyone who stood outside fell silent. Albert reached for his arm. Blood ran like a river through his fingers. Shoshana looked away to keep herself from vomiting.

"You didn't kill him," the more senior soldier said. "You shot him in the arm. I told you to kill him." He pulled his pistol and held it right in front of Albert's face.

Albert closed his eyes and covered them with his right hand. Then he began to recite the Shema again: "Sh'ma Yis-ra-eil A-do-nai Eio-hei-nu, A-do-nai E-chad . . ."

Shoshana felt bile rise in her throat. She turned away. She couldn't bear to see what would happen next.

"Well, Jew. It's your lucky day." The older Nazi laughed. "I don't think I'll kill you. Too big a mess," he said. His voice was cocky, but there was a strange undertone of fear.

The guard walked away. Albert lay on the ground. He held his arm where he'd been shot. The blood seeped through his fingers. Shoshana had never seen so much blood and she felt faint.

"Can you stand up?" It was Albert's father. He'd walked over to where they were standing. Albert's mother was close behind. She was crying. Naomi went to her and put her arm around her. Neither spoke.

Albert stood up, but he was shaking.

Just then a tall, slender man in his late forties, with laugh lines surrounding his kind blue eyes, walked over. "I'm Dr. Horwitz." He smiled. Then he tore a piece of fabric from his shirt and tied it around Albert's arm. "I'll take you to my office and fix you up." He smiled.

"You live here? In this place?" Albert's father asked the doctor.

"Oh yes. I have been here several months. I was a doctor in Warsaw."

"You're a Jew?" his father asked.

"Yes, I am a Jew. And this place where you have been brought to is called the Warsaw Ghetto. Everyone here is Jewish. Good thing there are plenty of Jewish doctors and dentists, right?"

Albert's father nodded.

"Will he be all right?" Albert's mother asked.

"He'll be fine. Why don't you two stay in line so you can get your address assignments. I'll take care of Albert."

"Thank you," Albert's father said.

"It's the least I can do. One Jew to another." The doctor smiled. He put his arm under Albert's and helped him as they walked away.

Shoshana glanced at her mother and then her father. No one in the Aizenberg family said a word. But a soft sigh of relief slipped out of Shoshana's lips. *I wonder what stopped him from killing Albert. Could it be possible that the Nazi was afraid of Albert's prayers? Is it possible that he really believes that Albert was casting a spell on him? Or was it God who stopped that Nazi's hand from pulling the trigger? Did Hashem hear Albert's prayers and interceded to save his life?*

The Aizenberg family was given an address where they were expected to live by the Judenrat. They began walking down the streets of the ghetto. Perle was softly weeping. Bluma was angry and defiant. Shoshana was frightened and confused. They had been forced out of the world they knew and loved and sent to a place unlike any they'd ever been before.

It wasn't long before Shoshana and her family realized that this prison where they'd been sent was a filthy, disease-ridden place, overcrowded and smelly. The contrast between the shtetl where she'd lived her entire life and this ghetto was shocking in so many ways. She'd grown up in a village where she knew everyone else who lived there. She knew their jobs, their families, even their life stories.

But here, inside this Warsaw Ghetto, there were so many different types of people.

When she lived in the shtetl, she'd seen a few secular Jewish salesmen who had come into their little village to sell their wares. But she'd never spoken to any of them. They did all of their dealings with the men in town. It was strictly forbidden for the women to be alone with any man who was not her husband, let alone a secular Jew. To the Hasidim, a secular Jew was not a Jew at all; he was considered a goy, a non-Jew. And that meant he did not know or respect the important Jewish laws and traditions.

She'd also seen the non-Jewish salesmen when they came to the shtetl, the goyim. It was easy to tell them apart, the way they dressed, the way they walked. And because her parents had been firm in telling her to beware of them, she had been careful to have as little contact with them as possible. They frightened her when they tried to speak to her, using words like "sweetie" or "darling." They would ask, "Sweetie, can you tell me where I can find the local locksmith?" or "Darlin', don't you look pretty today?"

She wouldn't answer them; she would run away, pretending not to understand them.

When they lived in the shtetl, her father bought things from the Jewish secular salesmen, and on occasion from the goyim, but he always reminded his children that they were to keep their distance from these people. And he made it clear that the secular Jews were the same as the goyim. "Remember, they are not to be regarded as Jewish. I have no respect for them. They are no better than the goys," he said.

Now, in the ghetto, the secular Jews were everywhere. The Nazi guards were the only goyim she saw, and they were horrible, frightening people. She could see why her father had been adamant about staying away from them. And the secular Jewish men were one thing. Shoshana knew what to expect of them, or at least she thought she did. But she couldn't help it. Although she would never tell anyone, the truth was that the secular women intrigued her.

They wore clothing that exposed their collarbones and even more. Their skirts were too short to be considered modest. And, married or not, they did not cover their hair. No married woman in her village would have allowed herself to be seen by men without covering her hair. Shoshana had to admit to herself, although she would never have told her parents, the secular women were beautiful. Their long, flowing hair, and the dark makeup around their eyes, as well as their red lipstick, struck Shoshana as enviable. A part of her longed to be like them. Although she knew their behavior was shameful, and each time she thought of how much she admired them, she prayed for the sinful thoughts to go away.

Shoshana's mother had always been a sensitive and emotional person, but no one had ever seen her weep as much as she had when they got off the train in the ghetto. Naomi Aizenberg had been a perfect example of good and frum, a pious woman. She'd been highly regarded by the other women in their village. And now, her entire way of life had been ripped away. She was nervous and uncertain as they waited in line for the Judenrat, the Jewish council, to assign their living quarters. The Judenrat, was a group of Jews chosen by the Nazis to rule their fellow Jews within the ghetto walls. They were put in charge in order to carry out the Nazis' orders. And even at first sight, Shoshana disliked them.

As Naomi stood in line weeping, her husband, Herschel, quietly reprimanded her. In a harsh whisper he told her that she should not cry. "You are fortunate to be alive. You must be happy that Hashem has bestowed the gift of life upon you. So, we are here. We don't like it. But we are all together, and we are alive. Stop your crying, woman." He had not hugged her or comforted her in any way. And Shoshana thought that if he had, it might have been more effective than his hard words. But she knew that this was her father's way, and he would never change.

Shoshana's family was assigned a small, dirty apartment, in a large building which they would share with the Klofskys. Ruth and Isaac Klofsky were a young couple who had a four-year-old son, Yusuf. Yusuf was full of energy, and the apartment was too small and crowded for a young child. Consequently, Yusuf was a terror. He ran through the apartment breaking things, and always getting into everyone else's belongings. The twins found him to be obnoxious. They hid their things from him. Then one afternoon, when Ruth, the child's mother, offered them money to play with him and keep him entertained, they refused. However, Bluma asked Ruth how she had money to pay them. Ruth just smiled and explained that she had been a famous singer before she was sent to the ghetto, and now that she was there, she earned extra money singing at one of the clubs.

"There are entertainers here in the ghetto?" Naomi asked.

"Oh yes, we have plays, and musicians who perform. We have comedians. If you don't already know this, you're going to find out that Jews are talented," Ruth said.

Naomi was shocked. "I didn't realize it. I thought this was a prison."

"Oh, but it is. However, Jews love the arts. And you are going to find that we have art. That's for sure, although we have no food; the rations are pitiful. We have no heat in the winter, and we're dying of disease. But the one thing we do have is art.

CHAPTER TWENTY-FOUR

EVEN BEFORE THE FAMILY WAS TAKEN TO THE GHETTO, WHEN THEY still lived within the protection of the shtetl, the twins had never needed any other friends. They had each other, and they did everything together. But now that they were in this strange and miserable environment, they were even less open to allowing anyone else into their lives. The only person they really loved and trusted other than their parents, was their older sister, Shoshana. She knew them better than anyone else outside of each other. Bluma was the strong one, the leader. She was healthier and more vivacious. Perle followed Bluma's directions. So if Shoshana needed the girls to do something, she knew she must convince Bluma to do it, and Perle would follow.

Often, when the weather permitted, the twins would sit together outside and play a strange game. One would think of a number, and then they would look into each other's eyes, and the other would guess the number. Shoshana would watch them playing. They could easily pass an entire afternoon playing this game together. Shoshana never said a word to anyone about what her sisters were doing, but she marveled at how often the number they guessed was correct. It seemed as if they were capable of reading each other's minds.

Poor Yusuf was terribly bored. His parents didn't like to sit on the floor and play with him. So he had no one to play with. He was in desperate need of attention; any attention was better than none. So Yusuf was a constant annoyance to everyone in the apartment. He was loud—shouting, crying, and constantly busy doing things. He got into everyone's possessions, including the precious items Shoshana's mother had brought with her for Shabbos.

One afternoon, Yusuf was desperately trying to get his mother to play with him. Ruth was busy taking the pin curls out of her hair. He brought her one of his toys and handed it to her, but she shook her head. "I'm sorry, darling, I have to finish my hair, so I can go to work. I don't have time to play now." Yusuf sat at her feet for a few moments. He looked angry. He pulled at the hem of her dress. "Stop that now," she said. Then Yusuf got up and got a spoon. Banging on a pot, he got everyone's attention but his mother's. "Stop, please," Naomi said. But it did no good. The twins could hardly stand to be around the little boy. They gave him a look of disgust, then went outside.

When Yusuf saw that his mother was not moved by the noise he was making, he stood up and began running around the apartment, reaching up and pulling things off the shelves. Then he grabbed a kiddush cup that had been in Shoshana's family for years. He threw it on the floor, and it broke into a million pieces. Naomi gasped. She ran to pick up the glass. "Oy vey, what have you done? This was my father's kiddush cup. He got it from his uncle for his bar mitzvah. It's irreplaceable." Her eyes grew glassy, and Shoshana was afraid she might cry. She went to her mother and put her arm around her shoulder.

"It's all right, Mama. It's just a cup," Shoshana said. "I'll clean it up."

For a few moments, no one said anything. They were waiting to see what the child's parents would say or do. And since Yusuf's parents didn't say a word, Shoshana's father yelled, "He's a vilde chaya, a wild animal. I blame the parents. You can't blame a child for what he has not been taught." Herschel had raised his children to be respectful and disciplined, so consequently he was exasperated by the boy and his parents' lack of concern. "This child has no discipline. He was not raised properly. He's growing up to be a monster." Herschel Aizenberg said it loud enough for everyone to hear. But it didn't matter to Ruth or Isaac; they seemed to have too many other things on their minds. So Herschel went over to Isaac and said, "That cup was of great value to my wife. Do you intend to pay for it?"

Isaac stammered. "Well . . ."

"I'll pay for it," Ruth said. "What do you want? How much?" She sounded annoyed and exasperated.

"Never mind," Herschel said. "Money could never take the place of a valuable memory anyway."

Shoshana knew her father would not take the money. He wanted to shame the parents, and it just didn't work. They didn't care. Shoshana felt sorry for the little boy. She knew that Yusuf just needed more attention. His mother was not home very often, and when she was, she seemed to be preoccupied with other things. To make matters worse, lately his father was not home either. He left the child alone in the apartment, depending on Shoshana's family to look after him. It seemed that Isaac had taken to spending his time with the woman who lived in the apartment across the hall. Shoshana tried to tell Ruth that Yusuf needed more attention, but Ruth refused to listen.

"I know he is a bad boy, but I just don't have the time to take care of him. I wasn't cut out for this."

"He's not a bad boy," Shoshana said. "He just needs mothering."

"I said I wasn't cut out for this. I mean it."

"For what?" Shoshana asked.

"For motherhood."

"Then why did you ever have a child?"

"Because I got pregnant. It's a long story. And I don't feel like explaining," Ruth said. "I'm sorry." Then she got up and went outside, leaving Shoshana to watch Yusuf and keep him from destroying everyone else's things. Shoshana was shocked that Ruth could be so callous about her son's needs. But she didn't bring it up again. There was nothing else to say. Ruth was a selfish woman.

Shoshana's father said so all the time. But even so, Shoshana didn't know why, but she admired Ruth and her strong independent streak. Ruth was beautiful, with her bobbed hair and red lipstick. She was strong willed, and she didn't care what anyone said to her. She wasn't afraid of angering her husband or Shoshana's father. Ruth did what she pleased. And Shoshana often wondered where she went in the afternoons. Most days she would sleep late, then wake up, get dressed and leave the apartment, not returning until just before curfew.

Meanwhile, her son was Shoshana's family's responsibility. Because his father, Isaac, was gone too. Sometimes Shoshana wondered if she should tell Ruth about Isaac spending so much of his time with the young woman who lived across the hall. Ruth should know, but Shoshana just couldn't bring herself to tell her. It was not something someone could bring up lightly. It was shameful, and she felt certain that Ruth's husband was acting against God's commandments.

Since she didn't have the courage to tell Ruth, Shoshana vowed to find time to spend playing with the little boy. She would do her best to mother him. It was a mitzvah, a blessing to help this child in need, she decided. When she wasn't caring for her sisters, or washing clothes, she invited Yusuf outside to throw a ball with her. The child was thrilled. At first, he was obstinate about having his own way. He refused to listen to her, and his behavior was not good. But when she threatened to take him back inside and stop playing with him, he started to behave. The more time Shoshana spent with Yusuf, the more endearing he became. He loved to run into her arms and be held and cuddled. He picked dandelions for her and made her a bouquet. *I love children. And I know I will be a good mother. So why am I secretly afraid to get married and have children of my own? It's my destiny. It's what I was put here on earth to do. And yet I am afraid of it. I could never tell anyone of this fear, not even Neta, because she would not understand.*

Unlike the Aizenbergs, Isaac and Ruth Klofsky were not religious. They did not keep kosher, which caused problems in the apartment. They were forced to share the use of the dishes and silverware in the kitchen. Shoshana's father put up a sheet between his family and the Klofskys in order to give everyone some privacy. But even so, it was difficult to have any privacy in such a small living space. And soon, Shoshana began to learn more about the Klofskys, especially Ruth.

She was surprised at how often Ruth Klofsky commanded her husband, Isaac, to do things to help her. Shoshana had never seen a woman make demands on a man before. All the women Shoshana knew were obedient to their husbands. Ruth was strong and outspoken and never obedient to anyone. When she was busy, she shamelessly told her husband to wash their clothes, and when she had to go to the market, she demanded that he stay at home to watch their son, so she didn't have to drag him with her. Of course, it was Isaac's responsibility to spend his days with Yusuf when Ruth was at work. However, as soon as she left, he went next door to see the woman who lived there, leaving his son in the care of the Aizenbergs. But when Ruth was around, Isaac Klofsky did whatever his wife asked him to do.

They kissed passionately, without shame, in front of Shoshana and her entire family, even the children. At night she heard loud sounds coming from their bed, and she felt certain that they were copulating. It made her face turn red with shame. They did not even attempt to be quiet or discreet. Of course, she knew that a young couple must have intercourse to produce children, but they certainly could have been less vocal, knowing that there were others in the apartment. She thought of the twins and how strange all of this must make them feel. They'd grown up in a very pious home, where sex was never discussed, let alone openly displayed.

Her father never said a word, but Shoshana could see by how he looked at the young couple that he was disgusted by their behavior. She could also see that it made him angry that he did not have the power to move his family out of this apartment and away from these secular Jews. He was appalled by the way Ruth spoke to her husband. Sometimes he was so appalled that he spit on the floor at how brazen Ruth was when she spoke to Isaac during an argument.

And no matter what Herschel Aizenberg said, which he always said loud enough for everyone to hear, Ruth didn't back down.

There was constant disapproval in Shoshana's father's eyes. And Shoshana knew why; religious women did not behave this way. But Shoshana couldn't help herself; she was intrigued. Never before in her entire life had she met anyone like Ruth. All of the women she'd known growing up were the same. They were obedient. They wore modest clothing. And they obeyed their husbands. Ruth did none of these things. But what struck Shoshana as most compelling was that Ruth went about her daily chores singing love songs. Not religious songs, but romantic songs of star-crossed lovers. There was a sensuality to her voice which was a haunting soprano, and Shoshana found she could lose herself in it. Sometimes Shoshana would close her eyes and imagine the lovers in the songs, and she would wish she could be one of them.

Ruth left the kitchen a mess most of the time. Shoshana's mother cleaned it without complaining. But her father made comments about Ruth's lack of cleanliness. It took a great deal of work for Naomi to manage to keep kosher because Ruth openly declared that she had no intentions of keeping kosher.

"It's just too much work," she said simply. "I have never done it. And I have no plans of doing it now. I just can't be changing dishes for your convenience. We're all stuck in this lousy situation. In this filthy, miserable place together. And I know we have to try to make the best of it. But I am getting sick and tired of your comments, old man." She was looking directly at Herschel Aizenberg. Shoshana held her breath. No one had ever spoken to her father that way. And especially not a woman. Then Ruth continued, "Quite frankly, when you make demands on me, it annoys me. I'm not your wife. And I would never want to be. Poor woman is afraid to breathe around you. You're such a damn tyrant. I don't know who you think you are. But to me, you're just a silly old man with a long beard and stupid-looking sideburns."

Herschel was struck silent. He'd never had a woman speak to him in such a curt and discourteous manner. He turned away from her and shook his head. But Shoshana had always feared her father.

She'd tried to love him, but he rejected affection and demanded obedience. So now, she secretly admired Ruth for standing up to him. It was something she'd always wished she had the courage to do.

Each day, Herschel got up and dressed himself, then he walked down several streets to an apartment where many of the men he'd known in the shtetl had set up a makeshift synagogue. All day he studied and prayed. In the evening, he returned to the apartment, where he cautiously tried to eat what he felt was acceptably kosher, from the meager rations that were given to each Jewish person. He did not tell anyone, but he believed that his family had fallen on such terrible times because he was being punished for the years that he did not believe in God, for the years he'd secretly questioned God's existence. He had been a brazen man then; he'd broken God's commandments. He had thought he was too educated and too smart to believe in God. In fact, when he had intellectual arguments with other lawyers, he called God a man-made superstition created to keep the ignorant in line. Then he spent almost a whole year eating non-kosher food and sleeping with a shiksa, who betrayed him in the end. Now he wanted to show God that he was ready to repent, that he was wrong, and he'd learned his lesson.

One night, Herschel came home from the shul and said to his family. "Nu, so, listen to this . . . today, while I was in the shul, one of the men talked about this place called the public kitchen. It's not far from us. It's just over on Nalewski Street. The man says it's glatt kosher. And they will accept our ration cards as payment. We don't even need any extra money. So instead of eating here by all these goyim, who keep the apartment so filthy and traif, unkosher, I've decided that we are going to eat all of our meals over by the public kitchen."

Naomi nodded. Shoshana cast her eyes downward. He would have the final say, and he had decided to call the Klofskys goyim, which was the strongest insult that Herschel Aizenberg could say about another Jew. Shoshana was ashamed to line up outside a public kitchen to eat. But what her father said was law. And she knew that although he would never admit it, he was ashamed too.

Before the ghetto, Herschel was a proud man who had taken pride in making a good impression on others. In fact, he had always made sure that everyone knew he made large donations to the shul, not because he believed in it, but because he wanted everyone to know that he was a successful lawyer earning far more than most of his neighbors.

The following afternoon, because Herschel demanded it, Shoshana took her sisters by the hand and followed her parents to Nalewski Street where they got into a line to collect their meal. It was humiliating, but it was just as well. The rations that were provided by the Nazis were very meager. And the Aizenbergs had no money, and nothing left of value to trade except Naomi's ring, which they decided to hold on to as long as they could. However, not having any money or valuables, they were unable to purchase extra food on the black market which had become the only outlet for obtaining additional food.

Whenever Shoshana had a moment alone, she would go outside and sing the songs she'd heard Ruth sing. She would sing them very quietly to herself, because if her father heard her, there was no doubt in her mind that he would be furious. But she found that she loved to sing; it gave a feeling of deep calm. And with all the changes in her life, she needed something to calm her nerves.

CHAPTER TWENTY-FIVE

ONE AFTERNOON HERSCHEL AIZENBERG DID NOT COME HOME FROM the shul. He'd still not returned by the time the family was ready to go to the public kitchen for dinner. "I'm worried about him," Naomi told Shoshana quietly. "He should have been home by now. Still, the children must eat. So you and I will take them together. Yes?"

"Of course, Mama," Shoshana said. She could see the deep lines between her mother's eyes.

"The girls are outside. They can't stand to be in this apartment with Yusuf. He is so noisy, but he is just a child and has no attention at all. Poor thing. Can you go out and find the girls? They are probably sitting behind the building. I don't like it that they sit outside all the time. It's too cold. But what can I say to them. I know they can't stand this way we are living."

"I'll go and get them, Mama," Shoshana said. She knew that since the winter had come, the girls had found another place to play. They sat under the stairwell in the lobby where it was not warm but still not nearly as cold as it was outside.

"Perle, Bluma," Shoshana said as she approached.

"Yes," Perle answered.

"Come, we have to go to eat."

"Papa isn't home yet, is he?" Bluma asked. "We didn't see him come in."

"No, he's not. But he'll be home soon. I'm sure of it. Now, come on upstairs and get ready. You know how Mama insists that you both wash your hands and faces and brush your hair before we go to eat."

"Yes, I know how she insists. But I can't see why," Bluma said, "Everyone at the public kitchen is dirty and smelly. I hate it there. And I don't know why she thinks we should take so much time with our appearances."

"Because you are young ladies. And it is the right thing to do," Shoshana said. "Now, come on upstairs. It's getting late. We have to eat before curfew."

The girls were hungry, so they followed Shoshana up the stairs. As they were about to leave the apartment, Shoshana saw Yusuf standing all alone by his little blanket on the floor where he slept. "Where's your papa?" she asked him.

Yusuf shook his head. Shoshana assumed his father was across the hall with his lady friend. She turned to her mother. "I'm going to tell Isaac that we are leaving, and he must return to the apartment to watch his child. I'll be right back."

Shoshana went next door and knocked. A woman in a housecoat answered. "Is Isaac Klofsky here?" Shoshana asked.

"Aren't you the girl who lives next door?"

"Yes, he lives in our apartment with his wife and son. I need to speak with him."

"Sure, just a moment."

Isaac came to the door. He looked disheveled. Shoshana looked away. She could not look directly at him. "My family will be leaving the apartment. Yusuf is too young to stay alone. You must come and get him or come home," she said. She'd never spoken so boldly to a man.

"Just leave him in the apartment. He'll be fine until his mother gets home," Isaac said.

"I can't do that." Shoshana glared at Isaac. "He could get hurt."

"He's my son, and I said he'll be fine," Isaac said insistently.

Shoshana hesitated for a moment. Then she said, "Would it be all right if I took him with me and my family to the public kitchen to eat?"

"Sure."

Shoshana nodded. "Please tell Ruth where we've gone and that we'll have Yusuf back as soon as possible."

"Sure," Isaac said, closing the door in Shoshana's face.

When the twins heard that Shoshana was bringing Yusuf with them, the girls scoffed. "Why are we taking him with us?" Bluma asked. "All I want to do is get away from him."

"I know. He's a little rambunctious. But he's a child and, well, would you really feel good about leaving him all alone here in this apartment? How would you feel if he fell out the window?" Shoshana asked.

Perle looked down at the ground. "All right, let's take him with us," she said. "I can't stand being around him, but I wouldn't want anything bad to happen to him either."

The twins held Naomi's hands, and Shoshana carried Yusuf down the stairs, but just as they were about to leave the building, Shoshana's father walked in.

"Where were you? Are you all right? I've been so worried," Naomi said.

"Yes, I'm fine. After the shul I met with Albert's father."

"Is everything all right? Did Albert recover from the gunshot wound to his arm?"

"Yes, he's fine, praise God. He was lucky that doctor saw the whole thing and took care of him. Anyway, come, let's go eat, and I'll talk to you and Shoshana as we walk to the public kitchen."

CHAPTER TWENTY-SIX

SHOSHANA WRAPPED HER SCARF TIGHTER AROUND HER HEAD AND neck as they headed down the street. Thin plates of ice hid under the snow and slush, and everyone had to be very careful not to slip.

As they rounded the corner to the public kitchen Shoshana's father began to speak. He was addressing Shoshana: "Nu, so we have no choice. You'll get married next month. Rabbi Paulsky is here in the ghetto too. I spoke to him at the shul before I saw Albert's father, and he has agreed to marry you."

"Yes, Papa," Shoshana said, hanging her head, but she thought, *There is no money for a banquet for the wedding. The Nazis took the dress Mama made for me. And the truth is, I just don't want to be married. Albert is a wonderful man; he's a good catch, but I just don't want this.*

So much had changed since they'd left the shtetl. Life was no longer simple. The lines of what was expected of a person were blurred now. The ghetto was harsh, but in a strange way, Shoshana had also found it to be enlightening. Here in this place within a big city, she had come in contact with people she would have never met if she had stayed in the shtetl where she was born. Here she'd seen other ways of life, and she thought she might like to explore them more.

She'd met women who had been career women, owned businesses, had lives other than wives and mothers, and had lived as equals in a world where men were not their bosses. Yes, she'd met women like Ruth, who didn't take orders from their husbands. And she wondered what it would be like to have a choice about when and who she would marry.

They arrived back at the apartment just before curfew. Ruth was already there waiting. Isaac was not at home.

"Thanks for taking Yusuf," Ruth said. "Isaac told me you took him with your family to eat"

"Yes, you're welcome; he was a good boy," Shoshana said.

"I'm glad. I know he can be a lot at times, but he's really just a little boy. You know?"

Shoshana nodded. She was tired and had too much to think about. Her future was about to be decided, and she wanted to go to bed so she could be left alone with her thoughts.

The following morning, Shoshana woke up feeling as if her body was frozen. Even so, she needed air. She needed to get outside and walk, to take time to think things through. The apartment was as clean as she could get it, considering she had no soap. And there was nothing she was expected to do right at this moment, except perhaps to pray. And she felt she could pray better while she was outside in the fresh air. So she grabbed her old coat and told her mother she was only going out for a quick walk to see Neta, who was living only a few streets away. Her mother nodded in agreement. "All right, go. But don't stay all day. I know how you and Neta can get lost in talking and laughing, and before too long the whole day is gone. Make sure you're home in time to go to eat."

"Yes, Mama." A gust of wind greeted her when she opened the door of the apartment building. It was chilly, but the air outside was cleaner and fresher smelling than the air in the apartment. A bout of dysentery had spread through the building over the past week, and the smell was overwhelming. Each of the twins vomited several times until they finally got used to the odor.

Shoshana breathed deep. Walking always made her feel at peace inside, so she took the long way to Neta's apartment. She wanted some time alone. And even though it was cold, it was pleasant. Singing softly to herself as she walked, she looked up at the sky.

"Shoshana." Someone called her name.

Shoshana turned around quickly to see Ruth standing a few feet behind her. "Hello," Shoshana said shyly. She'd never spoken to Ruth alone, without anyone else around before.

"Where are you going?" Ruth asked.

"I'm on my way to see my friend, Neta. She lives close by."

"I overheard you singing some of the songs I sing. You have a nice voice," Ruth said.

Shoshana blushed. "Was I that loud? I had no idea."

"It's all right. I sing all the time. And I sing loud," Ruth said. Her smile was sincere and open. Shoshana knew she was a selfish woman, but it didn't matter; she liked her. Shoshana smiled too. "Listen, I have an idea. There is going to be a concert here in the ghetto on Leszno Street tomorrow. The Jewish Symphony Orchestra is playing, and to make it even more exciting, Marysa Eisenstadt will be performing. Do you know of her?"

Shoshana shook her head. She'd never heard of the orchestra, or the woman Ruth just mentioned.

"Well, I've heard her perform before. And let me tell you, she has the most wonderful soprano voice, so pure and clear. I was lost in it. Would you like to attend the concert with me? I know you will enjoy it."

"Oh yes," Shoshana blurted out. "But . . ." She hesitated. "My papa would never allow it."

"Oh yes, there's him to think of, isn't there?" Ruth shook her head. "I honestly don't know how you can tolerate all of his control-ling ways. He gets on my nerves."

"Please, don't talk about my father that way," Shoshana said, but deep down inside, she agreed it was difficult to endure her father's constant restraints and demands.

"I'm sorry. I didn't mean to offend you. But you would like to go, wouldn't you?"

"Yes, of course. But I don't think I can."

"Well, if you can't go to the concert, maybe you can go with me to hear some live music. The concert is about two hours, but we could go to a café for a quick twenty minutes or so. Your father would never know you were gone."

"I don't know. It seems so deceptive."

"Aren't you getting married soon?"

"Yes," Shoshana said, looking down at her shoes.

"Well, I think you deserve some fun before you get tied down."

Shoshana's heart ached. She longed to go with Ruth, to see how it felt to sit in a café and listen to music. She'd never been in a restaurant or a café.

"So, I think we should start with something small, like the café. We can go and stay as long as you want. I promise we'll go home as soon as you say you're ready to leave."

Shoshana bit her lip. She juggled her handbag nervously from one hand to the other. "I am not sure what to do."

"For the first time in your life, Shoshana, why don't you do something that you really want to do instead of pleasing everyone else?"

This struck a chord with Shoshana. *Soon I will be Albert's wife. He will take my father's place in my life. I will no longer obey my father, but I will spend the rest of my days obeying my husband. I want to go. I want to go more than I can express. I know it's wrong, but I have to do this just once before I sign my marriage contract.*

"So, what do you say? How about if I help you get out of the apartment and away from your father for a while, then we can go to one of the cafés that's offering live music. It will be fun. I have a little money; we'll have something to eat and drink."

Shoshana's head was whirling. She'd never done anything like this. And the only live music she'd ever heard was the cantor in the shul. "I don't have any money," she said.

"I know you don't. I told you that I do," Ruth said, winking. "How about we go tomorrow night?"

Shoshana thought about it for a moment. She'd always been so obedient. But the thought of getting out and having just a taste of a different life was wildly exciting to her. A little voice in her head said *You'd better not. Your father will be furious if he finds out and it could ruin your engagement if Albert or his family find out that you have been carousing all over town.* But she and her family had lost everything, and she'd longed for something to take the place of her old life. She no longer had her home, her clothing, the way of life she'd grown up with. She tried to make the best of it, always smiling, and doing what was expected of her. Helping with children, the wash, the cleaning. Acting as if nothing had changed. Yet it had. All around her was sickness, hunger, and death. If she could steal just a moment of pleasure, what was so wrong with that? "Yes, I'll go," she said bravely. "Yes."

"Good. We're going to have so much fun. You'll see. You'll like it."

"I just don't know how I am going to get out of the apartment. My father is going to be full of questions."

"Don't you worry about that. You just leave it to me." Ruth winked.

CHAPTER TWENTY-SEVEN

THAT NIGHT AT ABOUT SEVEN IN THE EVENING, THERE WAS A KNOCK on the door to the apartment.

Naomi opened the door. "Yes?" she said to a handsome young man who stood on the other side.

"I need to see Ruthy," the man said.

"Come in, please. She's here." Naomi was shocked that a man was coming to speak to Ruth who was a married woman. But she didn't interfere. She just called out: "Ruth, someone is here to see you."

Ruth got up from her dressing table. She walked over to the door. When she saw the man, she hugged him. Naomi's mouth fell open when she saw Ruth have physical contact with the stranger. Then Ruth said, "Michael. What brings you here?"

"My wife, Sara. She's having the baby. She needs you."

"Oy, all right. She's early, isn't she?"

"Yes, she's not due until next month. I am very worried about her," Michael said.

"You wait right here. Let me gather my things. I'll just be a minute," Ruth said.

"You're a midwife?" Naomi asked. Suddenly she was impressed.

"Yes." Ruth nodded. She went over to her dressing table and picked up a small bag. Then she headed back to Michael. "Let's go."

"But . . ." Michael said, hesitating. "I can't take care of the other children while Sara is in labor. I can't do it all alone. I am too nervous right now. Is it possible maybe that this young woman can help us with my other children until the baby is born?" He indicated Shoshana whose face was hot with embarrassment.

"No! It's after seven o'clock; it's after curfew. She cannot go out of the apartment. If she's caught outside by the Nazi guards, who knows what they'll do," Shoshana's father said.

"But we need her. Please, I implore you, sir. It's a mitzvah," the young man said.

Herschel Aizenberg was genuinely conflicted. It was a mitzvah to help a person in a time of need, and he believed in treating his fellow man with goodness as it was instructed in the Torah. But this was dangerous. He didn't know what to do.

"You want to go and help, Shoshana?" her mother asked.

"She can't go with these strangers at night," Herschel said, dismissing the question.

"I am surprised at you, Mr. Aizenberg. You, of all people, should understand that this is a mitzvah. Your daughter is being called by a needy husband to help with his children. How can you deny your daughter this opportunity to be useful?" Ruth insisted.

"It *is* a mitzvah," Naomi said in a small voice.

"We need her help," Ruth said.

Herschel looked at his daughter. "I suppose it is all right. But be very careful," Herschel said.

No one waited for Shoshana to answer when her mother asked if she wanted to go. They made the decision for her. But she didn't care. She was awestruck by the genius plan that Ruth had put into action.

"Come, Shoshana," Ruth said. "I'll bring her home as soon as the child is born."

Herschel nodded. "Behave yourself," he said to Shoshana.

"Yes, Papa."

"And please, please be careful," Naomi added.

CHAPTER TWENTY-EIGHT

SHOSHANA FELT A WAVE OF GUILT COME OVER HER AS THE THREE walked toward the café in town. "I hate to lie. It's a sin," she said.

Ruth took a tube of lipstick out of the black bag she was carrying and applied it to her lips.

"I thought that was your medical bag. I believed you were really a midwife," Shoshana said. "The bag looks so real."

"It's my cosmetic bag." Ruth laughed. "Do you want to try some lipstick? I have a red that would look ravishing on you."

"Oh, no, thank you," Shoshana said, her guilt growing by the minute. There was a moment of silence, then Shoshana said, "I feel bad about this. I think I should go home. I lied to my parents. It's not right."

"Let yourself enjoy the evening. You are free from your father's heavy hand for a few hours. Don't use these hours to dwell on him. You'll be back under his thumb soon enough," Ruth said.

Shoshana thought about what Ruth said and she nodded. *Ruth is right. But somehow I have to stop these voices in my head that are telling me how this is a sin and how wrong it is.*

As they walked, Ruth asked, "Did you know that they have established a school here in the ghetto that your twin sisters should probably be attending. I mean, it's none of my business, but it seems a shame that they aren't learning with the other children. I know that I'll be sending Yusuf as soon as he's old enough. I want him to be able to read and write. I want him to be able to get along in the world once this government and Hitler are gone."

"Well, we can only hope that this will all be over. Who knows what can happen? This might never end," Shoshana said.

"It might not. But then again, it might. And if it does, your sisters should be able to read and write. Don't you think so?"

"My papa would never send them to a secular school like that. He hardly agreed when my mother's younger brother, Shlomoe, taught me to read and write. The only way Papa would agree was if Shlomoe promised him that I would never be permitted to read forbidden books. I would only be exposed to religious text. And Shlomoe agreed. My father was reluctant even so. But I was lucky, Shlomoe was insistent, and so now, I can read and write."

"Is he here?"

"Who?"

"Shlomoe."

"Oh no. Sadly, he was sickly his entire life. He died a few years ago from some sort of a blood disease. I don't know too much more about the disease, but he was very sick. I miss him often. You would have liked him. He was an advanced thinker. Sort of like you."

Ruth glanced over at Shoshana and smiled. Then she patted Shoshana's shoulder.

What Ruth had referred to as a café wasn't really a café at all. It was a small apartment where several musicians lived. There was an entrance fee to hear the music. Food and drink, which the musicians had purchased on the black market, were available for a price to the customers. "It's rather ingenious, really," Ruth said. "A group of these musicians got together and created this place where they could exercise their talents. You see, we are allowed to have cafés and entertainment during the day, but once curfew arrives, the Nazis want us to be at home. And who are they to tell us what to do? We are adults, no? We should be able to come and go after dark. And let's face it, here in the ghetto, we have an even stronger need to be entertained than we did when we were out in the world. Don't you agree?"

Shoshana shrugged her shoulders. She'd never been entertained in her life, unless you could call a service at the shul entertainment. So this was all new to her.

Ruth went on to say, "And what I really like about this concept is that it's in their home. Nu? So, once the doors close, the Nazis have no idea. Or if they do, they don't care."

The apartment wasn't much different than the one where Shoshana and Ruth lived. It was small and dirty. But tonight, it was filled with music and dancing. The cots where the musicians slept stood up against the walls. A middle-aged female singer with wavy black hair crooned a love song. There were only a few chairs, and they were already occupied. So Shoshana leaned against the wall and closed her eyes. Then she allowed the music to enter her soul. Swaying with the rhythm, she soon forgot where she was. The misery of the ghetto faded away. She even forgot about her father and the guilt she'd felt about lying to him. Her body was swaying back and forth, lost in the music. Except for the music, which was kept at a low volume, the room was fairly quiet.

Then a young man walked up to the front of the room. "Ladies and gentleman," he said. " I have an announcement to make. We have a special guest here with us tonight. I am sure many of you have heard her sing. Won't you join me in welcoming Ruth Klofsky. Perhaps if we give her some applause, she'll sing for us."

The crowd began to applaud. Ruth stood up and raised her hands. Then she nodded her head and walked up to the stage. Shoshana held her breath. She hadn't known that Ruth was a famous singer. *But, of course, how would I know? We never knew what was happening in the outside world when I lived in the shtetl.*

Ruth sang a lively song while the audience danced and clapped. When she'd finished, they yelled "Encore!" But Ruth raised her hands, then she just shook her head and went back to sit down with Shoshana.

"You sang so beautifully."

"Oh, thank you," Ruth said, rubbing Shoshana's hand. "I sing at a real café during the afternoons. As you know, they can't be open in the evenings because of the curfew. But I am sure you could find a way to escape your parents for a while and come to see me perform if you wanted to."

"Yes, I suppose I could say I was going out for a walk. But I do hate all this lying," Shoshana said, and she felt ashamed because she knew she would do it; she would lie. *How easily these lies are coming to me. I must truly be a sinner.*

When the music ended at ten that night, Shoshana was sad that the magical night was over. *That was so beautiful; if only it could go on forever.*

"Good night everyone, and thank you for coming. Be careful on your way home," one of the musicians said as the customers started to leave the apartment.

Ruth turned to Shoshana. "Well, this is the part where things become a little more difficult. We must be very cautious. We can't get caught on our way back to the apartment. There is severe punishment for being out after curfew."

Shoshana felt her heart begin to race. She began to wonder if she'd made a mistake. There were Nazis out on the streets. She could hear them talking loudly, sometimes laughing. Ruth held her hand as they hid in the shadows, quiet, waiting for the Nazis to pass, listening for footsteps, and then moving forward getting closer to home. Every so often, Ruth stopped to listen and glance behind them. Then as they turned the corner and were just a few feet from their apartment building, they heard the hard boot heels of two Nazi guards hitting the pavement. Ruth grabbed Shoshana and pulled her into the alley behind the building next door where they waited, listening to their own hearts beating and their frantic breath, until the danger passed.

"I've never been so frightened in all my life," Shoshana said as they began to walk toward their apartment building.

"Yes, I know. And there is the temptation to stay inside at night and allow these Nazis to have power over us. But we can't let them dictate our lives, can we? We must do the things we love even if there is danger involved; that is what living is. If we spend all of our time living in fear, we might as well be dead."

Shoshana nodded. But her heart was still pounding as she entered the building where they lived. Both women ran up the three flights of stairs to their apartment and then quietly opened the door. Shoshana had spent her entire life listening to her father snore. So when she didn't hear him snoring, she knew he was awake. But he didn't say a word as Shoshana and Ruth went behind their respective curtains to get ready for bed. Shoshana saw his shadow in the darkness, and once again, she felt guilty for lying. But as she lay down on her cot, she closed her eyes and heard the music in her head. She sighed softly; it had been an exhilarating experience. Then she fell asleep.

CHAPTER TWENTY-NINE

ONLY ONE WEEK LATER, SHOSHANA WENT TO THE CAFÉ TO HEAR Ruth sing. She loved it. She couldn't explain why the music served as such an escape for her; all she knew was that it did. When the music played, she didn't worry about the dysentery, or the typhus. She didn't worry about how she was going to cope with her new life as a married woman. She didn't worry about the sins she was committing by lying. All she knew was that within the haunting sounds of the violin, or the piano, lay freedom and bliss.

"You love the music, don't you?" Ruth asked as they walked home together from the café.

"Oh yes, I do."

"I can tell. You've changed. You're not so somber anymore."

"When I hear the music, I feel alive. I feel like life is worth living even though we are here in this terrible place."

"I know, that is why the entertainment is so important here in the ghetto. That's why it's even more important here than it ever was before. Music, theater, art, these are the things that will keep us alive, keep us wanting to go on. Do you understand me?"

"Yes, actually I do," Shoshana said.

"Well, then you know why I love to sing."

"Yes, I would love to sing too," Shoshana said.

"Would you really?" Ruth asked, amazed.

"Yes, but I couldn't."

"Sure you could."

Shoshana shook her head. "I can be happy just listening. My father would be angry if he found out I was at the café, but he would be furious if I was singing."

"All right, so you'll come and listen. I am glad to have you." From that day on whenever Ruth was going to sing at a café, she would whisper a secret message to Shoshana in the morning. Then if she was able, Shoshana would sneak away for an hour or two and go to the café. One afternoon when Ruth wasn't singing, and Shoshana's father was at the makeshift synagogue praying, Shoshana's mother, along with her sisters, and Ruth's husband and their son, had all gone into town to pick up their ration tickets.

"Do the wash while I am gone," Naomi said to Shoshana. "And try to straighten up as much as you can."

"Yes, Mama," Shoshana said.

"I wish this place weren't so dirty." Naomi shook her head. "But I am taking the children with me, and Isaac is taking Yusuf, so you should have plenty of time alone to get things done."

"I will, Mother."

They thought Ruth was asleep, but as soon as they left Shoshana and Ruth alone in the apartment, Ruth got up from her cot and stretched. "What I wouldn't give for a cup of real coffee," she said.

"I can make you some of this fake coffee, if you'd like."

"It's better than nothing," Ruth said.

Shoshana began to prepare a cup of coffee for Ruth. Then while the water was boiling, she turned to Ruth and asked, "How do you command such respect from your husband? He treats you like an equal. You aren't afraid of him at all. I can hear you talk to him, and from what I hear, you don't hesitate to tell him your feelings."

Ruth laughed. "Of course I tell him what I feel about everything. And you say he treats me like an equal? Ha! Actually, he should be treating me like a superior. When I met him, he was a fumbling alcoholic without a job, who was starstruck because I was a fairly famous singer. I liked him, mostly because I found his constant devotion endearing. But before I agreed to marry him, I told him what he could expect from being my husband. I made sure he knew that I planned to live my own life, my own way. I like girls and men. I do whatever I please, and he has nothing to say about it."

Shoshana looked at her, shocked. "What do you mean, girls and men?"

"I mean that I am not faithful to my husband, and he knows it. I sleep with women, and I sleep with men, whenever I feel moved to do so. No one owns me. Isaac knew when we got married that if we had children, he was going to be the primary caretaker of them. I would be the breadwinner. We talked about it. He agreed to it. And so we have a very good marriage."

"So you know about the woman across the hall?" Shoshana blurted out the words, then she was suddenly ashamed. Her hand covered her mouth. She was shocked that she'd said that, and even more shocked at what Ruth had just told her. Sleeping with men and women and having sexual relations outside of marriage were all sins she would never even contemplate.

"Of course I know about her. Do you take me for a fool? I never worry about Isaac. He's like a puppy. All I have to do is snap my fingers, and he'll fall at my feet. I could make him give her up any time I want to. But I figure, he needs something to make him feel adequate. I know that he has always felt as if he were beneath me. And this girl is only a substitute. It's my love and affection he truly craves."

"But, do you care for him?"

"In my way, I love him."

"You know, we did not talk of love when I lived in the shtetl. We talked of honor and respect, but never of love. However, even though I have never known it, I can see by the way Isaac is when he is around you that he loves you."

"Yes, that he does," Ruth said. "And I care for him. I really do. I know he does have some exceptional qualities. Isaac is a good listener, and he's a very kind person. Besides that, he's good in bed."

Shoshana blushed. "How can you talk about sex so causally?"

Ruth laughed. "Because it's not such a major issue. Sex is nothing more than a natural part of life. People make too much of it. They are afraid of sex because they put too much emphasis on it. Don't get me wrong, it's a wonderful thing. Very sweet, and if you have a good lover, it's quite satisfying. But not something that should be feared or restricted. It's something to be enjoyed. Now, I know you were raised to be very religious, and so sex is a taboo subject for you. But, I will tell you right now, that if you marry a man who your father has chosen for you, and if you don't have any passion for your husband, you will be missing out on the joys of passion and lovemaking. If I were you, before I would agree to this marriage, I would dip my toes in the water. Do you know what I mean?"

"Not really."

"All right, little innocent one," Ruth said, patting Shoshana's hand. "I think before you settle down for the rest of your life with one person, you should try a few different men in bed. Perhaps women too. You should know yourself and what you like and don't like, before you take on a spouse."

Shoshana looked away. "I could never do that."

"You could if you wanted to. And . . . if you were smart, you would. No one would need to know. It could be your secret. Especially with you being Hasidic, once you sign on the dotted line, it's hard to get out of a marriage. If I were you, I would explore the world before I committed myself to anyone."

Shoshana shook her head. "I could never do something so deceptive. Even if no one found out, Hashem would know. But, believe me, in my religious world, people would find out. I don't know how, but they would. Everyone is always watching each other, and the gossiping never stops even though gossiping is a sin in itself."

"So you mean to tell me that these people commit what they consider sins, but at the same time they condemn each other?"

"I suppose you could say that, yes. And I can imagine what a shanda, a scandal, it would be if I did that. I would be called

139

terrible names, and I could never make a decent match. No decent man or his family would have me."

"Why would you even want a man who was so judgmental of you? Your husband should know you and accept you for who you are. Otherwise, he doesn't deserve you."

"It's not like that for us. As a good pious woman, I must adhere to certain rules. It's just our way of life. My father would be mortified if I behaved like a kurveh, a slut. And I would be shunned by our community."

"Your father." She scoffed. "Shoshana, I don't want to say anything bad about your father, but . . ."

"Please, don't. I know he can be hardheaded and hurtful at times. But he is my father. And Hashem says that we must honor our parents."

"All right, so you honor them. But does that mean that you give up your entire life for them? Is their happiness more important than your own? Do you think it's right that you should marry and live with a man who you have no passion for because your father demands it of you? Well, I don't, Shoshana. Personally, I wouldn't do it. Not for my father or anyone else. This is my life. As far as I know, we only live once, and I am not sacrificing my happiness for anyone."

"You just don't understand. This is the way I was raised. It's impossible for me to see things differently. I don't know how to do that."

"I understand. But when your entire life is at stake, you learn how to do it. Perhaps you don't realize that you have choices. Perhaps you don't realize that it's you who is stopping yourself from living fully. If a man doesn't want to marry you because you have lived a full life before you met him, then he's not someone you would want to be married to anyway."

"Oh, you really don't understand," Shoshana said, shaking her head and getting up from the bench where she was sitting, and walking a few steps away. Her fists were clenched. Her eyes burned with tears just waiting to fall. She was shaking, and she did not turn around to look back at Ruth who was still sitting on the bench, when she said, "I wish I had your courage, your strength. I wish I could do the things you say. But I can't."

"But you do have courage and strength. And you can do whatever you set your mind to. I see all of this in you. I see your zest for life, Shoshana."

"It's too late anyway. I am already betrothed to a good man from a fine family. My life will be the same as my mother's life was and her mother's before her. My father has made the arrangements, and I will be married in a few months. From then on everything will change. I will no longer have time to come to the café, or to think so heavily about things. From the day I say I do, my life will be devoted to Albert and our children."

"Is that what you want?"

"What I want?" Shoshana gave a harsh laugh. "I have never thought much about what I wanted in life. Until I met you, I was just grateful that the man my father chose was handsome. He could have been old, ugly, and fat. But I am fortunate. Albert is handsome, and not only that, but he is brave too."

"That's all fine and good, but do you want to marry him? Are you ready to give him the rest of your life?" Ruth pressed on.

Tears spilled from Shoshana's eyes. She shook her head. She still did not turn to look at Ruth, and she did not speak.

"Well, are you ready to give up the rest of your life? To become a baby-making machine and a housekeeper?" Ruth asked.

"No. I want to do things. I want to see things. I don't want to get married." The words sprung from Shoshana's lips. She wiped her tears with the backs of her thumbs.

"Then don't."

"Easy for you to say. Not easy for me to do," Shoshana said. "Please, can we stop talking about this. It's very upsetting."

"Of course." Ruth smiled, then she added, "So, you'll come to see me sing, for an hour or so, once a week, yes?"

"I'll try," Shoshana said, but she still did not look at Ruth. Instead, she headed to her bed behind the curtain in the apartment.

"Good," Ruth called out as Shoshana walked away.

CHAPTER THIRTY

FOR THE NEXT MONTH OR SO, SHOSHANA WENT TO HEAR RUTH sing at least once, and sometimes twice a week. Whenever she went to the café, she lied and told her mother that she was going to visit Neta. The guilt was eating at her like a cancer. She not only felt terrible about the lying, but she also felt badly because she had cut back to only dropping by to see Neta once a week. Before she had met Ruth, she'd gone to see Neta as often as she could. But now, things had changed. Shoshana knew that she had changed. There was no denying that she loved those hours she spent at the café. The smoky room, the music, watching the people dance, all of it gave her a feeling of exhilaration. And the longing for a different life grew stronger with every passing day.

Then one afternoon, after Ruth finished a bluesy, torchy love song, in a raspy voice, she bowed as the audience clapped. Then Ruth smiled and said, "And now, I would like to introduce you to a good friend of mine. She's a singer too. But she's a little shy, so you're going to have to help me here. If you want to hear her sing, you're going to have to give her a big round of applause. We have to coax her up here to the stage. Her name is Shoshana Aizenberg. Come on up here, Shoshana."

The crowd began to applaud.

"Help me with this, everyone. I need even louder applause from you." The crowd roared and applauded wildly. Shoshana felt her face turning hot and red. She wanted to hide. But the applause continued.

"Come on up, Shoshana, don't be shy. Everyone wants to meet you. Don't you want to meet Shoshana?" Ruth said.

Shoshana couldn't believe how beautiful Ruth looked, how she bathed in the admiration from the crowd.

The crowd applauded even louder.

"Call her up here with me; let's chant 'Shoshana,' until she comes up."

The crowd, along with Ruth, began to chant Shoshana's name.

Shoshana stood up. Her knees felt weak, but she walked up onto the raised platform and stood beside Ruth. Ruth turned to Shoshana and started clapping. Then she raised her hands so everyone would quiet down.

"Shoshana has a beautiful voice," she said to the audience. Then she turned to her. "Won't you sing a song with me?" she asked.

Shoshana shook her head. "I couldn't."

"Should we start the applause again?"

Shoshana smiled. "No."

"Then let's do one song together. Come on, what do you say?"

What can I say? She nodded. "All right."

Ruth began singing a song that she had overhead Shoshana singing one day.

"He's the man that I love," Ruth crooned. "The man that makes me smile." Then Ruth nudged Shoshana's shoulder with her own. "Come on, Shoshana."

"He's the man that I need. Even if it's only for a while," Shoshana sang.

And soon they were singing together. When they finished, the crowd roared. Shoshana felt a charge of exhilaration shoot through her like a lightning bolt. Ruth started another song. Shoshana sang along with her, and this time her voice grew stronger. Ruth put her arm around her friend's shoulder. They finished the second song on a high note, and the crowd went wild.

From that day on, every time Shoshana went to see Ruth perform, Shoshana sang at least one song on stage with her. It was like a drug; she was addicted to the applause, to the magic of the music, to the freedom. When she thought about giving it up to marry Albert, she was so unhappy that she couldn't bear it. Two months passed. Each evening, after eating at the public kitchen, Shoshana's parents complained about their living conditions. Then they talked about the upcoming wedding between Shoshana and Albert. "There won't be any fancy food. But at least they will marry under a chuppah, a canopy," Naomi said.

"At least our daughter will have a husband. This is what is important."

"Yes, you're right. But I had made such a beautiful dress for her." Naomi sighed.

"Those are only material things," Herschel said, and his tone let everyone know that he didn't want to discuss the fact that they had lost so much. Then he continued. "But we must be respectful of the chasen, the groom. His mother has fallen ill. We will put the wedding on hold until she is well."

"Nu? And in this terrible place, she might not get well," Naomi said.

"Pooh, pooh, pooh." Herschel spit on the floor. "Don't even say that."

"You're right. God forgive me," Naomi said, then she turned to look at Shoshana. "Don't you worry. Your turn to be a kallah, a bride, will come very soon."

Shoshana nodded. She hoped her parents couldn't see how relieved she was that she had more time before she had to walk down the aisle and give her life to a man she hardly knew.

Then one afternoon Ruth and her family were not at home. Ruth was off work that day, and although it was rare, she decided to spend some time with her husband and son. They'd gone out for a walk together. And it was while they were gone that Shoshana's father returned from the synagogue. He slammed the door behind him when he entered. Shoshana's head whipped around. He stood there staring at her with his fists clenched. His face was red with rage. He looked at Shoshana and shook his head, then he spit on the floor in disgust. "What have you done?" he hollered.

"What do you mean, Papa?" Shoshana asked. She was shaking as she cast her eyes down to the floor. She knew she dared not look directly at him. Her heart was racing. *What has he heard?*

"Do you know what happened to me in the shul today?" Herschel Aizenberg said. "I was shamed. Yes, shamed. By you, Shoshana. I was approached by my old friend Mr. Fishman. You know him. He has a good reputation for always being a fair and righteous man. Oy, I am so ashamed of you. You may very well have ruined your life, your future." He shook his head, then he went on. "I was sitting in the shul when Mr. Fishman came over to sit by me. He said he didn't want to tell me what he saw, but he felt that for your sake, he must. He said that you were risking your future. I agree with him. My friend said he was walking by when he looked inside and saw you standing up on a stage in one of those cafés in town. You were singing like a kurveh, a whore. I am so ashamed. If Albert's family, your future machatonim, ever find out about this, and I have no doubt that they will, he'll never marry you. No decent man will marry you." He shook his head. "This will easily become a shanda, a scandal, that will not only ruin your future but will taint the future for your sisters. How will they ever find decent husbands with a sister like you? Is that what you want?"

"No, Papa. I would never hurt the twins. I love them with all my heart. But . . ."

"But? Nu? What, Shoshana?" Her mother had not spoken until now. She was standing in the corner of the room, shaking.

"I can't marry Albert."

"Oy, it's worse than I thought," Naomi said, shaking her head.

"Did you let some man ruin you?" her father said threateningly. "Did you do that, Shoshana?"

Shoshana shook her head and looked down at the floor. She was afraid to speak, yet she knew she must. Swallowing hard to find her courage, she said, "No, I didn't do anything improper with any man. And . . . I am sorry to have brought this shame on our family. I truly am. But, I can't marry Albert. He is a good person, a kind man. I know this. But, I just don't want to spend the rest of my life with him." Tears threatened to fall.

"You can and you will if I say you will," her father said.

"Please, Papa. I can't do this."

He slapped her hard across the face. She gasped. He had never struck her before. But in the past she'd never stood up to him. Having seen a different side of life since they moved to Warsaw, Shoshana found that she was bolder; she wanted more.

"I said you will, and you will. And if I hear any more talk about you going into town and behaving like a kurveh, I will make you sorry. You'll stay away from that Ruth. She's no good. I always knew she was no good." Her father growled like a grizzly bear.

Shoshana tasted salty blood in her mouth from where her father had struck her. She felt dizzy and sick to her stomach. How she wished that this apartment had more space so she could go off by herself and weep. She desperately needed privacy. But there was none in this tiny place. Her father seemed so large right now that he took up the entire apartment. Shoshana grabbed her coat from the hook on the wall and ran outside to sit on the bench. She heard her father's footsteps on the stairs, and she was petrified that he was pursuing her, coming outside after her to hit her again. Then she heard her mother say, "Let her go, Herschel. She'll come to her senses now that you've talked to her. She just needs a little time alone. I just hope and pray that her machatonim don't hear about this."

"But you know that they will, don't you?"

Naomi nodded. "I hope they will consider going forth with the wedding even so."

"Would you, if you were them? Be honest, Naomi. Would you want a girl like that in your family, bearing your grandchildren?"

Naomi didn't answer but sank down into a chair and put her head in her hands. Then she said, "What did I do wrong that my daughter should be so difficult? Was it my fault that we were forced to come here to this place? Was it my fault that she was exposed to such a person as this Ruth woman, who acts like a goy. Her and her husband live like goys. I would have thought Shoshana was smarter than that. At least I would have hoped. But now my own daughter, my Shoshana, my flesh and blood, has become one of them—a goy. I am pulling out my hair, I tell you. Pulling out my hair."

"I will never live down the shame she has brought upon our house," Herschel said.

Shoshana heard her parents yelling as her father retreated back to the apartment, with her mother following closely at his heels. Then she finally took a breath when she heard the door close. Walking outside, she smelled the open air. *Albert is a good man. I have nothing against him. And I was fortunate that he considered me good enough to be his wife. It's not his fault. It's mine. I can't marry him. I just can't,* she thought as she sank down onto the bench behind the building.

CHAPTER THIRTY-ONE

SHOSHANA SAT OUTSIDE FOR A LONG TIME. IT WAS CHILLY BUT SHE would rather endure the cold than see the accusations in her parents' eyes. Finally, she went back into the apartment after she saw Ruth and her family return. Shoshana was not shocked when she entered and saw that her father was sitting on a box, in stocking feet. He glanced up at the door when she came in. He had been waiting for her. The lapel of his coat jacket was torn. She felt her heart sink. She knew that the torn lapel, and the stocking feet, were signs that her father was in mourning.

"Nu? So, my daughter, my sweet little Shoshanaleah. The little girl who I held up to the sky when she would come running to me, has turned on her parents and her God. For me, she died today. And so, here I am sitting shiva," he said to no one, but loud enough for Shoshana to hear.

The sight of her father, so lost and forlorn, made her gasp. She felt the sin of defying him weighing heavy on her shoulders. She wanted to run to him and to tell him that she would do as he wished. But she couldn't. If she did, it would mean that she was ready to sign the rest of her life away and become a woman without any life of her own. A woman like her mother. Not that her mother was a bad person, or a poor example of what a wife and mother should be. *My mother always did what was expected of her. Everyone always said she was a good, pious woman..* But Shoshana could see in her mother's eyes that Naomi carried a deep sadness within her. She'd never let on about any of this to her children, but Shoshana had always known that there was something missing in her mother's life. And Shoshana often wondered what dreams lie in her mother's heart. Naomi had always been obedient, dutiful, and respected, but never happy. And if Shoshana had not come to the ghetto and met Ruth, she would have thought that this was the way of life for all women. She would never have expected to be happy. However, now that she'd sung in the café and felt the admiration of the crowd, now that she'd danced openly with men, now that she'd refused to follow her father's demands, she longed to go further. If this ghetto was ever dissolved, and she believed with all her heart that it would be, she didn't want to return to the shtetl and live out her life quietly as the wife of a good man. Shoshana had tasted the sweetness of a different life. And although the ghetto was hell, she didn't want to return to her old life. She longed to stay in Warsaw and become a famous singer like Ruth.

Ruth was watching from the other side of the room as Shoshana stood staring at her father. No one said a word. Finally, Shoshana's mother said to the twins, "Come, let's go eat by the public kitchen."

"Yes, let's go eat. Just the four of us. I will miss our daughter who is dead," Herschel said.

And Shoshana knew she was not invited to join them.

CHAPTER THIRTY-TWO

ALBERT HAD TO BE TOLD THE TRUTH. IT WAS ONLY FAIR THAT SHE tell him that she had changed her mind about marrying him. As she walked toward his apartment, she hoped that he had heard the gossip about her from their friends and neighbors from the shtetl. The Hasidic community, which they were a part of, was a tight-knit group, and news about one of their own traveled like lightning through it. If he already knew, perhaps she wouldn't need to say a word. Perhaps, Albert would break off the engagement. When she arrived at his door, Shoshana felt uneasy. Her hand trembled, and she felt a chill run down her back as she knocked. "Coming," Mrs. Hendler, Albert's mother, said. As Shoshana waited, she began to hope that the family had not heard the news, because it would be terrible to have to face Albert's mother if she knew. *Chances are good that if she has heard, she will slam the door in my face,* Shoshana thought.

"Who is it?" Mrs. Hendler asked through the door.

"Shoshana," she said in a soft, timid voice.

The door flung open. "Come in," Mrs. Hendler said. "Welcome, welcome. You want a cup of tea? I don't have any cookies, I am afraid. But I am making soup. You want a bowl? Are you hungry? You're so skinny. You should eat."

They haven't heard. I am still welcome in their home. I feel so bad. So ashamed. They are such good people. "No, thank you. I'm not hungry. How are you feeling?"

"Oy, much better. Thank you for asking. I am so glad that I am well, and we can get on with our wedding arrangements, yes?"

Shoshana tried to smile. She couldn't tell this woman how she was feeling. "I was just wondering if I could speak to Albert for a minute."

"He's down the street at the shul in the Ableskys' apartment with the rest of the men. I think your papa goes there, too, no?"

"Yes, he does."

"So, you want to sit down here, and we can have a nice chat while you wait for Albert? He should be home in a couple of hours. Or should I tell him to go by your home and see you?"

"Would you please ask him to come by my apartment? I really need to talk to him."

"Nu, Shoshana, is something wrong? You look so distraught. You can talk to me. Maybe I can help?"

"With all due respect, I need to speak with Albert."

"Of course. Of course you do. And don't you worry, I'll make sure he comes to see you right away, even before he eats."

"Thank you," Shoshana said.

She was having second thoughts about breaking the engagement as she walked outside and headed toward home. But even if she didn't break it off, he probably would, because he would soon find out what she had done, and his family would be mortified. *Even if I changed my mind, I have already made a mess of things. So I might as well tell him and get it over with.*

As she crossed the street, Shoshana noticed that two young Nazi guards who stood on the street eyed her with lecherous glances. She turned and looked away. Frightened, she began to walk faster. Hearing their laughter echo behind her only made her feel more terrified. Shoshana glanced behind her quickly. They weren't following her. Letting out a sigh of relief, she began running toward home. The Nazis were cruel, and she knew it was always best to steer clear of them whenever possible. If they wanted to, they could have their way with her, and she would have no recourse. She could not go to the police, because they were the police. The thought made her knees weak and her body tremble. She leaned against a building to catch her breath. The cold bricks against her face felt inviting. Then she heard a man's voice call out her name, "Shoshana."

Shoshana jumped. But when she turned around to see that it was Albert coming toward her, she forgot her fears and felt sad. His sweet smile touched her heart.

"I saw you walking, and, well, I just wanted to say hello," he said shyly.

"Hello," she said, not looking into his eyes. "I'm glad your mother is feeling better."

"Yes, so am I. We were very worried about her, but Hashem has healed her."

"I was glad to see it. She looks good."

"You saw her?"

"I was at your home. Didn't she send you to find me?"

"No, I was just walking home from the shul, and I saw you on the street. I know that it isn't proper for us to be speaking alone together like this on the street without a chaperone. I hope you will forgive me for being so bold." He cast his eyes down, then he added in a soft voice, "But . . . I thought because we are engaged and about to be wed that perhaps it would be all right just to say hello when I saw you walking."

He is such a good and kind person. It's probably only right that I am going to break this off. I am not worthy of such a man. "Albert," Shoshana said, her voice cracking, "I have something I must discuss with you."

"Of course," he said, nodding. "Shall we go to your home or to mine, where there will be others around to chaperone our meeting."

She shook her head. "No, I think it's best I just tell you here and now." She cleared her throat. Then she blurted out, "I can't marry you."

Shoshana saw the look of shock and hurt in his eyes. Then he said as calmly as he could, "Have I done something to offend you?"

She shook her head. "It's not you. You are perfect. Any girl would be very happy to be married to you. I just can't . . ."

He cleared his throat as if he understood. Then, in a gentle voice, he said, "The rabbi said that sometimes we must expect something like this. But don't worry. I understand how you feel. And I will help you. It's normal to be afraid. I am afraid too. But, you needn't worry. I will be a good husband to you and a good father to our children. You will be happy. I will do all that I can to give you a good life. Now I know that we are here in the ghetto, and I might have trouble providing for you here. But, if you allow me to be your husband, I will find a way to make sure that we have plenty to eat."

She wanted to cry. "It's not that," she said. "It's not that at all. Oh, Albert, I must tell you the truth. I have done some things that are not exactly proper. And I think it's only right I should tell you before you hear about it from others."

He cocked his head. "Go on. Please, tell me."

"I have made friends with a lady by the name of Ruth. She is a lady who lives with us, with her husband and young son. She is not one of us. She is a secular Jew."

"And because she is not Hasidic, you know that the other Hasids will say she is a goy, and you are keeping company with a goy. Is this it? You don't want to shame me by keeping company with a secular Jew? Because I don't care what people are going to say. If she is your friend, I believe she is a good person. I trust your judgment."

"I thank you for that. You have too much faith in me."

"A man cannot have too much faith in his wife. A wife is a gift from Hashem. Women don't need to study because they are naturally wise. They are born with all of the knowledge of the universe."

Now she began to cry. Shaking her head, she said, "I am not wise. I am a fool. I have been singing in cafés with Ruth. Not singing to praise Hashem but singing carnal songs, goyish songs. And dancing too . . . with men. I am not good enough for you, Albert. A man like you deserves a frum girl, who will make him a good wife."

He looked away from her and put his hands up to his temples. She could see that he was at a loss for words. But he didn't walk away. He stood there silently for a moment holding his head and thinking. Then he said, "People make mistakes. I don't care what other people say. I don't even care if my parents disapprove. I want to marry you. I want to be your husband and to go through life with you by my side. What's done is done. I forgive you."

She couldn't speak. She knew how hard it would be for him if he did marry her. His parents would be appalled. He would be forced to defend her past at every turn, yet he was willing to do this for her. *If I had a brain, I would marry him before he changed his mind. But that would mean I could never sing at the cafés again. I would have to give all of that up. It would be my job to be a good wife and mother. My life would be dedicated to caring for him, to keeping kosher, to having children, and being observant.* "I can't give up the singing in the cafés. It means too much to me. I feel elated when I am on the stage. I know, I am probably making the biggest mistake of my life and that any girl would be lucky to get a man like you as a husband."

"You can give up this singing. I will help you. You can do it."

"I'm so very sorry, Albert. You are a wonderful catch. And some girl will be very happy to have you. I wish that girl were me. But I am sorry, I just can't."

He nodded. "There is nothing more I can say," he said. Then he turned and walked away. Shoshana watched him until his black silhouette grew so small she could no longer see him. Then with tears in her eyes she headed back to her apartment.

When Shoshana opened the door to the apartment, Ruth was there waiting for her. "Shoshana, your parents moved out. Your father went to see the Judenrat, the Jewish Council, and somehow bribed them into sending him and your mother to another apartment. A new couple just moved in."

"So, where are they? Where am I to go?"

"Before he left, your father said that you were not to follow your family. He doesn't want to see you again. So, you can stay here with us."

"But my sisters, the twins, they need me."

"I know," Ruth said, her voice as gentle as possible. "I'm so sorry I caused you all of this trouble."

"I don't care if my father abandons me, but he has no right to take my sisters away from me. No right at all," she said, crossing her arms in front of her as she began pacing.

"I am sorry, but I have to be critical of your way of life. It allows men too much power. Your father feels that he can do as he pleases. He is a man, and men in his world are faultless. That's why I can't stand these Jewish fanatics."

"You mean like us, the Hasidim."

"Yes, I do mean the Hasidic."

She didn't know what to say or do. For a few moments, she looked out the dirty window without seeing the street. Then she said, "I am so confused. It hurts me when I hear you criticize my people, but at the same time, I have tasted freedom, and I am ashamed to admit it, but I no longer want to be Hasidic. I yearn for a more secular lifestyle."

"You can still be a Jew, no? Yes, of course, just not a Hasid."

"In my world, the only people that are considered to be really Jewish are Hasids. And even within the different sects of Hasids, there's feuding."

"Really. I had no idea. I never knew there was more than one type of Hasidic Jew."

"Oh yes, there are. And the different sects don't always agree or get along with each other. In fact, more often than not, they don't agree. But there is nothing worse to a man like my father than a girl like me who was raised to be frum, religious, and modest but now has turned away from all she has been taught and has embraced a secular lifestyle. I suppose you might say that I am a sinner."

"You are not a sinner," Ruth assured her. She put her hand on Shoshana's shoulder. "You are just a girl who longs for love and fulfillment. Shoshana, you're a beautiful, talented young woman who doesn't want to settle for an archaic way of life. And who could blame you?"

Yusuf was throwing a ball against the wall of the room, again and again. The noise of it was getting on Ruth's nerves. "Stop that. You are always busy doing something aren't you?" Ruth said sharply to Yusuf. "Why don't you sit still already?".

Yusuf looked at his mother. Shoshana was afraid he was going to cry. It was obvious that his feelings were hurt. But he stopped, picked up the ball and sat down on the bed next to Shoshana. Shoshana ruffled the little boy's hair. Then she reached over and cuddled him. The child responded by laying his head on her lap. Her heart melted.

"I blame myself. I am greedy. I want too much." Shoshana said.

"So, you want to go back to your old life? You can go back, you know."

"No, I can't. I broke my engagement with Albert today. My father doesn't even know that yet. He just turned his back on me for the singing and dancing. When he hears that I broke the engagement, he will be outraged. And he will never forgive me. Never," Shoshana said. "Besides, I don't want to go back. I wish I did, but I don't. I love my new life."

"So what can you do? You can sit here and scold yourself even though we have no idea what kind of horrors the Nazis have in store for us in the future. Look around you. Every day our people are dying from starvation and disease. These filthy, rat-infested buildings we live in are overcrowded; they stink like shit because of the constant bouts of dysentery everyone gets. Face it, we just don't know how long we have left to live on this earth. You can waste the time you have, or you can enjoy what there is of your life. You can embrace the arts and music that has sprung up all around us, or you can follow your father and hide in the dirty apartment. The choice is yours, Shoshana."

"You're right. I know you're right. Death and misery surround us. Why should it be such a sin to enjoy even a moment of pleasure?"

"It's not a sin. Grab it, Shoshana. Grab the joy; grab the music; grab the art. We have so little to enjoy. Every day, our stomachs growl because we don't have enough food. The air that we breathe is filthy with disease. But we have one thing and one thing only that makes us feel alive. We have the arts."

Shoshana nodded. "You're right. I know you're so right. But, I feel so alone, so abandoned. I never thought I would be alienated from my family, from my friends, from my community. And, I also never thought that I would be a prisoner in a place like this. So, now, I must change myself in order to survive. I will stop chastising myself for turning my back on the way I was raised. I will do as you say. I will turn my face toward whatever joy I can find. And I will sing. Hashem gave me a voice. I will use it to honor and to praise him. But I will also use it to bring joy to others by singing with you in the cafés."

Ruth took Shoshana's hand and held it in both of hers. "You will be all right. And who knows, maybe your father will come around. Maybe he will see how much he misses you, and he'll realize that a secular daughter is better than no daughter. Miracles can happen."

Shoshana smiled. "I doubt it, but who knows. You're right. Miracles do happen."

CHAPTER THIRTY-THREE

Although the relationship between Shoshana and Neta had changed significantly since Shoshana had become friends with Ruth, each week on Wednesday, Shoshana went to Neta's apartment to visit with her old friend from the shtetl. They talked, mostly about recipes, and how Neta's father still had not agreed upon any of the matches that had been offered to him for Neta. On one such Wednesday, Shoshana and Neta sat on Neta's cot and talked. "I worry that I will never find a husband," Neta said.

"You need not worry. Your papa will find someone for you. He is taking his time because he just wants the best for you, that's all," Shoshana said, trying to comfort her friend.

"My papa doesn't want me to leave our family. He would never admit it, but he doesn't. He likes the fact that I cook and clean. Mama is always getting sick, and he needs someone to take care of things. If I get married, there will be no one. Besides that, we are poor, so my possible suitors are not as plentiful as yours were. If he were to ever give his consent on a match, my father would like me to marry a Torah scholar. But, of course, he says that, because he knows it would take a miracle. Why would a scholar want a girl from a poor family when he could marry a girl whose father has enough money to allow him to spend his days comfortably studying? And . . . of course, to make things even worse, I am not as pretty as you. So, a man like Albert would never want me."

"That's not true. You're lovely, and you're kind and frum. Any man would be lucky to have you," Shoshana said.

"Well, we'll see. My mama tries to convince my papa to accept one of the matches, but so far he ignores her. I am not even sure she really wants me to get married either. She's not well, and I know she worries about what will become of my papa if something happens to her."

"Don't be in such a hurry to get married. It's nice to stay at home with your family. Once you are married, you will have a million extra responsibilities."

"But I have wanted this my entire life. And besides, I already have a million responsibilities. I do all my mother's work."

"Yes, I know. And I am sorry. I don't know what to tell you. I suppose our rabbi would say that you should pray."

"I do pray. I pray every day. But so far I am still here with my parents."

"Don't worry, I know it will happen. One day your papa will come home and tell you that he has found the perfect man for you. You'll see," Shoshana said, smiling. Whenever Shoshana went to visit Neta, she tried to bring small gifts of food. If she was unable to, she apologized for coming empty handed. But Neta just smiled. "You don't need to bring anything. I know times are hard for everyone, and our rations are small. I'm just glad to see you, my friend," Neta would say as she gave Shoshana a hug. Sometimes, Neta's mother would give Shoshana something she'd baked to bring back home with her. But it wasn't often. Not because she didn't want to. In the ghetto, they'd always exchanged gifts of food. However, now the rations were so low for Jews that everyone was barely surviving.

The following week, Shoshana went again to see Neta. She brought with her a few potatoes which would be considered a treasure. And giving them away was a true act of generosity.

When Neta's mother answered the door, Shoshana smiled. "Hello."

But Neta's mother didn't say hello. In fact, she didn't look directly at Shoshana. She stood in the doorway and did not ask Shoshana to come in.

"I'm sorry, Shoshana. Neta is not available to see you." Her voice was firm but sad.

"What do you mean? Is she all right? She knows that I come to visit her every Wednesday at one o'clock."

"Yes, she's fine," Neta's mother said, clearing her throat. "But she can't see you. I'm sorry. Go home," she said. Then she closed the door, leaving Shoshana standing out in the hallway. Shoshana felt a wave of sadness come over her. *This is because of my reputation. Everyone must be talking. And the gossip has reached my friend's parents*, she thought. As she turned and began to walk toward the stairway to leave the building, the door to the apartment opened. Neta stood there. Her face was pale and stained with tears. Shoshana walked back toward her. "Neta, what is it? You don't look well."

"My father forbids me to see you anymore. I couldn't let you go home without telling you the truth."

"But why?" Shoshana asked. She had to hear Neta say it, but she already knew the answer.

"Oh, Shoshana. You have done something terrible. You made a big shanda on your family name. Everyone is talking about you. They say you are singing and dancing in a public place with men. And . . . they say that you broke off your engagement with Albert."

Shoshana nodded and looked down at the floor. "It's all true. I did. I had to. I couldn't marry him."

"But why? He is everything any girl would want in a future husband. Why did you do this? Have you gone mad?"

Shoshana looked down at the ground and shook her head sadly. "I don't have an answer that will make sense to you. All I can say is that I just couldn't marry him."

Neta bit her lip. Her hands were clenched in fists as she shook her head. There were a few long moments of silence, then she said, "I think I understand. You are lashing out. You are angry because of what the Nazis have done to us, taking us from our homes and our way of life. Putting us here in this terrible place." Neta took a long, ragged breath, then she continued, "But don't you see? This is not the time to abandon our traditions. We must continue to live the way our people have lived since the beginning of time. We must preserve our precious ways. This is how our people have survived since the beginning of time."

"I understand what you are saying. But for me, it is just not possible. I have changed, Neta. I'm not the same girl I was when we first arrived here in Warsaw."

"I know. I can see the change. And it breaks my heart. I wish more than anything that we had been able to stay in our shtetl and live next door to each other. We always talked about how we would raise our babies together. That was our dream. Do you remember? I can still recall those days when we would sit on your bed and discuss how nervous we were about attending the mikveh before our weddings. We were so afraid to be naked in front of the attendants. But we both longed to experience immersion because we knew it would bring us closer to Hashem. I know you remember those talks. I know you do," she said, her voice pleading.

Then she continued, "Oh, Shoshana, you were like a sister to me. And I loved it when we would walk to the market together each Friday morning to buy the food for our Sabbath dinner. I waited all week for Friday, not only because it was the Sabbath, but because we were all alone for several hours, and no one could hear us. We were able to share all of our dreams and talk freely about the future. Then sometimes after we'd both finished our chores for the day, I would drop by your house, and we would sit in your room and giggle about what kind of marriage prospects our fathers might bring us, all the while hoping our future husbands would be handsome. Do you remember all of this, Shoshana?"

"Of course, how could I forget? I loved those days. We were so young and innocent."

"And if the Nazis had not taken over Poland, that would have been our lives. But now everything has changed. I hate the changes, Shoshana. I hate it. And now, I've lost you too."

"I know. Oh, Neta, I do know. And I am so sorry if I've hurt you. But even though this move to the ghetto has been the darkest hour of my life, there has been a flicker of light. That light came to me in the form of my friend Ruth. She lives with me, with her family. She's shown me that there are other options for my future. I don't have to live the way we were raised to live. I can do other things. And . . . I have chosen to give up our way of life and to take those options. I am afraid, believe me. I am afraid. It was difficult to make this choice. But I know, for me, it was the right choice."

Neta nodded. Then in a soft, small voice, she said, "I will miss you so much. But my father says that if I am seen with you, or if it is even rumored that I have spoken with you, it will ruin my chances for a decent match. And I know he's hesitant to allow me to get married. But every day, I hope and pray he will change his mind and bring home a prospective husband. So . . . Shoshana . . . I am sorry."

Shoshana nodded. "I understand," she answered in a small voice. "I'm sorry too."

"Do you hate me? Are you angry?"

"No, Neta. I could never hate you. And I am not angry. I understand. I truly hope you find everything you are looking for in life. I wish you all the blessings and happiness that life can offer," Shoshana said.

"I wish all of this for you, too, Shoshana." Neta was crying. She wiped her eyes on the sleeve of her dress. Then she turned and walked back into her apartment quietly closing the door behind her.

Shoshana stood paralyzed for a few minutes. She couldn't will her feet to move from the spot where she stood. She felt as if a part of her had just died. She'd made a choice. And now she was going to have to live with the consequences. *I hope I am brave enough to do this, because there is no turning back now*, she thought. Then slowly she began to move, and she turned away from the door to Neta's apartment, and headed back home.

CHAPTER THIRTY-FOUR

Winter 1941

The winter was cold; even inside the apartment, it was bitter cold.

The other family who had moved in when Shoshana's family had left, had a son a few years older than Yusuf, and Yusuf followed him everywhere, trying to engage him in play. Sometimes the other boy would play with him, because he had nothing else to do, but more often than not, he would go out into the yard and find older boys to play with, leaving Yusuf in the apartment crying and demanding his mother's attention. Ruth loved her son. Shoshana could see that, but she was not equipped to be a mother. Shoshana had never asked her about her childhood, but somehow she knew that Ruth didn't have any training in child rearing. Shoshana had taken care of the twins when they were little. And her mother had taught her all about children. When Yusuf became restless, which was often, Ruth became angry and frustrated. Many times Shoshana had cared for the child so Ruth could relax.

Shoshana knew something was wrong with little Yusuf when he did not get out of bed one morning in late February. Since the day she met him, Yusuf had always been awake before the sun rose. And he had never been one to play quietly. He'd always been so noisy that he'd disturbed everyone else in the apartment. But on this particular morning, Yusuf had no interest in getting into trouble. Shoshana was used to Yusuf waking her up. And when he didn't, something inside of her stirred, awakening her. Opening her eyes, she turned over and glanced at him. He looked so small where he lay on the floor wrapped in the blankets that made up his bed. Shoshana got up and walked over to him. When she got closer, she could see that he was shivering, and his teeth chattered as he sucked his thumb.

Ruth didn't notice that her son was in his bed much later than usual. She was fast asleep, snoring softly. No one else in the apartment, not even the other little boy was awake. But when Shoshana looked at Yusuf, she felt a chill run through her blood; something was not right. She bent down close to Yusuf. His eyes were open. But he lay quietly in his bed. When he saw Shoshana, he reached for her and put his arms around her neck. She leaned down and held him close to her for a while. She knew that since she'd started showing the little boy the attention he needed, Yusuf had come to love and trust her. Now as she held him in her arms, her heart was breaking. His breath was ragged, and he was wheezing. Shoshana lay him back down and softly put her hand on his forehead. Alarmed by how hot he was, she bent down and kissed his forehead. "I'll be right back," she whispered. Then as she walked over to Ruth, she thought *I'd rather be woken up by his loud antics than to ever see him like this.* She stood by Ruth's bed, then reached down and gently shook Ruth's shoulder. Ruth opened her eyes and stared at Shoshana, still half asleep. "I think Yusuf is sick," Shoshana whispered softly so as not to disturb everyone else in the apartment.

"Sick? Why? What's wrong with him?"

"I don't know. He's laying very quietly, and his head is hot. I'm worried."

Ruth sat up quickly. She rubbed the sleep out of her eyes, then she stretched and climbed out of bed. She ran over to her child. "Do you feel sick?" she asked him.

Yusuf nodded. His face was red and clammy. "I want Shoshana," he said.

Ruth glanced at Shoshana. There was terror and worry in her eyes. They both knew that people died in this ghetto every day, and children were the most vulnerable. Very few were strong enough to withstand the conditions.

"Can you go and get the doctor?" Ruth asked Shoshana.

"Yes, of course, I'll get dressed and go immediately. I'll be back as soon as I can," Shoshana said, thinking she'd have to be very careful because of the curfew.

"No, Shoshana, stay with me," Yusuf moaned.

Shoshana crouched down beside Yusuf and touched his hair. "Your mama will stay with you. I am going to get the doctor, so he can make you feel better. I'll be back as soon as I can." She leaned down and kissed Yusuf's burning forehead. Then she quickly got dressed and left the apartment.

It was not yet dawn. She knew she was not permitted to be outside of the building this early, and if the guards caught her, she would be punished. But she had to get to the doctor. If they waited, Yusuf could be dead before the curfew lifted. The sooner he received help, the better his chances. The closest doctor was three streets away. He lived in a small apartment above his office. Shoshana didn't see any guards on the streets, so she ran all the way. When she arrived, she knocked hard on the door. It was several minutes before a young girl's voice came through the door: "Who is it? What do you want?"

"My name is Shoshana Aizenberg. I live a few streets away from here. A little boy who lives in the same apartment as I do is very sick. He has a fever. His mother is at home with him now, but we need the doctor as soon as possible."

The door flung open. "Come in," the girl said. She was a petite little thing with wavy dark hair that hung loose about her small shoulders. The girl looked young, but because of her demeanor, Shoshana took her to be about fifteen. "Wait right here, please. I'll get my grandfather."

Shoshana waited in the dark by the door. She looked around

her. There were people asleep on the floor. She wasn't sure how many, but from where she stood, she counted five. The apartment smelled like a mixture of alcohol and sweat. *Well, it seems that being a doctor doesn't exclude one from living in a cramped and miserable apartment.*

"Yes?" The doctor came walking over to Shoshana; his white hair stood up straight. He looked exhausted and disheveled. His glasses hung down too low on his nose. If the situation had not been so dire, Shoshana would have found his appearance comical. But as it was, there was nothing to laugh at. The old man was trying his best to pull himself together in order to save another life in this horrible ghetto.

"There is a little boy who lives in the same apartment as me. He is very sick. His head is hot. And well, you see, he is normally very active, but today he is not getting out of bed. Please, we need your help. Please, can you come with me?"

The old doctor nodded. Then he said, "Wait here. I'll be a moment. I have to get my bag."

They walked together slowly, and silently, hiding in the shadows, from the guards. Shoshana had not realized how hunched over the doctor was until they were walking together. It appeared to her that every step the old man took was painful and she felt sorry for him. But his dedication to helping people was apparent, and for that she admired him. When they arrived at the apartment, the old doctor knelt down beside Yusuf, who looked up at him wide eyed and frightened. "Don't be afraid." the doctor said. "I'm here to help you." He touched Yusuf's cheeks and forehead. "He's running a high fever," he said to Ruth and Shoshana, who stood beside him waiting to hear the prognosis.

Shoshana nodded. Yusuf was eerily quiet. It was so unlike him to be so still, that it unnerved her. "Has he been coughing?" the doctor asked.

"Yes, and he says his head hurts," Ruth replied.

Isaac, Ruth's husband, had awakened. He was now standing at her side. There were tears in his eyes. "Will he be all right?" Isaac asked the doctor.

"Come," the doctor said." He led Shoshana, Ruth, and Isaac to

166

the other side of the room where Yusuf could not hear them. Then the doctor said, "The child is very sick. I wish I could say that he will be fine, but the truth is, I don't know. He is very small and very thin. And . . . I believe he has typhoid."

"Typhoid," Shoshana said, spitting three times. "What can we do for him?"

"Not much, I'm afraid." The old man sighed, then he continued. "Try to get him to drink some tea and to eat something, if you can."

"Is there any medicine that you can give him?" Ruth said.

"I'm sorry," the doctor said. "Just make him comfortable." Then he picked up his bag and left.

Ruth and Isaac stood staring at each other. It was as if they finally realized that their child was not invincible and that they should have appreciated him. Now they could lose him forever.

Shoshana went back to Yusuf. She knelt at his bedside and closed her eyes. Then in a soft voice, she began to pray. Ruth watched her. In the past Ruth had challenged Shoshana's belief in God. She'd made fun of Shoshana for having such faith in something she'd never seen. Ruth had intellectualized Shoshana's strong feelings about Hashem as nothing more than superstitious nonsense and she often said, "You wouldn't be so gullible if you hadn't been raised by such a religious family. I'm glad my parents allowed us to think for ourselves. And, personally, I don't believe there is a God."

Shoshana had not argued with Ruth. But she'd seen God's work. She'd felt his presence in her life. And no matter what Ruth said, she held fast to her faith.

But today, Ruth was not so arrogant. Today, she was desperate; she needed help. Deep worry lines had set in on her brow. She walked over to Shoshana and said, "I wish I knew what to do for him. He can't die. He just can't. He's too young. Hell, Shoshana, he's just a baby." Neither Shoshana nor Isaac said a word. Then Ruth knelt on the floor beside Shoshana. Trembling, she took Shoshana's hand, and quietly Ruth tried to pray along with Shoshana.

But God had come calling for Yusuf, and no matter how much

prayer Shoshana offered, it was not meant for Yusuf to recover. The time had come for the little boy to leave the ghetto. And so early one morning, three days later he took his final breath, Shoshana wept, and Ruth screamed curses at God and the doctor, and the Nazis, until her voice gave out. Then she threw herself down on the floor and wept.

CHAPTER THIRTY-FIVE

THE LOSS OF THEIR CHILD CHANGED THINGS BETWEEN ISAAC AND
Ruth. Because they were in mourning, it was to be expected that
they stopped their lovemaking all night. But now, Isaac hardly spoke
to his wife. And it didn't seem to get much better. Then one night as
everyone lay on their cots, Shoshana overheard Ruth demand that
Isaac have a talk with her. He did.

"We've lost our son. It's broken my heart," Ruth began, then she
continued, "but I feel as if I have lost you too."

"There is nothing left for us. I'm sorry. But I want a divorce,"
Isaac said. "I don't want to be with you anymore. I have come to
realize that I want a stable home with a wife who cares for me and
my child, and isn't running around with other men, and women,
and, well . . . you know."

"A divorce?" Ruth said. "I just lost Yusuf. Now you are going to
leave me too?"

"I just don't want to live this way anymore, Ruthy. And I know
you. And I know that you couldn't honestly promise me that you
would be faithful. You are like a bird. If I try to hold you captive in
my hand, you will die. You are too free of a person to be a wife and
mother. Your singing means more to you than family."

Ruth was silent. She didn't cry. Or at least Shoshana didn't hear her cry. But no one spoke for a long time. Then Ruth said, "All right. If this is what you want, then go. Go now. Get out of here. I don't want to look at you anymore."

The curtain between them was thin. Shoshana could hear movement. She assumed Isaac must be packing up his few possessions. Then she heard the heels of his shoes clicking on the floor. The door to the apartment opened and closed softly. Ruth whispered to herself, "Damn him."

Shoshana thought about going to Ruth. But she didn't know what she would say. So she lay in her bed pretending to be asleep.

The following morning when Shoshana awoke, Ruth was already awake, sitting on a chair sipping ersatz coffee, a bitter brew that was made from acorns. "This is miserable coffee, you know?" she said to Shoshana, shaking her head. "I miss the rich taste of the real stuff."

Shoshana nodded. Then she said, "It's all right. At least it's something hot to drink, no?"

Ruth nodded. "I suppose," she said. There was silence for a few moments, then Ruth said, "Isaac is a no-good bastard. He left me last night."

"I'm so sorry," Shoshana said. "Is there anything I can do?"

"What can you do? Maybe you have been right all along. Maybe there is a God. Maybe he's punishing me. He took my son, and now he's taken my husband."

"I don't know what to say," Shoshana said, but she thought, *He wants another type of life, and you can't give it to him. I don't believe that this is God's fault as much as it's your choice.*

"Then don't speak?" Ruth said harshly. Then she looked at Shoshana who was clearly offended by her last remark. "Listen, I'm sorry. I didn't mean to speak so unkindly to you. I'm just bitter. And to be honest, how could I blame Isaac? He wants something different than what we had. It's his prerogative, no?"

Shoshana shrugged. Then she nodded.

"Ehh, well, fine. There's nothing I can do. So, nu? Life goes on. Doesn't it?"

Shoshana nodded.

"I'm working at the café today. You want to come?"

"Yes, I'd love to. But first, we should go and pick up our ration cards."

Since Shoshana's parents left, Shoshana found that she was changing slowly. She had stopped keeping kosher. It was because in order to keep kosher, she would have had to be constantly cleaning up after everyone in the apartment. The dishes were traif; no one took the time to separate the food. They weren't kosher to begin with, and now they were just glad to have something to eat. She knew that she could have gone to the public kitchen. But she'd never felt comfortable there.

And now, even more pressing, as much as she would have loved to see her mother and sisters, she was afraid to face her father. So, out of convenience, she'd begun to eat her meals at the apartment. She'd told Ruth that she felt bad about not keeping kosher. But Ruth just laughed. "I'd never bother with it. It's too much extra work for no reason," Ruth said. "If you feel so bad, and want to keep kosher, that's fine with me. You can go to the public kitchen. Because I am just not going to keep two sets of dishes, and all the rest of it. There is hardly room for one set of dishes in this place."

Shoshana didn't answer. She knew that everyone who lived in the apartment felt the same way Ruth did. And although she would have kept kosher if her parents were still around, it was just easier now to let the practice go.

Most of the time, Shoshana loved Ruth. She found Ruth to be intellectually stimulating, entertaining, and fun to be around. But sometimes Ruth could be so coarse and offensive. And because of her thoughtlessness, she would hurt Shoshana's feelings. But Shoshana knew that she'd made her choice, and now she had no other friends, and no family to fall back on. Except for Ruth, she was all alone in the ghetto. No one from the shtetl spoke to her when she saw them on the streets. Ruth was all she had, so Shoshana put up with Ruth's occasional foul moods.

CHAPTER THIRTY-SIX

S<small>INGING AT THE CAFÉ BECAME A DAILY PASTIME FOR</small> S<small>HOSHANA.</small>
Each day, Ruth invited her to come up onto the stage and join her
in a song or two. For Shoshana, the music never lost its magic. It
was easy to sit in the café and lose herself in the beauty of it. Weeks
passed. She could have been happy. But there was a dark cloud over
her. Whenever she saw someone from the shtetl, they averted their
eyes, then crossed the street to avoid speaking with her. She knew
what they thought of her because she'd seen others who had been
ostracized from the community when she was young.

She'd heard her parents talk about these poor misguided people.
Now she was one of them, and it hurt her. She'd chosen this lonely
life, but sometimes when no one was around, she questioned her
choice. She wondered if she would have been happier as Albert's
wife. *I might even have been pregnant by now*, she thought. But it was too
late to change anything. She was a sinner in their eyes. And no
matter what she did, there was absolutely no possibility that Albert
would take her back now that she was openly living a secular life.
Even if he wanted to, his parents would never allow it.

Once when Shoshana had gone shopping, she spotted her father
across the street from her, in the marketplace. She looked directly at

him. She knew he saw her because their eyes met for a single second. But he didn't smile or give her any indication that he missed her. Instead, he stared right through her. Her heart ached when she saw that he still wore the suit coat with the torn collar, indicating to the world that he was still in mourning. It was as if she had died. The sight of this made her feel sad and sick to her stomach. She wanted to go to him and fall on her knees to beg his forgiveness. But she couldn't. Instead, she just stood there in the street staring at him with her palms sweating until he turned and walked away.

Once in a while, Shoshana would sing an entire set for Ruth. And on the days when she did, Ruth insisted on sharing some of the money she earned working at the café with Shoshana. Those days were Shoshana's favorite. Ruth would invite her to come on stage and sing the last set of the day. Shoshana would close her eyes and allow the music to take her. Oh, how she loved to sing, and she enjoyed the fact that the crowd had come to know her, and they cheered for her and loved her voice. As soon as she walked up on stage, everyone began to applaud.

Late one afternoon, after Shoshana had finished singing a final set for Ruth, she bowed and left the stage. As she walked back to her table, she was followed by a round of applause from the audience. A smile came over her face, and for a few moments her heart was full. But it was getting late, almost curfew, so it was time to head for home. She and Ruth always left the café and walked back to the apartment together. But today, she looked around and didn't see Ruth anywhere. She asked the owner if he'd seen Ruth. He nodded. "Yeah, I saw her. She's outside. Out back. Behind the building. But I don't think it is a good idea for you to go out there and get her. Maybe you should sit down at a table and wait for her."

"Is she all right?"

The owner shrugged. "I think she's a bisl meshuga. A little bit crazy, but who am I to say. You know how artists are."

"Perhaps. But it's getting late, and we have to get home, so I'll have to go out back and get her."

"Suit yourself. But, I think you're going to be in for a shock."

Shoshana didn't understand what the owner was trying to tell her. All she knew was that Ruth was outside, and they needed to hurry and get to the market to use what was left of their rations. There was nothing to eat in the apartment. And there was only an hour left before curfew began. Shoshana shook her head. *Sometimes I hate the way Ruth can be so irresponsible*, she thought. Then, walking out of the café through the back door, Shoshana looked to her left and saw Ruth pushed up against the building. She looked away quickly, embarrassed. *How could Ruth be so brazen.* But that wasn't the worst of it. Shoshana's mouth fell open when she realized that the man whom Ruth was having sex with was wearing the uniform of an SS officer.

CHAPTER THIRTY-SEVEN

SHOSHANA WALKED BACK INTO THE CAFÉ. SHE DIDN'T KNOW HOW to approach Ruth, so she waited inside until it was ten minutes before the onset of curfew. Ruth had still not come in. Steeling herself against the shame and embarrassment, Shoshana went back outside, but Ruth was gone. It was too late to go to the market; everything would be closed. So she hurried back to the apartment.

During the time Shoshana and Ruth had known each other, Shoshana had never once expressed anger at Ruth or even so much as disagreed with her. But tonight, Shoshana was worried about Ruth, and as each hour passed, Shoshana was more certain that something terrible had happened. *She's gone too far this time. I am afraid that Nazi had his way with her, then killed her to keep her quiet. Relationships between the Germans and Jews are illegal. He easily could have killed her and thrown her into the river because he wouldn't want to risk getting caught,* Shoshana thought. She was terrified. The very idea of Ruth lying dead somewhere made her sick, but at the same time, she was angry with Ruth for being so stupid and putting herself in such a vulnerable position.

There was nothing to eat in the apartment. Shoshana wasn't hungry anyway. She was too upset to think about food. The other family who had moved in when Shoshana's family left, were having their evening meal. It wasn't much, but the wife offered Shoshana a bowl of soup. "Oh no, thank you," Shoshana said, knowing that they had hardly enough for their own family. To give them some privacy while they ate, Shoshana went behind the sheet and sat on her bed. Listening as the other family talked to each other, how they told each other about the things they'd done that day, Shoshana felt very alone. *I miss my sisters. I can still remember how they filled our home in the shtetl with their laughter. And I miss my mama, her warm hugs, her chicken soup. And I don't know why, but I even miss Papa. When he was happy and in a good mood, he could make us all laugh.* Shoshana sighed aloud. *If I had married Albert, I might be blessed with a child of my own. But then again, would I really want to bring a child into this place? Our lives here in this ghetto are so uncertain. And so many of the children are dying. I should be grateful to Hashem that I don't have a child: at least not now, not here.*

Taking one of the religious books her father had allowed her to read, out of her small suitcase, Shoshana opened it and tried to concentrate. But she couldn't. The words blurred on the page. Ruth was all she had left, and for all she knew Ruth was dead. *How have I done this to myself? Why have I allowed myself to end up in this position?*

For a long time, Shoshana lay there thinking, drifting in and out of sleep. It was very late, a quarter past one in the morning, when Shoshana was awakened by the door to the apartment opening. The apartment was dark; the other family were in their beds asleep. Shoshana sat up, startled. But then she saw Ruth's shadow in the moonlight as she entered the apartment, and she felt relief. Quietly, she got out of bed and went over to Ruth.

"What happened to you?" Shoshana asked in an angry whisper. "Where were you? I have been worried sick."

"I was with my new boyfriend," Ruth said.

The arrogance in Ruth's voice infuriated Shoshana. She wanted to scream, to shake her, to do something to make Ruth more responsible. "I saw you with your boyfriend in the alleyway," Shoshana said. "You should be ashamed of yourself."

Ruth let out a short laugh. "You're reprimanding me? So, now, you are becoming your father?"

"There's no need to bring my father into this. You are behaving very badly. Shamefully. I am beginning to think I might have made a mistake thinking the sun rose on you. I wanted so much to be like you. I wanted to be free from all the constraints of my youth. But what I find is that I am not free; I am just alone."

"Shoshana, you've never been like this before." There was genuine shock and concern in Ruth's voice. "You have always been so accepting of me and everything I do. That's why I trusted you to be my best friend. But if you don't like my ways, I can find another apartment. I'll go to the Judenrat tomorrow and ask if I can be reassigned to another apartment."

Shoshana let out a long sigh. The worrying followed by the fight with Ruth had left her spent. Looking into Ruth's angry face, she said, "I don't want you to leave." Then seeing that Ruth had not softened at all, she added, "I'm sorry." She apologized but only half meant it. Clenching her fists, she felt angry with herself for being so weak. "I am sorry, but I have to tell you that I think you are really playing with fire with that Nazi."

"He's a good fellow. Not like some of the other guards in here. He's kind and funny, and well, I like him. You know, before we were taken to this place, I dated a lot of gentile men. I know that there must still be plenty of them who don't hate Jews. Plenty who were just forced to join the Nazi Party. He's one of those. Not like a real Nazi guard. Just a man who was forced into a position," Ruth said. "He enjoys my singing, loves swing and jazz, and all the music that these horrible Nazis forbid. And . . . by the way, he does have a name."

Shoshana nodded. "Yes, I am quite sure he does," she said, trying to hide the sarcasm in her voice.

"For future reference, his name is Hermann," Ruth said arrogantly. "He was born and raised in a small town outside of Frankfurt."

"That's nice," Shoshana said, "but I remember you once told me that you admired men who had principles. If he had principles, wouldn't he have resisted taking a job like this?"

"I don't want to discuss this any further with you," Ruth said.

Her tone of voice let Shoshana know that if she continued, there would be an out-and-out fight, and Ruth might leave. For a few moments, neither woman said anything. Then smiling, Ruth said, "Well, on a lighter note, I brought you something." Ruth reached into her handbag and took out a sausage wrapped in white cloth, and a thick slice of white bread. "Look at this. It's all for you. Real sausage, and real white bread. Not that lousy brown stuff they call bread that's made from sawdust—but real bread."

"Yes, it is real bread," Shoshana said, and for a moment her thoughts drifted back to the beautiful, braided challahs, the delicious egg breads she'd helped her mother bake for the Sabbath when they lived in the shtetl. A smile came over her face as she remembered how delightful the house smelled when the challahs were baking.

"And the sausage is real meat."

"Pork, I would assume," Shoshana said.

"That shouldn't bother you. After all, you aren't kosher anymore. I mean, you don't keep the dishes and all that nonsense. So, why not just the pork? We haven't had meat in forever. I thought that bringing you this would be a nice gesture. Try it."

"I'd rather not," Shoshana said.

Ruth put the sausage in front of Shoshana, but Shoshana did not look at it. Then in an exasperated tone, Ruth asked, "You're still angry at me?"

"It's not that I am angry, Ruth. It's that I am afraid for you. I'm afraid that you are dancing too close to the flame this time. The more invisible you are to the Nazis, the better. Getting involved with a guard in the ghetto is not a smart move."

"Perhaps, but perhaps not. Hermann can do us a lot of favors if he chooses to. And he likes me. So, why not? What have I got to lose?"

"Your life? I don't trust them, Ruth."

"He's a man, no different than any other man. Only this one wears a fancy uniform and has the power and connections to make our lives a little bit better."

"I just don't want anything bad to happen to you," Shoshana said.

"It won't. Now please stop being such a mother hen. And, at least eat this bread. I know you haven't had anything to eat tonight because we didn't have a chance to go to the market. So there was nothing to eat in the apartment."

"No, I haven't eaten."

"Come on, please, just the bread? Won't you?"

Shoshana nodded. She took the bread and began to nibble at first. Once she started eating, she realized that she was very hungry. She finished the bread and washed it down with a cup of water. But she still could not bring herself to eat the sausage.

"You're not going to eat this?" Ruth said, pointing to the sausage.

"No, I am sorry. I just can't. But thank you for bringing it for me. It was very kind of you," Shoshana said.

"You're always so polite and well mannered, my sweet little friend," Ruth said, and there was no hint of sarcasm in her voice. "Nu? So, you won't eat it. Why should it go to waste? I'll eat it."

Shoshana couldn't blame Ruth for devouring the sausage. She'd never kept kosher, and meat was hard to come by in the ghetto. The rations for the Jews were small, and everyone was always hungry.

Once they'd finished eating, Ruth said, "I'm exhausted. Let's get some rest."

"All right," Shoshana agreed.

They went to their beds. But Shoshana could not sleep. She lay awake for a long time after she heard Ruth's breathing slow down, indicating that Ruth was asleep.

CHAPTER THIRTY-EIGHT

THE FOLLOWING DAY, HERMANN CAME STRUTTING INTO THE CAFÉ. As soon as he walked inside wearing his uniform, everyone turned to look. Then they grew quiet. The only sound to be heard was Ruth's singing as she stood on the stage. Shoshana was sitting alone at a table in the back of the room, sipping a cup of tea, and watching. When she saw Ruth wave to Hermann, she shuddered. *Ruth is so stubborn. She has her own mind and refuses to listen to anyone else. She does what she wants and won't allow anyone to control her. That strength was one of the qualities I first loved about her. But now, I find that I think she is foolish, and I am afraid for her. These Germans are not our friends, and I don't trust any of them. I don't know what kind of game Hermann is playing with her. However, I doubt he really cares about her. And I am sure he will not put his own reputation or even his life at risk by openly breaking the law for her. I know Ruth, and I know she can't see this. She sees only what she wants to see.*

Ruth grew even bolder in her relationship with Hermann as the months passed. She began to behave as if there was no ghetto, and he was just a boyfriend and not a guard. Many times, Shoshana would see Ruth walk up to Hermann on the street, when he was speaking with other Nazi guards. Shoshana stood far away and watched, and shivers ran up the back of her neck as her friend laughed and flirted with the guards as if there was no possible danger.

All through the winter, Ruth and Shoshana sang at the café. It gave Shoshana purpose, a place to go, an escape from the filth, the starvation, and the misery. She often wondered how long the Nazis would allow the café to continue to exist. It was becoming more and more apparent that they enjoyed making the Jews miserable.

Ruth continued her affair with Hermann. And Shoshana had to admit he was kind to her, at least for the time being. He often brought her gifts of food, and once he even gave her a wool coat. It was an old coat, used, but at least it was warm. Life in the ghetto was always hard, but the winters were exceptionally difficult. Icicles froze on the tree branches and the sidewalks. Sometimes when Shoshana was on her way to the market or the café, she would walk past the body of someone who had frozen to death. Often the eyes were open, and she shivered, not only from the cold but from the unseeing eyes that seemed to stare at her.

The weather grew frigid outside, and it was not much better in the apartment. Illness ran rampant through the already weak and undernourished population of the ghetto. The husband of the family who lived with Ruth and Shoshana died of dysentery. He'd been sick for several days, and then one morning he just didn't wake up. His wife screamed and wept. There was no one to say Kaddish for him, the prayer of the dead. Their son was too young. So each day, Shoshana said the prayers for him. The wife who was lost and heartbroken, was very grateful. She offered Shoshana a portion of her food rations in exchange. But Shoshana refused. "You have a young child to feed. I am fine. Please don't worry about me. I don't mind doing this for you," Shoshana said.

CHAPTER THIRTY-NINE

1942

IT SEEMED AS IF IT TOOK FOREVER, BUT SPRING FINALLY ARRIVED. And even though Shoshana missed her family, and she was still locked in the ghetto, the arrival of spring had the same effect it had always had on her. The budding trees, the tiny blades of grass struggling through the concrete sidewalks in search of light, the golden heads of dandelions, the smell of the earth as the snow melted. All of these things made her heart soar and filled her with hope and a feeling of well-being.

But lately Hermann had stopped coming to the café. Ruth was in a foul mood. She no longer brought home extra rations or warm sweaters. Shoshana wanted to ask Ruth what had happened between her and Hermann, but she dared not. Ruth was not herself. She didn't want to sing. Instead, she stayed home and allowed Shoshana to work at the café for her. When Shoshana got home, Ruth was quiet and if she asked Ruth any questions, Ruth was on edge and quick to anger. Shoshana finally couldn't take it anymore, and she said, "I know something is bothering you. Is there anything I can do to help you?"

Ruth didn't answer. She just shook her head.

Then one late evening when Shoshana and Ruth were sitting at the table in the apartment, watching the fireflies through the window down below in the alleyway, Ruth said, "He's grown tired of me."

"Hermann?"

"Yes, of course. Who else?" Ruth snapped. "This is the first time any man has ever grown tired of me before I got bored with him. I feel betrayed. I feel like I've lost my appeal. Do you know what I mean?"

"I don't know what to say. I've never had a lover," Shoshana said. *She has always been the one to break it off with her lovers. She's hurt because this one is walking away from her. It was bound to happen at some point. But how can I explain that to her. I can't tell her that. She is so quick to get angry and mean.*

"Do you know what to do when you don't know what to say? I'll tell you. Just keep quiet." Ruth snapped in an angry tone. Then she wrapped her arms around her chest.

There were a few moments of silence, then Shoshana said, "Ruth, please listen to me. You are such a pretty girl, and you're not only pretty, but you are also talented. Very talented. You don't need a German. Any man would be happy to be with you. To marry you."

"Marry me? Who says I want to get married? And, why would you think I want just any man? I really liked having a German boyfriend. Hermann gave me things that the poor Jews who are here in this ghetto can't get their dirty hands on. They are worthless to me in comparison to him."

Shoshana didn't speak. There was nothing left to say. Why even try? Ruth wouldn't have listened anyway.

In the sweltering heat of mid-July, the Judenrats put up an announcement that there was to be a mandatory meeting in the center of town. Everyone was required to attend. It was scheduled for the following Monday. Shoshana and Ruth went together. When they arrived, one of the Judenrats, a middle-aged man who had been a lawyer, greeted the group by standing up on a podium.

"Thank you for coming," he said to his fellow Jewish inhabitants of the ghetto. "I have good news for you. Things are about to change here. For the better, of course," he said, smiling. "You should be pleased to know that you will now have the option to board a train which will take you to a work camp where you will be given an important job. And because you will be important to the Nazis as you will be doing work for them, when you get to the work camp, you will be given better food and lodgings. And, to make the deal even sweeter, because they need us to work, when you arrive at the train station while you are waiting to board the trains, you will be given bread and jam as a gift of goodwill."

The crowd let out a cheer. The Judenrat smiled and waited a few minutes, then he put his hands in the air to quiet the crowd. Once it had grown quiet, he began to speak again, "The Germans want us to be more productive for them. Right now, as things have been, we are a burden on the German economy. Those of us who board the train and agree to work, will be favored by the Nazis. Their lives will be much better," the Judenrat promised.

Shoshana was skeptical. But Ruth loved the idea. Because she was so heartbroken over her breakup with Hermann, she wanted to leave the ghetto and start over somewhere else. "This is our perfect opportunity to get out of here," Ruth said, "and I am ready to go."

"I don't think we should rush into anything. After all, Ruth, we know this place. We have the café to go to, where we sing. We know our customers. If we leave, we have no idea where we will end up. It could be worse than here," Shoshana said.

"I don't care. I am sick and tired of this place. I can't stand the smell, the disease, the lack of food. I hate it," Ruth said.

Shoshana looked into her friend's eyes. "Are you really sure you want to go?"

"Yes, I am sure."

"I don't know if this is a good idea. I am afraid of where they'll send us. What if they won't let you sing? What if you have to work another kind of job?"

"You silly little fool. Why would they do that? I am a singer. A famous singer. I'll sing their lousy German songs. I know most of them. They'll like that."

"You can't be sure of that," Shoshana said.

"Sometimes you get on my nerves," Ruth said "Where do you think they are going to send us? They are going to send us someplace where we will have work to do. I am a singer. They'll use me for my talent. But as for the rest of the people, they must need them to fill these jobs. I am an entertainer. That's my job. But once the Jews become necessary to them, they will treat us all much better. Makes sense, no?"

Shoshana hated it when Ruth talked down to her. But she had to agree that it did make sense. Shoshana nodded. "All right," she said. "If you want to go, I'll go with you. But I am not sure you are going to be a singer."

Ruth smiled. "You leave that to me. I know how to get my way from any man. I'll get what I want when we are moved to the new camp. You'll see. I am ready to go. I think this is a good idea."

Ruth told everyone in the café that she planned to leave on the train. She enjoyed hearing them tell her that they would miss her and that things would never be the same in the ghetto without her.

The next transport was to take place the following Wednesday. Shoshana accompanied Ruth to the Jewish Council to add their names to the list of people who would be boarding the transport. As they stood in front of the Judenrat who was adding their names to his list of people who would be on the upcoming transport, Shoshana looked down at the paper he was filling out. There she saw the names of her parents and her sisters. "Sir," she said humbly, pointing to the names of her family that were written on the paper, "can you please arrange it so I can go on the train on the same day as these people?" *If he agrees, then I will see my family at the train station. I would love to see my mother and sisters. And, who knows, it's been a long time since I last saw my father. Perhaps he has forgiven me. I will say a prayer in the hope that he will speak to me,* she thought.

"Certainly. They are leaving this Wednesday. Shall I put your names down for Wednesday?" the Judenrat asked.

Shoshana looked over at Ruth, who nodded. "Yes, please," Ruth said. "Add us to the list. We'll be ready to go on Wednesday."

For the next week, Shoshana and Ruth were busy making all of their preparations to leave the ghetto. They were both nervous and excited. "It will be a new life for us," Ruth said. "I'm tired of it here. It's gotten to me. I've lost my zest for life. After things ended with Hermann, I found it impossible to bear the misery of this place. At least when Hermann was around, we had some extra food. But now . . ." She sighed. "Now, it's time to go. That's how I see it."

"I am glad my parents and my sisters will be going too. Then at least I will have a chance to see them again."

"Yes, that will be good for you. I can't wait to get better rations. I'm starving to death on what they give us," Ruth complained. "Someone said it's about six hundred calories. Who can live on that, I ask you? Just look at me, I am so skinny that I am losing my beautiful breasts."

Shoshana only nodded. *Ruth is so impetuous. I just hope everything works out all right with this move. She gets an idea in her head, and she won't listen to anyone. Well, at least I know my family will be moving to the work camp, too, and no matter what my father does, because I am there with them, I will have an opportunity to see my sisters once in a while. So, perhaps, Ruth is right. Maybe it is time for us to leave this place. I just don't know why I have this nagging fear. I shouldn't. It's only logical that the Nazis would want to use our labor. But, no matter what I do, I can't seem to shake these feelings of dread.*

On Wednesday morning, Ruth and Shoshana ate a single slice of brown bread and a cup of ersatz coffee without milk or sugar. Then Shoshana took a single last look around the apartment. She remembered when she had first come here. So much had changed since that day. She thought of poor little Yusuf and of Isaac and the woman next door. But most of all she thought of her family, her precious twin sisters, her sweet and gentle mother, and her stubborn and self-righteous papa. Even though he made her angry, she wished she could talk to him, to hear his voice, to lean on the wisdom he had always shared with her from his religious studies. "Are you ready to go?" Ruth asked, interrupting her thoughts. "I don't want to be late."

"Yes." Shoshana nodded.

"Well, come on, then. Let's get going."

Both women carried the suitcases that they'd packed, and walked side by side to the holding point in the train station called the Umschlagplatz. When they arrived there, they found that they were surrounded by crowds of excited people talking loudly about how ready they were to be leaving the ghetto. They were ready to work; they thought it would benefit them greatly if they had jobs which made them a necessity to the Germans. And they longed for the better treatment the Judenrat had promised. Their mouths watered as they ate the bread and jam and dreamed of a future that held sufficient food and clean lodgings.

Ruth set her suitcase down on the ground and got into the line which had formed to board the train. Shoshana put her suitcase beside Ruth's as she stood beside her. But her eyes searched the crowds frantically for her parents and sisters. There were so many people, she could hardly see anyone she knew. But because Albert was so tall, he stood out from the crowd. Shoshana saw him standing quietly beside his parents. He looked as handsome and serene as she remembered. But then to Shoshana's surprise, she saw that Neta stood beside him, and she had a large pregnant belly. Shoshana's mouth hung open as she watched Albert give Neta his slice of bread with jam, and her heart ached. Neta tried to refuse the bread, but Albert insisted. Finally she took it and began to eat it. *He would have been a good husband to me. I know that I chose not to marry him. But I would never have thought Neta would swoop in and make him her own. She always envied me, and now he is hers.* Shoshana felt betrayed. *Neta and Albert must have gotten married. And now she is pregnant with his child.* Shoshana tried to turn away, but she couldn't look away; her eyes were glued on Neta and Albert. He was so gentle with her. And for a moment, Shoshana felt a pang of regret. *That could have been me. It should have been me, if I had not been so headstrong. Did I make a mistake?*

"It's so damn hot out here," Ruth said, shaking Shoshana away from her thoughts.

"Yes, well, it's July. It's always hot in July," Shoshana said quietly, but she didn't look at Ruth; her eyes stayed fixed on Albert and

Neta. *I don't know why I should feel this way. It was my choice. My decision. I wanted freedom more than I wanted family. And now, I have freedom from my parents, but like Ruth, I have no one who loves or cares about me. I am alone.* She felt a deep emptiness in the pit of her stomach. Ruth sat down on her suitcase and lit a cigarette. She'd started smoking when Hermann had brought her cigarettes as a gift. Shoshana had never liked the habit. She thought it was dirty and smelly. But Ruth thought it made her look sophisticated. However, now that Hermann was gone, and Ruth was addicted to the nicotine, she was having a terrible time trying to get her hands on cigarettes through the black market.

"I can't wait to get on that train and get the hell out of here," Ruth said. "All this place holds for me is bad memories. Yes, nothing but bad memories."

Shoshana looked away from Ruth. Lately, she'd been finding a lot of faults with Ruth, and today she was finding her to be annoying and almost unbearable to be around. Then a space broke in the line and Shoshana looked up. She was now able to see more. And she scanned the crowd until she saw her parents at the front of the line. She looked for but couldn't find her sisters. She assumed it was because they were too short to be seen over the heads of the adults.

"Mama, Papa . . ." Shoshana yelled. But there was too much noise for them to hear her. "Mama. Mama," she yelled again.

Just then an open-back truck pulled through the crowds, honking its horn, forcing the people to scatter, until it came to where Ruth and Shoshana were waiting. Hermann was standing up in the back bed of the truck. He had a gun at his side. "Right here. Stop," he yelled to the driver who stopped the truck immediately.

Shoshana's heart was pounding. *Why is Hermann here?*

"Get in the truck," Hermann shouted to Ruth.

She glared at him. "Why should I?"

"Because I am telling you to," he said. "I can make you do it if I want to. But I don't want to do that. So just listen to me and get in."

"I don't want to go anywhere with you," Ruth said as she turned away from him.

"You will do as I say." He pointed the gun at her.

"You wouldn't."

"I would," he said, and his eyes were dark and fixed on her.

Ruth turned and pointed at Shoshana. "I'll come if she can come with me," Ruth said. "Either Shoshana comes, or I won't go. I swear it." Ruth was shaking. Shoshana could see Ruth was afraid. But she was angry at Hermann. And even though she knew he had the power to shoot her, she was still so stubborn.

Hermann nodded. "All right. Your friend can come. Now, let's go. Both of you get in the truck. Mach schnell."

Shoshana felt a tug on her arm. She turned to see that no one was there. But then she looked down. It was Perle tugging at her sleeve, and Bluma was by her side. Shoshana let out a gasp. "I've missed you," she said as she grabbed them both into a bear hug and squeezed until Bluma said, "You're hurting me." Then she laughed. "I missed you so much," Bluma said.

"Me too," Perle said.

"I missed both of you too."

Shoshana looked up to where her parents stood. She could see her mother was waving.

"When Mama saw you, we told her that we wanted to come over here to say hello to you," Bluma said.

"I'm so glad you did." Shoshana waved back to her mother. Then as tears began to form in her eyes, she added, "I love you, Mama." But she knew she was too far away for her mother to hear her. Then she looked over at her father who was standing rigid beside her mother. Their eyes met. "Papa, Papa, I miss you. I love you," Shoshana said. Now the tears came full force and ran like a river down her cheeks. For a moment, her father's eyes held her gaze, then he turned away from her. And pulled at the torn lapel on his jacket, to let her know that she was still dead as far as he was concerned, and he was still in mourning for her. Shoshana felt her heart breaking. She knew he was not ready to forgive her. She called out as loud as she could, "Papa, Papa, please. Please turn back and look at me. Please forgive me." But her father took her mother's arm, and turned away. Then he forced her mother to look away too.

"I must go to them," Shoshana said.

"You can't. You must do as I say. The train is starting to board," Hermann said.

"But the crowd is so thick, I must help my sisters get back to my parents. They could never get through here alone."

"They got through to get to you, didn't they? They'll get back to your parents. Let them go and get on the truck," he said.

"I must help them. I'm sorry. Go on without me."

"No! I won't go without you," Ruth insisted. "Go ahead and shoot me, Hermann. I won't go without Shoshana."

"You can't take your sisters back into the line. There is no time. I am risking too much to help you as it is. Get in the truck, now," Hermann demanded.

Shoshana couldn't move. Her feet felt as if they were glued to the ground.

"Get in the truck. I am telling you to do what I say. Get in—now," Hermann said, "or I am leaving without you."

Shoshana saw that her mother was trying to get to her. She knew that her mother was coming for the twins. But a guard with a gun stopped her. He pushed her forward. Shoshana screamed. She could see her mother was in distress, begging. Her father was begging too. She was certain that they didn't want to board without the twins. But the guard shoved them both into the boxcar. And then they were gone.

"Get in the truck. I don't know how many times I have to tell you," Hermann repeated. His voice was strained. He sounded exasperated and even a little frightened. "If you don't get in right now, I will promise you this. I am leaving without you," he said to Shoshana. "And as for you, Ruth, I will shoot you. I swear it. I will."

Ruth crossed her arms over her chest. "I'm not afraid of you," she said. But Shoshana could hear the fear in her voice.

There was nothing else to do but obey Hermann. Her parents were gone. "Can they go with me?" Shoshana asked Hermann indicating the twins. "Please?"

"Yes, yes, just hurry."

Shoshana took her sisters' hands and led them both onto the truck where they sat down beside Ruth.

"All right. Let's go," Hermann yelled to the driver.

Shoshana was afraid. She had no idea where she was going and if she might not have been better off just boarding the train without Ruth.

Then as if Ruth had read her thoughts, she said to Hermann, "Where are you taking us?"

"To a better place than you would have gone if you had followed the rest of those stupid Jews."

"What do you mean?" Ruth said boldly.

"If you had stayed in that line and boarded that train, you would be dead within a few days. That train is on its way to Treblinka. All those Jews are going to be murdered."

"You're wrong. That train is on its way to a work camp where Jews can get jobs and better food and lodgings," Ruth said arrogantly.

"You silly little fool. It's on the way to a death camp. I saved you because, well, I like you. We have a sort of history together. And, for the sake of what we had, I saved you."

The twins heard what Hermann said, and they huddled into Shoshana and began to whimper. She felt like she might start crying too. "Mama and Papa are on that train. Are they going to be murdered like the guard said?" Bluma whispered to Shoshana.

"Shhh, no, of course not," Shoshana said. But she wasn't sure what to believe. She'd seen how cruel the Nazis could be. *It was hard to fathom that anyone would take an entire trainload of people away just to murder them. It is far more logical that they were going to use these people as free labor,* Shoshana thought, trying to comfort herself.

There was a long silence. No one spoke. All that could be heard was the sound of birds chirping and the twins softly sobbing as they clung to Shoshana.

Then Hermann, who had been standing up until now, plopped down beside Ruth. "I know you are angry with me because I haven't been coming around. And I want you to know that I feel that we did have a good time together. But, you must understand, I had no choice. I had to break up with you." He was speaking softly, but Shoshana could still hear him. "My superior officer said that I had to get rid of you. He said I was putting myself and my family in grave danger by carrying on with you. Don't you understand? You are a Jew, and I am an Aryan. Not only an Aryan, but a guard. My hands were tied. I was forced to stay away from you." He added, "I have my wife and my children to think of."

"I didn't know you were married."

"There was no reason to tell you. It had nothing to do with you, or with us. I liked you. I liked you a lot. I enjoyed your company. If it had been my choice, we would have gone on the way we were. But, it was not my choice. So, as a kindness, I am going out of my way to save your life. You should be grateful."

She looked at him and cocked her head. "You didn't want to break it off with me? You weren't tired of me?"

"How could anyone ever grow tired of you. You are the most challenging woman I've ever known. But, more importantly, you must realize that you are a Jew. And there are laws that forbid this thing between us."

"So, then why did you decide to take this one last risk by trying to save me? Why didn't you just stay away?" Ruth asked.

"Because, I couldn't sleep at night. I knew where the train was going. And even though I know we can never be together, well . . ."

"Well, what?" she asked.

"I still care for you."

Ruth snorted, then she shook her head and said, "So then, let me ask you this, where in hell are you taking us?"

"Auschwitz."

"Auschwitz?" She cocked her head. "What the hell is that?"

"Yes, I am taking you to Auschwitz. It's a work camp," he said. "You would have been better off staying in the ghetto. But when I saw your name on the list of prisoners who were scheduled for the transport this morning, I knew you wouldn't listen or believe me if I tried to explain everything. You would have gotten right on that train just to spite me. And worse yet, if I had told you that the train was headed for Treblinka and that it was a death camp, I could have gotten myself into even more trouble. I hate to imagine what would have happened to me if I had told you the truth about where those people were headed, and then you had decided to tell the others who were boarding that transport. There would have been panic. No one would have boarded that train willingly. That's why the Judenrats tell the prisoners that they are going to a work camp where they will have better treatment. They get a little piece of bread and some jam, and they go willingly because they have no idea what is in store."

"The Judenrats know where the train is going?" Shoshana couldn't help but speak out.

"They know. But they are Jews. They think that if they collaborate with us Nazis, they'll be spared. However, in the end, they will go to the death camps too. Just like the others."

Shoshana shivered. "My parents are on that train," she said. Perle let out a loud whimper. Shoshana patted her sister's head.

"I'm sorry, but this is the way it is. I did what I could for Ruth. You and your sisters are lucky you were with her today, or you would have the same fate," Hermann said.

"So you got a hold of a truck and came to my rescue." Ruth let out a short laugh. "You did all this for my own good? I suppose you must feel bad that you won't be able to see me again. Now that I know you never really stopped caring for me."

"No, I never did. But I do know it has to be over between us. And yes, I am sorry about it. But not sorry enough to continue to risk everything," he said, then he sighed. "You're a hardheaded person, Ruth. You should be kissing my feet for what I have done here for you today. Taking you and your friends away by truck before you boarded that train has put me at risk. But I know you, and the last thing you would ever do is show me your appreciation. It's all right. The truth is, I did it for myself. I couldn't have lived with myself if I had just let you be murdered."

BOOK THREE

CHAPTER FORTY

Marseilles, France, 1940

Fourteen-year-old Gisele Lenoir wrung her hands as she sat staring at the bedroom door in disbelief. This all felt like little more than a dream. A nightmare actually. It had happened so fast. One minute her mother was baking a bread, the next minute she was on the floor, not breathing.

For two days, Gisele washed her mother's face with cool water, trying to help her regain consciousness, but it hadn't worked. She counted out all of the money her mother had in the jar that she kept in the kitchen. A lifetime's worth of savings. She paid the doctor most of it; the rest she returned to the jar. But even with all the money she had spent, it only paid for a single visit from the doctor who declared that there was nothing he could do.

The following day, her mother, Simone Lenoir, died. Gisele felt as if there should have been some sort of earth-shattering sound or drastic movement to let her know that the terrible moment had arrived. But nothing like that happened. No alarm had sounded. Her mother's ragged breath just slowed down and then stopped quietly. *This is the end,* Gisele thought. *How could a woman who had been so vibrant, be gone so quickly?* A chill came over Gisele. *I am an orphan. But how can this be? Perhaps I will wake up and this will have been a dream.* Her mother had been a constant in her life. She'd never given a single thought to what might happen if her mother died. It had always seemed to Gisele that her mother was invincible. She would live forever, or at least until Gisele was much older. It had always been just the two of them. Gisele never knew her father. According to her mother, he'd died before she was born. But she'd always wanted to know more about him. He had been absent but always a part of their lives. And from the time Gisele was a small child, she'd asked her mother about him. Her mother had responded with stories of her father, the great fisherman. Painting pictures of a man who everyone in town adored for his easy laugh and gentle nature. "He was kind and loving and took good care of us," her mother had said. "You should have seen how excited your father was when I told him I was pregnant. You should have seen how eagerly he awaited your birth."

Gisele loved to hear how much her father had wanted a child. But then when she asked how her father died, her mother said, "Each day your father went out on the water to fish, for it was his livelihood. One day when he had gone fishing, a storm kicked up. It had been a sunny summer afternoon when he left, with hardly a cloud in the sky, but then without warning the winds swirled, rain fell, lightning lit up the sky, and the sea swallowed the small boat." Gisele pictured her father in his little boat, the giant waves and wind tossing him around like a paper doll, and she hugged her mother tightly. "Now, it's just the two of us," her mother said. And although Gisele had never known her father, she adored this fisherman with the warm smile who had loved her even before she was born.

But children are cruel. And far too soon Gisele would learn that her mother's tale of her father was a lie. It began when she started school. The other children put an end to the fantasy that her mother spun. They teased Gisele mercilessly, saying that their parents told them that Gisele's mother had never had a husband. They taunted the small, weeping Gisele, saying that her mother was nothing but a common prostitute, and for a few francs the woman was anyone's wife for the night. Gisele asked her mother for the truth, and finally her mother admitted that she'd lied. So the story of the fisherman, the wonderful loving father who wanted to be a part of the little girl's life, disappeared in a cloud of black smoke.

At first Gisele was angry with her mother and refused to speak to her for almost two days. But her mother was all she had in the world, and she soon forgave her for lying. Her mother loved her; of that she was certain. In fact, she knew that was why her mother had made up the story in the first place.

They were poor, dirt poor. Men came to see Gisele's mother; they stayed sometimes for an hour, other times for the night. After they left, there was money to pay the rent and buy a little food. Her mother never complained, but Gisele hated the strangers, and as she grew older and entered her early preteen years, she began to wonder if any of the men who visited her mother was her father. She didn't bother asking her mother because, by this time, she knew her mother had no idea. Or at least that was what she thought. However, questions about her father were never far from her thoughts.

And as the men came and went from her mother's bed, Gisele watched them. She longed to know who this man was who had fathered her. *Had he been one of the men who came for the night, only to walk away in the morning? Had he ever known about her? And if he did, how could he have been so cruel as to abandon her mother and his child? How could he permit her mother to go on selling her body to support a child he helped create?* The more she thought about her father, and the more she saw the men who came to see her mother with lust in their eyes, the more she began to hate men.

It seemed to Gisele that her mother's clientele had gone from French fishermen to German soldiers within a few days. After the Germans conquered France, the Nazis were everywhere. They walked the streets proud and victorious. Gisele hated them because they'd conquered France, but she was determined to learn their language. That way she would understand them when they spoke among themselves. When the men came to see her mother, she listened to them trying to communicate with her in their broken French. She knew her mother would never approve of Gisele talking to the Germans who came to visit, so she found ways to slip out of the house. Once she was on her own, Gisele flirted with the German soldiers who were all over town, asking them to help her learn their language. And they were glad to oblige. They were proud of their mother tongue, and it seemed that they loved everything German.

They made it clear that anything German was superior to anything French. Gisele just smiled, but she hated their arrogance.

Her mother never so much as allowed any of her male visitors to see her precious daughter. When she expected a visitor, Gisele was firmly instructed to stay in her room. Gisele did as she was told, but she watched them through her window when they knocked on the door.

On Gisele's fourteenth birthday, which was only two months prior to her mother's death, her mother had somehow been able to get a cake for her. Gisele thought it might have been a gift from the baker who sometimes came to visit her mother. Trying not to think about her mother and the baker, she and her mother were sitting on the old sofa, talking and laughing and enjoying the sweet icing when one of her mother's male callers, a heavyset fisherman with a thick, black beard, dropped by unexpectedly. He knocked on the door. Her mother turned to Gisele and said, "Stay right here. I'll handle him."

"Yes, René? What do you want? We don't have a date tonight."

"I wanted to see you," René said. He pushed past Gisele's mother and walked inside. Gisele felt the hair on the back of her neck stand up.

"Go home. You have no right to come into my house without my permission. You want to see me? You make a date."

But René wasn't listening. He was staring at Gisele. She felt his eyes bore into her, and her flesh felt hot and uneasy. Then he turned to her mother and smiled. "I heard you had a child. But I've never seen her before. Pretty little thing, your daughter is. I'd give you ten francs for a night with her."

It was true, Gisele was already showing signs that she was going to be a beauty. She had her mother's golden curls and long, shapely arms and legs.

Ten francs was a fortune. And they could use the money, desperately. But her mother just glared at the man. "How dare you," she growled. "Don't you ever look at my daughter that way. You disgusting pig. And don't you come back here ever again. Your business is not welcome here. Now, get out. Get out," she screamed. The man called René left.

Outside the window, Gisele heard the man say, "You aren't worth the time or money I pay you. I could get ten whores better than you. You're getting old and skinny, Simone. You should be very careful how you treat your customers, or you might just starve to death."

Gisele was shaking. Her mother closed the window shade, and then she turned to Gisele who had been staring at the door with wide eyes. Her mother's voice was stern. "Never, never, never are you to let any one of these men see you. When they come into this house, make sure you hide. Make sure you are nowhere to be found. Do you understand me?"

"Yes, Mother. I always do. This one came unexpectedly today. If I had known he was coming, I would have gone into my room."

"I know. And he forced his way in. We're lucky he left when I told him to."

"He scared me," Gisele said.

Her mother nodded. "Now, listen to me good. If any man ever tries to lure you to go somewhere with him when you are on the street, make sure you don't go anywhere with him. Do you understand me? They are pigs; they are all brute pigs, and they will hurt you." Her mother had begun to cry. Then she grabbed Gisele's shoulders and shook her hard. Gisele was frightened. She had never seen her mother behave so irrationally. With tears running down her cheeks, Gisele nodded. "Yes, Mother, I promise." Her mother's rage terrified her. It was rare that she would even scold her. But then, when her mother saw that Gisele had started crying, she came to her senses. She gathered Gisele into her arms, whispering, "I love you. You have no idea how much I love you. Everything I do, everything I have ever done, has been to protect you. And I am so sorry that this terrible man ruined your birthday. I promise you that next year we will do something very special."

Mother, she thought as she remembered those words. *Next year? Next year on my birthday, you will not be here with me, but at that time we didn't know it.*

There was a knock on the door. Gisele jumped. Then she stood up and went to see who was there.

"Who is it? What do you want?" Gisele asked.

"It's me, André."

André was a friend of her mother's. He wasn't one of the men who came to spend the night. He was different. He was the only real friend her mother had. A tall, slender man with a full head of dark hair, handsome and kind, André had been coming to visit Gisele and her mother for as long as Gisele could remember.

"I've been friends with André since I came to Marseille from the country," Simone had told Gisele when Gisele was five years old. André was different than any man Gisele had ever known, and she often wished he had been her father. He was funny and charming, but when she asked her mother why she and André had not gotten married, her mother explained that André was effeminate. "He doesn't like women that way," her mother explained. Gisele didn't quite understand, but it didn't matter. All she knew was that he was always kind to them both. When Gisele turned six, he bought her a puppet, a gift she still treasured today.

"How is she?" André asked when Gisele opened the door. He'd been at the house visiting when her mother passed out.

"Come in," Gisele said. André walked inside. After closing the door, Gisele broke down crying. André put his arms around her. "She's gone. My mother is gone."

"Oh no. I am so sorry," André said, his voice soft. "I'll take care of everything. All of the funeral expenses. It's the least I can do."

"No, André, really. I can't take your money."

"Do you have any money, Gisele?"

"A little, but I gave most of it to the doctor. He didn't do a thing for her. He just took my money."

"Well, don't you worry. I am going to pay for her burial. We wouldn't want her to be buried in a pauper's grave."

"Are you sure you can afford it?"

"Of course, dear. Of course," André said.

Gisele was grateful to André for paying for her mother's burial. He was right; it would have devastated them both to see her mother laid to rest in a pauper's grave. But had it not been for his help, she would have had no other choice.

"I am going to go into town and get the undertaker," André said solemnly. Then he patted her shoulder. "I'll be back."

Gisele nodded. She watched him leave. The door closing behind him. The room suddenly silent. Her mother's lively spirit no longer filling the small space. She sank down into the worn chair in the corner where her mother usually sat. Then she lifted the bottle of whiskey her mother kept on the table next to her chair and took a swig. It burned the back of her throat. But it gave her courage. She took another. Then she spoke aloud to herself in a soft voice, "I have to see her one more time. I have to say goodbye before André returns." Steeling herself against the pain and grief of loss, she walked into the bedroom. Her mother lay there. When Gisele looked at her, she seemed so much smaller than she'd been in life. And Gisele imagined that she heard her mother say, "Will you read to me, Gisela?"

That had been her mother's greatest pleasure because she had been unable to read. But she was proud that she'd sent her daughter to school and that Gisele was literate. So she had often asked her to read to her. Gisele walked over to her mother's body. Taking her mother's cold hand into her own, she sat on the edge of the bed. "Mama, I can't believe that I will never see you again. I feel so desperate and alone. I wish I could have even one more minute with you." There was so much she wished she could say, and yet, none of it mattered. Because none of it would change a thing. Gisele was on her own now. She lay her head on her mother's breast and wept. For several minutes, heart-wrenching cries came from deep within the young girl's throat. Then she wiped her face with the back of her hand and picked up the Bible that she had been reading to her mother. Her voice trembled, but she began to read aloud as if her mother could still hear her. And . . . in the words, she found comfort.

CHAPTER FORTY-ONE

THERE WAS A SOFT KNOCK ON THE DOOR. "GISELE, IT'S ME, André. Open the door, please."

She wiped her face again. Then she got up and let him in. He didn't say a word. Instead, he took her into his arms and held her tightly, whispering, "I'll miss her too." Then adding, "The undertaker is on the way."

Gisele couldn't speak. She was crying again.

"Let me make us some strong coffee," he said. "I have some things I want to talk to you about."

She watched him prepare the coffee. The water began to boil, and the aroma filled the small, airless room. He took two cups down from the shelf and then poured the coffee. Setting one in front of her and the other in front of himself, André sat down at the kitchen table across from Gisele. He took a sip of the steaming brew, then he began to speak.

"So, you'll need a place to live. I've talked it over with Pierre. He agrees that you should come and live with him and I," he said.

"I'd rather stay here."

"Gisele," he said gently, "you are only fourteen. You need someone to care for you."

"I don't want to move in with you and Pierre," she said. *Pierre and André are lovers. They are like a married couple. There is no room for me in their home. I'd rather go it on my own.*

"I insist. We'll provide for you. I owe it to your mother."

"But why?"

"It doesn't matter," he said.

"I want to know. Tell me, please. Why do you feel so obligated to her?"

"Because she helped me out when I needed her."

"How?"

"It was a long time ago. When your mother and I first met. I was going through some very hard times. As you know my family had some money. Not a great deal, but more than most. They left the lion's share of it to my brother when they died. But at the time my parents wanted to disown me because I am . . . well, different. You know?"

"Effeminate?"

"Yes, exactly." He smiled. "Your mother must have told you that?"

"She did."

"When I first met your mother, my parents were coming to town to visit me. I had to hide my secret way of life, if you know what I mean. So, I asked your mother to help me. She agreed, and so, she posed as my fiancée. My parents were so glad that I had a female lover that they never looked into it further. Later I sent them a letter telling them that your mother and I were married in a civil ceremony. And it was enough to keep them happy until they passed away. Even so, they always liked my brother best."

"My mother loved you. She said you were always a good friend to her. Pierre too."

"And that's why I insist that you come and live with us. Say you will."

"André . . ."

"Yes."

"I have a question for you. I've always wanted to know the truth about my father. Please, I need to know. Please, tell me everything you know about my father. Did you know him? My mother wouldn't tell me anything about him.." Then her voice caught in her throat. "Did my mother know who he was, or was he just one of the men who came to visit her?"

André sighed. "I knew the day would come when you would want to know the truth. Simone told me that she made up that story about your father being a local fisherman."

"My mother finally admitted that story wasn't true, but she wouldn't tell me the truth." Gisele said, shaking her head, then she continued, "When I got into school, my classmates told me that there was no fisherman. They were so cruel. They said my mother was a putain, a whore. They said she probably didn't know who my father was. I made her admit that my father was not a fisherman. I was very hard on her. She so wanted me to believe that lie."

"She wanted to protect you."

"I know, but now, I want to know the truth. I have a right to the truth, André. It's my story. It's my life. Please tell me. Did you know my father?"

André ran his fingers through his thick, wavy hair. He looked down at the ground and softly said, "I never met him. But I knew of him."

"You did? Tell me, please, was he one of my mother's male customers? One of those men?"

"Oh no. He was a German boy she met years ago, when she was about your age. She said he was very handsome. He was here in France with his parents. From what your mother said, he was just a young boy too. They were both only fourteen when they met, and you were conceived."

"Do you know how it happened?"

"He was here in France on holiday. At the time, your mother lived in Paris with her family. Anyway, it was a first romance for both of them. At least that's what your mother said. I believe they spent a little less than a week together, and then he returned home to Germany." André let out a long sigh, then he said, "Your mother was pregnant. When her parents found out, they threw her out of the house. She had nowhere to go. She had brought shame upon herself, and everyone in her neighborhood turned their back on her. Old childhood friends and relatives would not speak to her on the streets because they didn't want to be associated with a girl who had gotten pregnant out of wedlock. Poor thing, she was just fourteen when she left Paris, alone and penniless. That's when she came to Marseille where she got a job working at one of the local bars.

"You are a beauty, just like your mother. Simone looked older than her years, and she had that same allure that you have. She worked hard, but even so, she couldn't earn enough money to save a few francs so she could take off from work when you were born. That was when she decided she must find a way to supplement her income. This was how she began to have male visitors. Then by the time you were born, she had saved some money. But she had no one to leave you with if she continued to work at the bar. So she quit her job, and the men visitors became her only means of earning a living."

"She could have left me with you."

"I didn't know her yet. I met her when you were almost five years old. Before that she was on her own."

"Did she tell you all of this?"

"Yes," he said. "She told me everything. That was because she knew I would never judge her. We had an understanding. I had a tough time as well, because of my . . ." He hesitated. Then he looked down at the floor, and in a soft voice he said, "Because I wanted to be born a woman instead of a man."

Gisele patted André's arm. For a few moments, neither of them spoke. Then in a small, cracking voice, Gisele asked, "I have another question."

"All right. Go on. Ask me."

"Did my father know about me? Did his family know? Did she ever tell him that he had a daughter?"

"She never told him. She wouldn't have known how to get in touch with him, once he left France. He didn't give her an address. He told her he would be in touch. He said he would write to her every week. But he didn't. He never wrote to her. She was devastated. Heartbroken. This was her first love. And from what I understand, her only love. Except for you, she never loved another person in her entire life. And . . . maybe me. Maybe she loved me like a brother."

"Do you know anything else about my father?"

"Only that he was very handsome, with dark hair and deep, dark eyes. She said he was from a wealthy family. I do remember her saying that he had a small space between his two front teeth that she found incredibly attractive. I know that a gap in the front teeth should have been considered a fault. But she said it was his only fault, and it made her love him even more."

"That's all? That's all she told you?"

"Only that . . . and that his name was Josef Mengele."

CHAPTER FORTY-TWO

SIMONE'S BURIAL TOOK PLACE ON A RAINY MORNING WHEN THE WIND threw gusts of dirty gray rain into Gisele's face.

André and Pierre stood at her side. Except for the three of them, no one came to see Simone Lenoir laid to her final rest. As they walked away from the grave site, André took a cigarette out of the breast pocket of his coat and lit it. He inhaled deeply. "So, little one. I guess you could say, Pierre and I are your parents now," he said. "You will come home to live with us." Then he gently put his arm around her shoulder. "Don't worry, everything will be all right. We'll take care of you."

"I know," she said, but she felt sick to her stomach.

"You will go to school, and you will make something of yourself. Yes?" André said, trying to be as cheery as he could, considering the circumstances. But she could see that there were tears in his eyes.

"Yes," she said softly. "I hope you won't mind, but I would like to go home for an hour or so to say goodbye to my home. I have so many memories in that house. It's where I grew up. It's where my mother raised me as best she could. I am sure you must understand."

"Would you like us to go with you?" Pierre asked. "You shouldn't be all alone at a time like this."

She'd been staying at André and Pierre's home for the last two days since her mother passed.

"No. Please don't get me wrong. I appreciate all you have done for me. But, I need to do this alone. I hope you understand. I must have some time by myself, time to grieve."

Pierre and André looked at each other. "All right," André said. "Go, but please be home before it gets dark outside. Can you do that for us? If you are out when it's dark, we will worry."

"Yes, André. Of course," she said.

They separated when they came to a fork in the road; one way led to Gisele's house, the other to the home of Pierre and André.

Once Gisele arrived back at the small shack she'd shared with her mother, she sat down at the table. The emptiness deep in the pit of her stomach was so painful that she reached up and put her hand on her belly for comfort. *My mother is gone. She was not perfect. But she was my strength. I leaned on her and depended on her for everything. I can't believe I will never see her again. Somehow, it doesn't make sense, but I still expect her to come walking in the door any minute. In my mind I can see her smiling, carrying a basket of food for us to prepare for dinner. But the reality is I know she will never be with me again. We will never again sit at this table and peel potatoes or carrots together.*

Gisele shivered, then took the threadbare gray blanket off the bed and wrapped it around her shoulders. As she did, her eyes caught a glimpse of her mother's shoes on the floor, and seeing them there brought such pain of loss that she hugged herself and began to rock. Gently she reached down and touched the worn shoes. Tears began to fall from her eyes. One of them dropped on the shoe, leaving a small stain on the gray leather. *I don't care what people said about you, Mama. I don't care that you were a prostitute, or even that you lied to me. I just wish you were here beside me now. I miss you so badly.*

Gisele picked up the shoes and put them in the back of the closet where she would not see them. Then she lay down on the bed and buried her face in her mother's pillow. It still smelled like gardenias. This was because of the soap that her mother used. It was a gift that one of her mother's customers gave her. Gisele pushed her face into her mother's small, hard pillow, and for a few moments she lay there breathing in the essence of her mother. And as she did, it brought back too many memories. All she could do was weep.

Time passed, and Gisele lay there lost in the past and frightened of the future. Afternoon turned to evening. It was growing dark outside. She remembered that she had promised André she would return before dark. *I am not going back there*, she thought. Gazing out the window, she wiped the tears from her face with the back of her hand and whispered aloud, "I am alone now. I must be strong. I must be very strong."

Gisele reached for the small suitcase. She packed everything she owned, including the small piece of soap her mother had treasured and the handkerchief that her mother always carried with her. On it was embroidered her mother's name, Simone, in blue thread. *I feel terrible about not returning to André. I like him and Pierre. I truly do. But I don't want to live with him and Pierre. I am not comfortable there. They have their life. I must make a life of my own. I loved my mother with all my heart. And if my mother was still here, I would stay. But since she is gone, I must go on my own. I know she meant well, but for as long as I can remember, my life was filled with rules and restrictions. I don't want more rules from André and Pierre. I need to be free now to make my own decisions. I know that I am young, only fourteen. But it was at this age that my mother came to Marseille, all alone. And she was pregnant. Even so, she made her own choices. Now it's time for me to make mine. I hope André will understand and not be too angry with me. I hope he will forgive me for not returning to his house.*

She picked up the valise. Then she took what was left of the money her mother had saved, out of the tin where she kept their cash. Her heart was beating wildly. It was difficult not to lose her courage and go to live with André. Steeling herself, she took a deep breath. *I must be strong*, she thought, then she walked out of the house. Gently, she closed the door. Not only was she closing the door to her house, but she was closing the door to her past. "It's time," she said out loud. "I'm on my own. I'm going to Paris."

CHAPTER FORTY-THREE

Autumn 1940

PARIS WAS BOTH EXCITING AND FRIGHTENING IN GISELE'S EYES, AS she stepped off the train. Peering into the windows of fancy restaurants, she saw waiters with white gloves and women in fancy clothes sitting beside Nazi officers in their dark, well-made uniforms. Flags with swastikas hung from the buildings, blowing softly in the wind. The harsh, guttural sounds of the German language could be heard on the streets as groups of Nazis walked by talking and laughing together. It was hard to believe that it had only been a few months since France fell under the German boot.

The Germans are everywhere, she thought. *They were in Marseille, it's true, but not nearly as many as there are here in Paris.* She remembered how her mother had told her to be careful of them. How she'd said that they had no respect for the French people because they'd conquered them. *I'll just stay out of their way. There are so many beautiful and fancy-dressed French women here in Paris that they won't even notice me.*

Her stomach growled with hunger as she walked past a street vendor. She hated to spend any money. But she had to have something to eat. Stopping, she bought a pastry. The woman who sold it to her was an older woman with dyed red hair, thick eyebrows, and shifty brown eyes.

"You look hungry," the woman said. "I gave you two for the price of one."

"That was very kind of you. I appreciate it very much," Gisele said. She knew she only had a little money left after paying for the train ticket And she still had to find a place to live. *I must hold on to whatever I can until I can find work. I am so hungry I could easily eat both of these pastries, but I shouldn't. I should save one for later.*

"Yes, well, we French must stick together in these hard times, no?"

Gisele nodded. "Yes, thank you again." Then she began to walk away. But she stopped and then turned back. "Excuse me, ma'am. Can I ask you a question?"

"Yes, is something wrong with the pastry?"

"No, not at all. It's delicious. But, well, you see, I am not from here. I am from Marseille. But, I am here, in Paris. And . . . I am alone. Do you know of anywhere that I can rent a room cheaply?"

The woman studied Gisele. "How old are you?"

"Eighteen," Gisele lied.

"You look younger."

"I am eighteen," Gisele insisted.

"I see." The redhead studied her. "Are you looking for work?"

"Yes. I will need a job."

The older woman nodded. "Well, if you want to work, I know just where to send you," she said, smiling. And when she smiled, Gisele noticed that she was missing one of her front teeth. "I'll give you directions. Now, listen closely. Are you ready?"

"Yes, ma'am," Gisele said.

"You will walk down to the end of this street. Then you will turn left. Follow that street all the way to the end, and there you will see a big house made from red bricks with a heavy mahogany wooden door. Knock on the door, and tell the girl who answers that Annie from the pastry stand sent you. She'll introduce you to the woman who lives there. That woman can help you find work and a place to live."

"That is very kind of you, Annie."

Annie smiled at her again. "But, of course. But don't forget to tell her that I sent you."

"I won't forget. And . . . thank you."

Gisele had meant to wrap one of the pastries up in a handkerchief that she carried in her purse. But once she started eating, she was so hungry that she couldn't stop. She gobbled up both pastries as she walked toward the house, following Annie's directions. The pastries had left her throat dry, and she wished she had a cup of hot coffee or tea to wash it all down. But she didn't want to spend any more money until she had secured work and a place to stay.

CHAPTER FORTY-FOUR

THE RED-BRICK HOUSE AT THE END OF THE STREET WAS LARGE. There was a massive oak tree that covered the front lawn with a blanket of colorful leaves that it shed. Gisele walked up the path and then climbed three stone steps up to the door. She was a little nervous as she knocked.

A young woman wearing a short, pink silk robe that revealed her long, slender legs opened the door. Her brown hair was in pin curls that had been neatly placed about her head. For a moment, she studied Gisele. "What do you want?" she asked curtly. "We don't accept solicitors."

Gisele was taken aback. She'd hardly expected such rudeness. "Annie sent me. Annie from the pastry stand."

"Yes, I should have assumed as much. It seems you have a full bag of flour on the front of your dress."

Gisele looked down. Her face grew red with embarrassment when she saw that her dress was covered in flour. She began to brush it off frantically.

The girl in the silk robe laughed. "Come on in," she said.

Gisele did as she was told.

"Have a seat in there." The girl indicated a room filled with three thick burgundy sofas and two matching chairs. Thick velvet drapes covered the windows. On the floor was a heavy Persian rug in shades of burgundy and gold with deep forest green. And in the corner was a shiny black piano. Never in her entire life had Gisele seen such a beautiful place. It was truly magnificent. *This is what I imagine a palace would look like. The people who live here must be very wealthy. I doubt I am going to be able to afford to rent a room here. But Annie did say that they might be looking to hire someone. I could be a maid, or even a cook, although I am not very good at cooking. Still, I would try my best. It would be glorious to live in such a place.* She was still frantically brushing any trace of flour from her dress.

"Bonjour." A stately older woman with curly blonde hair and an hourglass figure stood in the doorway of the room. "I'm Madame Auclair. And who are you, may I ask?"

"Gisele Lenoir. I am here looking for work and to rent a room," Gisele said in a small voice. She was intimidated by the woman. "Annie sent me. She said you would know her, the pastry lady."

"Yes, of course, I know Annie. I've known her for years. She delivers bread and pastries to the house each morning."

"Yes, ma'am," Gisele said nervously. "Well, Annie said you might have a job for me. I can clean very well." She cleared her throat, then continued. "I can cook too. I'm not as good at it as I'd like to be. But, I will work very hard. And, I can learn. You see, I do need a job desperately."

"I see. Where do you live now?"

"I don't have anywhere to stay just yet. I arrived in Paris this morning. That's why I was hoping to rent a room from you."

"Hmmm . . ." the older woman said as her eyes traveled over Gisele. "Why don't you sit down, and I'll have the cook bring in some refreshments. Then we can have a nice chat."

"Thank you, madam. That would be very kind of you," Gisele said, sitting down on the plush sofa.

A tray arrived with tea and cookies. Gisele wanted to grab all the cookies and put them in her purse, but she forced herself to remember her manners.

"Well, now, go on and help yourself," Madame Auclair said.

Then she waited while Gisele poured herself a cup of tea and put two cookies onto a plate. "So, you need a place to stay, and you need work?"

"Yes, ma'am, I do."

"Hmmm." The woman ran her hand over her chin and looked into Gisele's eyes. "You are a very pretty girl. I'm sure you've been told this before."

"No, ma'am, not really. Only by my mother."

"I see. And where is your mother now?"

"She's passed on," Gisele said, trying not to think about her grief. The last thing she wanted to do was start crying right now. She needed this job, and she didn't want this woman to think of her as an emotional disaster.

"A maid and a cook." Madame Auclair nodded her head. "Yes, we could use the help. And . . . perhaps . . . once you see what we do here, and how we live, we just might be able to give you a promotion where you could earn real money. For now, though, you'll start by keeping the place tidy and helping the cook. You'll have a room of your own to sleep in, and food. And, in addition, I will pay you three francs a month. Does that sound agreeable to you?"

"Oh yes! Thank you, thank you so much, ma'am," Gisele gushed. She was so nervous that a small piece of cookie fell out of her mouth. "Oh, I am so sorry. I'm so embarrassed."

"It's all right. Just relax. This is going to be your home now. Why don't you finish eating, and then I'll have someone show you to your room." Madame Auclair rose gracefully. Then she turned to leave.

"Thank you again." Gisele stood up. "Thank you," she called after Madame Auclair, who strolled like a film star on her way out of the room.

CHAPTER FORTY-FIVE

ABOUT TEN MINUTES LATER, A TALL, THICK-WAISTED WOMAN IN A flowing housedress came walking in. Her steps were heavy on the wooden floor. "I'm Marie, the cook. The madam told me to show you to your room. She said you are going to be our new maid. But, I have to say, with that figure and long legs like yours, not to mention that angelic face, you could earn a small fortune."

"Doing what?"

"You don't know?"

"I'm sorry, but I don't."

"Well, then I sure won't be the one to tell you. But don't worry. You'll find out soon enough." Marie laughed. Then she added, "Have you been given a list of your responsibilities yet?"

"No, ma'am. I haven't."

"All right. Let me tell you what will be expected of you. You'll get up in the morning and go to the market for me. I'll tell you what I need to feed everyone for the day. When you return, you'll clean the main room, that's the living room where you were. The room with the sofas and chairs. Once you have finished, you'll do the bathrooms. Then as each of the girls wakes up, you'll clean their individual rooms."

"How many girls live here?"

"Eight. Eleven people including the madam, me, and you. Tonight, you'll meet Jacques. He plays the piano. He doesn't live here. But he comes to play every night."

"You have a piano player?"

"Yes, we do."

"It's really nice here."

"I like it," the cook said. "But then again, I don't have anything to do with the customers. It's nice, but it was a lot better before. Since the Germans took over, it's not the same. They're a rougher bunch. That's for sure."

Gisele wasn't sure what the cook was talking about. But she was certain she could fulfill her duties. And she was glad to have a job, money coming in, and a place to stay.

"Get settled in today. You don't need to do any work until tomorrow. You'll start work in the morning. Come on, follow me, I'll show you to your room."

"Thank you," Gisele said. She took two more of the cookies that were on the tray and put them into her handbag.

The cook laughed a little. "Don't you worry. You won't be needing to horde food. We won't let you starve. Didn't the madam tell you that you'd be fed the same food as the rest of the girls?"

"She did, but I don't have much money, and I wasn't sure if I could count on it."

"You're a nervous little thing. Relax. You're going to be just fine."

Gisele followed the cook up a long flight of stairs and then up another. On the third floor of the house, there was a storage closet, a bathroom with a toilet and a tub, and two bedrooms. "Our rooms are up here on the third floor. The girls who work here have rooms on the second floor. When you go to clean their rooms, you will find that they are much nicer, more elaborately furnished than ours. Even their bathrooms are elegant. Ours are simple. Our rooms are small and simple too," she said as she opened the door to a bright sunlit room. "But, at least we have rooms of our own, and they are clean and well lit as you can see. This will be your room."

Gisele looked around. The bedspread, which covered a small bed in the corner, was white with tiny red rosebuds embroidered into the fabric. A whitewashed wooden dresser with three drawers stood beside it. "This is beautiful," Gisele said.

"You think so?" the cook said. "If you like this, just wait until you see the rooms the girls have. Well, of course they need them to be lovely because they entertain the guests in their rooms."

Gisele looked at Marie but asked no questions. Then Marie smiled and said, "Now, why don't you take a few hours to get settled. Dinner is at four. It may seem a bit early, but we like to be finished eating before the customers start coming."

"What time do they come?"

"Usually, they begin to arrive when the sun goes down and continue to show up through the night. Sometimes you'll see one or two leave in the morning. Make sure you never ask them any questions, like their name, or where they live. Or anything at all. Just be polite, and if they ask you for something, try your very best to get it for them. If you don't know where to find it, just ask me. Follow these rules, and you'll be all right here."

"Thank you."

"I'll see you downstairs in the dining room at four," Marie said.

"Yes, ma'am. And thank you."

Once Gisele was alone, she sat down on the bed. It was so soft and clean. Gingerly, she ran her hands over the bedspread. Then she lay down, and to her delight she felt a pillow beneath her head. *A pillow, my mom had a pillow. But not a pillow like this one. Hers was small and hard. This is fluffy and soft. That was the only pillow I have ever felt before. I never slept on one.* She cradled it in her arms. The house where she'd lived with her mother was old and dirty. The paint was peeling off the walls, and her bed was little more than a hard wooden box with a blanket. *This is like heaven*, she thought.

CHAPTER FORTY-SIX

THAT AFTERNOON, GISELE HELPED THE COOK SERVE THE GIRLS WHO were seated at the table. She brought out steaming plates of food, but the girls were so caught up in their conversations with each other that they seemed not to notice her at all. Gisele was awestruck by their lovely dresses and their perfect hair. They wore red lipstick and dark eye makeup. She thought they were beautiful. After the girls finished their meal, Gisele and Marie cleared the table. Then they went into the kitchen and had their dinner together while everyone else in the house prepared for the visitors who would come by night.

"You should know, so you aren't shocked, that this is house of prostitution," Marie said matter-of-factly.

"I had no idea," Gisele said, but she wasn't frightened or offended. Her mother had been a prostitute. She didn't want to be one, but she had seen this before, and it didn't frighten her.

"Yes, the customers will begin arriving soon. You should know that with your looks, the madam will probably try to recruit you as one of her girls."

"Me?" Gisele shook her head.

"Does the idea sicken you of working here?" Marie asked.

Gisele shrugged. "I am not one to judge anyone. My mother had men visitors when I was growing up. It was the only way we had of surviving. However, she never wanted me to do it. And I would rather not, if possible. You see . . . I don't know how to say this, but . . . well, I am a virgin."

"Don't let the madam find out. She can make a lot of money from a girl like you who is untouched. If you don't want to be a prostitute, keep that to yourself."

"Yes, ma'am."

"You don't have to call me ma'am. Just call me Marie."

Gisele nodded, then smiled. "Marie," she said.

"So, I suppose you're familiar with a house like this?"

"Like this?" Gisele shook her head. "No. Not at all. We were dirt poor. We never had meals like this or clothes like the girls here have. I never had a bed like the one I have now, with a real pillow. These girls are earning far more money than my mother did. I am sure of it. But, of course, we didn't live in Paris."

"Where are you from?"

Gisele realized she'd said too much. "Oh, I would rather not say."

"You ran away from home?" Marie asked.

"Something like that. Please don't ask me anything more," Gisele begged.

Marie reached across the table and patted Gisele's hand. "We are all running away from something here in this house. No one asks anyone any questions. I won't ask you anything else."

"Thank you."

Marie was a friend. The only friend Gisele had in Paris, and she was glad to work with her. And except for Annette, who was the most popular girl in the house, the others hardly noticed Gisele. But for some odd reason that Gisele could not understand, Annette took a strong dislike to her. She ordered Gisele around, giving her extra work just to make her miserable. She would spill things on the floor just to watch Gisele get on her hands and knees to clean up the mess. But what Gisele found to be so strange was that everyone— the customers, the girls, the madam—they all said Gisele and

Annette looked so much alike that they could be sisters. Gisele, being so young and naïve, thought that because they resembled each other, Annette would have befriended her rather than made her an object of her hatred.

"I don't know what I have done to make her hate me so much," Gisele asked Marie as they were eating together one afternoon.

"She hates you because she's threatened by you. You're a prettier and younger version of her. She knows that her men customers are looking at you. She doesn't want to lose them."

"But I don't want to be a prostitute. I wouldn't take her men. Besides, she has all of those German officers who come to see her. And to be truthful with you, I am afraid of them. They scare me. I would never flirt with them. Besides, I wouldn't know how to flirt. I have never been around men. Even though I was the daughter of a prostitute, I grew up rather sheltered. My mother wouldn't let any of her men near me. She was a good mother, very protective."

"It doesn't matter if you would flirt or not. Just knowing that you could take her customers. Just seeing how pretty you are, drives Annette mad. She has been the queen around here for a long time. When she looks at you, she sees the possibility of losing her crown to you. Do you understand?"

"Not really. I just know she makes my life difficult. Go and fetch this for me, Gisele. Go and find my necklace, Gisele. There's a bit of dust on my dresser, Gisele. All day long she is finding extra work for me. I've thought about talking to the madam about it."

"Don't do that. If you think Annette hates you now, she would be worse if you did that. Just try to stay out of her sight as much as you can," Marie warned.

Gisele nodded.

Most of the girls didn't pay any attention to Gisele or Marie. But a few of the girls were kind to Gisele. In their spare time, they had fun putting makeup on her and dressing her up like a doll. She enjoyed it too. They gave her advice about men and told her amusing stories. And sometimes she would help them get dressed for their evening callers. When one of the prostitutes became involved with a highly ranked Nazi officer, who gave her several new dresses, she cleaned out her closet to make room. Then she offered her old dresses to Gisele, who was delighted to have them.

The girls knew by her clothes that she had very little, and a few of the more generous girls gave her a tube of lipstick, a pretty blouse they had long discarded, or a mascara. Gisele loved to wear makeup because it made her look older. But she never wore it when Madame Auclair was around. She knew she looked very attractive with the red stain on her lips and cheeks and the dark makeup around her eyes. And the last thing she wanted was for the madam to start trying to recruit her into a life of prostitution. She needed this job, and if Madame Auclair demanded that she turn tricks, she might be forced to oblige. *So far, I have been lucky*, she thought. *She hasn't bothered me yet.*

CHAPTER FORTY-SEVEN

OVER THE NEXT THREE YEARS, GISELE AND MARIE GREW VERY close. Occasionally the madam tried to convince Gisele to join her girls. "You will make money as a prostitute. Far more than you could ever earn as a maid."

However, Marie stood up for Gisele even at the risk of losing her job. "She's not cut out for this," Marie told the madam. "She's a good girl."

When Gisele and Marie were alone, Gisele felt comfortable enough to tell Marie her secret hopes and dreams. "I want more than this out of life." Gisele told Marie as she gestured with her hands to indicate the brothel that surrounded them. "I want a rich, successful husband who is handsome and who takes good care of me. I don't want a man who is a good paying customer. I don't want to be a prostitute. I want to be loved. My dream is to have a man who thinks enough of me to make me his wife. A man who treats me with respect."

"You are such a delicate, precious girl. You remind me so much of my own daughter," Marie said.

CHAPTER FORTY-EIGHT

1943

"RUDOLF IS COMING TONIGHT. I WANT EVERYTHING TO BE PERFECT," Annette declared that morning at breakfast. "He is very good to me; he brings me gifts, and he brings extra food for all of you, so I want to be sure everything is perfect when he comes to visit me here. That is, of course, until he takes me away with him to be his wife in Germany."

"Of course, Annette," the madam said. Gisele frowned. The madam was always bowing to Annette's demands. Marie said it was because Annette brought in the most revenue. Then the madam turned to the other girls who sat at the table. "All of you, make sure you do whatever Annette asks of you."

Annette smiled smugly.

Over five weeks passed. During that time Gisele had come to know each of the girls. She liked most of them. But not Annette. *Annette thinks too much of herself,* Gisele thought as she started to climb the stairs to begin her cleaning. Annette called after Gisele, "Make sure you clean the toilets. I wouldn't want to be embarrassed when Rudolf arrives tonight."

Gisele didn't answer, but she trembled with anger.

That night Annette was in the main room entertaining Rudolf, a German officer. They had been laughing and talking. But then out of nowhere Annette let out an angry cry, "Gisele, this is your fault. How is it that we are all out of German beer? My friend would like a beer, and we have none. You are so lax at your job." She snorted.

"I'll be right there."

"No, you wash the dishes; you belong in the kitchen," Annette said. "Marie, Marie, get in here."

Marie scrambled quickly into the living room. "Yes, Mademoiselle Annette?"

"It seems we have no German beer."

"We should have. Let me check." Marie scuttled back to the kitchen. Gisele was washing dishes when she heard Marie curse. "Damn, we are all out of that bitter German trash that the Nazis drink. Gisele, can you please help me?"

"Of course. What can I do?" Gisele wiped her wet hands on her skirt.

"Can you go to the corner to the liquor store, and have them help you bring back plenty of that dark German beer? The guests drink it like water."

"Of course. Let me get my sweater, and I'll go right away."

"Thank you so much, dear. Thank you."

It was getting cold outside. Soon it would be winter. Her sweater was thin, and she wished she'd taken the time to go up to her room to get her old coat. But Marie had seemed so flustered that she wanted to go and get the beer as soon as possible. Walking quickly toward the corner store, she heard a voice.

"Hey, Frenchie." It was a man's voice with a strong German accent. Gisele recognized it immediately as Rudolf's. "Wait up. I came after you to make sure you returned safely."

There was something in the way he said "Frenchie," something in the way he spoke to her . . . perhaps it was the hint of sarcasm in his voice that made the hair on the back of her neck stand up. She remembered how her mother had warned her to stay away from the male customers. She shivered. He caught up with her. He was smiling. "You know me, I am a customer at the house where you work. I visit Annette sometimes, but I would rather visit with you."

She felt her heart begin to race, and then she began to run.

"Come on. I just want to talk to you," he said, letting out a short laugh. "What are you running for?"

Something inside was telling her that she was in danger. She ran faster. He was tall and although she was tall, his legs were longer than hers. He started to run after her, and he caught up with her in seconds. Grabbing her arms, he stopped her.

"Where are you going in such a hurry?" Rudolf asked, "You know, Frenchie, I've been watching you. And I can see how arrogant you are. You walk around that whorehouse where you work, like you are some kind of special virgin queen. Now, I think that we must do something to rectify that. Where are your manners? How dare you treat those who conquered your pathetic country that way." He was very drunk, and he was slurring his words, but even so, the hold he had on her arm was strong. She struggled, trying to free herself, and he squeezed tighter until she winced in pain.

"Please, let me go," she begged as she started to cry.

"Come on, Frenchie," he said. "Show me a little of your French charm. I know you French are inferiors, but I must admit, I just love you French girls. You're all so good in bed. But nobody fucks you, do they? That makes you a special prize. You're such a beautiful blonde with those long legs of yours. You could pass for a German, an Aryan." He smacked his lips as he grabbed her thigh and squeezed hard.

"Please. You're hurting me."

His face was so close to hers that she could smell the alcohol on his breath. The look of cruelty and desire in his eyes sent a shot of fear through her entire being. Gisele tried hard to push him away, but he held her tightly. "Let me go. Please, please, let me go," she begged.

Laughing, he groped her breast. And she knew he wasn't going to release her. She was terrified, so she kicked and punched at him, but her blows never reached him. They landed in the air. Then he pulled her into an alleyway between two buildings and threw her on the ground. Gisele's elbow hit the pavement, and an intense pain shot through her arm. She reached over to rub her elbow. But then he pushed her skirt up over her waist, and she began to cry.

"If you stop fighting, this won't hurt at all," Rudolf said. "In fact, I'll bet you'll like it. Not to brag but the women I fuck, love it. I'm good at it. I'm big too."

"No, please, no," she said. "Let me go. I won't tell anyone what happened. Please."

She was trying to get away from him, kicking her feet and punching his chest. But all he did was laugh. "You're a feisty little thing, aren't you?" he said, grabbing her hands and holding them so tightly over her head that she winced in pain. "Now, are you going to lie still, or am I going to have to really hurt you. Is that what you want? Maybe you like it rough?" he said, squeezing her wrists a little tighter.

"Please, I am not a prostitute. I have never been with a man. I am begging you to please let me go."

"That's what all of you whores say, 'This is my first time.'" His voice was high and whiny as he imitated her. Then he added in his own voice, "Well, if it really is your first time, which I highly doubt, you should know that there is a first time for everything. And tonight, I am going to have you. Now, we can do this painlessly, and you can let yourself enjoy it, or you can resist me, and I'll take you by force. You might enjoy that, too, but I doubt it. It's your choice. Are you going to be a good girl?"

She was crying. "Yes," she whimpered. "Please let my wrists go."

He released her wrists. Then he said, "Don't make me sorry I did that. If you hit me, I'll break your jaw."

She couldn't move. She was afraid to fight and afraid not to.

She saw him undo his pants, and she let out a whimper. Then she tried one more time to get away, but he punched her in the jaw. The pain was so great, it paralyzed her where she lay. Then she felt him as he pushed himself inside her. Her body closed tightly against the assault. But he was strong, and he forced himself farther in. Then he grabbed her wrists again and squeezed them tightly, holding her hands above her head. She closed her eyes tightly, wishing she could disappear.

The pain was so intense that it overshadowed the pain in her jaw. She bit her lip and screamed. He let go of her wrist and slapped her face hard. Gisele tasted the saltiness of her own blood. *I hate you*, she thought, *I hate you*. She turned her head to the side so she would not have to look at his face, and it was then that she saw a rock. It was heavy one, but not too heavy for her. In her agony, she was stronger than usual. His eyes were closed as he moved inside her, breathing heavily in ecstasy. He was moaning as he rammed himself inside her.

Gisele moved slowly, carefully, as she reached over and picked up the rock. He didn't notice. It was as if he were in a trance. His eyes were closed, and a small string of drool fell from his lips. He was completely unaware of what she had in store until she hit him in the temple with the rock as hard as she could. His eyes flew open. Blood poured from the wound. He was stunned. Before he could fight back, she hit him again and again. She felt his manhood grow small and leave her body. She kicked him between his legs. He let out a cry. Then she kicked him in the stomach. And once again she hit his head with the rock. He fell off her onto his side. His eyes were open, staring at her but unseeing.

The anger inside of her took hold, and she continued beating his face with the rock until he was unrecognizable. Then, her anger spent, she looked down at him and gasped. His face was a bloody pulp. *I've killed him*, she thought as she pulled her dress down. Her dress was covered in blood, and her heart was pounding as she got up and ran through the back alley so that she would not be seen.

When she arrived at the house where she lived, she went in through the back door. She could hear Annette complaining to the madam downstairs. "I am so angry, I could spit. Rudolf left because we didn't have any German beer. I warned Gisele to make sure we had everything he would want. But she is so lazy and forgetful that she forgot the most important thing."

"I'm sorry, Annette," the madam said, "but I am sure he will return later tonight."

"I doubt it. I am not going to sit here and wait. I could lose him forever. I am leaving. I'm going to go and find him and apologize again."

Gisele heard the door slam. She knew Annette had left, and she trembled hoping Annette would not find Rudolf's body.

Gisele knew why Rudolf had left. It had nothing to do with the beer. He'd left to follow her. She felt sick to her stomach as she ran to the bathroom outside her bedroom where she washed the blood and dirt from her thighs and her face. She scrubbed her body until it was raw. Then she carefully cleaned all the blood from the sink, not leaving a trace. She quickly slipped into her room and put on a clean dress. Not wasting a second, she ran down the backstairs and out into the alley, where she burned the bloodstained dress and torn underclothes. Then she sat down on the pavement outside and tried to catch her breath.

It was almost a half hour that she sat there not realizing how much time had passed before Marie found her.

"What are you doing out here? I sent you to the liquor store. Why are you sitting outside in the cold? Annette is livid. Rudolf left because we didn't have his beer," Marie said, then she looked closer at Gisele, and she saw that Gisele had been crying, and that her lip was cut. "What happened? What's wrong?" Marie asked gently.

Gisele tried to speak, but she couldn't; the words wouldn't come. She shrugged her shoulders. Then she looked into Marie's kind eyes. The older woman looked at her with such compassion that Gisele began to cry. Without asking anything else, Marie took Gisele into her arms and let her weep for several minutes. "It's all right," she said. "It's all right. You take the rest of the night off, and I'll go to the liquor store for the beer."

Gisele finally stood up. She went to her room where she lay down on her bed relieved that she didn't have to face anyone. But when she closed her eyes, she saw Rudolf's empty and cold eyes. He was lying dead on the pavement. I hope no one witnessed what happened. *He is still a German officer, and I am nothing but a French girl. If the Germans find out what happened, they won't care what he did to me; they will come and arrest me.* She shuddered, unable to sleep.

CHAPTER FORTY-NINE

THE FOLLOWING EVENING, THE MAIN ROOM OF THE BROTHEL WAS full. There were many German officers with young prostitutes perched on their laps. The alcohol flowed freely; the room was filled with cigarette and cigar smoke. A pianist played as two Gestapo agents entered the bordello. They had come to ask questions.

"Your attention. Your attention," one of the agents called out. The music stopped. Everyone turned to listen. "When was the last time anyone here saw Rudolf Altner, the German officer?"

"He was here last night. I am hoping he will drop by tonight. He is my customer," Annette volunteered, then smugly she continued. "We are in love. You see, we are promised to each other."

"Not anymore," the Gestapo agent said.

"What do you mean? Did he say something to you?" Annette asked, her eyes wide.

"He has been found dead. He was murdered."

Annette let out a scream. She fainted. The madam turned to the Gestapo agent. "How horrible! Are you sure it's him? Are you sure he was murdered?"

"It's him. And he was found hit on the head with a rock with his pants below his knees. This is a murder."

"Go look somewhere else," one of the high-ranking SS officers, who had been visiting the brothel, said to the Gestapo agent. He was annoyed at having his evening of entertainment interrupted. And just like that, the two Gestapo agents apologized for interrupting. Then they left without another word, afraid to anger their superiors. But when Gisele caught Marie gazing at her, she could see Marie had put it all together in her mind, and she knew what happened. Still, she didn't mention a word. She didn't ask Gisele any more questions, and that seemed to be the end of it. That was until Gisele missed her period that month.

CHAPTER FIFTY

I CAN'T BE PREGNANT. I JUST CAN'T, G<small>ISELE</small> <small>THOUGHT.</small> *N<small>OT</small> <small>BY</small> <small>THAT</small> man, that horrible man who raped me. I would rather die than bear his child. Maybe my period is just late. My mother used to say that if something happened that was very upsetting it could mess up a woman's cycle. So, perhaps that's what happened.*

Another month passed, and she still had not bled. Her breasts began to ache. And she was always tired. *I am pregnant,* she thought, and fear coursed through her veins. *I'll kill myself rather than have this baby.*

When Marie was not looking, Gisele slipped a kitchen knife into the pocket of her dress. Then late one night, when the girls and men had all paired up and settled into their rooms, Marie and Gisele went to their respective rooms. It was quiet, so quiet and eerie that Gisele shivered as she took the knife out of her drawer. She looked at the pale skin of her slender wrist in the moonlight, and she thought of dying. *I will never laugh again or enjoy a pastry. I will never take a long walk on an autumn morning. Or enjoy listening to children sing Christmas carols.* Tears came to her eyes. *I don't want to die. I'm only seventeen. I have a whole life to live. But I can't have this baby. I just can't.* She poised the knife over her wrist. She trembled as she thought about her blood spilling on the floor. Then she began to weep, loud, gasping sobs which she couldn't control. *I can't do it. But I have no choice. I refuse to raise a baby by that man. Especially after I killed him. I would always see his face in the baby's face. And I would hate my own child.*

Her hands were trembling as she was about to make the slice across her wrist, when there was a knock on her door. The knife fell from her hand and hit the floor with a thud.

"Gisele? Open the door." It was Marie. "Let me in."

Gisele stood up. She wiped her face on her skirt, and then she opened the door. Marie surveyed the room. Her eyes fell on the knife. "I heard you crying," Marie said. She closed the door behind her, then sat down on Gisele's bed. "I think you'd better tell me everything. You know you can trust me."

"My life is over," Gisele said, shrugging her shoulders.

Marie sighed and picked up the knife. She held it and shook her head. "You're very young. Your life is hardly over. I can see that you're in trouble. Tell me everything."

Gisele's face crinkled, and she began to cry as she told Marie everything that had happened and then added that she was pregnant.

"I knew you were the one who killed him. I knew it as soon as the Gestapo came. But don't worry; your secret is safe with me. Now, listen. I know a doctor who can help you get rid of your pregnancy. I haven't met him, but several of the girls here have gone to see him. He will do something to get rid of it."

"Is he expensive? I don't know if I can afford it."

"It doesn't hurt to go and talk to him. Tell him your situation. See what he says, then you can at least see what he will charge you."

"You're right. I have to try. Where is he?"

"Right here in Paris. I have his name and address. You can go tomorrow. I'll take care of everything in the house for you."

"I haven't taken a single day off since I started. Do you think the madam will give me a day to go into town to see him?"

"I'll tell her you're sick in bed. She won't care as long as I tell her that I'll handle your workload. Just go and see the doctor."

Gisele nodded. "How can I ever thank you?"

"No need for thanks. You remind me of someone I once knew. Someone who died so unexpectedly that it left a wound inside of me I thought would never heal. But then you came, and, well . . . you made me feel a little better."

"Who was she?"

"I had a daughter. She was just a small child when she came down with the flu. She was so thin and frail that she was gone within a day." Marie wiped the tears that threatened to fall. Then she forced a smile. "It was a long time ago. Anyway, I'll give you the name and address for the doctor. Can you read?"

Gisele nodded. "Yes"

"Good. Some of the girls who come from the country are illiterate. I'm glad you can read," Marie said as she searched the drawer next to the table. "Where do you keep pen and paper?"

"I don't. I don't have any."

"All right. I'll go to my room and write the information down for you. I'll bring it to you in the morning."

"Thank you again."

Marie left, taking the kitchen knife with her. And for the first time since Gisele realized she was pregnant, she slept well.

CHAPTER FIFTY-ONE

IN THE MORNING, AS SHE PROMISED, MARIE KNOCKED ON THE DOOR.
When Gisele opened it, she handed her a slip of paper. "Here's the
information about the doctor. Good luck. Come and find me as
soon as you get back from his office."

"I will." Gisele tucked the paper into the pocket of her robe.
Then she quickly got dressed. Before any of the girls were awake,
she quietly slipped out the back door. The sun had just risen, and
the streets were already beginning to fill with people on their way to
work. The address Marie had given her was too far away to walk, so
she took the bus. She hated to spend the money on the bus because
the small sum her mother had left her was almost gone, and the
madam was not the most generous of bosses. She paid her, but it
was a very small salary. Most of her earnings were paid in benefits:
she had a place to live and food to eat.

It was a long ride, but when she got off the bus, she was only
one street from her destination. As she walked toward the doctor's
office, she felt queasy and nauseated. She had to turn into an
alleyway and vomit even though her stomach was empty. After
gagging on bile, she wiped her mouth with the back of her hand

and continued on her way. When she arrived, she read the name on the sign: Dr. Marcel Petoit. *This is it. I'm here. I'm so scared, I could vomit again. I wish I could turn around and run all the way back to Marie and the house. But I can't. I have to do this. This baby isn't going anywhere on its own, and I don't want a child, especially a child from a man who raped me.*

Gisele steeled herself and entered the office. The waiting room was full of people.

"Good morning. How can I help you?" a young woman who sat at the reception desk asked.

"I need to see Dr. Petoit."

"Do you have an appointment?"

"No," Gisele said in a small voice. "But, please . . ."

The young woman shook her head. "As you can see, we are very busy. I don't have any openings today. Let me see how the rest of the week looks."

"I can't come back," Gisele blurted out. "Please. I took the day off from work, and I spent money on bus fare to get here . . ." She began to cry, from nerves, and from fear that her trip had been for nothing. "I can't spend more money to come back again." She was rambling; her voice was getting louder. "I hardly have any money, and I am going to have to pay the doctor."

Just then a man came walking out of the back office. His back was straight, and there was a calmness about him. He'd combed his dark, thick, wavy hair back with oil so it was plastered down away from his face. He wore a starched cotton white coat and a silver stethoscope hung around his neck. When he saw Gisele, he looked her up and down, and then a smile came over his face. "What is going on here?" he asked the young receptionist.

"This woman wants to see you, but I told her that you didn't have any open appointments today. She is very upset, but I don't have any time slot open where I can fit her in."

"Hmmm," the doctor said, leaning over the book. "Yes, it seems I am very busy today."

Gisele groaned. She turned to leave.

"Wait, young lady. What's your name?" the doctor asked.

"Gisele Lenoir."

"Hello, Gisele. Don't be running away just yet," he said, and he looked at her with such kind eyes that she suddenly felt almost at ease. "I understand you need a doctor. So, don't you worry. I'll see you right now."

"Oh, Doctor, thank you, thank you so much."

He smiled. "Come around the corner, open the door, and that will take you into the office. I'll be waiting there for you. From there you will just follow me."

Gisele entered by a door that was around the corner on the right side of the reception desk. Dr. Petoit was waiting for her. She followed him back to one of the examination rooms.

"Sit down, won't you?" he said graciously.

Gisele sat down.

"Now, dear, why don't you tell me what seems to be the problem."

She felt her face grow red with embarrassment. But she had to tell him that she was pregnant.

He listened while she explained that she had missed her menses for the last two months, and she feared she was going to have a baby. "I can't have this child. I just can't," she said.

"You are not married, I assume."

"No, I am not."

"And the father? Where is he?"

"G-gone," she stammered. "He left me," she lied.

"I see. And your family?"

"I have no one here in Paris. My family is all dead. I am alone. I need help. I am desperate, Doctor."

"All right," he said calmly. "All right." Then taking a long breath, he added, "You do realize that what you are asking of me is an expensive procedure."

She shivered, although it wasn't cold in the room at all. "I don't have much money. But I'll work, and I'll give you everything I earn each month."

He let out a small almost cruel laugh. The first small sign of callousness that she'd seen in him. It unnerved her. But it was gone as quickly as it appeared. "I can't trust you to pay me. I could take care of this for you, and then you could disappear. How would I ever find you? Let's be logical."

She shook her head and began to cry again.

"Now, now. Don't cry. I have an idea. I think I can help you so long as you're willing to do some very important work for me."

"Work? Of course, I'll do whatever you ask. Do you want me to work at your front desk? Or help you in surgeries? I could clean up. I would scrub the floors."

"No, my dear. I have a cleaning woman. You're not a nurse, and you have no secretarial experience. Do you?"

"No." She shook her head.

"Well, no matter. I have something special that you can do for me. Something that I keep under wraps and only share with very special people. However, if you do as I ask, and you fulfill this job I ask you to perform, I will help you get rid of your unwanted pregnancy."

"I'll do it," she said.

"You really should ask what it is first, shouldn't you?" he said.

"Yes, perhaps. But it doesn't matter. No matter what it is, I have no choice. I must do it."

"I see." He smiled.

Then she added, "By the way, what is it?"

He took a deep breath, sighed, and then said, "Why don't we have dinner together tonight, and I'll tell you."

He wants me to have sex with him, she thought, shivering. The very idea of it made her cringe. *My mother always told me that men would want sex from me. I hate the idea of it. But, I'll let him have his way with me as long as he can rid me of this pregnancy.* "Dinner, tonight. All right," she said as flirtatiously as she could manage. "Shall I meet you here at your office?"

"Or I can pick you up."

"No, I live far away. I'll meet you here. What time?" she said, not wanting him to know that she was living and working at the brothel, even if she was the maid and not a prostitute. *Even though I am not a prostitute, he will think poorly of me if he knows I live at a brothel.*

"Six this evening."

"I'll be here," she said, smiling. Then she winked the way she'd seen the girls at the house wink at their customers sometimes.

Gisele would have loved to return home and rest. She was so tired all the time. But she didn't want to spend the money on the bus fare home and then back to the doctor's office later that evening. Instead, she wandered the streets, gazing longingly into the store windows and wishing she could buy one of the stylish frocks that hung so fetchingly on the mannequins. By one o'clock she was famished, but again, she didn't want to buy food for lunch. She hated to waste the money when she knew she could eat for free at the brothel. However, as the hours passed, she couldn't stand the growling of her empty stomach. *It will be hours before the doctor and I go to dinner,* she thought as she stopped at a small, inexpensive café, where she bought a sandwich and a cup of tea. She ate slowly.

Across the room she noticed that a group of Frenchmen were sitting and enjoying their afternoon meal. And . . . they were eyeing her. The looks on their faces reminded her of the look in the eyes of the German who raped her, but maybe not as harsh. Still, she was leery of them. They were talking loud enough for her to hear. "A beautiful woman is like a precious gem, always to be admired," one of them said in French.

"True beauty is rare," said another. Then he smiled at Gisele.

She looked away quickly, suddenly frightened. *What am I thinking? I don't know if I can let that doctor have intercourse with me. After what that German did, the very thought of a man touching me terrifies me. Yet, I have no choice. I can't afford to pay him, and I certainly can't have this baby.*

"May I buy you a glass of wine?" one of the men asked from across the room.

Gisele's heart thumped in her chest. She shook her head quickly, not looking at the man. "No, thank you. No." Grabbing what was left of the half sandwich she had been eating, she wrapped it hastily in the napkin, and then put it in her purse. *I can't eat when I am on display,* she thought.

Hurriedly, she walked to the front of the restaurant. "How much do I owe you?" she asked the heavyset woman with graying hair, who was standing behind the counter arranging pastries in a display case.

"Well, I don't know. Let me see." The large woman looked up and smiled at her. "Ahhh, well, you don't owe us anything. You see, your meal was paid for by that older gentleman who was sitting in the back of the room."

"What? What older gentleman? I didn't even see him." Gisele trembled. *Someone was watching me, and I didn't even know it. I could get raped again. It could happen.*

The woman behind the counter laughed. "Well, he said to tell you that because you are so pretty, and he enjoyed watching you so much that he thought he would pay for the entertainment."

Gisele tried to smile, but her lips quivered. She was truly frightened. Yet she couldn't explain this to this woman whom she didn't know.

The heavyset woman continued to speak: "It's nice to be young and beautiful. And you, my dear, are very beautiful. Exceptional, really. Believe it or not, I was once young and beautiful. Perhaps not as pretty as you. But pretty enough."

"Oh?" Gisele gasped. She didn't actually hear what the woman was saying. She was unnerved by the whole situation. The idea that some old man was watching her eat while she had no idea he was even there, frightened her.

"I was. Young and beautiful," the woman said, sighing as she remembered. "And you should know and understand that there is power in beauty. It doesn't last forever. It's fleeting. But while you have it, men will dance on a string for you."

Gisele's throat felt like sandpaper. "Thank you," she said. Then she turned and hurried out of the restaurant.

She looked behind her as she walked quickly. There was no one following her. Letting out a deep breath of relief, she turned the corner. Then she checked again to see if anyone had turned the corner behind her. She was alone and safe. As she strolled through the streets, she thought of what the woman had said. She'd never really thought of herself as a beauty. But she remembered that even when she was a small child, everyone in their little village always said that her mother was beautiful. And somehow Gisele had come to know that it was because of her mother's beauty that they were able to survive. Her thoughts turned to Annette, the girl at the brothel who was the most popular. *Annette is stunning, by far the best looking of all the girls in the house. And that's why she earns the most money. If it is really true, and I am truly beautiful, then I should use that beauty to get what I need from this doctor. It's my only chance. I must overcome my fear and just act on this.* Swallowing hard, she closed her eyes for a moment and wished that she were a small child again.

Gisele looked around to make sure no one was watching her. Then she sat on a bench in the park and finished her sandwich. After lunch, she walked for a while until it was time to return to the doctor's office.

The doctor had changed into a dark suit with a white shirt and tie and was waiting outside. As she approached, his face lit up when he saw her. "You must be hungry?" he said. "I know I am."

She nodded, not wanting to explain that she'd eaten earlier. Besides, she was already hungry again. It seemed that she was always hungry. *Tired and hungry. That's what being pregnant means to me.*

They walked for a while until they came to the entrance of a restaurant.

"This is so fancy. Am I dressed all right?" she asked.

"Not really." He let out a laugh. "But it will be fine. Come, let's go, and we'll have dinner."

They were seated by the window. When the maître d' handed her the menu, she felt awkward not knowing what to order. Everything was so expensive. "I will just have a coffee, please," she said.

"A coffee?" the doctor said, shocked. He studied her for a moment.

"I can't afford anything on this menu," she said, embarrassed.

He laughed again.

Why is he always laughing at me? she thought.

"This is a date. I'm paying for dinner. I would like you to order something from the menu. Don't worry about the cost. Just order something you would enjoy," he said.

She cocked her head. "I . . . I don't know what to order."

"Then I'll order for you."

CHAPTER FIFTY-TWO

WHILE THEY ATE, MARCEL TOLD HER FUNNY STORIES. SHE LAUGHED and found herself actually enjoying his company. She saw Marcel watching a man at another table just across from them. The man was writing something down in a small book, with a gold pen that looked as if it might be real gold. Marcel turned to the man and said, "What a handsome pen. Is it gold?"

"Actually, it is. My parents gave it to me. They hoped I would use it at college; however, I have decided to write poetry instead."

"The world needs more artists," Marcel said. "Would you honor us and read us one of your poems?"

"Oh, but I couldn't read it aloud."

"I understand. May I come over there to your table and read it myself?"

"I suppose." The poet looked a little taken aback, but he allowed Petoit to read it.

"It's quite good. Here, let me have your pen for a moment, and I will make some notes on it for you."

The poet didn't know what else to do. He handed the book and pen to Petoit, who took them back to his table. He took a moment and wrote some things down. Then he handed the book back to the poet, who read the comments. The poet's face turned red. He was obviously unnerved and uncomfortable. He threw some money down on the table and ran out of the restaurant.

"What happened?" Gisele asked.

"Oh, nothing. He was just too sensitive. I was only trying to help him be a better poet," Petoit said sincerely.

She didn't ask any more questions.

The food was excellent, and the atmosphere, with the round tables covered by starched white tablecloths, and adorned with single candles, was exquisite.

"Dessert?" he asked when they'd finished their meal.

She shrugged. "If you'd like," she said.

"Of course, let's have dessert."

While they finished their meal with a crème brûlée and cups of steaming coffee, he gazed into her eyes. "Do you know that you are quite lovely?" he said.

She blushed. "Thank you."

He took her hand in his and held it to his lips. She shuddered a little.

"It's all right. I don't expect you to spend the night with me. That's not what I have in mind for you. When I said I had a job I want you to do, that was not it. Not at all."

"Then what is it?" she asked.

"Come, let's take a walk. We can go back to my office where we can speak privately."

I'm not sure he is telling the truth. I'm not sure that he isn't going to try to have sex with me in his office, she thought. *I'd like to go home. But I can't. I have to do whatever he asks. I must get rid of this pregnancy.*

He paid the bill and helped her with her sweater. Then he opened the door, and they walked outside.

A chilly wind was rushing through the trees when they left the warmth of the restaurant. "It's rather cold out here, isn't it?"

She nodded; her teeth were chattering. The thin sweater she wore was no match for the weather. He took off his suit jacket and put it around her shoulders. She looked up at him, and he smiled. "There, how does that feel?" he asked.

"Much better," she admitted.

"Well good. I'm glad to hear it."

"But aren't you cold?" she asked.

He laughed. "My heart is cold, or so my wife says. So, I guess I don't feel the cold the way others do."

"You're joking, right? Are you really married?"

"Yes, I am married. But that has nothing to do with us, you and me. When we are together, I am yours, completely."

She thought of his wife, and the strange comment he made about having a cold heart. But she said nothing.

When they got back to the doctor's office, he unlocked the door and turned on the lights. Then he led her into the back room, where there was a sofa and chairs.

"Please, sit down," he said, taking a bottle of brandy and two shot glasses out of his drawer. He lifted the bottle and poured two drinks and handed her one. She took a sip and frowned. "Ohh, this is bitter," she said.

He laughed.

"Why do you always laugh at me?" she asked.

"The truth?"

"Yes, of course. Please tell me the truth."

"Because your naïveté is so adorable and funny to me. I am so used to hard-boiled women."

Now, she laughed. "What's a hard-boiled woman? Is it like a hard-boiled egg?"

"Sort of. I guess you could say it is. A woman with a crusty, hard exterior," he said.

She giggled. Then she added honestly, "I really don't understand."

"It's all right. No need to understand. Just know that I am not laughing at you. I am just enjoying your charm," he said, taking a sip of the brandy. "Now, here is the job I have in mind for you."

She sat back ready to listen, but she was wishing that the brandy was a cup of coffee instead of a glass of alcohol.

"Are you aware of what is going on with the Jews here in France since the Germans took us over?"

"Jews? Not really. I haven't paid much attention, I'm afraid," she said.

"It's all right. I'll tell you all about it," he said. Then smiling, he lit a cigar that smelled sweet, like the cigars the men at the brothel smoked. And he began. "Our German conquerors hate the Jews. Most people do, I suppose. Anyway, the Germans have been rounding the Jews up and sending them off somewhere. I don't know where exactly; however, the Jews know that if they go, it's not going to be good for them. So, they are trying like hell to get out of France. But they can't get out. They have nowhere to go. And even if they did, the Germans won't let them out. That's where I come in. I have created a code name for myself. It's Dr. Eugene. I have put the word out in the Jewish communities that for a nice sum of money I can get the Jews out of France and into South America. The ones who can pay, can be free of the Germans forever."

She looked at him. "Aren't you afraid of getting arrested?"

"I'm careful," he said, smiling.

"They must pay you a lot of money?"

"Yes, they do. But besides all of that, I'm a genuinely nice fellow."

She smiled at him. He smiled back. "So, what do you want me to do?"

"You?"

She nodded.

"I would like you to go to the Jewish neighborhoods and seek out Jewish families who can afford my services. They might very well be in hiding, as it is not safe to be a Jew. However, put the word out among those people that you have a way to help them escape. They will seek you out. They need your help."

"So, I would be doing a good thing?"

"But of course. And you would be earning some nice money as well."

"How much money?"

"How does one hundred francs sound?"

"Like a lot of money." She blushed. "A lot of money."

"Yes, it is. And all you have to do is help people in exchange for such a hefty sum."

"That is very generous of you, Dr. Petoit. But . . . what about my pregnancy? I can't have this baby."

"You needn't worry about that. I will take care of it for you. Like I said, my dear, I am a nice fellow." He smiled. She smiled back at him, but her lips were trembling. "Here is how we will do it. I will rid you of your unwanted pregnancy in exchange for the first group of Jews that you bring to me. After that, you will be paid in cash. How does that sound?"

"Wonderful. I am so grateful to you, Doctor."

"Good. I am glad I could help. Now, can you read and write?"

"Yes. Both."

"Well, that's good, isn't it?" He reached into the breast pocket of his jacket and took out the gold pen that had belonged to the poet in the restaurant. She looked at him, puzzled.

"You must have forgotten to return that man's pen." *But I wonder if he really forgot it or if he took it on purpose. It's a beautiful pen.*

Petoit let out a small laugh. "I must have forgotten." He handed her the pen and paper.

The gold pen was heavy and felt expensive in her hand.

"Are you ready?" he asked.

"Yes."

"Now, write this down. I am going to tell you where the Jewish neighborhoods are. This is where you must go to recruit."

She wrote down everything he dictated. When he'd finished, she asked, "So, when will we take care of this pregnancy?"

"After you bring me the first group, of course. I need to be sure that you are going to go through with your part of the bargain. It's only fair. But you'd better not wait too long to go and get me a group. The earlier you terminate this pregnancy, the easier it will be on your body."

CHAPTER FIFTY-THREE

WHEN GISELE RETURNED TO THE HOUSE, SHE WENT TO MARIE'S room and knocked on the door.

"Thank you for covering for me today."

"Where were you all day?" Marie asked. "It's so late, and I was starting to worry. I thought you'd be home by late afternoon but it's already night."

"I saw the doctor. He asked me to stay and have dinner with him. I did as he asked, because I need his help."

"Yes. I understand. And what happened? Did he fix the problem"?

"No, not yet. But he will. And he's very nice."

"Yes, that's all fine and good, but tell me what happened. Can he help you get rid of the pregnancy? Will he help you?" Marie asked nervously.

"Yes, but since I don't have enough money to pay him, he wants me to do something for him."

"Sex?"

"No, he wants me to work for him." She wanted to tell Marie everything. She needed someone she could trust. Someone older. Since she'd lost her mother, she felt alone in the world. And since she'd come to the house, Marie had been like a mother to her, at least as close as one could be. So she told her everything.

Marie listened quietly while Gisele explained what the doctor had in mind. When she'd finished, Marie shook her head, then she said, "This is all so dangerous. He wants you to go to the Jewish neighborhoods to find him families who want to get out of France?"

"Yes."

"If the Germans should catch you, they would arrest you. And they are not kind when they are angry," Marie said, biting her lower lip.

"I know. I am afraid of them. My mother said to be careful of them. But, what else can I do? I can't have this baby. Not only that, but how could I ever raise and love a child who was fathered by a man who raped me. I have to get rid of it. And I feel I should be grateful. At least Dr. Petoit is willing to help me. So, I must do as he asks."

Marie nodded. "Oh, Gisele," she said. "You must be very careful."

"I know."

"You must go to these neighborhoods at night after you've finished working, because even if I try to cover for you, if you are gone from the house every day, the madam will notice, and she will fire you."

"Yes, I know that too."

"Oh dear, what a mess this is. When are you going to start?"

"Tomorrow night after we are done with work for the day. I'll leave by the back door."

Marie nodded. "It's getting late; you should get some rest. We have to be awake in a few hours to receive the food deliveries for the day. I would tell you to sleep in, but lately the madam has been awake when the deliveries arrive. She's been complaining about the quality of the food since the Germans took over."

Gisele nodded. "I know."

"Good night," Marie said. Then she leaned down and unexpectedly kissed the top of Gisele's head. "Sleep well."

"Good night."

CHAPTER FIFTY-FOUR

THE FOLLOWING NIGHT, AS SOON AS THE KITCHEN WAS CLEANED, Gisele ran up to her room and got ready to leave. She waited until Marie came upstairs and gave her the okay. Then she slipped out the back door and took a bus to the first neighborhood that the doctor had suggested.

Walking through the Jewish neighborhood was like walking through a ghost town. It was late in the evening and dark. There was no one out on the street. She hated the dark, empty streets. They scared her. But as she walked, she remembered what the doctor had said the night before: "Now, remember this when you go to these neighborhoods. The Nazis have been rounding up the Jews, so it might not be easy to find them. If they haven't been taken, they have probably gone into hiding. But the good thing is that they'll want to get out of France. And Jews have plenty of money. They're all rich, you know. Just let everyone you meet know that you have a connection who is able to get the Jews out of the country."

"But how can I do that? If I am caught by the Nazis, I'll be in trouble."

"That's your problem," he said, smiling. "You need my help. I need you to do this. Now, go."

There was nothing more to say. So she'd left.

Gisele had never met a Jew, at least not that she knew of. And because of all she'd heard about them, before the Germans came, but especially since the Nazis took over, she was afraid of them. When she was a child, she'd once overheard two old women in Marseille talking about Jews. They said that the Jews were sorcerers with horns and tails.

As she walked the empty neighborhood, shivering from the cold, she decided it was hopeless. No one was around. *I've wasted money on bus fare*, she thought. Gisele had been about to leave and return home when she overheard the voice of a young boy.

"How much farther do we have to go, Papa?"

"Not much farther. But you must be quiet."

"My feet hurt, and I am tired," the boy said.

"It's all right. We will be there soon."

"But Papa. I don't want to leave our house. Is Mama coming?"

"Yes, she'll meet us there. Now, enough talking. I told you to stay quiet. We can't get caught out here. We must be very careful. We must get to the Heinzes' home before sunrise. If we are caught, it will be the end of all of us."

Gisele hid in the alley and watched the boy and his father. They hurried quickly down the street. *They must be Jews*, she thought. She was frightened, but she forced herself to come out of the shadows. And that was how she met the Goldsteins.

"Hello," she said, her voice just above a whisper.

"Should we run, Papa?" the young boy asked.

"Who are you? What do you want?" the father asked pleadingly.

"I am Gisele Lenoir. I . . . I . . ." *How do I ask this?* She cleared her throat. Then she looked at the yellow Star of David badge on their coats. "You are Jews?"

Then a young woman came out of the shadows. The little boy said, "Mama," and he began to cry.

"Please, I beg you; let us go. Don't report us. We mean no harm to anyone," the woman said.

"I am here to help you," Gisele said. "I know of a man, a

respectable doctor who can help you get out of France. For a sum of money, he can help you escape."

The father came into the light from the streetlamp. Now that she could see him better, she could see he was a lot older than the woman. Perhaps twenty years. His hair was steel gray, but he was handsome and distinguished looking. "Go on, please tell me more," he said.

"It's not inexpensive, I am afraid. But the man's name is Dr. Eugene, and he has been helping other Jewish families leave the country safely."

"And where would we be going—China?"

"No, South America. He has set up a small settlement of Jews who are now living there safely. He has helped them escape from France. But the cost is twenty-five thousand francs per person."

The older man glanced at his young wife and then at his son. "How many can you take?"

"As many as you have," she said simply.

"We wouldn't have to leave my mother behind?" the young woman said. "We could take her with us?"

"Yes," the man said. "I know how hard it was for you to leave her when we found out that the Heinzes' didn't have enough room. But if we were all to go to South America, she could come with us," he said.

"The money?" Gisele asked. "But can you get the money?"

The man nodded. Then he swallowed hard. "I'll get it," he answered.

"You must get it quickly. Can you do it by Monday of next week?"

"Yes."

"All right. Now, listen to me," Gisele said. She was breathing hard. "You go home and get the money together. Be sure you have it. Don't show up without it because if you do, Dr. Eugene will not help you. Do you understand?"

"Yes, we'll have it," the man said.

"All right. Then be at this address on Monday night of next week at eight o'clock." She handed him a piece of paper with an address that she'd written earlier just in case she'd found a group. "Now, listen to me closely," she continued. "You must pack only your valuables and the things that you will absolutely need because you will be making a long journey. So, extra things will just weigh you down."

"So, we will be leaving next Monday?" the woman asked.

"Yes. You will be leaving France on Monday," Gisele said.

"What if you are lying to us? What if we get there, and you take our money and turn us in to the Gestapo?" the woman asked.

"I don't have any way to prove to you that I am not lying. You'll just have to trust me."

The man studied Gisele. "All right. We'll do as you ask. We'll be there . . . eight o'clock, on Monday."

"Good," Gisele said. "You won't regret this."

"By the way, once again, what did you say was the doctor's name?" the woman asked.

"Dr. Eugene. His name is Dr. Eugene," Gisele said, then she turned and disappeared into the shadows.

CHAPTER FIFTY-FIVE

On Monday, the Goldsteins arrived on time. But they'd brought two additional people with them. There was the original father, mother, and young boy that Gisele had met the other night, but there were also two elderly ladies, one of them wearing a mink coat. "We brought my mother and her friend, Minnie. I hope it's all right. We have enough money for everyone," the young woman said.

"Of course it's fine," Gisele said as Marcel Petoit walked into the room.

"It's nice to meet all of you. I'm Dr. Eugene," he said.

"Here is the money." The man handed Petoit an envelope.

"Good, very good. So, let's get started." Petoit smiled. "The sooner we get you out of France, the better, right?"

The old woman nodded.

Petoit turned to Gisele. "Thank you, my dear," he said. "You've done a wonderful job. You have helped this family so much." Petoit smiled. "Now, go on home and get some rest. I'll take care of things from here. You are going to need to be well rested for your procedure tomorrow."

"*Yes, Doctor,*" Gisele said. *He is a good man, a kind man,* Gisele thought as she walked out of the office. *He'll take good care of me tomorrow when he aborts this pregnancy.*

CHAPTER FIFTY-SIX

GISELE WOULD HAVE LIKED TO TAKE A SHOWER BEFORE GOING TO SEE the doctor, but she dared not. The sound of running water would surely wake up the other women in the house, and she didn't want to explain where she was going at such an early hour or why. Marie was awake earlier than usual. But even so, she was getting ready to receive the day's deliveries. She was downstairs in the kitchen when Gisele came down and walked into the kitchen through the back door to let her know that she was leaving.

"He's going to do it today?" Marie asked.

Gisele nodded. "Yes," she said in a half whisper. Her entire body felt weak.

"I wish I could go with you; I hate to let you do this all alone. But we both can't leave. The madman would be furious."

"I know. I'll be all right. I appreciate your covering for me. I really do."

Marie touched Gisele's cheek. "You look so pale. Are you sick?" she said.

"It's just early in the morning. And I'm a little nervous. But, I'll be fine."

Marie nodded. "Yes, you will." Then as Gisele started to walk toward the door, she added, "Are you sure you want to do this? I mean, you could have the baby. Babies have been born in this house before."

"I must do this. I hate the man who fathered this child. I killed him. And even worse, I know I would hate the child because of its father. That wouldn't be fair to an unborn infant."

The night before, when Gisele returned, Marie was awake and waiting for her.

"Do you trust this doctor?" Marie asked Gisele in a small voice.

"I have to. I have no other choice," Gisele had answered. "He seems to be a good person."

Now as Gisele was about to leave, Marie looked into her eyes. Then she rushed over to Gisele and hugged her tightly. "I'll see you later," she said, and Gisele could hear in Marie's voice that she was holding back tears.

"Yes, later." Gisele tried to sound reassuring but was afraid. *Women have died from aborting babies. Many women have died. This could be the last time I will ever see Marie.* She forced a smile. Then she walked out the door.

When she arrived at Dr. Petoit's office, she walked up the stone walkway to the door. Her hands trembled so badly that she could hardly open it. She thought about running away, having the child, and muddling through. But then in her mind's eye, she saw the face of the Nazi who forced himself on her. She saw his face as he entered her, and then she saw his face as he lay dead, and her strength returned. She opened the door and headed into the office.

Dr. Petoit was there waiting for her. "Good morning," he said cheerfully.

"Good morning," she moaned.

"Awww, don't be afraid. You're going to be just fine." He smiled. "Do you think I would let anything happen to my best accomplice? Last night went so smoothly, didn't it?" he asked, not waiting for her to answer. "Together, you and I can make a small fortune off these pathetic Jews."

She felt sick. "Will it hurt?" she asked.

"A little, but I'll be as gentle as possible. So, let's get started," he said.

The cold steel table against her bare buttocks sent waves of fear through her. She shivered so hard that her teeth began to chatter.

"Don't be so afraid," Dr. Petoit said gently. "It will be over very soon."

Then he began. She felt sick to her stomach, terrified, and violated.

It hurt. She let out a piercing scream and bit her lip until it bled, filling her mouth with salty tasting blood. It hurt more than she had anticipated. The pain was so intense that she wished she could die. He used no painkillers, no anesthesia. It was hard to lie still. Her entire body was shaking so badly. And to make matters worse, when she looked at him, she could see he was smiling. He made no effort to hide the fact that he was enjoying her pain. Bile rose in her throat, but she swallowed hard and forced it back down.

"Well, it's all over," he said finally.

She took a deep breath. She was weak, and the pain had not yet subsided. Gisele wondered if it ever would.

"I'm not pregnant anymore?" she asked, putting her hand over her eyes for a moment, blocking out the blinding light that was shining right over the operating table.

"No, you're not."

"Are you sure?"

"Very sure." He smiled.

She felt relieved, but strangely enough, she also felt a little sad. But she couldn't figure out why.

Marcel patted her thigh, and she automatically pulled her hospital gown down to cover herself. Then he said, "You'll bleed a little for a while. Then the bleeding should stop. If you start bleeding heavy, you had better get back here to my office as quickly as you can. How far do you live from here?"

"Far. Several miles. I can't walk it. I have had to take the bus to get here. But that could be because I was weak due to being pregnant. I can't say for sure."

"Who do you live with? A lover?"

"No. I live at a brothel," she admitted, too exhausted and in too much pain to keep it a secret. "They don't know about my being pregnant, but I am sure that they have probably seen women there who have gone through things like this before."

He laughed. "I should have guessed it. That's how you found me. You must have come from Madame Auclair's place. I have helped many of her girls get rid of unwanted pregnancies."

"Yes, that's right. That's where I came from. Marie the cook, who works there, sent me."

"I have never met her. But, like I said, I have helped plenty of the girls from that house. So, you are a whore? I really would never have guessed. You have such a sweet, innocent face. But why didn't you have enough money to pay me?" Then he laughed. "You little minx; you tricked me, didn't you?"

She shook her head. "No, Marcel. I didn't trick you. I'm not a whore. In fact, I have never been with a man before this. I'm the maid at Madame Auclair's house. She hardly pays me anything. Most of what I earn is paid in room and board. That's why I didn't have enough money to pay you. If I had been a whore, I am sure I would have had the money."

"Well, your days of cleaning toilets are over. From now on, you will have a job that pays you well. You will be my recruiter for my special Jewish clients." He smiled. "You did a wonderful job last night. And because you did, I want to give you this." He walked out of the room but returned in a moment carrying a fur coat. It was the coat that the old woman had been wearing the night before.

"Doesn't that belong to one of the old Jewish women who I brought to you last night?"

"It did. Now it's yours."

"But won't she need it to travel?"

"Not where she is going." He smiled. "Like I said, it's yours."

Gisele held the coat in her arms. It felt soft and smelled faintly of an expensive perfume. *South America is warm. Perhaps the doctor is right; she won't be needing a fur when she gets there.*

CHAPTER FIFTY-SEVEN

GISELE SURVIVED THE ABORTION, AND WITHIN A WEEK SHE WAS feeling well enough to go back to the Jewish neighborhood to see if she could find another family. It almost felt noble to her to be doing this work with Marcel, although she was still afraid of getting caught by the Germans.

This time it was easier to find a group who were desperate to escape the Nazis. News spread when Mr. Goldstein told his friends about the pretty blonde who, along with Dr. Eugene, was helping the Jews to escape from the Nazis. As Gisele walked down the dark, empty street, she was approached by an older man. She saw that he was trembling as he walked up to her. "I'm looking for Dr. Eugene," he said. "I am a friend of Harry Goldstein."

"Oh yes. I work with Dr. Eugene," Gisele said, smiling. "I know Mr. and Mrs. Goldstein."

"Harry said that you and Dr. Eugene might be able to help me and my family. We want to get out of France as soon as possible."

"Of course. It's expensive. Twenty-five thousand francs per person. Can you afford it?"

He nodded.

She handed him an address. "Bring yourself and your entire family to this address on Monday at eight p.m."

"We'll be there," he said.

CHAPTER FIFTY-EIGHT

THE ROSENBLATTS ARRIVED ON TIME: TWO YOUNG BOYS; AN OLD,
but still attractive woman; a young, beautiful woman; and a wealthy,
distinguished-looking man. They were nervous. Gisele reassured
them that everything would be fine. She promised them that they
had nothing to worry about. "I have the utmost confidence in Dr.
Eugene," she said. "He will take good care of you."

Dr. Eugene arrived and introduced himself. Then he explained
that in order to be permitted to enter the South American country
where he was sending them, they must be vaccinated. He carried a
tray of syringes. "My nurse, Gisele, will administer your vaccines,"
he said.

The two boys started crying. "I don't want a shot, Papa," one of
the boys said.

"Me neither."

"You boys must do as the doctor says," the father said.

"Give them the injections, Gisele."

"But, Doctor . . ."

"Do it now."

Gisele was nervous. She didn't know how to do this. No one had
shown her how to give an injection. Her hands were trembling.

Then, as if he knew, Petoit took the syringe from her hand and said, "Watch me. I'll do the first one."

Gisele watched, and then, with trembling hands, she administered the rest of the vaccines.

Once that was done, Petoit said, "All right, now let's all get into the car."

Gisele looked at him. "Shall I go home like last time?" she asked.

"No, this time you are going to join us." Petoit smiled, and she felt a shiver run down her spine.

CHAPTER FIFTY-NINE

THEY DROVE FOR A LONG TIME BEFORE THEY ARRIVED AT AN OLD farmhouse outside of town. Marcel stopped the car, and Gisele turned around to speak to the Rosenblatt family. But to her horror they were sitting huddled together in the back of Dr. Petoit's automobile: all of them were dead.

"They are dead?" she said, her voice filled with shock and horror.

"Of course they are. I injected them with cyanide. However, I did give them what I promised, didn't I? After all, they did escape the Nazis." He laughed. It was a terrifying laugh that broke the stillness of the night. It was then that she realized what she'd done. She felt sick; bile rose in her throat. She tried to rationalize it by telling herself that they were only Jews. But she couldn't. She'd seen them, spoken to them, and they weren't monsters; they were just ordinary people. The very idea that she was responsible for their deaths, that she had brought them to Dr. Eugene and filled them with hope, only to have them murdered, made her feel frightened and guilty.

The area was very dark. They were out in the country far from the city lights. Gisele was in shock. She had not known that the family was going to die. Dr. Petoit had told her that these were vaccines and that this Jewish family was on their way to South America. Her body was trembling so hard that she could barely stand up. *I am alone with a madman. No one knows where we are, so if something happens to me, no one will know where to look. I don't dare let him know what I think of him. I don't dare question him. Although I would like to. I would like to ask him why he lied to me. But as long I do as he says, I believe that I will be all right.*

"Help me drag them into the house. We have to get them into the furnace. But first take all of their jewelry, money, and anything else of value."

"Furnace? You have a furnace in that place?" Gisele asked, indicating the farmhouse.

"Yes, I built it especially for this purpose. Brilliant, don't you agree?"

"Yes, Marcel," she said. *I must praise him. I must not let him know my real feelings.* "Of course. Everything you do is brilliant."

"Have I told you today that you are beautiful."

"Dr. Petoit, you flatter me too much." She laughed nervously.

Gisele looked at him. *I must admit I am frightened at how cool he was through the entire evening. He never let on what he had in store for those people when he injected them with cyanide. And I have to admit, I'm really scared of him. He is insane, completely and utterly insane. Terrifyingly mad, and no doubt, quite dangerous, even to me. However, I have just earned a hundred francs for a few hours' work. It wasn't difficult at all. And I needn't fret because, even if we're caught, I doubt anyone would care. Especially not the Germans. They hate the Jews. I doubt they would arrest us. After all, they wouldn't see the victims as human; they would agree that the victims were just Jews.*

Dr. Eugene, as he was nicknamed, didn't have any such feelings of guilt. He told Gisele to get out of the car and help him. Together, they carried the bodies of the Rosenblatt family into the farmhouse and put them into the incinerator that Marcel had built. Then, once they were burning, Marcel put his arm around Gisele and escorted her outside the farmhouse.

They'd stripped the family of all of their valuables, which now lay on the ground. "We can go through their luggage later this evening, and if you find any clothing that you would like to have, you can take it, as a gift from me. I'll bet the wife had beautiful dresses. The man seemed to have plenty of money."

Gisele didn't answer. She couldn't speak. Her throat hurt as if she'd been crying. But the weeping was all inside.

He looked at her; his eyes were glittering. "I am feeling exhilarated. Everything went so well, didn't it? I'm hungry, first for you and then for food." He laughed.

She was overcome by the smell of the burning bodies and the guilt of what she'd done.

The last thing she wanted to do was have sex with him.

"Here's the money I promised you," he said, counting out one hundred francs and then handing them to her. Her hands were trembling as she put the money into her purse. Then before she realized what was happening, he pulled her into his arms and began to touch her body. She gagged when she looked at his face and noticed a small string of drool hanging from his mouth. He was breathing heavily as he reached inside of her coat and ran his hands over her breasts. Gisele felt nauseated and dizzy. She was shivering, not only from the weather, but from anticipation of what was to come. She wanted to push this terrible man off her and run as fast as she could, run away from the horrible things she'd done that night. Run away from his groping hands that now pinched her nipples. *If only I could escape into the darkness far from this monstrous man and these horrific murders I helped him to commit.* But she knew that even if she ran, ran for miles and miles, she could not escape from the memories that she would carry with her for the rest of her life.

She felt herself gag; she tried to stop it, but she couldn't control it. The bitter taste of bile filled her throat. He didn't notice. She looked away from him, but her eyes were fixated on the smoke belching out from the chimney of the house. *That smoke is the burning of the bodies of the Rosenblatts. They are burning,* she thought, and she felt the bile rise in her throat. Again. This time it came all the way up and Gisele vomited.

"Putain de merde!" Petoit said angrily. Then he slapped her hard across the face. "You puked on me. You are nothing but a low-class slob."

"I'm sorry," she pleaded. She was crying. "It's just, the smoke and the smell. It's not you. You are a handsome man. But I am cold, and we are outside . . . and the smell of those bodies burning . . . I didn't mean to throw up on you. I tried to stop it. Please, I beg you, don't be angry with me."

Then the anger left his face, and he let out a laugh. "You are such a delicate one, my dear. But you'll get used to this. You'll see. Soon it won't bother you at all."

She looked away from him.

"Don't worry. I can wait to have you, my dear. And, perhaps you're right, our first time together shouldn't be outside in the cold. It should be in a warm bed."

She was relieved that he was going to let her be, at least for the night.

He helped her to her feet, then he smiled and said, "Well, your days of cleaning toilets are over. You will no longer spend your time catering to a bunch of whores. From now on, you will have a good job that pays you well. You will be my recruiter for my special Jewish clients." He smiled. "You did a wonderful job tonight. That family never suspected a thing."

"I am sorry. I am not feeling very well."

"You can take a few days off before you recruit the next Jewish family. I understand that this is taking some getting used to. However, I can see you are going to be good at it."

"Yes, I could use the time off before the next one," she lied to him. She was afraid to tell him the truth, that she couldn't recruit another family. She just couldn't bring herself to do it again. He would be angry once she told him this, and she had no doubt in her mind that he was dangerous when he was displeased. *I can't do it anymore. But I don't dare tell him that right now. He'll be furious, and I feel too weak to fight him off if he decides that he wants to kill me. And he might just decide to do that. I am feeling so vulnerable and tired.*

"Of course, my dear. Why don't we get you something to eat?"

She wasn't hungry at all. "I think I would rather just go home."

"Yes, I understand. Like I said, take a few days." He smoothed her hair out of her face. "I hope I didn't scare you off with my advances tonight," he said. "I was just overwhelmed by your beauty and charm. Please, won't you forgive me?"

It was amazing how gentle he could be and how soft spoken, and yet she knew he was a madman. She'd seen the look on his face when he threw the bodies into the furnace. *I know I can't trust him. He likes me now, and he will like me as long as he thinks I will serve a purpose for him, but once he knows that I am not going to recruit Jews for him, he could easily kill me. Easily. Without feeling a thing,* she thought.

CHAPTER SIXTY

"I AM GOING TO STOP WORKING WITH THE DOCTOR. I AM DONE WITH him." Gisele told Marie when she walked into the kitchen. Her arms were wrapped around her chest protectively.

"Well, at least you got rid of the pregnancy. But why are you quitting your job with him? It gives you extra money and it doesn't really interfere with your work here at the brothel."

"I don't want any part of what he's doing with those Jews. I can't do that anymore."

"Have you paid him all you owe him? You don't owe him any more money for the abortion?"

"No, I am all paid up. But, he wants me to continue with this recruiting of Jews."

"I think it's wise for you to quit. If the Germans find out that you have been having any association with Jews they won't be happy with you."

Gisele took a deep breath. "It's so much more than just that." She said. Then she told Marie everything that happened with the Rosenblatt family.

Marie shook her head. "Oh, Gisele. I had no idea. That is horrible," Marie said. She was trembling.

"He pays me well. But I can't do it anymore. It's a disgusting, horrific business. I am the lure. It is me. I am the one that brings these poor people to the slaughter, like the Judas goat or something. Then once he kills them, there is the horrible smell when he burns their bodies. It's all just too terrible. And too dangerous."

"So what will you tell him?"

"I don't know. I am afraid of him. I am thinking I just won't go back there ever again. He'll find someone else to help him. I am sure there are plenty of girls that he could find who would love to earn that kind of money."

"Why don't you go and get ready for bed. I'll bring you something to eat."

Gisele nodded. "Thank you, you are such a good friend to me."

CHAPTER SIXTY-ONE

AN ENTIRE WEEK PASSED, AND GISELE DIDN'T HEAR A WORD FROM Dr. Petoit. She believed that she was free of him until one night when she was emptying the ashtrays in the main room, she looked up. There he was sitting in a heavy chair with Annette curling onto his lap. But he wasn't paying any attention to Annette who was gently rubbing his upper arm. Instead, his eyes were fixed directly on Gisele.

"Hello, Gisele," he said. He was smiling, but she could feel the wrath behind his trembling lips. "I came all the way here to find you. And do you know why that is? It's because I haven't seen you for a while. You were supposed to come back to my office. You still owe me . . ."

"I-I was recovering," Gisele stammered. "I was going to return as soon as I felt up to it."

"Recovering from what?" Annette asked in a snippy voice.

"That's none of your business." Marcel glared at Annette. Then he slapped her behind. "Go on. Get away from me. I'm tired of you."

Annette shot Gisele a look of pure hatred mixed with jealousy. But she stood up and left the room.

"I see. Well, I could be wrong, but from what I can see, you are looking quite well right now. You are able to do your duties here as the cleaning woman in this house, aren't you?" Marcel said to Gisele in a sarcastic tone of voice. He waited for a few moments for her to say something, but she didn't speak. Gisele stared at the floor. "You do look very well, actually. Very well indeed," he said as he ran his hand over his chin. "In fact, I am thinking about asking Madame Auclair if you and I might go up to one of the rooms."

"I am only the maid here. I am not one of the prostitutes," Gisele said. Her voice was shaking. "Did you forget that? I am sure any one of the other girls would be happy to go upstairs with you."

He let out a cruel laugh. "Did I forget? The question here is, did you forget? You seem to have forgotten a lot of things—first of which, your obligation to me. We had a bargain; we made a deal. I fixed your situation, and you were going to be my special recruiter. Do you remember that, or have you forgotten that too? I don't know what happened, Gisele. All I know is that I waited for you to keep your end of the bargain, and you just never came back." He shook his head. His tone of voice was mocking. Then pretending to be sad, he frowned and said, "How could you do it? You broke my heart."

She shook her head. "I'm sorry." It was all she could manage to say.

He let out a loud laugh that unnerved her. She trembled.

Gisele felt a chill run up her spine. "I have to finish cleaning," she said weakly.

"Do you? And what if I get angry with you? What if I pay the madam to take you out? And then once we are alone, I take you to that farmhouse. You know the one I am talking about. I am quite sure you remember it. What if I take you there and . . ." He got up and stood close to her, so close he could whisper in her ear: "What if I throw you into that furnace while you are still alive? I could do that, you know. The madam would let me take you out if I paid her well enough. And you wouldn't dare tell her about the farmhouse. Because if you dared to try to explain, whatever you told her would implicate you in the murders. So, you would have to keep your cute little mouth shut and go quietly, wouldn't you?"

"Leave me alone. Leave me alone, please. Just go away or I'll scream. I swear I will."

"AND THEN WHAT will you do? What reason will you give them for screaming? Will you tell Madame Auclair that you helped me murder a whole family? If you don't, I will tell her. But I won't tell her you helped me. I'll tell her you did it alone. And even better, I'll tell her, and I'll tell the Germans that you were raped by that German officer who was killed. Once they find that out, you'll be their prime suspect in his murder. Of course, the Germans won't care what he did to you. All they will care about is the fact that you had a motive to kill one of them. And, Madame Auclair won't care about you either. All she cares about is her house and her income. You see, my dear, all of these people, might not give a damn about a family of Jews, because they're nothing but rats. But I can assure you that they will care greatly about one of their own. You killed a German, a Nazi. They won't take that lightly, I promise you. How will you feel when the Gestapo comes and takes you away to one of the German prisons? I hear those places are barbaric. I hear the Nazis are masters of torture."

"But you were responsible too. They will take you too."

"You are such a silly, naïve fool. Gisele, I am a respected doctor. You are nothing but a filthy maid. Who do you think they will believe?"

She shuddered. "I know what you want from me but I can't do it anymore. It was too horrible. I am still haunted by the faces of the Rosenblatts. The Rosenblatts were just a family; they were only trying to survive. They never did anything wrong to me."

"You will continue to work for me, or I swear I will have you arrested. Or better yet, perhaps you would prefer that I finish you off. I could do that to you, you know. Easily. I could find a way to get in here at night when everyone is asleep. I am sure Annette would help me, especially if I paid her. Then, when no one is around, I could find you sleeping in your bed and finish you off. I'd cut your pretty little throat and let you bleed out all over your bed. Just think, you'd never know when it was coming. It might even be tonight." His eyes twinkled, and he laughed again. This time his laughter rang out, filling the room and filling her heart with fear.

She looked into his eyes. They were so dark. His brows were so thick and black. And as his gaze bore into her, it seemed to burn like hot black flames. It was then she realized that fighting him was of no use. He was capable of anything. She knew he had no conscience. He could turn her in, or he could kill her. She'd seen him kill before, and he'd walked away without any feelings of remorse. It would be easy for him.

This is not the way to go about this, she thought. *I must change my tactics with him. He is stronger and more diabolical than anyone I have ever met. Making an enemy of him is dangerous. Instead, I have to find a way to make him trust me. I have to change how he feels about me.* In a soft voice, she said, "Marcel, you're right about all of this. I was nervous because of what we did. You see, I have never done anything like that before. But I shouldn't have avoided you. I am sorry; it was a mistake. I should have talked it over with you. I know you could have helped me to feel stronger and more capable carrying out our task. It's just that I was feeling so sick after getting rid of the baby. I guess my hormones were going crazy. And I just needed some time to get back to myself. But if you are willing to have patience with me, I will come back and work with you again. I would rather earn the one hundred francs than go on being a maid in this house. I hope you can forgive me for not being ready," she tried to smile. Then she touched his hand. "Please, forgive me." She could see he was softening. So she touched his cheek and ran her fingers along the contours of his face down to his chin. "I am glad you came here to find me. Because now that you are here, and now that I see you again, I remember how handsome you are. I don't know how you feel, but I think perhaps now that I am no longer pregnant, there could be something special between us."

He smiled. The glimmer in his eyes told her that he was truly insane. "I'm intrigued," he said, "but how can I know if I can trust you, my little beauty?" You have already betrayed me once."

"Give me another chance. I am young. You know that. And, I was just afraid. That's all. Why don't you wait until we close tonight, then come to my bed after I finish work. Once we are alone, I'll show you how much you mean to me. And then we can make plans to carry out our work together," she said fetchingly.

He stared at her and licked his lips. "So, you are willing to be my little recruiter after all. That's wise of you. Well then, I suppose everyone deserves a second chance. And I would love to spend the night with you. So, I'll come to your room once the house is closed for the night. I look forward to it. I hope you do too," he said.

She knew she had no other choice but to make him her lover. The very idea was revolting to her. *But it will make him trust me.*

Although she had never told him which room was hers, he arrived at her bedroom door after things grew quiet in the main room of the house. His knock on her door was as soft as a mouse, but she knew he was there, and she shuddered. *How does he know which room is mine? He is so dangerous.*

Gisele opened the door, and Marcel Petoit entered. "You look lovely as always," he said as he walked in and sat down on her bed. She didn't say a word. She was afraid if she did, her voice would betray the revulsion and fear she felt. Instead, she put her arms around his neck and kissed him. *Don't gag,* she told herself *You must pretend to like this.*

That was all she had to do. He took the lead from there, and before she knew it, he was inside of her. She shut her eyes tightly and held her breath. He was surprisingly gentle. It didn't hurt the way she'd feared it would after the abortion. Once it was over, she lay her head on his chest so that he couldn't see her face. Then in a soft voice she said, "You've restored my desire for men."

"For all men?" he said. There was a threatening catch in his voice.

"No, Marcel. Only for you."

He smiled. "It was our first time. After we are together and doing this for a while, it will be even better for you. You'll see."

She ran her hand over the hair on his chest. "I know you have a wife."

She felt him tense up.

"It's all right. I don't care," she said. Then she continued. "I was thinking that perhaps you would like to set up an apartment for me somewhere near your office. I could leave this brothel and move in there. Then you could come and see me whenever you liked. And together we could devise a plan to work together recruiting the Jews."

"What kind of a plan? We have a plan," he said, his voice growing defensive. "You bring them to me. I take care of it from there."

"All right. So we don't need a new plan. We will keep the same one. I was just thinking that I could help you recruit more girls to do the same thing. Then you would have even more Jews to pay you."

"You're a smart little minx, aren't you? But I am not sure we want to open this up to so many people. It's best, I think, if we keep it a secret. Just the two of us." He smiled. "We are less likely to get caught that way."

"That's true. But, if you set me up in an apartment near your office, you could come to see me whenever you wanted to."

"That sounds good. I do like that plan a great deal. All right, I do have some pressing meetings tomorrow, but I'll try to get out of my office, so I can rent you an apartment. Can you move in on Thursday?"

"Yes, Thursday would be perfect. I'll come to your office on Thursday evening with my things, and you can take me to the apartment from there. Then I'll move in, and I can start recruiting again on Monday. What time should I arrive on Thursday?"

"Eight o'clock?"

"We are busy on Thursday nights, so I can't get out of the house until a little before ten. Would ten be all right?"

"Who cares what the madam thinks. You are quitting."

"But I would rather she didn't know what we have in mind. I will get nervous if she asks me any questions. If I got to my room, then slip out the back door, I won't have to talk to her. Would ten be all right?"

"Of course, if you feel better leaving that way, then that's the way we'll do it. I'll meet you at my office at ten thirty. That will give you time to catch the bus."

Marcel stayed with her in her bed until the sun rose. Then as the sun lit the sky, he stretched and slowly got out of bed. He picked up his clothes from the floor and got dressed. "I'd love some coffee, but I don't suppose it's a good idea to go down to the kitchen. I'll get it from a café on my way to the office," he said. "I'll take the backstairs to leave. That way no one needs to know that I was with you last night."

She nodded. But she thought, *How does he know about the backstairs? He knows everything. Everything.*

"Did you know that people call me Dr. Satan?" he said, then he let out that terrifying laugh again. "I can't imagine why, can you?"

She shook her head nervously. "No." she said, but she thought, *I know why. It's because you're the devil.*

"How I do hate to part with that young, supple body of yours," he said. "What pleasure you give me." Then sighing, he added, "I'll see you on Thursday, my dear."

"Yes, Thursday evening. I am looking forward to it." She forced a smile.

He leaned down and kissed her softly. Then he walked out of the room and quietly closed the door.

She jumped out of bed and ran to the window where she watched him come around from the back door and climb into his automobile which he'd parked right in front of the house. For a moment, she didn't move, and she was worried that he might take the day off from work and return to her room. *Please just go, just leave,* she thought. Then she heard the car start. He slowly maneuvered it out of the parking place and onto the empty street. Once he drove far enough away that she could no longer see his car, she immediately pulled her suitcase out from under her bed. Then she packed everything she owned, and with suitcase in hand, she went down to the kitchen where she found Marie baking bread.

"I don't know what to do," Gisele said. Then she told Marie what had happened with Marcel. She explained that he had returned, and he was angry. She told Marie the promises she'd made to him. Marie listened without saying a word.

"He's a dangerous man," Marie said in a whisper. "You must get away from him."

"I know. You're right."

The girls began coming down to the dining room for breakfast. They were quiet as they were most mornings, because they kept such late hours.

"We'll talk about this later," Marie said, "I don't want to risk anyone hearing us. Especially Annette."

Gisele nodded and began carrying the platters of eggs and toast to the table. She had just picked up a pot of coffee when there was a knock on the door.

"Come in," the madam said.

It was the same two Gestapo agents who had come the night of Rudolf's murder. They looked around the room suspiciously. "We have returned because we now have a witness who says he saw Rudolf Altner with a blonde girl who he recognized as one of you whores the night he was murdered. So, we need an alibi from each of you for that night."

The investigation took all morning. Marie covered for Gisele. She told the Gestapo agents that Gisele was up in her room feeling ill. Marie said that it was she, not Gisele who had left the brothel to purchase the beer.

Gisele was as white as the china dishes when she confirmed Marie's story.

But when the Gestapo agents questioned Annette, she was livid. She pointed to Gisele. "She is responsible for this. I know she is. She has always been jealous of me. And she was jealous of my engagement to Officer Altner."

"You're crazy," Marie said, then she turned to the Gestapo agents and said, "Annette is the one who was always jealous of Gisele. I know for a fact that Gisele was in the house that night. Annette followed Officer Altner out after he left."

"That is true," one of the other prostitutes said.

Then Annette took a small handkerchief out of her pocket. Gisele gasped when she saw the hanky embroidered with the blue thread. "That's my mother's handkerchief," Gisele moaned.

"Yes, it is," Annette said. "Now, tell me what happened that night. Tell me the truth, or I swear I will throw this lousy old thing in the fire."

Gisele was crying. But she could not tell the truth. She just shook her head. "I don't know what happened," she said.

Annette threw the handkerchief in the fireplace. Gisele put her hand on her throat. But in seconds the thin cloth was nothing more than ashes.

"Don't you think she would have told you if she knew anything? After all, that handkerchief was the only thing she had left from her mother," Marie said. "That and a small piece of soap."

"I already threw the soap in the trash two days ago," Annette said.

"Well, the fact that Gisele said nothing means she knows nothing. I told you she didn't. If she had known, she would have tried to save her mother's memory," Marie said.

Finally after two hours of intense questioning, the Gestapo agents left.

Marie closed the door behind them. Annette stormed upstairs to her room. Then Marie turned to Gisele. "Come into the kitchen with me and help me clean up. We've wasted half the day with those Germans," she said.

Gisele and Marie were washing dishes when Gisele whispered in Marie's ear, "I'm leaving," she said. "I have to. I must get away from here as soon as possible. I have two days until Thursday, before Dr. Petoit comes looking for me. I must use that time to put as much distance as I can between myself and Dr. Petoit. If not, he expects me to start working with him. If I don't, he might kill me himself. He is a terrible man. Besides that, now the Gestapo is looking for the killer of that German officer. They have a witness who says he saw him with a blonde girl from this house. Things are getting too hot here for me. Unfortunately, I must go. But I want to say that I love you, Marie. Thank you for being a friend to me. I wish things were different, but as they stand, I must say goodbye."

"Where are you going?" Marie asked.

"I don't know. I am going to take the first train out of here. I am going to get as far away from Paris as I can. I pray that Marcel won't find me. I pray that the Gestapo wont search for me if I am no longer here. At least I have the one hundred francs Petoit gave me for that job I did, to help me get settled in my new home."

Marie put her arms around Gisele. "Be careful. I'll miss you."

"I will. I promise to be careful, and I'll miss you too," Gisele replied.

CHAPTER SIXTY-TWO

THE NEXT TRAIN THAT WAS SCHEDULED TO LEAVE THE STATION IN Paris that day was headed for Berlin. *Everyone says I look German. Perhaps I can blend in there. I am not the only blonde in that whorehouse. They will question all of the others, and by the time they try to find me, I will have a new identity. Besides that, they would never think I would go to Berlin to escape them. And, even better, I can speak enough German to help me find work in Berlin. I can always be a maid.* So Gisele purchased a one-way ticket and then sat down on a bench to wait. She had stuffed the fur coat into her suitcase feeling that she looked less conspicuous wearing her old wool one.

As she waited for the train to arrive, she looked around nervously, afraid that somehow Marcel was toying with her and that he knew she was going to try to escape. She imagined that he might have followed her. Her heart raced; her palms grew sweaty. She felt dizzy and sick to her stomach. But as time passed, and she saw that he was nowhere to be found, she began to relax a little. And as she did, she thought about Berlin and what André had said about her father. *I know he came to Paris with his parents on a holiday from his home, in Germany, but I don't know where in Germany. However, André said he came from a wealthy family. I am his daughter. Perhaps he would help me if he knew of my existence. I wonder if he is still alive. Who knows? He could be dead. But I know that since André told me about him, I have both loved him and hated him at the same time. I've often thought about what our lives would have been like had he stayed with my mother and faced his responsibilities. Yes, he was young, but then again, so was she. And she was all alone. There is no way to know if he even knew she was pregnant or not. If he didn't know, I would have to forgive him. But if he did, and then he left us anyway, he was truly a good-for-nothing fellow. I have so many things I wish I could ask him, yet I can't imagine I will ever have that opportunity, even in Berlin. I doubt that with all the people who are there, I will ever find Josef Mengele.*

Then the train whistle blew announcing the train's arrival. Gisele's legs felt like rubber bands as she stood up. The sound of the whistle startled her back to the present time, and immediately her eyes searched the depot one last time to be sure she had not been followed by the doctor. *He's not here. I'm safe.*

Gisele glanced left and then right as she boarded the train. Then found a seat by the window. She was exhausted, so she laid her head back and tried to rest. But in her mind, she heard Marcel's laughter as he said, "Did you know that they call me Dr. Satan?"

And she couldn't relax.

CHAPTER SIXTY-THREE

December 1943

WHEN GISELE ARRIVED IN BERLIN, SHE COULD HARDLY BELIEVE THAT it had been four years since her mother had died. She remembered the young innocent child she'd been when she was living with her mother in that small shack. A bittersweet tenderness came over her. She'd been through so much over these last four years. And it had changed her. There was a time when she thought that the fears her mother instilled in her about men were unwarranted. In fact, she'd sometimes thought her mother to be a little crazy. But she'd learned the truth; her mother was far from mad. Her mother knew that men could be dangerous and must be handled with care. And now Gisele knew it too. However, there was another side to all of this. Yes, men were dangerous, but they were also easily manipulated with sex, and if a girl was smart, and very careful, she could have anything she wanted in this world. And Gisele was determined to live a better life than her mother did. She was not going to let fear keep her down. *I will find the most successful man I can find, and then I will make him love me. My mother was a prostitute for many men. I will marry for money and be a prostitute for only one.*

As Gisele stepped onto the main thoroughfare in downtown Berlin, the first thing she noticed was that the streets were filled with German soldiers. Nazi flags hung from the buildings. Her heart beat fast as she studied her surroundings, a little unnerved by the sight. Her mother's voice came back to her, warning her to be careful of the Germans. The face of the young German soldier whom she had killed entered her mind's eye. He had been the beginning of all her problems, causing her so much misery, raping her, and then leaving her pregnant. If it hadn't been for him, she would never have met Marcel. *But these people who live here in Berlin, don't know that I am not German. I can speak their language fluently. They will only be dangerous if they find out that I am not one of them. And there is no reason they need ever find out,* she reassured herself.

It wasn't difficult to find a women's boarding house in Berlin. It seemed to her that they were everywhere. Signs hung outside several of the houses she passed as she walked down a main street, advertising rooms for rent. Gisele went to see several of them. Some were very nice, but too expensive . Finally, she decided upon an inexpensive room off the main street. It wasn't as pretty or as brightly lit as the room she'd left behind at the brothel, but she didn't need much. *All I want is a place where I can be safe from Marcel. That horrible Dr. Satan. And I don't think he would ever be able to find me here.*

Gisele paid her first month's rent and then began to unpack. Once she'd finished, she realized that she'd been so nervous, she'd forgotten to eat that day. She glanced at the fur coat, wishing she could wear it because it was freezing outside but deciding it was safer not to. *It's best not to draw any attention to myself.* Wrapping a scarf around her neck, she walked quickly down the stairs and out onto the street. There were plenty of restaurants all with varying price ranges to choose from. But when she heard noise and laughter coming from a biergarten, her youthful blood stirred. She wanted to laugh, to be happy, to enjoy life. So she walked inside. With her face made up the way the girls at the brothel had taught her, she looked glamorous. Taking a seat on a barstool, she ordered a dark German beer. She'd tasted the bitter beer at the brothel, and she liked it. When her mug of beer arrived, she took a large gulp, and then another. *I am going to like it here in Berlin. I am going to be safe here. Marcel might search for me, but he would never suspect that I have gone to Berlin. He would think that I am somewhere in France, probably still in Paris or perhaps back in Marseille.*

She ordered a sandwich, a bowl of soup, and another beer. She finished the first beer so quickly that she felt a little dizzy. But when the second beer arrived, she began to drink it just as quickly. It made her feel relaxed and at ease. And she liked the feeling. She liked it very much. At least until a man wearing a dark coat and hat sat down on the barstool beside her.

CHAPTER SIXTY-FOUR

ERNST LOVED BERLIN. HE WAS GLAD THAT DR. MENGELE HAD suggested he take a holiday. *I needed to get away from that horrible place. It's good to be home, back in Germany.* He was sitting at a table in the back of the noisy biergarten eating alone and remembering the days he'd spent at the university in this wonderful, exciting city. *Maybe Mengele was right. Maybe all I needed was to get away from that place for a while. Perhaps a little time away will make it easier to do what he asks of me.* Ernst gulped his beer. *Still, when I think of going back to Auschwitz and doing those ghastly things, I feel sick. If I thought I could reason with Mengele and explain how I feel, I would tell him that I prefer to find work at a real hospital here in Berlin. But I am afraid that he would be angry, and he is not the kind of man to forgive. He could hurt my career. I might lose my license, who knows what damage he might do to punish me. Let's face it, he has the power. He is an important man in the Nazi Party. He could see to it that I never practice medicine. I don't want to, but I have to go back to Auschwitz and work for him until I can think of a way to leave there with his blessing.*

A pretty young waitress with blonde braids wrapped around her head brought his food. "Is there anything else I can get for you?"

"Oh no, this is fine," he said as she set the plate of steaming noodles with schnitzel down in front of him.

The smell was delightful, and he inhaled deeply. Ernst was very hungry. He had always had a good appetite, and he could have easily eaten two plates of this wonderful food. He closed his eyes, savoring the flavor of real German cooking. *How I have missed this*, he thought, when the bartender yelled, "Is there a doctor? This woman needs help."

Immediately, Ernst got to his feet. He rushed to the bar and saw a beautiful young girl lying on the floor. She was perhaps the most beautiful girl he'd ever seen. But she was unconscious. He got down and knelt beside her, taking her pulse. She was alive.

"Give me a wet rag. Wet it with cool water," he said to the bartender, who came out from behind the bar to see what was happening.

Within seconds, someone brought Ernst the wet rag. He gently washed the girl's face. She wore black mascara and eyeliner that had smeared under her eyes. But even so, she was beautiful, and when she finally opened her deep-blue eyes, Ernst was instantly smitten.

He helped her to sit up. "How do you feel?" he asked.

"I don't know. I feel strange. Dizzy."

"What happened?" he asked.

She looked around frantically. "I thought I heard the voice of someone."

"Who?"

"A man. A man I used to know," she said looking at the man with the dark coat and hat, who was still sitting on the barstool. But now he was looking down at her with a strange curiosity. "Him," she said, then looking closer at the man, she added, "but it's not him. He's a stranger. He's not the man I thought he was. I thought I knew him. But I don't. It's not him," she said more to herself than to Ernst.

"She's crazy," the man in the dark coat said.

"It's all right," Ernst soothed the girl. "Come and eat with me at my table." Then he called out, "Waitress, please bring her food to my table."

The waitress nodded.

CHAPTER SIXTY-FIVE

ERNST LOCKED HIS ARM UNDER HERS AND LED HER TO WHERE HE'D been sitting. She sat down. "I haven't eaten today. And I guess I drank too much while I was waiting for my food."

"Here, have some water," he said, handing her his water glass. She drank it slowly. Then he gave her a piece of bread, which she nibbled on.

"How do you feel now?"

"Better. Actually, much better."

The waitress brought her food and set it down on the table. Ernst smiled at the young waitress and nodded. "Thank you." Then he turned to the beautiful blonde, who had started eating her bowl of soup. "May I be so bold as to ask your name?"

"Gisele Lenoir." She gasped. She realized after she'd given him her name that she had meant to adopt a German name. Now he would know the truth; he would know she was French.

"I'm Ernst Neider," he said. "Your name tells me you're French."

Her shoulders fell. "Yes, I am," she admitted.

"How long have you been here in Germany?"

"About five hours."

"Welcome!" he said, smiling. "How do you like it so far?"

She nodded and continued to eat. *He doesn't seem like the other Germans I've met. He doesn't seem to think he's superior to me because I am French. But it could be because he is so unattractive. He's significantly over-weight and not at all handsome. Still, he's kind.* "Are you from Berlin?" she asked, trying to make conversation.

"I went to the university here in Berlin, but I don't live here now. I am on holiday."

"Oh, where do you live?"

"Poland. I am a doctor. I am apprenticing under Dr. Mengele. Have you heard of him? He's very famous." Ernst sat up straight.

"Dr. Mengele." She dropped her spoon. *Could it be? Was it possible? Josef Mengele. André said my father's name was Josef Mengele. Could it really be him? It might not be. It could be someone else with that surname.* She was suddenly filled with interest, curiosity, fear, hatred, love, need, pride. "I think I've heard of him." She tried to sound casual. "What's this doctor's first name?"

"Josef Mengele. Have you heard of him?" Ernst asked again. She could tell by his tone of voice, he was trying to sound important and impressive.

"You are Mengele's apprentice?" she asked.

"Yes," he said. "I am. He chose me to come and work with him. I guess you could say I saved his life during the war. He thought I was a hero, but I only did what anyone would have done.

"That's impressive, very impressive," she said, but her thoughts were spinning. She hated her father for leaving her mother to bring up a child alone. And yet she wanted to have a family. She needed to meet him. In fact, she wanted it more than anything, now that she was so close to finding him. Gisele was filled with so many conflicting feelings toward her father. "Tell me about him," she said.

"There's nothing to tell." Ernst looked away. "He's a famous doctor."

"Nothing else? Nothing at all?"

He shrugged. "Not really."

She wanted to press him to tell her more about her father, but she couldn't because she felt him close up—as if he didn't want to say any more. He seemed to grow cold. At first she thought he was proud of working for this famous doctor. But when she wanted to know more about Mengele, Ernst's demeanor had changed. She couldn't imagine why he didn't want to talk about Mengele, but she decided not to press him.

I won't tell him that I think Mengele might be my father because, if he knows, he might decide to run away from me. He might be afraid Mengele would be angry that he found his illegitimate child. How many men, especially successful men, would want their bastard coming out of nowhere to destroy the life they built. No, I must not tell this man anything. She watched Ernst try to act as if he were at ease in her company even though it was obvious he was clumsy and uncomfortable.

Studying him, Gisele made a decision. She decided that if she could make this sad, clumsy man fall in love with her, he would be willing to take her to Poland with him. And once she was in Poland, she would find a way to meet her father. If she could just speak with her father, she would know just what kind of man he was. And she would no longer be haunted by questions. She would no longer spend her time wondering why her mother had invented a father figure who was a fisherman and why she had been so careful to hide Josef Mengele's true identity from her. *If my poor mother had not passed away, I would still not know anything about my real father. Why? Why had she been so reluctant to tell me? What is it about him that she was hiding?*

"Tell me more about your time at the university?" Gisele asked, trying to look interested in Ernst's every word. She remembered how the girls at the brothel had asked their clients questions and always pretended to listen intently to the answers.

"It makes the clients feel important. But never ask personal questions that might make them feel uncomfortable. Try to find things that they feel proud of. Men love to brag," one of the girls at the brothel had told her. At the time she hadn't thought she would ever want to make a man feel important. But now, she needed to do just that. If she could make Ernst feel important, he would enjoy her company so much that he would feel he'd fallen in love with her.

Ernst suspected nothing. He'd had very little experience with women, and so he was easily charmed. He told her about his studies, how he'd worked very hard. Then he told her about the tragic loss of his parents and how much he missed them. But he never mentioned his Jewish friends. She propped her chin onto her fist and gazed into his eyes as he spoke, just the way she'd seen the prostitutes do with their customers. When he made a joke about confusing two classes and how he'd gone to the wrong room, she laughed with him. And then she reached out to touch his hand. He looked at her, shocked, as if no one had ever touched him before. But then she smiled, and she gently ran her fingers over his. He softened and smiled back at her, his eyes gleaming with emotions. *This is working. He is falling for me*, she thought.

It was getting late. Gisele thought she might fall asleep at the table, so she said, "I am very tired. I've been traveling all day."

"How thoughtless of me. Of course, you must be exhausted. I am a little concerned because you fainted earlier."

"Do you think I am all right?" She was suddenly a little worried.

He must have seen the genuine fear in her eyes. In a gentle and reassuring voice, he said, "Please don't be afraid. I am sure you are all right, but just to be cautious, why don't I walk you back to your room. Where are you staying?"

"I rented a room in a cheap boarding house. It's right down the street from here."

"Wait here for a moment while I pay the bill, and then we'll go."

She didn't offer him any money, and he didn't seem to care. He took a large roll of reichsmarks out of his pocket and paid. Her eyes lit up when she saw the money. *It's just as I thought. He must be someone important working with Dr. Mengele who he claims is famous. I can see by the money he has that he's very successful, and rich. Besides that, I have to admit that he is a nice fellow. He's kind, and I can tell he really likes me. I sort of like him too. This is all going very well.*

He opened the door for her, and they walked outside. Then together they strolled slowly, in spite of the cold, all the way to the boarding house where she was staying. When they arrived, they were both shivering so they stood in the lobby for a moment. "Thank you for dinner. And . . . thank you for saving me," she said, looking up into his eyes.

He blushed. "I didn't save you. I just helped you get some food into an empty stomach."

"But you were there for me when I needed you." She reached up and touched his face. "And . . . also, thank you for a lovely evening. Your stories are fascinating. You are facinating."

He beamed. "I don't know what to say. Except, thank you for . . . well . . . for everything."

"Perhaps we can see each other again?" she asked.

His face was the color of ripe cherries, partially from the cold but also from the flattery. She knew he was flattered. She'd watched and learned so much about men from the girls at the brothel. And now that she was using that knowledge, she could see how easy it was to manipulate a man.

"I'd like that," he said. "I'd like it very much. Can I take you to dinner again tomorrow night?"

She nodded. "Yes. That would be just lovely."

"What time?"

"Is seven all right?" she asked.

"I'll be here in the lobby at seven tomorrow night."

She put her hands on his shoulders and reached up to plant a soft kiss on his lips. Then she turned and walked up the stairs to her room.

CHAPTER SIXTY-SIX

ERNST HAD NEVER KISSED A GIRL BEFORE. HE'D THOUGHT ABOUT IT, and many nights he'd dreamed about it, but he'd never done it. And she had kissed him so casually. Now as he walked back to his hotel, his feelings for her were already growing. *I can't believe a beautiful woman like her would be interested in me. I am not an attractive man. However, my position sounds like it would be admirable, especially since she doesn't know what really happens at Auschwitz. She thinks I am a doctor apprenticing under a very famous doctor. It must sound extraordinary. And that is all she really needs to know. If she ever found out the truth about what happens at Auschwitz, she would be repelled by me, and I couldn't blame her. But I am concerned that what she likes about me is my job. When I first mentioned it, she was obviously impressed.* He sighed. Then he thought, *Now that I have met her, I don't dare leave Mengele and go to work at some small, unknown hospital for a meager salary. I wouldn't want to risk losing her attention. No, I'll stay where I am. At least for now, until her and I get to know each other better. I realize that Mengele and the other German officers might not approve of my relationship with a French woman. But, I don't care what they say, or what they think. I am wild about her. And I will do whatever I can to keep her.*

That night he hardly slept. He replayed the kiss in his mind over and over again. He tingled with excitement and anticipation as he thought about their upcoming dinner date. *I wonder if she will kiss me again. Do I dare try to kiss her?*

The hours passed slowly the following day. At five o'clock, he took a shower and carefully combed his hair. Then he started to get dressed. First, he tried on the two sweaters he had with him but decided they were too casual. Then he put on several different shirts with gray trousers. Finally, he decided on a black suit, white shirt, and dark gray tie. It was the same suit he'd purchased to wear when he arrived at Auschwitz the first time. He didn't own another. Not because he couldn't afford it, but he hadn't needed it until now. At six thirty, he walked to the candy store where he bought the most expensive box of chocolates available. He paid extra to have them wrapped with a pretty pink ribbon which he thought would look lovely in her hair. Then he took his purchase and began walking to the boarding house. He was ten minutes early. Sitting in the lobby, holding the box of candy in his hand, he fidgeted. *What if she doesn't show up? What if she realizes that I am nothing special, and she just doesn't show up? Everyone who walks through that door stares at me. I can imagine what I must look like to them. Even the girl at the front desk is eyeing me. I'm sure she thinks I'm pathetic. She sees a fat, kind-of-ugly guy with a box of candy in his hand. That certainly is pitiful. I would be so embarrassed if Gisele stood me up.*

But she didn't. At precisely seven o'clock, Gisele came walking down the stairs. She was stunning in the high heels she received from one of the girls at the brothel who had discarded them, and her dark mink coat. Her golden hair fell in waves around her beautiful face. But it was her deep-sapphire-colored eyes that made him gasp. He stood up, flabbergasted. The candy fell to the floor. Picking it up quickly, he was embarrassed by his clumsiness. She walked right up to him and stood on her toes to plant a kiss on his lips. His hands trembled as he handed her the box of chocolates. "This is for you," he said. "It's chocolates. The best ones the candy store had."

"How sweet of you," she said. Then she reached up and touched his cheek. Ernst melted. He was in love.

CHAPTER SIXTY-SEVEN

AFTER DINNER THEY STARTED TO TAKE A WALK. IT WAS COLD, BUT IT was a beautiful clear night. Gisele looked up and said, "Look at the stars," her breath looking like white smoke as she spoke.

Ernst turned his head toward the sky. It was so dark with tiny specks of twinkling silver light. *I have been so lonely for so long*, he thought. He wanted to tell her that he loved her, but he was afraid it was too soon, and he might scare her away.

"My heavens, but it's so cold outside," she said, pulling her coat tighter around her. "Perhaps we can go to your hotel room and have a brandy or something after dinner."

"My room?" he said, then he realized how stupid he sounded. Clearing his throat, he said, "Yes my room. But, of course, what a brilliant idea. Of course, yes, let's go to my room." *Damn that stutter. I haven't had it in years, but I am afraid it will come back tonight because I am so nervous. I have never been with a woman before, let alone one who is such a beauty. I feel so afraid that I will do or say the wrong thing.* His hands were trembling. *How can she possibly see me as anything but a clumsy, overweight, fool. And now she wants to go to my room. Oh, how I wish I had straightened up the room before I left. I left all the clothes I tried on, on the chair. She's going to think I am a slob.*

Gisele hooked her arm into his, the way she had seen the girls at the brothel do when they took a man up to their rooms, then she turned her head so she could gaze up into his eyes and smiled as they walked down the street to his hotel room. When they entered the hotel, the heat immediately warmed them. "It's nice in here," she said, smiling.

"Yes," he answered, leading her to his room. His palms were wet as he turned the key in the door. Ernst looked around as she entered. He was embarrassed. "I'm sorry for the mess. I wasn't expecting company."

"It's all right," she said, reaching up and touching his face. She put the box of chocolates that he'd given her down on the night table and slipped off her coat. Then she began folding the clothes he'd left on the chair. Watching her carefully fold his things made his heart grow warm, and he began to think of what it might be like if she were his wife.

"I don't have any wine or brandy," he said. "Would you like to wait here while I go and purchase a bottle?"

"Sure. I would be happy to wait," Gisele said, sitting down on the chair in the corner and gazing out the window.

"I'll be right back," Ernst said. He had not yet taken his coat off, so he left the room quickly.

Once she was alone, Gisele searched through the dresser drawers. She found a huge stack of reichsmarks. *I was right; he is rich*, she thought as she counted the money. *This is a lot of money. I could take it all and run away. Of course, if I did, I'd have to check out of my room and look for another so he wouldn't be able to find me. But then I would never have an opportunity to meet my father. No, I won't do that. Ernst is a shy man who is easily manipulated. Poor thing. Well, he is easy, that's for sure. And I know I can make him love me. I could probably make him take care of me, maybe even marry me. Then, since he is a doctor, working under a very famous doctor, I would be well provided for. I would be a doctor's wife, and I would never want for anything. I would finally escape the poverty I grew up in.*

Ernst returned less than a half hour later. His face was bright red from the cold, but he had a bottle of fine brandy in his hand. "Sorry I took so long. You see, I had to go to a few stores to find this, but I didn't want to bring back just anything. I wanted to get something nice."

Gisele smiled. She loved wine with her meals and had come to enjoy the German beer, but she didn't care much for hard liquor. Still, she knew it would help him relax. And it was easy to see how nervous he was.

"Oh damn, I forgot to get glasses," he said, hitting himself in the forehead with the heel of his palm. "I'll be right back. I'll have to go and find a store where I can buy two glasses."

He was going to leave again, but she grabbed his arm. "It's all right. We can drink from the bottle. It will be more intimate that way."

Ernst stood there looking dumbfounded. He nodded, and she helped him take off his coat.

"You're so cold," she said, taking his hands in hers and putting them up to her lips. Then she softly blew hot air onto them. "Sit down, and let me take off your shoes."

He looked at her, puzzled, and she knew he didn't know what to say or do. But she did. She'd seen so many women seduce men that it was easy for her to imitate what she'd witnessed. She removed his shoes and socks. Then she removed her high heels. Gisele sat on the floor and took his feet into her small, delicate hands and massaged them. "There, that should help you warm up," she said.

He nodded. "Thank you," he said nervously.

She stood up in one graceful movement and opened the bottle of brandy. Then she took a swig and handed it to him. The hot liquid burned her throat, but it felt good, warm, and soothing. Then she sat down beside him, close enough that they were touching. "That's good brandy," she said, not really knowing the difference, but she was certain he'd bought good quality.

"I got the best I could." He smiled; his lips were quivering.

"I wish we had some music," Gisele said. "I'd love to dance with you."

"Oh, I don't dance."

"Why not?" she asked.

"I never learned how," he said.

"Come on, stand up. I'll teach you," she said. Then she stood up and took his hand. Melting into his arms she began to sing softly in French, and he moved with her. There were no actual steps to their dance, but her body flowed like a river over his. Then she moved slightly away from him and began to unbutton her dress. It fell to the floor. His eyes grew wide. She ran her index finger over his lips. Then she smiled. Standing before him in her slip, she took his hand and led him to the bed. He was trembling. "This is your first time?" she asked.

"I'm afraid so," he said.

"It's all right. Everyone must have a first time for everything, yes?" She smiled as she began to undress him. He stood there, not moving until she asked him to step out of his pants. "Now, come and lie down with me."

He did as she asked.

Gisele took the lead. She saw his penis respond to her quickly. But she made love to him slowly, building him up to a powerful climax. Once it was over, she lay in bed beside him.

"That was the most wonderful thing I've ever experienced," he said. "You are so beautiful." He was no longer stuttering.

She smiled. "You are a fantastic lover."

"Really, was I all right?"

"You were." She turned over and kissed him. "In fact, you were better than all right," she said as she reached for the box of chocolates on the nightstand and opened it. "And so . . . I give you a sweet reward." She giggled, popping a chocolate into his mouth.

"You are a sweet reward," he said. "The chocolate is delicious, but it doesn't compare to you." Then he took one of the candies out of the box and put it into her mouth.

"Oh, how I love chocolate," she said, closing her eyes and savoring the sweet flavor. "Mmm," she moaned, then she leaned down and kissed him. "You know what else I love?"

His heart was racing. "What?"

She giggled and winked at him. "I'm not telling you," she said flirtatiously. "At least not yet."

Gisele kissed him and then straddled him. She put his hands on her breasts. He felt encouraged as his shyness melted away. Gently he caressed her as if she were the most precious creature on earth.

They made love again. When they'd finished, Gisele stretched her back and lay down beside him. Then in a soft voice she said, "I have to go home. I have to get up early in the morning so I can go out and look for work."

"You can't stay the night with me?" His voice was clouded with disappointment.

"I'm sorry, darling. I can't." She touched his cheek, then she got out of bed and began getting dressed.

He looked at her with such strong disappointment in his eyes. A little smile curled the corners of her lips because that was just how she wanted him to feel. Gisele remembered how one of the girls told her, "Never give a man too much of your time. You don't want him to grow bored. Instead, send him away while he still wants more. That way you will make him hungry for you." At the time Gisele had laughed because she never thought she would need to use such information. But now as she lay with this man whom she had already decided she wanted to go to Poland with; the advice she'd been given by the prostitutes had certainly come in handy.

Ernst forced himself to get up. He reluctantly put on his clothes. "I do wish you could stay," he said. "In fact, I wish you could stay forever. You make me feel so good. You have no idea."

"I'm glad," she said, touching his arm. "But we should go. It's late."

He nodded. Then he helped her with her coat and carried her box of chocolates as he walked her back to the boarding house. When they arrived, he asked, his voice almost pleading, "Can I see you tomorrow?"

"I don't know. I am afraid I might be tired. After all, we are getting in so late tonight, then I will probably be job searching the entire day. Unless I find something right away, but that is doubtful."

"When can I see you again?"

"Perhaps the day after tomorrow?"

"Dinner? I would love to take you for dinner."

"All right." She smiled.

"Seven p.m.?"

"Yes, I'll meet you here in the lobby," Gisele said.

"I'll miss you. I will count the minutes until then."

She smiled at him. Then she turned and went inside. It was cold. The wind blew across his face, chilling him to the bone. But he stood outside the door of the boarding house for several minutes mesmerized by the wonder of it all. He stood there closing his eyes and just remembering her face. Finally, a gust of wind woke him out of his dream state, and he turned and walked back to his hotel room alone.

Oh, how he did miss her. The following day, he could think of nothing else. He buried his face in the pillow where she'd laid her head. *It smelled like soap. If she were my wife*, he thought, *I'd buy her the finest shampoo from Paris. I would buy her the most beautiful clothes and jewelry. In fact, she would want for nothing.*

When he awoke the following morning, he was depressed because he knew he would have to wait another day until he saw her again. The hours seemed like years. He decided that he needed to distract himself, so he made a trip to the university to visit with one of his former professors. But even as they spoke of old times, his mind was elsewhere. He thought of Gisele's golden hair, the softness of her touch. The warm and wonderful secrets of her body.

"What are you smiling about?" the old professor asked.

"Was I smiling?"

"You certainly were."

"I'm just happy to be back here visiting with you," Ernst lied.

The professor laughed a little as he knew that Ernst was lying, but he didn't say anything about it; all he said was, "It's good to see you again."

Night finally arrived. Ernst lay awake in his bed thinking about Gisele. *What if she was lying to me? What if she didn't want to see me tonight because, after we made love, she didn't like me anymore? I had no experience. What if I was a terrible lover, but she just didn't want to tell me? Then again, if she didn't like me, would she have agreed to see me tomorrow, or would she have made up another excuse? Maybe she didn't know how to get rid of me.* He agonized, going back and forth, arguing within himself. *And to make matters worse, I only have two days left in Berlin, then it will be time for me to return to Poland and to return to work at that horrible place. I can't bear the idea that I must say goodbye to her, forever. I don't know what I am going to do. I must see her again even after I leave here.*

He was too anxious to sleep, worried that he'd finally found happiness, only to lose it. Ernst sat up in bed and stared at a small beam of moonlight peeking through the drapes that covered the window. He picked up the bottle of brandy he'd bought—it was over half full. Neither he nor Gisele had consumed much. Taking a long swig helped him calm down a little. *She knows I am a doctor. She knows I have a good position. I wonder if she would consider marrying me and moving to Poland. It's probably too soon to ask, but I don't have time to waste. I could promise her prosperity and a good life filled with all the comforts she could ask for. Putting up with Mengele and that horrific place would be worth it if I had Gisele to go home to every night. I'm so afraid that it might scare her off if I ask her to be my wife. But if I don't, I will soon be on my way back to Poland, and she will find someone else. A woman as beautiful as she is won't be alone for long. Some man will scoop her up for his own. I must try. I will put my fears aside, and find a way to make her see that she would be happy with me. I must.*

CHAPTER SIXTY-EIGHT

THE FOLLOWING DAY, GISELE CONSIDERED GOING OUT TO LOOK FOR a job, but she found the idea of walking in the cold repugnant. Instead, she turned over in her warm bed and pulled the blanket over her. Then she closed her eyes and imagined what life would be like if she were the wife of an important doctor. Not only an important doctor, but the apprentice of an even more important doctor, and to make things more interesting, she was fairly certain she was his daughter. The stigma of being the child of the town prostitute would be gone. She would never again be forced to wash a floor or clean a toilet or take orders from a girl like Annette, who thought she was better than her. And Ernst was nice, not attractive and not exciting, but nice. Making love with him didn't cause her soul to dance. She'd heard the girls at the house say that some men had that effect on them. But she couldn't imagine it. After all, no man had ever touched her heart. And she preferred to keep it that way.

Gisele liked being in control. Falling in love, even falling into lust, would strip her of that control. *I know I did the right thing making him wait a day to see me. If all goes according to my plan, he should be thinking about how much he will miss me when he returns to Poland. And he won't want to go back without me. But I do so wish I could rush things. I hate the uncer-*

tainty of waiting. What if it all fails, he leaves, and I am here in Berlin without a job, and with a terrible future looming over me. She didn't like that thought, so she climbed out of bed, got dressed, then she tossed on her old wool coat and went downstairs. *I'll talk with the manager of the boarding house. Maybe he has an opening for an employee. After I speak with him, I'll go to the store and purchase a little food and some inexpensive ersatz coffee to bring back to my room.*

"I'd like to see the manager here," Gisele said as she walked up to the receptionist at the front desk.

"Is something wrong? Is there something I can help you with?"

"No, nothing is wrong. I just had a question for him. Perhaps you can help me. Do you know if they need any help here? I need a job," Gisele asked.

"We always need maids," the girl said.

On my hands and knees scrubbing floors again, Gisele thought. *I'll take it if I have to, but maybe there is something else I could do.* "Do you know if they need any other help?"

"What skills do you have?"

Gisele shrugged. *I have no skills. I can't type or take dictation. I wish I knew how to work a switchboard like the receptionist. So, what can I do? All I can do is work as a maid. Oh, how I hope this plan I have with Ernst works.* "I don't really have any skills to speak of."

"Then it's going to be rather difficult for you to find work other than cleaning. You could look for a job caring for someone's child," the receptionist offered.

"Well, thank you anyway," Gisele said. Then she tossed her scarf around her neck and left the boardinghouse. As she walked down the street she thought, *Well, if things don't work out with Ernst, I suppose I'll be forced to take the job as a maid. But before I do that, I could always sell that fur coat.*

She walked into a bakery. It smelled wonderful, and it was warm and cozy from the baking. "Do you need any help here?" she asked the woman at the counter.

The woman shook her head. "I'm sorry. We don't," she said.

Gisele nodded. *I would have liked to work here, at least during the winter.* "I'll take one of those brown breads," she said.

"Yes, Fräulein," the woman answered, and she began to wrap Gisele's purchase.

As she waited, Gisele remembered how the girls at the brothel had turned up their noses at the brown bread that was made with sawdust. They demanded that the madam purchase only white bread. And Gisele, too, had preferred it. But the brown bread was much cheaper, and she couldn't afford to spend unwisely. *I must watch every penny until I have some idea of what the future holds for me.*

Next, she walked to a general store where she purchased a small amount of coffee. Then she took all of it up to her room to eat. She was hungry, so even the sandy-tasting bread and black, sugarless coffee tasted wonderful. As she nibbled the bread, she remembered the scrumptious dinner that she'd eaten the night before with Ernst, and she wished she had agreed to see him tonight. *If only to have another good meal. But it was wiser to keep him waiting*, she reminded herself.

The following evening, Gisele got ready for her date. She wore her prettiest dress. It showed just a small bit of cleavage. *I wish I wasn't so skinny. My breasts are almost nonexistent*, she thought as she stared at herself in the mirror. It was true; she was slender, but she was tall and lanky and very graceful. Once she applied the lipstick, eyeliner, mascara, and rouge, she looked stunning instead of just innocent.

At 7 p.m. that evening, Gisele pranced down the stairs to the lobby where Ernst was waiting. He had another box with him. This time it didn't look like chocolates. He looked up at her just as she started walking toward him.

"You look beautiful," he said, and she could see the admiration in his eyes. Then he handed her the box.

"It looks too big to be chocolates," she said.

"It's not. Actually, I couldn't figure out what to do with myself yesterday when I couldn't see you. So, after I visited with my old college professor, I went shopping. I saw this dress, and I thought of you. I hope you're not offended."

"Offended? By a new dress? What girl would be offended by receiving a new dress." She excitedly tore the string off the box and opened it. When she saw the deep-blue dress, she gasped. "It's gorgeous," she said.

"It's cashmere. Feel how soft it is?"

"I've never owned anything so lovely."

He smiled. "I'm really glad you like it."

"Like it! I love it! Can you wait for just a few minutes while I go and put it upstairs in my room?"

"Of course."

After Gisele put her new dress away, they walked to a famous German restaurant a few streets away. As they entered, Ernst said, "I've never been here before, but I know that a lot of the important officials in the party eat here. Dr. Mengele said he always comes to this place when he is in Berlin. So, the food should be good."

"It's so pretty. Like a fantasy," she gushed as she observed the white tablecloths, the cream-colored china plates with tiny gold swastikas engraved all around the trim, the candles burning on each table even though candles were scarce and should be rationed. At the tables she saw SS officers dressed in dark, well-made uniforms sitting beside women in elegant dresses with silk stockings and leather high heels.

The food was expensive, very expensive. Gisele was intimidated. She didn't know what to order. "I don't know what to have," she said, feeling that she sounded less worldly than she wanted to appear.

"Do you like schnitzel?"

"Of course," she said, not sure what it was.

He ordered two plates of schnitzel with potatoes and carrots, and a green salad. "How about a bottle of wine?"

"Yes, I would love that."

Ernst had plenty of money to spend. He hadn't spent much since he'd started working. He'd eaten modest meals at home and never went shopping unless he absolutely needed something. So now, in order to impress her, he ordered a bottle of good red wine.

They ate slowly. "Tell me all about you," he said.

"What do you want to know?" she said, wishing he hadn't asked her anything.

"Where did you grow up? What were your parents like? Do you have any brothers or sisters? I want to know everything there is to know about you."

She put down her fork. Her appetite was suddenly fading. *How can I tell him the truth about me? If he knows who I am, he will surely lose interest.* "Must we talk about the past? I don't want to talk about where I came from. I would rather discuss where I am going."

"I'm so sorry. I offended you."

She shrugged. "You didn't. I mean, your question shouldn't have offended me. It's just that I had a rough beginning. I think you already know that I am not German."

"I know, you're French. You sang that delightful little song to me in French. I thought it was terribly charming." He smiled.

"I didn't want to tell you that I wasn't German."

"I could tell by your accent right away. You do speak excellent German though." Then he added, "But why would you not want me to know the truth?"

"Because a man like you, an important man, would never take a girl like me seriously. I mean . . . you would probably be looking for a girl who is a, how do you say it, an Aryan?"

He laughed. "Yes, that is how we say it. But you needn't worry. I do take you seriously. Very seriously." Then he boldly reached for her hand. She looked up into his eyes.

"You look stunning by the candlelight," he said.

She looked down and batted her eyelashes.

"I don't know how you feel about me. But I know how I feel about you," he said, and she could hear his voice cracking; his hands were trembling. "I like you a lot. In fact"—he cleared his throat—"I . . . think I am falling in love with you."

She reached up and touched his cheek. "I think I am falling in love with you too. And that's why it's so important to me that you don't see me as just your good-time girl. Do you know what I mean by that?"

He shook his head.

"I don't want to be the girl who you bed during your holiday.

But then once the time comes for you to return to your life, you marry a girl who is more appropriate. A German girl."

"I would never do that to you," he said earnestly. "I don't see you as a good-time girl. In fact, I realize that we hardly know each other, but there is something about you that makes me feel that . . . well . . . h-how do I say this?" he stammered. "I think you are the one for me. When I look at you, I see the woman I want for my future wife." Then he giggled. "I can't believe I just asked you to marry me. I hope you don't think I am crazy. I mean, after all, we just met. But what I said was true. I don't want to go back to Poland without you. Since we've met, I can see a wonderful future for us." He looked into her eyes, then he looked away. "I'm sorry. I hope you aren't angry."

"Angry? Why would I be angry?"

"I hope you don't think I am moving too fast."

"I don't. Because I feel the same way."

His heart swelled. It felt as if it would jump right out of his chest and twirl and dance with joy. Suddenly he felt fearless and jubilant. "Gisele," he said in a serious tone, "would you ever consider marrying me? I don't know if you would want to move to Poland, but I think you would be happy if you did. I have a good job there. I earn a lot of money, and I could give you a good life. I would treat you well. I promise. And if you don't want to live in Poland, I'll quit my job and move back to Germany, or even to France. Whatever you'd like."

"Definitely not France," she said almost under her breath. Then she shivered a little in disbelief. "Are you really asking me to be your wife?" she said. *I can't believe it worked. I can't believe he is falling right into my plan. He wants to marry me. My days of poverty are over. I should take it slow though. I can't grab at his offer, or he'll have second thoughts. I must seem like I am unsure. I must make him wait while I decide.*

"Yes," he said, his palms wet with sweat. "I am asking you to marry me."

She hesitated for a moment, took a long breath, then said, "Well, I don't know. I will have to think it over."

"I am supposed to return to work in Poland in a couple of days .

. ." he said. "Shall I tell Dr. Mengele that I've decided to quit my job and will stay in Germany? That way we can continue to see each other, and you would have time to decide."

"Oh no. Don't quit your job. You mustn't do that." Then quickly, she added, "I'll move to Poland."

"You'll marry me?" he said, his voice trembling.

"Yes," she said. "I will." *Why should I make him wait? I can see no reason. He already likes the idea. I know he wants to make love tonight. But I won't let him. I'll keep him hungry, so he is crazy with his desire to have me. Then I'll suggest we get married at the courthouse tomorrow morning. I'll tell him that if we are married as soon as possible, I will go with him when he leaves for Poland.*

"You will? You really will?"

She nodded.

He stood up and walked over to her. Then he pulled her to him and hugged her tightly and kissed her. "Gisele, you will be my wife?"

"Yes," she said again. Then she hesitated for a moment. "In fact, why don't we go to the courthouse and get married in the morning?"

"Tomorrow? Tomorrow morning?" he said giddily.

"Yes, tomorrow."

"All right. I would like that very much," he said. Then blushing shyly, he added, "Perhaps you would like to spend the night in my room with me? Tonight, I mean?" He felt good, confident. Alive.

She touched his cheek. "No, we must not. You see, it's bad luck for the bride and groom to sleep together on the night before they are wed. I'll go back to my own room and pack my things. Then I'll meet you at the courthouse in the morning."

"All right," he said. "You have made me so happy."

She smiled. "And you have made me happy too."

Gisele went back to her room and packed the small suitcase she'd brought with her when she left her childhood home in Marseille. Everything she owned fit into that small, well-worn valise. But as she packed, she smiled because she was certain that soon she would have everything she'd ever dreamed of: lovely clothes, a nice home, and a secure future.

That night Gisele was so excited she could hardly sleep. She wished she were more attracted to Ernst but reminded herself that he was the doorway to the new life of her dreams. *Ernst is very kind, generous, and considerate. That should be enough,* she thought, but still, it was difficult for a girl of eighteen to settle for a marriage that held no passion for her. There was a restlessness inside of her that she was fighting against.

Dawn finally broke. It had snowed the night before, and the ground was lightly dusted with soft white flakes. She looked out the window at the snow-covered tops of the trees. *It is so lovely. And my future will be lovely too. It's an omen.* She smiled to herself.

She tried to eat a slice of the brown bread she'd purchased the day before, but she had no appetite. She was too excited and even a little nervous. *I hope nothing goes wrong. I hope he doesn't change his mind for any reason,* she thought as she put on the blue dress he'd given her as a gift the previous night. When she looked in the mirror, she gasped. "I am beautiful," she uttered. "I am almost as pretty as Annette was." She glanced at the wooden table where she'd left the loaf of bread, and because she'd always lived in poverty, she wrapped what was left of it in a towel and put it in her purse. Then she took her suitcase and made her way to the courthouse, careful not to slip on the ice with her high heels.

Ernst was already waiting for her. He was sweating, dressed in his suit with his hair carefully combed. And he was pacing back and forth.

When Gisele walked in, wearing her fur coat and blue dress, he stood staring at her, stunned by her beauty. She smiled at him. He returned her smile, but his lips were trembling. Walking over to him, she stood on her toes and kissed him. He let out a sigh. "I am so glad to see you," he said.

By noon they were husband and wife. His heart sang. He was beaming from head to toe as they walked hand in hand to a small, quiet café where they had a peaceful lunch. Then the newly married couple walked back to his hotel room where they made love until they fell asleep. When they awoke, it was the middle of the night;

they were both very hungry, so they finished what was left of the box of chocolates and then they made love again.

"We should get some sleep. The train to Poland leaves at nine tomorrow morning," he whispered in her ear. "I'll call Dr. Mengele first thing tomorrow and tell him the good news about us getting married. I'll let him know that I am bringing the new Frau Neider back to Poland with me."

"It sounds so funny to hear. I am Frau Neider," she said proudly. "I am Gisele Neider."

"Yes, you are," he said.

And I will never have to scrub another floor or clean another toilet again. Now I will have maids to do it all for me! she thought.

CHAPTER SIXTY-NINE

DR. MENGELE HAD JUST FINISHED WITH A TRANSPORT AND WAS ON his way to have something to eat when one of the guards came racing toward him. "Dr. Mengele, I have something to tell you."

"Yes, what is it?" Mengele said, annoyed.

"A friend of mine, you might know him. His name is Hermann Weber. He is a guard at the ghetto in Warsaw."

"The name is not familiar. What is your point, Breuer?" Mengele said, not hiding the annoyance he felt. He hated the way Hans Breuer was always trying to win his favor. It got on his nerves.

"Well, the last time I saw Weber, which was last year, we were talking about you. Only good things were said, of course."

"Of course," Mengele said even more annoyed. He started walking faster, making it hard for Breuer to keep up with him. "Would you get to the point already. You're just rambling, wasting my time."

"Yes, yes of course. Yes, well, at that time I told Weber how much you liked twins and, well, I guess he saw two identical twins when he was at work in the ghetto. So, because of our conversation last year, Weber drove them here to bring them to you."

"He brought me twins?"

"Yes, two little girls. Jews."

"Hmmm," Mengele said as he stopped walking, "let me see them."

Breuer ran back to where he'd left Perle and Bluma hugging each other and their sister, Shoshana, tightly. Perle was softly weeping. But Breuer didn't notice. He just yelled at them, "Come on, follow me." He pushed Bluma and she almost fell. "Mach schnell," he said as he rushed them over to where Dr. Mengele was standing. Ruth followed behind. Mengele looked at the girls. "Hmmm. Cute little things, even if they are Jews," he said. "And who are these two older ones?" He was looking at Shoshana and Ruth.

"I am their sister, sir," Shoshana said, looking down at the ground.

"And you?" Mengele looked at Ruth.

"You don't know me? You don't know who I am?" Ruth said.

Shoshana cringed. She knew how arrogant Ruth could be, but this was not the time for arrogance. And she was afraid for Ruth.

Mengele let out a loud guffaw. "Know you? Why would I know you? You're nothing but a Jew rat."

"I am a singer. I'm famous. My name is Ruth Klofsky," Ruth said proudly.

"A famous singer. I see. Well, you're no one but a filthy Jew here. Jews are rats; perhaps you are a singing rat." He laughed hard, amused at his own joke. Then he turned to Breuer and said, "Send the singing rat to the showers," Mengele said to Breuer, then he turned to look at Shoshana. "Not this one. Send this one with her twin sisters so she can look after them. She's a pretty one; quiet too." He chuckled a little. "I might just have something special planned for her."

"Erich," Breuer called out to one of the guards. Then indicating Ruth, he said, "Take this Jew to the showers for Dr. Mengele. I have to bring these three other ones over to Mengele's room because of the twins."

Erich nodded and pulled Ruth by the arm.

"Don't touch me," Ruth said.

Erich hit her across the cheek with the butt of his gun. Ruth let out a scream. Shoshana gasped. A deep, gaping wound opened on Ruth's cheek.

Perle began to weep loudly. "I'm scared. I'm so scared," she said, clinging to Shoshana.

"It's all right," Shoshana tried to reassure her little sisters. But she hardly felt confident in her statement. She was terrified too. But she took both of their hands and followed quickly behind Breuer.

Once Breuer was gone, and Shoshana and her sisters were left in the room with the other twins, Bluma sat down on the floor and started to cry. "I want to go home. I want to go wherever Mama and Papa went. I don't want to be here."

"We can't leave. You heard what Hermann, Ruth's friend, said before he left us. He said if we try to escape from here, we'll be shot. I saw a guard with the gun sitting up in the tower when we arrived. He was watching our every move. And even if we could get past that guard, you must remember what was said about the barbed wire. It can slice your head off. We can't try to escape. For now, we'll be safe here. Let me think about what to do. I promise I will try to figure out some way to get us out of here."

"Do you think you can get us out?" Bluma asked.

"I don't know. But I am certainly going to try my best."

"Shoshana," Perle said, "do you remember my dream of the doctor? That nightmare I used to have of the evil doctor?"

"I remember," Shoshana said.

"That was him," Perle said. "That doctor was him."

Shoshana trembled. *How could I ever forget that dream?* she thought.

The room was silent for several minutes.

"Where did that guard take Ruth?" Bluma asked.

"I just wish I knew. For some reason the doctor thought she needed to take a shower," Shoshana said.

A girl, who was sitting beside her twin sister on the floor, looked over at Shoshana and said, "No one ever comes back from those showers. You see the fires in those chimneys over there?" She pointed a dirty finger toward the window where Shoshana saw smoke rising from a chimney. "Those fires are burning up the bodies of the people who were sent to the showers."

"That's insane," Shoshana said.

"It is insane, but it's true," a young boy, the other twin, said. "From what we hear, the showers aren't really showers. They don't spray water; they spray poisonous gas."

Now Bluma and Perle turned pale. They were holding each other tightly and weeping.

"All right. That's enough. We don't want to hear any more," Shoshana said to the others, then she turned to her sisters and said, "Let's get settled in here."

"Who are you?" a little girl asked. "What are your names?"

"I'm Shoshana. This is my sister Bluma, and this is my sister Perle."

"I'm Esther, and this Rachael."

"I'm Jacob and this is Daniel."

"I'm Renate. I don't know where they have taken my brother, René, or our parents."

The introductions went around the room until everyone had been introduced.

Bluma and Perle had never had outside friends, but when the other twins came over and began to talk to them, they seemed to enjoy the conversation. As they were talking with Esther, Rachael, and Renate, Shoshana watched them, and she was reminded of how young and innocent they were. It seemed that they forgot their fears for a moment, and the four of them were just children at play. It made her sad and terrified to think of the reality of the situation. Sitting down in front of the window, Shoshana watched the smoke shooting out of the chimneys. She thought of Ruth and what the little boy had said. It was cold, very cold in the room. She shivered. Then softly, under her breath, she said a prayer in Hebrew, but she found she could not dismiss the child's words. And she was hoping that the little girl was wrong about the showers.

CHAPTER SEVENTY

THE PHONE RANG IN DR. MENGELE'S OFFICE. HE WAS NIBBLING ON A piece of raisin strudel and sipping a cup of coffee.

"Who is it?" he called out to his secretary.

"It's Dr. Neider," she said. "He asked to speak to you."

Mengele picked up the receiver. "This is Dr. Mengele."

"It's Ernst. I am on my way back today. But, I also have some good news."

"Oh? Do tell," Mengele said, a little annoyed at being disturbed.

"I got married."

"Married?" Dr. Mengele said. "You're joking."

"No, I met a wonderful girl in Berlin. She's the love of my life. We're on our way to Poland today. I'll be back at work tomorrow."

"Well, well, perhaps I was right. Perhaps this little holiday was exactly what you needed."

"It was just what I needed, Dr. Mengele. It was."

Mengele sat back in his chair and sucked on the end of his pen. *The love of your life, huh? Well, this should be fun.* Mengele enjoyed testing human nature. It intrigued him to see how people would react when they were put into unimaginable situations. *This marriage will give me an opportunity to test Ernst's inner strength. I can see what he is really made of. I know he thinks I am a monster. Let's see how much misery he can endure before he snaps. Once he does, he will discover that he is no angel. He will be appalled, but he will find that the very same monster he sees within me, lives within him too.*

AUTHORS NOTE

I always enjoy hearing from my readers, and your thoughts about my work are very important to me. If you enjoyed my novel, please consider telling your friends and posting a short review on Amazon. Word of mouth is an author's best friend.

Also, it would be my honor to have you join my mailing list. As my gift to you for joining, you will receive 3 **free** short stories and my USA Today award-winning novella complimentary in your email! To sign up, just go to my website at www.RobertaKagan.com

I send blessings to each and every one of you,

Roberta

Email: roberta@robertakagan.com

Turn the page to read the first chapter of book three in The Auschwitz Twins Series, *The Auschwitz Twins*.

THE AUSCHWITZ TWINS

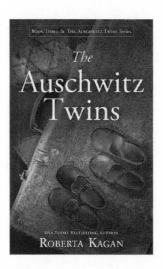

The Warsaw Ghetto, in Poland, Winter 1943
An Overcrowded Cattle Train

The entire box car trembled as the door slammed shut. The sound penetrated right through Naomi Aizenberg's heart like a butcher knife. The train car was dark. The only light came in tiny slivers that entered through the small cracks in the wooden slats.

The train shuddered and shifted as it sprung to life. Everyone was jittery and nervous. They are stuffed wall to wall leaning against each other. Naomi has never been so close to strangers before. The frightened people chatter until they are silenced and unnerved by the sound of a loud whistle. An odor of sweat filled the air. It is mixed with a strange smell, acidic, dirty, nauseating. Naomi decided that it was the stench of fear and desperation but most of all loss of hope.

Her body trembled with anxiety. Not only was she worried about where they might be going, but when they boarded the train, Naomi was separated from her three daughters. She has no idea where her children are and she is terrified. They are her life, without them she knows that she cant go on. Hershel, her husband is standing beside her. She longed to turn to him for reassurance. If only he was the kind of man who would put his arms around her and hold her tightly. But she knew better. Herschel was cold, and when he was frightened or threatened instead of turning to her so they could comfort each other, he grew even more distant. Still, even though she knew he would not give her much warmth or affection, right now, she needed him. And she would take whatever crumbs he might be willing to provide. Theirs had been an arranged marriage, one that her father had wanted. And although Naomi had succumbed to her father's wishes, things between her and Herschel had never been quite right. They were different in too many ways. He was prideful and hard refusing to ever show weakness. But Naomi was warm, and she craved human touch. Right now, as they stood surrounded by strangers, she was panicked inside. She desperately needed Herschel to ease her mind. and so she hungered for anything that might calm her. And although he'd never been one to lessen her anxiety, she still craved any small amount of help that his familiar voice might bring. There was no one else she could talk to. She didn't know anyone else on the train. And she was finding it unbearable to be in the darkness bumping along the rails all alone with her thoughts.

"I am shaking. What will become of our girls? I don't know where they are." Naomi asked Hershel in a small voice. "I am sick with worry about them. OH, how I wish they were here with us. At least we could face whatever happens in the future together as a family. Right now all we can do is worry about them."

"Don't worry so much. You're always worrying bout something. They'll either get on the next train or they have already boarded this one and they are traveling in another box car. Everything will be all right. You'll see. Shoshana will watch them." He said coldly.

It was just as she had expected. Hershel had withdrawn into himself. *I might as well be all alone here.* She thought. *He can't give me what I need. He has never been willing or able to give me what I need.*

Naomi leaned against her husband, but he moved away. "This is not what the guards promised us when they told us that if we boarded the train we would be transported to a place where we would have a better life. They said the train would be comfortable. But that's a lie. This is anything but comfortable. Look at us. We're stuffed in here. I can hardly breathe. And people have started using the bucket to relieve themselves. The smell is making me sick. I want to vomit" Naomi said

"I know. You're right. It's true. The Nazis are good for nothing liars. And I should have seen this coming. But I didn't. I let them lie to me. I wanted to believe them. And I am kicking myself for trusting those bastards. I am not stupid man. How could I fall for such a trick?" Herschel said there was anger and bitterness in his voice. He wrapped his arms around his chest and tried to push away from the strangers who were smothering him on ever side.

"Where do you think they are taking us?" Naomi asked

"Who knows. They have their own agenda, their own ideas about us and everything else. Nazis look like men, but I tell you they are not even human."

"I wish I knew where we were headed and how long we are going to have to be on this train."

He sighed "If I were to wager, I would say that I believe they are taking us somewhere where they can work us good and hard. Why not? They figure they'll use us for free labor. They see us as nothing but Jews." He said

"What kind of work do you think they will have us do?"

"I don't have any idea. But my guess is they're going to work us and work us hard. But if they want us to have the strength to work, they're going to have to feed us. So, we can only hope that in the end we find out that we made a good choice getting on this train."

"I hope so. We were always hungry in the ghetto. They hardly gave us enough in rations." She said

"The rations in the ghetto were terrible. If it weren't for the young boys who worked on the black market that sold me the extra food we would have all starved to death.

"Oh Herschel. We wasted so much time hurting each other before the Nazi's came to power. If I had known then what I know now, I would have tried harder to make our lives better."

"Yes." He said softly

"You have regrets too?" She asked

"What good do regrets do anyone?" He said "We are here now. Let's make the best of it. Perhaps we are going somewhere where we can get more food and live a better life."

" I just wish I could hold my daughters." She wanted to lay her head on his shoulder and weep, but she knew that he would not welcome her affection. He would gently pry himself away from her the way he always did when she got too close.

"All right, listen to me." He said with his usual voice of author-ity. "If we can't find our girls we arrive at our destination, we'll tell the Nazi's we want to go back to the ghetto to get them." Hershel said

"And you think they'll let us, just like that?"

"We'll see. I have a some money. I'll pay them off if I have to." Then he sighed "I'll do whatever I have to do to take care of this. Now, if you don't mind, I don't feel much like talking. I need some peace and quiet. I can't hear myself think and I need some time to sort out my thoughts. Why don't you lean up against the wall and try to get some rest. I know it's not easy to sleep standing up. But, you won't fall down if you fall asleep. You couldn't there are too many people in here. We're all stuck holding each other up."

She nodded. "All right." She said in a small voice. Tears ran down her cheeks. *I'm glad it's dark and he can't my face. He would be angry that I am crying. But I can't help myself. I know it's a sin, but I can't help myself, I wish Eli were beside me instead of Hershel. He would understand my feelings. And even though he, like the rest of us, would be powerless against these guards, he would at least hold me and comfort me." She thought. Then she reminded herself " These are selfish thoughts; I should be glad he is in Brittan with his wife. He is safe there. Our love for each other was a sin. I knew it was wrong, I was a married woman and he was a young scholar. But we couldn't help it, we fell totally and desperately in love. It was wrong, but those were the best days of my life. Our love affair has been over for years. And,I am sure he has gotten over it. But I never did, not even when he got married. I don't think I ever will.*

Chapter

Even with all the degradation and mistreatment that he and his family had been forced to endure, Hershel Aizenberg had never felt so humiliated, angry as he was stuffed in to this train. And although he was too prideful to ever admit it to anyone, he was terrified. Before he arrived at the ghetto he'd been a high powered lawyer in Warsaw. He'd always been in control. But the Nazis had stripped him of everything. He looked around him. In each tiny ray of light he could see expressions of fright and terror on the faces of his fellow passengers. Other's had fallen asleep and were leaning against thee strangers beside them.

He was remembering how he and Naomi had been separated from their children. It was Shoshana's fault. Shoshana, his head strong eldest daughter. They hadn't spoken in months, because she had defied him and refused to marry the boy he'd arranged for her. During those months, he had forbidden his two younger twin daughters from having any contact with Shoshana. But when they saw Shoshana at the train station, they went running to her. He'd asked the guards to allow him to wait for his daughters to return, but they had laughed at him and forced him and Naomi at gunpoint to board the train without the twins. And now he had no idea where they were. Naomi had stopped talking and for that he was grateful. He had no answers for any of her questions, and he hated to admit that he just didn't know. She was standing beside him. He could hear her weeping softly. He wanted to put his arm around her, to hold her close to him and to comfort her, but he knew that if he showed even the slightest bit of weakness this whole hard exterior of his would crack and he would be nothing but a useless, blubbering, and pathetic excuse for a man. The train ride was rough, no water and no food. As the hours passed, some of the passengers became motion sick, other's just needed to relieve themselves. And the smell of vomit, urine and feces grew strong in the already stifling air.

A woman was standing just a few feet from Naomi was embracing an infant who had been crying when the train ride began. Now the baby was silent. Herschel thought that the child must be dead dead. As the train took a sharp turn a ray of dust filled light illuminated the woman's face. Hershel caught the dull look in her eyes as she sang the same song in Yiddish to the dead infant, rocking the child over and over again. From the silhouette of her shadow, Herschel could see she was tall slender girl who wore a head covering of some kind. Her voice c cracked like tiny broken bells, as she sang the familiar lullaby to her child. This sight of her made Herschel feel sick to his stomach because she reminded him of his eldest daughter. *She is probably about Shoshana's age.* He thought. *And if Shoshana had listened to me and married Albert, she might even have had a child by now.*

As time passed, Herschel felt worse and worse. His lack of the ability to control the outcome of this situation made him want to panic. But he knew better. If he went into a rage it wouldn't help anything. All it would do was weaken him. So, he sat quietly chewing on his lip, but his hands trembled. He watched the dancing tiny rays of light as they disappeared when night fell and then return hours later at dawn. And by this system of dark and light, he figured that they had been riding on this train for three days.

Then one morning as the rays of light began to enter the box car again, the train came to an abrupt stop. The train jerked everyone forward. Those who'd drifted off to sleep were awakened. Several people began banging their fists on the sides of the train car. They shouted "Let us out. It's hot in here. We need food. We need water. Help us please. People are dying."

And it was true. It was hard to tell who was alive and who was dead because of how tightly packed they all were. But, there were those who no longer spoke or moved.. Hershel wondered how many other people were dead in the other overfilled box cars. The passengers kept pounding on the walls and doors, but no one answered. They were so relentless that Herschel wondered if their fists were bleeding. But, finally, after a long while they stopped beating on the wood. There was snoring and Herschel knew that at least some of them had fallen asleep from the heat, hunger and pure exhaustion.

The train began to move again. Naomi lay her head against the wall and slept. Hershel watched her. *God bless her, she can sleep anywhere.* That is such a gift. He thought and a sad smile came over his face. *I know that she is worried sick about our daughters, Bluma and Perle. I know she's worried about Shoshana as well. I must admit that I am worried too. But worry doesn't do anyone any good. And I know she likes to talk things out, but I've found that discussing things that are upsetting only makes them worse. I am relieved that at least for the moment, she is quiet, not asking me any questions. And, she is resting.* He longed to reach out and touch her shoulder, to caress her and let her know that no matter what the future held for their family, they would face it together. But he couldn't bring himself to do it. His fingers trembled with the longing to caress her. Herschel turned his head away so as not to look at her. He had learned as a child to close himself off from feelings. His father had laughed at him whenever he was emotional, he'd laughed and called him weak like a woman. This hurt young Herschel deeply because he admired his father, and so, he fashioned himself to be like him. At first it was difficult, but as the years went on, the wall Herschel built became thicker and unable to penetrate. By the time he was married, he was strong, to his father's delight he never wept like a woman, but he was cold. And now, because he was used to pushing his feelings aside, he could not open his heart and tell Naomi what he wanted her to hear. He knew that they might be close to the end of their lives and he wished that for once he could tell her just how much she had really meant to him all of the years of their marriage. Herschel opened his mouth to speak, to say the things his heart longed to express, but the words would not come. Instead, he just sighed and watched her sleep. A slight wind blew through one of the openings in the slats. He sucked the fresh air in and swallowed it deeply. Then he leaned his head back against the wood and closed his eyes. Hershel thought about his oldest daughter, Shoshana, they had not spoken for almost a year. He was regretting that decision at the moment. He knew that the twins had missed her terribly as did Naomi who was devastated when Hershel had thrown Shoshana out of the apartment where they lived in the ghetto. At the time Herschel was angry, and when he was angry he was stubborn. Naomi begged him to reconsider, but he refused. He'd had gone through the motions of sitting shiva, mourning as if Shoshana were dead. In fact, even now, as he stood in this crowded train car he still wore the torn cloth of mourning on his lapel. He reached up and touched the piece of cloth. *I don't want to scare Naomi but I don't trust the Nazis. I don't know where they are taking us. The truth is we may never see Shoshana again, and I may never have had the chance to tell her that I forgive her and that I love her. So many regrets. I have so many regrets.* He thought. *And my little ones, my sweet little twins, Bluma and Perle. I should have spent more time with them, but I was too busy trying to impress the world. I wanted to be an important man, the kind of man my father would have admired. What I failed to realize was that my father was dead, and my children needed me much more than they needed all the material things I provided. Ahh, the mistakes I made. So many. And now, it might be too late to redeem myself.*

When they were boarding the train, he remembered how angry he was at Bluma and Perle for running to their sister. The whole scene was chaotic. He stood there glaring at them. But, they must have been afraid of the future too, because they had defied him when they saw Shoshana, they ran to hug their older sister. And, before the twins had a chance to return to their parents the Nazi guards began to load the train. Naomi and Herschel were at the front of the line, and there was no way to step out of line. The Nazis forced them on to the box car without the twins. Herschel shook his head as he remembered the morning at the train station. Until he was separated from Bluma and Perle, leaving them in Shoshana's care, Hershel had not seen how any good could come from Shoshana's independent streak. He'd despised her strength. Women were not supposed to be tough; they were supposed to depend on men. But now he was relying on Shoshana's vigor. It was the only hope he had for the survival of his daughters. His head ached with worry. If he had been alone on this train with no one who relied on him to be strong, he would have shown how angry he was. He would have roared, and pulled out his hair. However, he knew if he did it would scare Naomi and he wanted to keep her calm. Besides that he wouldn't give the Nazis the satisfaction of seeing him weak and vulnerable. No matter what they did to him and his family, he would laugh in their faces, because he knew that he was not a man to beg. And besides, begging would do him no damn good.

Then once again, the train came to an abrupt stop. Everyone was thrown forward. A woman screamed. But the guards paid no attention. Naomi woke up and grabbed Hershel's arm. "Where are we? What's happening?"

"its nothing." He said reassuringly although he didn't believe his own words. "Everything is fine. We've just stopped for a few minutes. Probably to refuel. We'll be on our way soon enough. Go back to sleep."

She did as he asked.

Hershel could not say how long he stood there, sweat beading on his brow, worrisome thoughts filling his mind. Hours passed. Hershel knew day had turned to night and the sun had gone down.

Most of the people in the box car fell asleep even though there was no room to lie down. But, Because they were sardined so close together, they kept each other from falling down. Hershel was alert. He felt something was happening. He was tired, but it was not safe to let his guard down and go to sleep. *These filty Nazis will not sneak up on me. I will stay awake and keep watch.* He was still furious with himself for believing the lie the Nazi's told them, that this train was on its way to a better place and that the ride would be safe and comfortable. He quickly glanced over at Naomi. She slept quietly. *I am glad that at least for the moment she is at peace.* The silence in the box car was Erie. The baby had died so it's incessant crying was silenced forever. That thought made him sad. Not even one of the passengers snored, or farted, or coughed. It was as if all them were all dead, all of them were ghosts. Then the wind howled and somewhere outside an owl hooted. Hershel closed his eyes for a moment. But then he overhead the voices of two guards. They were speaking right outside the box car. Although they spoke in German, he understood them completely because not only had he studied German in law school, but he was fluent in Yiddish and the language was very similar.

"I know they're nothing but rats. But I still feel a bit sorry for them." One of the guards said to another guard.

"Do you really? It's not as if they are really human. We know they are not. In fact they are nothing but a stain on the fatherland. And they are Christ killers."

"But I can't imagine just murdering all of them. Did you see how many of them we loaded onto this train?"

"Yes, I did. And by the end of the week, they'll all be dead. No longer will they be a plague on society. You know, one day the world will thank us for riding them of the Jews"

"But, there are women and children here. We will be murdering little children. That makes me ill."

"Rolf, you sound like a weak fool. Please don't speak this way to anyone else. I am your friend. We have known each other since childhood. So, I will keep my mouth shut about all these treasonous things you've said today. But make sure you don't talk like this in front of the other guards. The things you are saying make You sound like you are unfit for your position. And believe me, they will tell on you. Everyone wants to get recognition. By turning you in, they could get a promotion. They don't care what happens to you."

"You're probably right, Bert."

"I know that I am right. You must keep your mouth shut about feeling sorry for Jews. NO matter whether they are women and children or not. They are still Jews. An Aryan man must be strong. You should know that from the days we were in the Hitler Youth together."

"I'll try to be strong.."

"Try hard, because the future of your career and maybe even your life depends on it." Bert said.

Hershel pushed through the crowd of sleeping bodies and

looked out through the slats of the train car. He saw one of the guards walking away and the other remained standing there staring up at the stars.

When the guard was alone, Hershel began to try to signal him without waking anyone "shhhh. I have something to tell you that you will want to hear." Hershel said

The guard turned to look at Herschel, and their eyes met through the slats.

"Come closer so I can talk to you." Hershel said

Rolf walked over suspiciously.

"It's all right. You're safe. Look, you can see that I can't get to you. I couldn't break out of here if I wanted to, I am securely locked in this train car. Come closer, I just want to tell you something." Hershel said in a conspiratorial whisper.

Rolf edged closer. "What do you want to tell me?" He asked suspiciously

"I have a proposition for you."

"You hardly look like you're in any position to proposition anyone."

"That may be true. But perhaps not." Hershel whispered. He was nervous. *This could all go wrong and backfire on me. But I have to try.* "In my former life, before the Warsaw ghetto, I was a successful lawyer and I was a very rich man."

"So how does this benefit me?"

"I am about to tell you. You see, I have a four carat that hid when we were being arrested. No one knows about it. But, it's a blue white, perfect stone. Worth a lot of money. If you had it you could quit work. You could buy a home somewhere and live in peace."

"So, how do I get it?" Rolf asked "What do you want to tell me where it is?"

"I want you to let my wife and I go. Free us so we can go into the forest and try to survive on our own. We will need two days worth of food and water."

"No chance. If I let you two go, what guarantee to I have that there is a diamond? By the time I go to look for it, you and your wife will be far away from here."

"All right. How about this then," Herschel said clearing his throat. *I will sacrifice my life for hers. She deserves that much for putting up with me all these years. He thought sadly.* " if you will just let my wife out of here. Give her two days worth of food and water. I will tell you where to find the diamond. You can keep me for collateral. If it turns out that I am lying, you can kill me."

"You will tell me where it is anyway or I will kill you right now."

"I overheard you and your coworker talking. You have plans to kill us when we arrive at our destination. And if you murder my wife and I then what will you have? Only our dead bodies. If you don't agree to my terms, you will have no diamond."

"Interesting idea."

"Yes, a flawless blue and white diamond is Worth a lot of money. A lot of money."

"How do I know you aren't lying to me?"

"Because, you will still have me in your grasp. You can torture me if you find that I am lying. Now do you think I would want to suffer at your hands? Not at all. Once you have the diamond, I would expect you to show some integrity and free me. But for now, all I ask is that you free my wife."

"Why didn't you pack the diamond when you were told you were being sent to the ghetto in Warsaw?"

"I didn't because I planned to someday escape and go back and get it. I'll give you a clue. I hid it in my office. Once you know where to look it will be easy for you to find. And it will be all yours. All, yours."

Hershel had been a lawyer long enough to know when he was winning an argument. He saw Rolf's eyes twinkle with greed and he breathed a sigh of relief. *I am probably going to die. But at least I will be able to help Naomi.* Hershel knew that there was power in silence. He did not say another word. Naomi's life hung in the balance as he trembled waiting for the guard to speak. He remembered the words of his favorite law school professor " Silence is your most powerful negotiation tool."

Several moments passed, finally Rolf said "I could probably arrange this. However, if I find out that you are lying, Jew. I will make you wish you had never made this deal with me. Do you understand me?"

"Of course."

"And…to sweeten things I will make you a promise?"

"Oh?"

"I will let your wife go now. And, if you are telling the truth and I do find the diamond, I promise you that I will let you go too as soon as I have the stone in my hand."

He's lying. But he's smart. Hershel thought. He is aware that I know that we are all on our way to our death and he thinks that once he's let Naomi go free there will be no diamond and nothing he can do to punish me. So, he is offering me my life and my freedom. But I know that he won't keep his promise. Once he has the diamond, I'll be murdered just like every other Jew on this train.

"And, you needn't worry. You will have the jewel. It will be yours. Of course I want to live, so I wouldn't lie to you. I believe you will set me free once I have proven to you that I am trustworthy. Now, Just let my wife go, as I asked."

"Very well. you have ten minutes to say goodbye. I will have some food and water ready for her to take with her. But she must be leave the train in ten minutes because it is almost dawn and then the other guards will be awake. This is your only chance, Jew, we will not be making another stop before we reach, Treblinka."

"She'll be ready to go in ten minutes." Hershel said

"Ehhh, wait a minute you trickly little vermin. Where is the diamond?"

"Not until my wife is gone. Then I'll tell you."

"You are a real Jew." Rolf laughed "But I'll indulge you because your life depends on it."

"All right, go now and say goodbye. You have ten minutes. No more."

Hershel sat back down beside Naomi who was still asleep. Gently he nudged her shoulder "Naomi." He whispered her name into the darkness, and the vocalizing of it brought back the memory of the first time his father told him that Naomi would be his wife.

"Hershel, what is it? Are you all right?" She asked

"I have to talk to you and there isn't much time." He said

She wiped the sleep from her eyes "Yes, what is it?"

"You are leaving this train."

"Me? You mean us?"

"No you are going alone."

"What? Hershel, I can't. I must get our destination to be reunited with our daughters."

"I am hoping they never boarded the train."He said and there was such a tone of doom in his voice that she shivered.

"What do you mean."

"I overheard the guards talking. You must get out of here. I've arranged it."

"What did they say, Hershel?"

And he told her.

She couldn't speak, but her body was trembling.

"Naomi, I haven't always been a good husband. I know I am not an easy man to love, or to live with for that matter. But…" he hesitated and knowing that this would be his last chance to speak to her, he forced himself to say all that was in his heart "I love you. I have always loved you. I could not always show you, because that's my weakness. I have a hard time with expressing myself. But, I have chosen to save your life rather than my own and that is because I love you. Now, you must go. Stay in the forest. Make sure you stay far away from the main roads where you could be spotted by soldiers. Try to remain hidden as much as you can. The guard is going to give you two days worth of food. After that you must steal from the farms at night. Be careful. Please be careful."

She couldn't help herself. She knew he hated to be touched like this, but she needed to feel human contact. So, she put her arms around him lay her head on his chest as she openly wept. "I can't go. I cant let you go to your death alone. And what about our daughters?"

"I will be all right. I'll find a way to survive, you know me. I am a clever one, yes?"

She tried to smile and nod, but she couldn't. She was weeping even harder.

"And, listen to me. You must survive so that when this is all over you can find our girls again."

"I'm scared Hershel. I'm scared for the girls, but I am scared for you and me too. I want to stay with you." For a mere second she considered telling him the truth about Shoshana, that she was not his daughter. That Shoshana was the child of her lover Eli. It would feel good to finally unburden herself of that terrible secret that she had carried deep in her heart since the day Shoshana was born. But she looked into Herschel's eyes and decided against it. It would not help him to know the truth. It could only hurt him. And if by some miracle, he was to survive and be reunited with his daughters, he would never feel the same way about Shoshana. They already had problems getting along with each other, and she didn't want to say or do anything that might further separate them. She took a long ragged breath "I am not going without you."

"I forbid you to stay here. You will do as I say."

She sighed. In her way, Naomi loved him. She knew that he was making a great sacrifice for her right now. He was trading his life for hers. She'd never known that he cared that much about her, and she wished they had more time together to try and make things better between them. But there was no time. In the next few minutes she would be escaping into a forest, dark and frightening. All alone.

MORE BOOKS BY ROBERTA KAGAN

AVAILABLE ON AMAZON

The Auschwitz Twins Series

The Children's Dream

Mengele's Apprentice

The Auschwitz Twins

Jews, The Third Reich, and a Web of Secrets

My Son's Secret

The Stolen Child

A Web of Secrets

A Jewish Family Saga

Not In America

They Never Saw It Coming

When The Dust Settled

The Syndrome That Saved Us

A Holocaust Story Series

The Smallest Crack

The Darkest Canyon

Millions Of Pebbles

Sarah and Solomon

All My Love, Detrick Series

All My Love, Detrick

You Are My Sunshine

The Promised Land

To Be An Israeli

Forever My Homeland

Michal's Destiny Series

Michal's Destiny

A Family Shattered

Watch Over My Child

Another Breath, Another Sunrise

Eidel's Story Series

And . . . Who Is The Real Mother?

Secrets Revealed

New Life, New Land

Another Generation

The Wrath of Eden Series

The Wrath Of Eden

The Angels Song

Stand Alone Novels

One Last Hope

A Flicker Of Light

The Heart Of A Gypsy

ABOUT THE AUTHOR

I wanted to take a moment to introduce myself. My name is Roberta, and I am an author of Historical Fiction, mainly based on World War 2 and the Holocaust. While I never discount the horrors of the Holocaust and the Nazis, my novels are constantly inspired by love, kindness, and the small special moments that make life worth living.

I always knew I wanted to reach people through art when I was younger. I just always thought I would be an actress. That dream died in my late 20's, after many attempts and failures. For the next several years, I tried so many different professions. I worked as a hairstylist and a wedding coordinator, amongst many other jobs. But I was never satisfied. Finally, in my 50's, I worked for a hospital on the PBX board. Every day I would drive to work, I would dread clocking in. I would count the hours until I clocked out. And, the next day, I would do it all over again. I couldn't see a way out, but I prayed, and I prayed, and then I prayed some more. Until one morning at 4 am, I woke up with a voice in my head, and you might know that voice as Detrick. He told me to write his story, and together we sat at the computer; we wrote the novel that is now known as All My Love, Detrick. I now have over 30 books published, and I have had the honor of being a USA Today Best-Selling Author. I have met such incredible people in this industry, and I am so blessed to be meeting you.

I tell this story a lot. And a lot of people think I am crazy, but it is true. I always found solace in books growing up but didn't start writing until I was in my late 50s. I try to tell this story to as many people as possible to inspire them. No matter where you are in your life, remember there is always a flicker of light no matter how dark it seems.

I send you many blessings, and I hope you enjoy my novels. They are all written with love.

Roberta

ACKNOWLEDGMENTS

I would like to thank my editor, proofreader, and developmental editor for all their help with this project. I couldn't have done it without them.

Paula Grundy of Paula Proofreader
Terrance Grundy of Editerry
Carli Kagan, Developmental Editor

Made in the USA
Las Vegas, NV
09 August 2022

52956302R00201